THE ULTIMATE PRICE

by

Gerry Ware

Copyright 2016 Gerry Ware

Gerry Ware has asserted his right under the Copyright, Designs and Patents Act, 1988 to be identified as the author of this work.

This novel is a work of fiction. Names and characters are the product of the author's imagination and any resemblance to actual persons, living or dead, is entirely coincidental.

ISBN-10: 1523311444
ISBN-13: 978-1523311446

To Sheila, whose help and support over the years
I'll never forget.

Chapter 1

JUNE 1958

"Bet you don't beat me this time," young Tommy Nelson's voice was full of enthusiasm and exuded an unusual air of confidence as he limbered up outside the gates of Southfields Junior School. His best friend and fiercest sporting adversary Steve Baker, for once was not relishing the race that lay ahead. Tommy's spirits were high however. Friday afternoon had arrived and the weekend beckoned. School could be forgotten for a couple of blissful days and Tommy Nelson was more than happy.

"It's about time I won," he said with a big grin on his cheeky face as he continued his extravagant exercises, oblivious to the chatter and banter of the steady stream of fellow pupils leaving the school premises with their own agendas for the weekend ahead.

The race in question was the two eight year old boys customary after school run back to the Barton Bridge flats in Felgate Road, where they both lived. Even at primary school there was intense rivalry between the inseparable pair, and the half mile trip through the suburban streets was always competitive and both of them took it very seriously,

This particular Friday it was Steve Baker's turn to look after the class's pet hamster Goldie for the weekend, and his eagerness to compete was tempered by the fact that the hamster's cage, with Goldie inside and covered with a cotton sheet, was tucked under his arm. Handicapped or not, he wasn't about to back down and Tommy's cockiness and confidence only cemented his resolve not to concede victory to his good friend.

"You take good care of Goldie now, young Steven." The authoritive voice belonged to the boys teacher Miss Bidwell who stood, arms folded, overseeing the Friday afternoon's exodus in the playground. Steve Baker looked across at her through the railings.

"Yes miss," he said rather sheepishly. Tommy looked away, giggling and smirking.

"She got her arms folded?" he asked in a whisper. Steve nodded.

"Over her big tits?" Tommy continued, gesturing with his hands cupped in front of him. Steve couldn't help laughing. He was one of Miss Bidwell's favourites in class and it was rare for him to incur her wrath, but he could see she was not amused.

"Is she coming over?" Tommy chortled, still with his back to her. He was eager to get the race underway and his impatience was noted by their rather buxom, middle aged class tutor.

"You *walk* home now, do you hear me? Don't you dare run carrying that poor hamster?"

"No miss." Steve was desperately trying to keep

a straight face.

"And you Tommy Nelson, don't think I don't know what you're up to. Do you hear me?"

Their after school contest was common knowledge even amongst the school staff. Tommy ignored her.

"I will personally check Goldie's state of health first thing Monday morning. You have my word on that. Now....off with you....and no running....do you hear?"

Miss Bidwell stood motionless as the pair slunk away ignominiously towards the junction with Hamilton Road and beyond their teacher's gaze. As soon as they turned the corner the race was on and Tommy dashed into an early lead.

He was quite small, lean and wiry and full of nervous energy. He huffed and puffed and his arms flailed wildly as he surged ahead. He desperately wanted to win and didn't care one iota that his best friend was disadvantaged and limited by the cumbersome object he was obliged to carry. Steve Baker, on the other hand, was composed and collected and wasn't fazed by Tommy's initial strategy. In contrast, he was tall and a bit plump and his gait could be compared to a palomino thoroughbred in an equestrian dressage event. It was high stepping, controlled and imperious and even carrying Goldie's cage he looked a relaxed and inherent athlete.

He was also somewhat conscientious by nature

and Miss Bidwell's words of warning had tentatively sunk in, whereas had Tommy been charged with the safe conveyance of the animal, her advice would undoubtedly have fallen on deaf ears, as his philosophy was to laugh in the face of anything authoritarian. As a result Steve, who was accustomed to winning most times, felt the classroom's pet hamster's well being was, on this occasion at least, more important than beating Tommy in the race home.

The winning post was the bus stop outside the Barton Bridge flats and Tommy duly reached it first, raising both arms in a triumphant gesture as he did so. Steve was magnanimous in defeat and could only look on as Tommy took the acclaim from the illusory crowd lining the street and surrounding the finishing line. Steve took a peek under the dishevelled cotton sheet and found Goldie alive and well, even if she did look petrified hiding in the corner of the cage.

Tommy was ecstatic and laughing loudly.

"Said I'd win didn't I," he boasted, coming over to take a look at the poor creature. "Still alive then?" he added looking closely at the furry rodent. Seeing the state the animal was in he then immediately went into a rendition of Elvis Presley's massive American hit of the previous year, *'All Shook Up'*. His hand went to his mouth and he sang into an imaginary microphone. He was very good. Steve looked on. He'd seen it all before but it *was* Friday and he couldn't help but get into the spirit of the moment and joined in with the occasional lyric.

He was soon in stitches and clapped along enthusiastically. Tommy's hips were gyrating just like Elvis's but his short grey school trousers were too baggy and a little on the long side and as much as he tried, he couldn't quite pull it off. He did his best though and by the end of the song he even had an audience. A young female audience in the shape of Carol Dooley and her friend Sandra. They both went to Southfields Junior School and lived in the same block of flats as Tommy and Steve. Their walk home from school had been a lot more leisurely than the two boys, however, and they were also in a good mood looking forward to the weekend ahead.

Seven year old Carol Dooley was a pretty girl with a bubbly personality and came across as a bit of a tomboy. Her short, blond hair was neat and tidy and her features, especially her big blue eyes, made her look attractive beyond her years. She was outgoing, confident and liked the boys. In the afternoon sunshine she looked a picture in her floral cotton dress and bobby socks and she and her friend stopped to watch Tommy's impromptu performance. She couldn't help laughing.

"You're such a show-off Tommy Nelson," she said.

He grinned, swivelling his hips as he moved.

"I'm proud to say that she's my buttercup" he sang, *"I'm in love........I'm all shook up."*

That was it. He stood motionless with his arms akimbo and waited for the applause. Steve, Carol and Sandra cheered loudly. Their flirtatious interlude came to an abrupt end though when a voice called down from a second floor balcony.

"Up here now you. How many times do I have to tell you about dawdling on the way home from school?"

It was Carol's mum, sounding irate.

"Every time we have a bit of fun she's there, spoiling it," Carol moaned.

"That's because your dad's a copper," Tommy quipped, mindful to keep his remark out of earshot of Carol's mother.

"I wish he wasn't sometimes. Come on, Sandra," Carol replied and the two girls walked slowly off.

"See you tomorrow?" Tommy called after them but he got no reply.

Carol's father was uniformed police constable Derek Dooley, who was based locally at Southfields Police Station. The police headquarters were located in Barchester city centre some eight miles away and although Derek Dooley hoped one day to be promoted there, at the moment he had to be content with where he was, in the less salubrious surroundings of Southfields.

The area had the reputation of being a somewhat rough suburb and had its' fair share of rogues and villains. Just a few years previously it had been a sprawling district of run down Victorian back to back terraced houses and grid-like dreary streets. It had also suffered at the hands of German bombers during World War Two and the locality left a lot to be desired. In recent times however, Barchester city council had designated Southfields, along with one or two other municipalities, of areas of special needs requiring regeneration.

The Victorian backstreets were cleared and low rise council flats with every modern convenience were built to house the post war population explosion that was steadily gaining momentum. The technology to construct high rise towers was also now available and a couple had sprung up in the area, but generally four storey blocks like the Barton Bridge flats were the norm. As a result the low rise developments kept alive the community spirit and small town values.

Whilst Steve Baker rearranged the sheet over the hamster's cage he noticed a gleaming black Humber limousine parked amongst the more common Austins and Fords in the street.

"See your dad's home," he said to Tommy, nodding towards the shiny, ritzy vehicle. Tommy looked and his heart sank.

"Just my sodding luck," he said. Immediately the euphoria of winning the race had vanished. "Sod it," he added, kicking a stone along the pavement. His disappointment was tinged with anger.

"He'll be asleep on the settee in the front room, I just know it. Means I can't listen to the radio or anything.....and he'll be in a mood when he wakes up. Damn and blast, it's not bloody fair."

Tommy's father Harry Nelson was an enigmatic character to many. To others he was looked upon as a bit of a spiv. In many ways he led an unconventional life but nearly everyone he met liked him, even if they didn't quite understand his slant on life or his idiosyncratic attitude to many things. The opulent motor car wasn't his. He was merely a chauffeur for Prestige Cars in Southfields Lane nearby and the weekend was his busy time.

On a Friday he usually started work around seven in the evening and his driving duties wouldn't finish until the early hours. So it wasn't unusual for him to cat nap on the sofa prior to donning his chauffeur's uniform in readiness for his evening shift in the metropolis. He was also a chancer and gambler, which sometimes made life very difficult for the family and didn't enamour him to everyone. PC Derek Dooley kept a close eye on his wheelings and dealings and although he liked and got on well with the man, kept his friendship at bay for obvious reasons.

Fundamentally, Harry Nelson was a good man though and worked hard to provide for his family even if it wasn't fully realised by others generally and Tommy, although peeved his dad was messing up *his* afternoon, wouldn't have changed him for the world.

"Tell you what," Steve said noticing Tommy's

mood change, "We'll go down the park on our bikes, see what's happening down there."

Tommy looked pensive, but only for a few seconds.

"Yeah," he nodded "That'll be great. Yeah...good idea Steve, we'll do that. I can listen to the radio tonight, when he's gone to work."

"Ten minutes then?" Steve asked. Tommy nodded. His ebullience had quickly returned and the two boys headed for the entrance to the flats, their weekend still very much on track.

Saturday morning in the Baker household was relaxed and organised. Breakfast was a family affair and although Steve was an only child the importance of mealtimes together in a fast changing world was seen as paramount by both his parents. His father George never worked at the weekend. He was strictly a nine to five man. His position as assistant buyer for an engineering company was salaried and office based, and George was happy in his role as a white collar worker. He earned enough to run a family car and splash out occasionally on luxury consumer items like a television and washing machine. He appreciated his weekends with the family and that was the status quo as far as he was concerned. His values were so far removed from those of Tommy's dad, Harry, yet they got on well socially. Class difference did raise its' ugly head sometimes, but it never threatened their friendship and they enjoyed each other's company. There was no getting away from the fact that they both lived in council accommodation on a council estate and in that respect, George Baker and Harry Nelson were equal.

Young Steve looked up to his father and respected him, but it was his mother, Mary, he turned to for love and affection and there was a special relationship between them that surpassed the usual bond between mother and son. Steve looked forward to Saturday mornings because of his love of football. He was a regular in the school team and the season was coming to a close. He was a centre forward and even for one so young he was a powerful, intimidating and skilful striker who many thought would go a long way in the sport. His mum and dad were also of that belief and gave him all the encouragement and tangible support they could.

Tommy also played for the team but he wasn't a regular like Steve. He was a winger and on occasions he was quick and elusive, but he lacked consistency and wasn't as fully committed as Steve. Even when his name wasn't on the team sheet Tommy still turned up to support both the team and his best friend and wasn't really bothered whether he played or not. His passion was music and singing.

There was no television set in the Nelson household. There was a record player though and more than one radio and Tommy was smitten by the new phenomenon, rock and roll. He lived it, breathed it and spent every spare minute listening and singing along to his idols. His mum June, and his younger sister Emma thought he had potential but Harry, his dad, was a big band enthusiast. He hated the modern stuff and took no interest in Tommy's burgeoning talent whatsoever.

The Barton Bridge flats were a great place for youngsters to grow up in. At the rear of the block, along with the usual utility areas for drying clothes and housing waste bins, there were well thought out recreation and play areas that made for a safe environment for children of all ages to enjoy.

Beyond the back perimeter fence was the suburban railway line which carried commuters into the centre of Barchester. Although noisy at times, it added interest and amusement to the daily lives of those living there. Steve and Tommy were never at a loss for something to do. Whether tearing around the place on their roller skates, scaring the living daylights out of the toddlers on their home made go-karts made from rickety orange boxes and old pram wheels, or playing football amongst the billowing sheets on the washing lines in the forbidden environs of the drying area.

It was as if the whole had been built just for them and although they were nearly always in trouble with one or other of the residents, they didn't care. It was their playground and they were determined to have fun. Some of their pranks incurred an aspect of danger though, like climbing the back fence onto the railway track and putting a penny on the line and watching as the train thundered by, crushing and defacing the coin as it did so. They also sailed close to the wind by tossing lengths of cable onto the track and watching the sparks fly when the wire shorted out on the live rail, the electric one. They were seen once by an old biddy who lived on the top floor. She threatened to tell Constable Dooley, but the boys sweet-talked her out of it, or so they thought. Consequently, it was a stunt they didn't do very often after that episode.

Away from the flats, on their bikes, they explored the area and had a marvellous time. The bond between them was growing stronger and their friendship developed and flourished. The biking trips kept them fit and active, and away from any parental control, their characters evolved and their personalities were shaped to lead them into young adulthood.

There was also the social interaction between the families living in such a tight knit community. Some didn't get on, but most embraced and enjoyed the closeness yet retaining an important degree of independence. Street parties weren't uncommon in the summer months, especially on occasions like Derby day and the Queen's birthday. Any excuse to wine and dine in the afternoon sun and dance the night away under the stars late into the night was embraced zealously and wholeheartedly.

Bonfire night celebrations were also high on the social calendar. Every year Tommy, Steve and the rest of the kids collected wood and rubbish and piled it high round the back of the flats, and every year, on the morning of November 5th, the council would turn up and take it all away citing hazardous fire risk as the feeble excuse. The intrepid youngsters soon thwarted the spoilsports from the town hall though, by keeping a huge reserve of old timber, car tyres and junk in a secret hideout behind the bin store, and building the real thing after the men from the council had left. The night was always a success with each family in turn letting off their own individual boxes of fireworks around the crackling fire under the friendly supervision of PC Derek Dooley.

Chapter 2

In May 1960, shortly after Tommy's tenth birthday, he fell in love. It was no surprise when his sweetheart turned out to be pretty Carol Dooley. Although a year younger than him, she was growing up fast and was already an inch or so taller than he was. She was still only nine though and both she and Tommy were very much at the pre-puberty phase in their lives and to those around them, including both their parents, their relationship seemed innocent and harmless.

That's not how they saw it however. Carol had always thought Steve was more her type with his good looks, blond crew-cut and his sporty outward attitude but Tommy made her laugh. She was happy in his company and what he lacked in charm and charisma he made up for with his sheer enthusiasm and vitality for life. His singing voice had also improved and matured, and although he was a natural boy soprano, he did his utmost to sing in a much lower register like his hero and idol, Elvis Presley.

He also pestered his dad into buying him a cheap, second hand acoustic guitar for his birthday and had mastered, albeit rather clumsily, three or four of the basic chords needed enabling him to strum and sing along to the simpler songs from Elvis's repertoire. Carol loved it and was generous in her appreciation of his undoubted talent and sang along sometimes. They both knew she couldn't sing for toffee and it amused him, but she knew when to stop, so it didn't become an annoyance to him.

On her part, Carol had been given a bicycle for her birthday and instead of sitting uncomfortably perched on Tommy's crossbar, she now had her own transport and they regularly went off cycling together. Her dad laid down the law though when it came to how far they could venture. The furthest they were allowed to go was Dunsbury Park, three miles west of where they lived. Derek Dooley had even mapped out a route to the park where the High Street and other main roads could be avoided. Tommy took no notice however, and he and Carol took great pleasure in choosing their own route, whether it was deemed dangerous or not.

Dunsbury Park was a brilliant place to go. It was an oasis of wide open spaces, trees and shrubs, amongst the concrete jungle of the western suburbs of Barchester. The amenities within the municipal park were excellent. There was a boating lake where skiffs could be hired on an hourly basis. There were wooded walks and grassy meadows ideal for walking dogs, a bowling green frequented mainly by the oldies and for the more energetic there were tennis courts and an undulating nine hole pitch and putt golf course. The centrepiece was a small Roman artefacts museum and an adjoining refreshments pavilion which sold the best ice cream for miles around.

Tommy and Carol loved the freedom they had in the park and cycled there as often as they could. It wasn't all to their liking though. There was one particular place in the park they gave a wide berth to, the public conveniences inside the main gates. It was rumoured that the men's toilets were the clandestine and furtive meeting place for homosexuals. Both Carol and Tommy didn't really understand the nature of homosexuality, especially where the sexual connotation was concerned. It certainly wasn't a subject openly discussed around their respective breakfast tables. It was in the school playground the tittle-tattle about the subject was rife, and the giggling and sniggering came to the fore every time homosexuals, or queers as they were more commonly known, were brought up.

It was in Dunsbury Park where Carol and Tommy had their very first tentative and exploratory sexual encounter. One warm July afternoon in the school holidays, they cycled there and after stopping and watching the activity in and around the boating lake, they sought the peace and quiet of the south side of the park which bordered the cemetery. It was an area less frequented by visitors and they chose to stop in a grassy meadow full of pink and white wild campions interspersed with brilliant red poppies.

The scents were intoxicating and the two innocent young lovers lay in the long grass soaking up the sunshine. It was here they shared their first fleeting, hesitant kiss. It was brief and innocuous but to them it was something infinitely more than a simple peck on the lips.

"Why don't we play that game," Carol said with a mischievous look on her face.

"What game?" Tommy had no idea what she was talking about.

"You know," she replied searching for the right words. She giggled.

"Don't know what you're on about," Tommy replied. He genuinely didn't know what Carol was proposing.

"Come on then," he added, his curiosity getting the better of him. Carol wasn't sure whether or not to continue. She decided it was now or never.

"The one when you show me yours, and I show you mine," she blurted out the words rather awkwardly. It took a few seconds for the penny to drop, but in the end Tommy got the gist of what she was saying. He laughed nervously. He'd heard of it, of course, in the school playground, but he'd never actually done it. Furthermore, he was taken aback that someone so naive and childlike could suggest such a thing. It excited him though and he decided that if she was willing, he would give it a try. He looked around but could see no one in the vicinity.

"I'll go first," Carol said, keen to take the

initiative. Tommy could hear the excitement in her voice. She stood up, lifted her dress and slid her knickers down to her ankles. Tommy could hardly believe what was happening. He'd seen his younger sister Emma naked many times so he knew what girls' genitalia looked like but this was different. This was close up and personal and he took a sharp intake of breath as she stood before him. He was lost for words.

"Cat got your tongue?" Carol teased, letting him have a good look. His eyes were fixed on her girlish triangle as she pulled her knickers up and let her dress once more cover her modesty.

"You like?" she asked. Tommy nodded feeling a bit guilty.

"Your turn," she said sitting back down on the grass. Tommy looked uncomfortable.

"I'm not standing up," he said stubbornly. He knew he was putting off the moment of truth but Carol was having none of it.

"Kneel instead then. Come on Tommy....it'll be okay."
He did as he was told and knelt in front of her. After a quick look to see if the coast was clear he undid his shorts and pulled them down.

"And these," Carol urged tugging at the waistband of his underpants. Tommy felt decidedly embarrassed. Carol waited but said nothing. He eased his pants down to his knees.

"Oh Tommy," she said looking on with interest.

She'd never seen a boys' penis before and didn't know what to expect in relation to its' size. But Tommy didn't know that and his peccadillo, as his mum used to call it when she bathed him as a toddler, seemed on the small side to him.

"It's bigger than I thought," she said suddenly, which reassured Tommy, but he still felt awkward. Inevitably, he felt his loins stirring. It had happened before, but not in front of anyone, especially a girl. He was mortified.

"It's moving," Carol said, the excitement in her voice quite distinct, but it was Tommy who was getting excited and he frantically yanked up his pants fearing further embarrassment and humiliation. Carol laughed sensing his self-consciousness.

"Fancy an ice cream?" she asked changing the subject. Tommy pulled up his shorts and did his best to compose himself.

"Got no money," he replied.

"I have," she said gleefully taking half a crown from a pocket in her dress. Nothing more was said on their impromptu, yet risqué diversion. They retrieved their bikes and headed for the refreshment kiosk next to the museum.

They were both growing up fast, and they knew it. Tommy still saw a lot of Steve, but there was a discernible change in their relationship as a result of his association with Carol. Against his better judgement he confided in Steve about his sexual arousal in the park with her. Steve was fascinated but asked his mum if it was possible at his age. Tommy was horrified to find out Steve had told anyone, let alone his mother. Even when Steve told Tommy his mum thought it possible and quite natural, it was some time before Tommy was placated. It was even longer until he could face Steve's mother, such was his embarrassment.

The time was fast approaching when both of them would have to face their potential scholastic nemesis, the eleven plus exam. Due partly to his parents persistence and to some extent his own volition, Steve became more studious leading up to that momentous exam. Gentle coercion, especially by his father, on the merits of continuing his education at grammar school rather than secondary school, was enough to persuade Steve to spend less time both in Tommy's company and in the pursuit of sporting activities, and more in an academic way.

George Baker wanted the best for his son and although some in the Barton Bridge flats thought his attitude rather snobbish, he genuinely believed in his principles on the subject. He wanted nothing less for his only child. His mother's approach was more subtle but the result was the same, with Steve spending less time on the football pitch and more on his school work. His teacher, Miss Bidwell, had no doubts that for Steve, Dunsbury Grammar beckoned. As for Tommy, she wasn't sure whether he would make the grade or not.

Tommy hoped to go, but it was mainly because he wanted to continue his friendship with Steve, and he feared his relationship with his pal would suffer if they ended up at different schools. He was under no illusion that he wasn't as academically gifted as his best friend and intellectual greatness wasn't high on his list of objectives. He just wanted to sing, to follow a musical career. Anything else wasn't on the agenda.

He'd breezed through his early school years and not learnt a lot. His father Harry hadn't been much help either. He had a more pragmatic approach to life and lived off his wits most of the time. The knowledge he passed on to his son was of greyhound racing tracks, casinos and betting shops, and the ability to develop street-wise credibility which kept him just on the right side of the law and enabled him to attain an acceptable standard of living within the community.

His mother June did her best to guide him in the right direction, but she had her hands full just keeping Harry on the straight and narrow, and although she was always there for young Tommy, he rarely asked her for advice. Also, in that final period leading up to the exam his time was spent more in the company of Carol Dooley than academic study. Carol, being a year below him at school, had ample time to prepare for *her* eleven plus exam, and had no reason not to be his constant companion during that period, and because of her age and immaturity, didn't even contemplate the bearing it might have on Tommy's future.

Chapter 3

In the summer of 1961 Steve Baker duly passed his eleven plus examination, but Tommy Nelson, not surprisingly, failed his. Steve made the transition from Southfields Junior School to Dunsbury Grammar with a natural self assurance and confidence which even surprised him. His parents were proud and happy to kit him out in the smart school uniform and Steve looked dashing and handsome in the distinctive formal attire as he began a new and exciting era in his life. His stature also gave him an advantage as he was already as tall as most of the second formers. His boyish plumpness was giving way to a more muscular frame and his blond crew-cut completed his new look at his new school.

Dunsbury Grammar was a modern, impressive group of buildings, built in a contemporary style. It had everything, a dedicated science wing, indoor swimming pool, well equipped gymnasium and a hall that doubled up as a six hundred seater theatre complete with state-of-the-art stage lighting and sound system. The grounds covered four acres, with tennis and netball courts, a cricket pitch and a running track.

Everything seemed just right for Steve except

for the disappointment of not having Tommy with him to share the experience. He genuinely felt their friendship would continue as before, but his optimism was misplaced because of his youthful naivety. Tommy, on the other hand, was under no illusion their relationship would remain the same and quickly came to terms with the situation.

His new school, Heathfield Secondary Modern, came a poor second in nearly every aspect to its' illustrious neighbour, Dunsbury Grammar. The austere Victorian building had started life as the workhouse for the district and it was ironical that, some one hundred years later, it still served some of the more underprivileged in society. Its' facilities weren't up to much, however, but the staff were excellent and cared passionately about imparting their knowledge to those who were deemed by some to be academically challenged. Paradoxically, Heathfield had produced more entrepreneurial millionaires, sportsmen and media celebrities than its' nearby counterpart, Dunsbury Grammar, and it was this legacy which kept the school going in the competitive educational market place.

On his first day at this school Tommy promised himself he would leave on his sixteenth birthday. There was a school uniform of sorts but, unlike the grammar school, it wasn't compulsory so hardly anyone wore it. Harry Nelson was certainly not going to spend his hard earned cash on something he felt was frivolous and unnecessary, so Tommy wore what he was most comfortable in, tee shirt and blue jeans. He thought he looked quite fashionable and put on a persona of being lean, mean and moody.

His scrawny body was maturing quickly and although still quite small, he was becoming deceptively muscular and his big brown eyes further accentuated the boyish good looks he had retained. His moodiness came naturally, however, the degree of which he could turn off and on as he pleased. He believed if he acted that part for long enough, he would become that smouldering, mercurial character.

He joined the school choir, much to everyone's amazement. His boy soprano voice hadn't yet broken and was pure and quite special, when he chose to be disciplined enough with it. He even landed a small part in an opera, along with half a dozen other members of the choir, when a woman from the operatic society came scouting on behalf of the esteemed Barchester Opera House. He enjoyed the experience and he *loved* the time off from school to rehearse and perform even more. His deviousness eventually got the better of him though when he was thrown out of the choir for consistently taking advantage of their *'time off in lieu'* policy once too often.

All the same, he was a hardworking lad when it suited him, but not where the school curriculum was concerned. He knew if he wanted money of his own he wasn't going to be given it by his parents. He would have to earn it. Paper rounds were the answer. Not one like most kids did, but two, for two different newsagents in the High Street. He was up at the crack of dawn every day, come rain or shine, pedalling the streets of Southfields on his bike delivering the morning papers to hundreds of households. Sometimes the workload made him late for school and detention was almost inevitable. But Tommy didn't care. The money he earned was far more important to him than the prospect of a worthwhile education.

Motorbikes had also grabbed his interest in a huge way. He was fascinated by the big, powerful machines and the romantic notion of being king of the open road fuelled his imagination even more. The leathers the bikers wore also appealed to him and the camaraderie which existed within the biking fraternity generally, and within the Hells Angels gangs in particular, he found alluring and beguiling.

Every month, when the glossy motorcycle magazines hit the newsagents, Tommy was there, thumbing through the pages, drooling over the photos of the sleek machines like other boys of his age were slavering over the contents of Playboy and other girlie publications. He was determined to have a motorbike of his own and nearly every penny of his paper round earnings he put away for that special day when he would fulfil his dream of owning one.

He discussed his passion with Steve on one of their diminishing cycle trips, but Steve didn't share the same zeal or enthusiasm for the motorbike as Tommy. He was taken in with the new form of two wheeled transport that was taking the world by storm. Motor scooters. Low powered, fun machines like the flamboyant Italian Lambretta and Vespa models that were grabbing the attention and imagination of sophisticated young people everywhere.

Tommy hated them. He hated their accessory laden quirkiness, their dumpy, fashion conscious lines and most of all he hated their lack of power, acceleration and performance. As much as he tried, he couldn't persuade Steve the motorbike was supreme and in the end he gave up trying. It was yet another crack in their once impervious, rock solid friendship they had forged growing up in the Barton Bridge flats.

Truancy was another aspect of Tommy's life that was on the increase. It was a secret part of his world he shared with no one, not even Steve. Boredom was the main catalyst, listening to tedious, monotonous ramblings on subjects he had absolutely no interest in. Subjects like geometry, physics, English literature and religious knowledge. Tommy loathed them and bunking off those lessons was his way of dealing with the escalating situation of his disenchantment.

Somerset Place market was the area he

frequented most when he skived off school. It was always busy there and he could easily get lost in the bustling crowd. Subway Records was his favourite market stall where he could listen to the latest rock and roll singles and while away the time knowing the chances of him being found out by the school were minimal. He struck up a friendship with the lad that worked there, Dennis Carter. At sixteen, Dennis was only three tears his senior and they were very similar in a lot of respects. Dennis was slim, good looking with dark blond hair and blue eyes.

The market stall environment suited Dennis's cheeky, happy-go-lucky, mouthy personality and he had a good rapport with the customers. He flirted with the girls at every opportunity and Tommy thought he could certainly learn a thing or two from the likeable guy and decided to cultivate the friendship further. At first that proved to be difficult because underneath Dennis's charming outward facade he was a person who was inherently distrustful of everyone, and it took some time for him to realise Tommy was no threat to him and accept him more as a friend than merely an acquaintance.

Tommy enjoyed singing along to the records and although his voice had not long broken, he was fortunate his vocal chords were still in excellent shape, even though his natural pitch was now that of a high tenor as opposed to the soprano voice of his childhood years. He was happy with the transformation however and, given the chance, would sing at every opportunity. Dennis Carter didn't mind him singing along at the record stall either, because it was both entertaining and drew a crowd, which usually meant more record sales and more money in his pocket at the end of the week in the form of a cash bonus from his boss and proprietor of Subway Records, Victor Slade.

The market wasn't the only place Tommy visited on his truancy jaunts. The High Street shops were also a Mecca for the impressionable teenager, and it was in one of these where he was caught shoplifting on yet another illicit excursion, when he should have been at Heathfield School. His luck had run out. He was arrested and taken to the police station where, to his horror, PC Dooley was waiting to question him.

Tommy thought his neighbour and family friend would come down hard on him and make him an example to everyone in the Barton Bridge flats and beyond. Even ridicule him. He wouldn't have blamed him if he had. But there seemed little animosity from the police constable as he went about his business.

Tommy's parents were informed, as was the school, but the shop manager took an unusually lenient approach and realising the theft of a bar of chocolate wasn't the crime of the century, decided not to prosecute. Tommy was fortunate and was released into his parents charge with no more than a stern warning from PC Dooley.

It wasn't until later when he was off duty that Derek Dooley, in his civvies, caught up with Tommy and told him in no uncertain terms his association with his daughter Carol was over. Tommy saw another side of the man on that occasion, and it was one he wasn't going to argue with. Carol Dooley had passed her eleven plus exam and, as expected, went on to Dunsbury Grammar. They were now mixing in different circles and, not surprisingly, were drifting apart. They still saw each other back at the flats, but as friendly neighbours not inseparable young sweethearts, so Derek Dooley's ultimatum wasn't as big a blow as it might have been and Tommy, not wishing to rile the man further, agreed to his demands.

For a while after that, Tommy's trips to Subway Records were confined to the weekends and after school. He knew he had to bide his time and curb the rebellious streak that was manifesting itself within him, at least for the time being. This he found difficult and frustrating and his bubbly personality became more subdued and suppressed. He made a conscious effort not to be morose and moody though, and concentrated on improving his guitar playing and within a short time his endeavours paid off and his guitar skills, especially his rhythm playing, improved greatly. His pride was restored which had a direct result on his temperament and soon he was back to his brash and confident self.

Steve found it highly amusing when he found out what Tommy had been up to. It was Carol Dooley he'd gleaned the information from, not Tommy. But as soon as the pair got together it was obvious there was no animosity on Tommy's part and he also had a good laugh at his own expense whilst relating the somewhat embellished and exaggerated details of his misdemeanour to his good friend whilst they shared a bottle of brown ale in Dunsbury Park one Sunday afternoon.

Steve was a few months older than Tommy and was now approaching his fourteenth birthday. For him, grammar school was the perfect learning environment and he excelled in both academic studies as well as sporting activities. The latter edged it for him though and his footballing prowess was getting better and better as he matured into adulthood. His talent and ability in that sport was matched by his inner belief, hard work and self imposed fitness regime, and he was now a regular in Dunsbury Grammar's senior team. He was the youngest player in that team, yet his height and developing physique combined with the fact he made goal scoring look easy held him in good stead, and he never looked out of his depth or out of place in the side.

His parents were justifiably proud of both his academic achievements so far and his developing football skills and his father George was on the touchline every Saturday morning encouraging and cheering Steve on at every opportunity. George wanted the best possible future for his only son but he was slightly concerned Steve's efforts seemed to be concentrated on the football field more than in his educational study, but he also knew there was plenty of time ahead for him to put his mind to serious academic matters and left it at that.

Steve and Tommy's relationship was moving on. They were no longer the mischievous, inseparable twosome from their primary school days. Their friendship wasn't the same. It was tenuous and more fragile because of their differing circumstances and it would be up to both of them to determine whether they wanted it to continue into adulthood and later life.

The test came sooner than they anticipated however, when they found themselves in a spot of bother outside the entrance to their block of flats. Their path's were blocked by four older youths who purposely stood in their way.

"What's going on?" Tommy said curtly. The youths laughed. He vaguely knew two of them from Heathfield Secondary. They were the Mantovani twins, sixteen year old Angelo and his younger brother by fifteen minutes, Frederico. Their father Luigi ran the popular Santa Marina fish and chip shop locally.

"We live here," Angelo replied, his voice confident and articulate.

"Since when?" Tommy asked abruptly.

"Cheeky little sod this one...eh Freddie?" Angelo said to his brother Frederico who was standing next to him. He then turned to Tommy.

"None of your business you little turd. But as you asked, and we want to be really friendly, we moved in yesterday.....top floor. So we're your new neighbours."

"How do you know *we're* from here?" Tommy said showing no outward signs of fear. Steve looked on but said nothing.

"We know everything that goes on round here, me and my brother....and from now on everything round here goes through us." Angelo replied. Steve decided he wasn't going to be left out of the conversation.

"And you are?" He asked quite politely. Angelo laughed. His brother and the two other youths laughed in unison.

"We're the Mantovani's, and we don't like poofs," Angelo was quick to reply. Frederico came in suddenly.

"No...we don't like poofters who go off down the park together. Nancy boys....fucking down the park," he said. Tommy was furious. The Mantovani family *had* just moved in to Barton Bridge council flats and were already making their mark. Angelo turned to Steve.

"Mods, the pair of you. Poncy mods....that's what you are."

Tommy took offence at that comment.

"Right...that's it. Get out of our fucking way, the lot of you." His voice had changed in an instant and he sounded menacing, but the four youths stood their ground. Tommy continued.

"If there's any queers round here....I'm looking at them," he said. Steve looked on dumbfounded as the red mist descended around Tommy. He made a move towards the biggest of the four youths, a strapping lad of nearly six foot who towered over him. Tommy poked him in the chest.

"You, ya fucker....I'll 'ave you first." Tommy wasn't mincing his words. He strode over to the grassy area by the pavement. Steve couldn't believe what was happening. He knew Tommy had a temper but he'd *never* seen him like this. The big fella was gobsmacked.

"You deaf as well as stupid?" Tommy shouted, removing his jacket. "Said I'll 'ave you first. Clear enough you fucking moron?"
Then he pointed to the other three in turn, the last being Angelo Mantovani.

"Then you....and you....and I'll finish with you, pretty boy....pretty greasy dago....that fucking clear enough?" Tommy's voice, although sounding agitated to the extreme, was coherent and precise and took *everyone* by surprise. Angelo Mantovani, in particular, was stunned and was briefly lost for words.

Tommy didn't say anything else. He stood

there, fists raised, his jacket lying on the ground nearby. No one moved. No one said anything. It was like time had stood still. Eventually the silence was broken by the elder Mantovani twin, Angelo. He laughed nervously.

"We were only messing about....having a laugh," he shrugged. "Weren't we Freddie?"
Frederico nodded, "Yeah, he's right. Just a game it was....yeah, just a game."
Tommy looked across at Steve and gave him the merest of surreptitious smiles. Steve knew Tommy had just pulled off a feat of blagging of the highest quality and nodded knowingly.

"We're off down the park now....me and my *friend*." Tommy said as he picked his jacket up off the grass. The four laughed again, but this time the sardonic aggression had gone.

"Tell you what," Angelo said "You've got balls...I'll give you that."
Out of the corner of his eye he caught a glimpse of uniformed Constable Dooley approaching. He was heading straight for them.

"Come on fellas, let's go," Angelo said quickly to the other three. They looked awkward as Derek Dooley passed them on his way towards the entrance to the flats.

"Alright lads?" he said in his usual authoritative voice, giving them a cursory glance as he did so. He disappeared inside. Tommy didn't miss a trick.

"Bet he's heading to the top floor...to your gaff,"

he sniggered, unable to contain himself. Angelo and Freddie took the bait. Together with the other two youths they slunk off down the path. Tommy called after them.

"Shows just how much you lot really know. He's Derek.....Derek Dooley....lives here in the flats!" His laugh was loud and gaudy. "He's our neighbour....a copper in our midst." He couldn't stop himself. "Know everything do we?" he cackled. The four youths didn't look back as they ambled off along Felgate Road.

Steve patted Tommy heartily on the back, laughing loudly.

"That was priceless Tommy. I'll remember this moment forever."

He knew then whatever the future held for the two of them, he would do his utmost to keep Tommy as a friend for life.

Chapter 4

Angelo and Freddie Mantovani's parents had come to England from Italy just after the war in 1946. There were too many people chasing too few jobs in their home city of Milan, and they'd heard reports from post war Britain that it was a resurgent land of opportunity and for those willing to work hard, could aspire to a much better standard of living than that which existed in their homelands. From the Caribbean to Ceylon, from Poland to Pakistan, folk were heading to the British Isles in search of a new life for themselves and their families.

Luigi and Chiara Mantovani were no exception, making their home in the Barchester suburb of Southfields. Luigi opened the Santa Marina fish and chip shop in lock-up premises along The Parade shortly after the two boys were born in 1947, and rented two rooms in a dilapidated Victorian terraced home not far away. They integrated well into the community and were well on their way to creating a prosperous and thriving business. The family was re-housed when their rented accommodation was condemned by the council and Barton Bridge Flats became their new home.

Two years had passed since the move and the

twins, Angelo and Freddie, now aged eighteen, had certainly made their mark on the tightly knit neighbourhood in Felgate Road. Out of the two, Angelo was the driving force. His smouldering, Mediterranean good looks belied the ruthless streak which existed within him and his burning desire to succeed and control those around him. He was suave and articulate and his deep brown eyes, jet black hair and dark olive complexion all combined to make him a stunningly handsome young man.

Freddie, on the other hand, wasn't blessed with the same striking good looks. His features were more pronounced and although they were sometimes mistaken for identical twins, there was an innate, congenital difference between the two of them on closer examination. He was also not as assured and confident as his brother Angelo, but what he lacked in intellectual acumen he made up for in his dependability and unwavering loyalty towards his slightly older twin sibling.

They had both left Heathfield Secondary Modern just before coming to live in the flats and at the time Luigi, their father, had big plans to open a chain of Santa Marina chip shops throughout Barchester and beyond for his sons to manage and eventually run the family takeaway empire providing security and wealth beyond his wildest dreams.

At first the plan went well and the two brothers started their unofficial apprenticeship at the establishment in The Parade, but Angelo soon became disillusioned with the greasy, hot and humid working environment and the anti social hours and began to formulate his own get-rich-quick scheme, where he could make his fortune quickly and with the least possible effort. His powers of persuasion soon got the better of Freddie and within a few short months they left the chip shop business to pursue an entrepreneurial vocation of covert dealings within the Southfields district and beyond.

Luigi Mantovani was initially stunned and despondent when his sons chose to leave the family business, especially as he thought they were far too hasty in making their decision. Family still meant everything to the hard working Italian and although his first reaction was to disown them and kick them out of the flat, he soon mellowed and they were allowed to remain in the family home.

Angelo was both shrewd and sharp when it came to business matters and he named their new company the Zanetti Corporation. It was a clever choice because the name sounded internationally trendy and important at the same time having a respectable ring to it. But more importantly to Angelo it was abstract and transparent and gave no clue as to what type of business ventures the company was involved in. Angelo and Freddie were equal partners but again Angelo was smart enough and had the foresight to proclaim himself managing director of the Zanetti Corporation and, as such, would have the casting vote on matters of business. Freddie, unaware of the implications, was happy to go along with the ruse.

Up to now, the benefits of living with mum and dad in Felgate Road had outweighed the disadvantages, but now, approaching nineteen, and with the success they had achieved so far they both felt it time to flee the nest and embark on a more independent life. They both had cars. Freddie's was a bright red MGB roadster convertible. It had sporty lines, was fun to drive and it was a great success when it came to pulling the girls. Angelo didn't need a flash car to attract the opposite sex, and he chose a more sophisticated marque, the Jaguar , to lavish his attention on. It was the classic British racing green colour and was sleek and powerful. It oozed style, elegance and individuality and Angelo loved everything about it.

The two years the Mantovani family had lived in the Barton Bridge flats hadn't gone unnoticed by Derek Dooley. Although he knew Luigi and Chiara were decent, hardworking people and respected them, he didn't have either the same high opinion or regard for their sons. As a policeman he was naturally inquisitive but he was especially curios as to how Angelo and Freddie sustained their somewhat lavish lifestyle when he knew they no longer worked in the family business.

He kept an eye on the Zanetti Corporation but

everything seemed above board with the company and, as far as he was aware, the two young men hadn't broken the law in any way, which left him bemused and a little frustrated. His professionalism didn't allow him to dwell on the matter though, or look for something that wasn't there, so he merely kept his eyes open and left it at that.

Tommy Nelson was another resident of the flats Derek Dooley kept an eye on, but as far as he knew, he'd kept his nose clean since his truancy and shoplifting escapade and he made sure his daughter Carol mixed with him as little as possible. Tommy hadn't completely forgotten about his childhood sweetheart but there were other, more important things on his mind.

He was rapidly approaching his sixteenth birthday and the day he vowed to leave school, but more significantly, the wages from the Saturday job he managed to get at Subway Records and his paper rounds had accrued into a tidy sum and the momentous day had arrived when he was able to take delivery of a black and silver Norton Manx motorcycle, the machine of his dreams. Although second hand, he bought it from a dealer in Barchester, so it had been cleaned and serviced and looked immaculate. Tommy thought it was the prettiest thing he'd ever seen, let alone owned.

He was still only fifteen though and wasn't old enough to legally ride it, let alone hold a license to do so. He had nowhere to keep it and the only person he'd told about his impending purchase was Dennis Carter at the market. He'd never even ridden a motorbike but this didn't deter Tommy in the slightest. His obsession for the two wheeled vehicles had grown over a number of years and nothing was going to stop him realising his vision of owning one and taking to the open road on his very own machine.

He donned his crash helmet and kick started the engine, but the sheer weight of the Norton took him by surprise and they both nearly ended up on the ground, but he steadied himself, flicked it into gear, gingerly let out the clutch and he was away, albeit at a snail's pace. Luckily for him the traffic was light and his confidence soon grew as he made his way sedately towards Somerset Place market in Southfields to show off his latest acquisition to his new pal and fellow biking enthusiast, Dennis Carter.

He approached Subway Record's stall with the proficiency of a complete novice, picking his way carefully through the crowd. Whilst the Norton's engine grunted and spluttered in protest over the low revs Tommy was subjecting the machine to, Del Shannon was blaring out of the speakers when he finally brought the motorcycle to a halt outside the record stall.

Tommy took off his crash helmet, switched off the engine and grinned. Dennis Carter looked on, open mouthed. Tommy spread his arms wide.

"Say something then, Denny," he shouted over the loud music. Dennis just stared.

"Not lost for words eh, Denny. No...come on....what do you think?. Suits my style? Mouthy Dennis Carter....lost for words?"

"Jesus Tommy," Dennis finally exclaimed, his eyes glued to the Manx 500. "Yours?" he asked tentatively, fearing Tommy might just have stolen the bike for the crack. Tommy nodded extravagantly, his face still beaming. He struggled to get it onto its' stand.

"All mine," he said gleefully not letting go of the thing, afraid his pride and joy might fall into the gutter and get damaged. It didn't and Tommy gave the fuel tank an exaggerated polish with his arm before having the courage to walk away and join Dennis at the stall.

"Just bought it," he said proudly, "With the dosh from my paper rounds."

"But you're only fifteen."
Tommy shrugged.

"You're fucking fifteen, Tommy. Jesus Christ."
Tommy didn't say a word.

"What you going to do with it?" Dennis probed further. Tommy was confused. Out of everyone he knew he thought Dennis would be the one person who would share his passion and enthusiasm and wouldn't be in any way judgemental. He certainly wasn't ready for a lecture and went on the offensive.

"Don't you like it?" he blurted out. Dennis could

see everyone admiring the motorbike as they walked by.

"Come on Denny....you're my mate. Don't you fucking like it....tell me?"

Dennis reached over and took Del Shannon's single off the turn table.

"It's fab Tommy. Fucking fab. Bloody marvellous!"

Tommy's fist went into the air.

"I knew you'd like it," he said, his spirits lifted once more.

"But what about the law?" Dennis added.

"Sod the law."

"Yeah, but you just can't say that."

"I can."

"You'll get done."

"So what. I don't care. I've got this now....I've worked bloody hard for this."

"Keep your knickers on Tommy. I'm with you....you know that. Just looking at things. that's all. Like where you're going to keep it."

"I'm glad you brought that up 'cause I need a favour."

"Here we go. I just knew there'd be a catch," Dennis said.

"I was wondering if we could put it in the lock-up, just for a little while."

"We?" Dennis replied. "You were wondering if *we*?......come on Tommy, you know what Slade's like with the lock-up."

"You can swing it. If anyone can, you can swing it, Denny. Just for a few weeks....'til my birthday. Stick it in the back and put a sheet over it or something."

"And tell him it's mine?"

"Yeah, I didn't think of that. Brilliant....you're a pal Denny. I'll take you out on it, you'll see....it's fast...fucking fast, I can tell you that."

Dennis Carter knew when he was beaten and a wry smile came to his face as he nodded to Tommy.

"Oh, you are a *real* fucking pal, Denny. I won't forget this. I won't. Never."

"Yeah, yeah Tommy, Whatever." Dennis replied, the casual air in his voice belying the deeper apprehension within. He knew his boss, Victor Slade, wouldn't take kindly to his lock-up premises being used to store a motorbike but he just couldn't let Tommy down.

"We'll do it when we close up.....and I've got some extra special weed to try. We'll celebrate with a smoke. How's that, Tommy?"

"That's fucking ace," Tommy enthused. He couldn't be happier.

Meanwhile, whilst Tommy was basking in his secretive glory having fulfilled his very first ambition of owning a motorbike any Hell's Angel would be proud to own and ride, his childhood best friend, Steve Baker, was about to steal his thunder and stun not only Tommy, but everyone at Dunsbury Grammar, and most importantly, his ever supportive parents, George and Mary.

He dropped his bombshell on Wednesday January 17th, *his* sixteenth birthday. After school lessons had finished he went to see the head teacher and coolly told him he was leaving school there and then to pursue a career in football. The experienced headmaster had seen it all in his illustrious and extensive career, but even he was astonished to hear that a model pupil, and one almost certain to progress to university and beyond, was exercising his legal right to terminate his education and schooling there and then. In the somewhat hallowed and esteemed surroundings of the head teacher's office, Steve briefly gave his reasons for the decision he'd made. He didn't stay long. He had a far more important meeting to attend to at Southfields FC. He was about to sign professional terms with the third division club and he was due to meet the manager and coach Will Grealish.

Leaving Dunsbury Grammar after nearly five studious yet enjoyable years, he barely glanced back as he cycled out of the main gates on his way to the football stadium. He arrived at the small reception area slightly embarrassed as he was still wearing his school uniform, and proudly announced he had an appointment with the manager of the club. The receptionist nodded and smiled as she informed Will Grealish of Steve's arrival via the office intercom. She'd seen it all before. Young hopefuls aspiring to reach the heights of the top footballing fraternity, and escorted him to the manager's office.

"Come in lad," Grealish said, his voice deep and confident. He was an ex-pro himself and although he never reached the top level, he attained almost cult status as an uncompromising centre half whose career spanned more than a decade in the lower leagues, and was well respected in footballing circles as a result.

Southfields FC, nicknamed the '*Hornets*' because of their black and yellow striped shirts and black shorts, was a relatively small club whose halcyon days in the first division, football's top flight, had long since gone and had now been confined to the history books. For some time the club had languished in the shadow of Barchester United, the city's big first division outfit, and Will Grealish had been brought in to revitalise the fortunes of the club and bring the long awaited success its' loyal fans had hoped for and dreamed about for years.

Money was still a problem though, hence the need to look towards promising youngsters like Steve Baker who could be plucked from within the community and hopefully moulded into top players who could, in time, bring Southfields Football Club back into the higher echelons of football society. The club scout had been watching Steve for a while. He'd introduced himself more recently and invited Steve to hold talks with the club about joining them as a professional. Steve had kept all this a secret from everyone, including his parents. There were a handful of his team mates from the school eleven who guessed what was going on but they'd said nothing so no one was the wiser.

"Sit down Steven," Grealish gestured towards a chair the other side of his desk. "Oh....and no calls Marion," he said to the receptionist as she pulled the door to and left.

"Have you had a chance to think things over since our last little chat?" he asked, turning his attention to the young striker.

"Yes sir, I've given it a lot of thought and...."

"Hold on Steven," Grealish interrupted, "You're not in class now. Nobody calls me *sir*.....Mr Grealish or just plain boss will do. Savvy?"
Steve nodded and immediately became more relaxed in the big man's company.

"Go on," Grealish encouraged. Steve explained his willingness to join the club there and then and even told him he'd left school that very day. Will Grealish listened with interest. Steve's grammar school education had resulted in him being well spoken and articulate and left Grealish knowing exactly what his intentions were.

"We're a family club here, we pride ourselves on that, and family values are important to us. So have you discussed this with your mum and dad?" Grealish sat forward. Steve shook his head.

"No, I haven't."
"Why not?"
"They wouldn't understand."

"What do you mean, wouldn't understand?"

"My dad would never agree. University's what he wants for me......I know it."

"But that's not a bad thing, surely?"

"It is for me. Football's what I want, and if you think I'm good enough, then that's what I've decided."

"Yeah yeah, hold on lad. It's not quite as simple as that."

Steve thought it *was* and hoped his dream of becoming a professional footballer wasn't going to come crashing down around him in Will Grealish's office under the main stand.

"With someone your age we like to involve the parents as much as possible. I know you think you're all grown up and can go it alone, but it's not that easy, Steven, believe me."

"But I don't need their permission, do I? Sixteen year olds didn't need permission from their mums and dads to sign up for the army in the war, did they? To fight for their country.....and die for it, surely?"

Grealish didn't have an answer for Steve's argument, because he knew he was right.

"If you're that committed young man, I'll tell you what I'll do." He reached into a drawer and took out an envelope. "In here I have two contracts," he passed one across the desk to Steve.

"I'll do a deal with you, lad. This is the contract you're so keen to sign. Take it. Read it. Show your mum and dad. Involve them. Get them on your side if you possibly can, you're probably going to need them. Then come back and tell me what you want to do. I'll respect your decision then. Deal?"

Compromise was something Steve knew inwardly he would have to embrace occasionally if he was to get out of life what he so desperately wanted. He also knew his dream of having a successful footballing career was very much alive. The contract was there on the desk, within his reach. Will Grealish stared across at him. Steve's eyes were fixed firmly on the contract. He looked up and met Grealish's gaze.

"You've got a deal," he said boldly.
Grealish looked long and hard into Steve's eyes. In his job, man management was second only to his footballing coaching skills, and eye contact, in his dealings with those under him, was of prime importance. Steve's gaze was unwavering. Grealish smiled.

"You've got a good head on you, lad.....I like it. I like what I see. Now scarper....I've got a team to pick for Saturday!"
Nothing more was said. Steve picked the contract up from the desk and left. As he cycled away from the ground his euphoria was tinged only by the thought of his impending confrontation with his mum and dad, which he decided to tackle that very evening.

Not surprisingly, his dad was lost for words

over Steve's revelation, and initially refused even to discuss the matter. It was only when he threatened to leave home that his father, George, began to take his son seriously. His mum was torn between siding with her husband or her only child. It was something she couldn't do on this occasion and said nothing. Steve knew by the look on her face that her sympathies lay in his direction and doing battle with his dad was the only option he had.

His youthful obstinacy was steadfast though and George began to realise perhaps his son's forthrightness, self belief and inner confidence were traits he and Mary had not only passed on to him, but had been instilled and nurtured by them during his informative years. Steve sensed his dad was beginning to mellow when he picked up the contract and read it through. When he saw the wages the club were offering Steve it suddenly made him think. He was now chief buyer at work, a seemingly well paid and respectable middle management position. It had taken him fifteen years to reach that senior status within the company. Yet Steve was being offered only marginally less at the tender age of sixteen, with the opportunity to earn a great deal more in the not too distant future.

George studied the contract thoroughly and even discussed some of the less rudimentary points with his son. Eventually he had to agree it was an opportunity no one in their right mind would cast aside, and to Steve's amazement and delight, he agreed he should seize the chance to play professional football and pledged his support and backing unconditionally and unequivocally.

Mary was so happy with the amicable outcome she shed a few tears of joy and gave Steve a huge cuddle. He also realised how magnanimous his dad had been and asked if he'd go with him to the club and witness his signing of the contract. He knew Will Grealish would approve of the family involvement and George said it would give him great pleasure to do so. Steve went to bed happy that night and dreamed of scoring a hat trick on his home debut for the club he'd supported since he was eight years old.

There was one person he had to tell about his news and good fortune. He *had* to tell Tommy. He also knew he had to do it before he signed for Southfields F.C. and caught up with him at the Wimpy Bar in the High Street the following afternoon when Tommy had finished school.

"I'm stunned," Tommy uttered when Steve finally plucked up the courage to tell him when they were on their second bottle of coke.

"Jesus Steve.....I'm just fucking stunned. There's me, counting down the weeks....the days...'til I can quit frigging Heathfield...for good. And you, you come up with this."

Steve was as matter-of-fact about the whole situation as he could be. He knew Tommy wasn't happy at school and although they had drifted apart, he had no intention of gloating over his good luck and the way life was panning out perfectly for him. Their friendship went back too far for him to ever act in that way, but he also couldn't hide his excitement about playing professional football, especially for the team they both supported and Tommy was altruistic, generous and enthusiastic on congratulating Steve on his pending success.

"What about you," Steve said, changing the subject. "What you going to do when you leave?"
Tommy shrugged.

"Why don't you do what *you're* good at?" Steve persisted.

"What....thieving and smoking dope?" Tommy half laughed at his own quip.

"No. Singing, you silly arse."
Tommy shrugged again.

"You're bloody good Tommy, and you know I'm not just saying that."
Tommy perked up suddenly. "You really think so?"

"I know so. If I can make something of myself playing football, you can do the same then with the talent you've got......your voice......your bloody voice Tommy. Wise up mate, go for it.....yeah?"
Tommy couldn't help but laugh. His singing career had been put on hold but meeting and talking with Steve had certainly given him food for thought.

"I'll think about it," he said casually. Inwardly though, he was buzzing with new found excitement. He lifted his bottle of coke. "Here's to your success

Steve Baker, and I really mean that."
Their glass bottles chinked as they once again enjoyed each other's company. Even so, apprehension and, to a point mistrust, still existed inside Tommy's head and he wasn't about to divulge *his* little secret about his pride and joy, the Norton Manx, to Steve that particular afternoon.

Chapter 5

Steve Baker signed for the club the following week. It was a low key affair and Will Grealish was pleased Steve had taken his advice and involved his father. A photographer had turned up from the local paper, the weekly Southfields Gazette, at Grealish's invitation and he happily clicked away when Steve put his signature to the contract in Grealish's office. That was followed by a glass of champagne each and a short speech from Grealish welcoming Steve to the club and wishing him a long and successful career as a professional footballer.

Then it was out onto the pitch where Steve was handed a black and yellow striped team shirt. More photos were taken with him and Will Grealish shaking hands in the centre circle, and a couple of Steve on his own, holding the club shirt above his head. He enjoyed the occasion and wasn't overawed by the proceedings or the special surroundings of his favourite football club. It was over far too quickly though as far as he was concerned. Grealish instructed him to report for work at ten the following morning, then he and his proud father left.

Family celebrations continued into the evening however, as George had booked a table for three at

La Vigna, the stylish Italian restaurant in the High Street. This time Steve's mother Mary could share in the revelry, and after a couple of glasses of Chianti, Steve was content to reflect on the day happy in the knowledge that they *were* still a family and he wasn't embarking on the most important part of his life on his own. Even his mum looked happy and contented as she tucked into her tiramisu dessert.

His first day at the club wasn't quite the romantic occasion he'd envisaged. He walked into the changing room at ten o'clock precisely, kit bag over his shoulder. He was overwhelmed. The cacophony of laughter and banter alone took him by surprise. His heroes were all there, within touching distance. He didn't know where to look. He stood bemused, believing all eyes were on him, the new kid on the block. Some were. But to most of the seasoned campaigners there, a new team member in their midst was something they were used to seeing. There was a tap on his shoulder.

"Over there," a voice said. Steve turned around. The voice was unfamiliar but the person it belonged to wasn't. It was the diminutive figure of tricky left winger, Joey Masters, who Steve had watched and admired from the terraces for years. He was pointing to a space along the far side. A numberless plain blue training kit hung on a hook and pinned to it was a scrap of paper with the name Baker scrawled across it. At six foot, Steve dwarfed the skilful thirty year old and was lost for words when he recognised who it was.

"Thanks," is all he said, rather awkwardly. He went over to his designated spot and sat down.

Changing rooms weren't new to him. He'd been in the school team long enough to be well used to the surroundings. The smell of sweat and horse liniment were familiar to his nostrils. The joking, the swearing, none of it was new to him. But this was a room full of men, with hairy backs and muscular bodies, not pale adolescent boys, and that *was* a new experience. Although it didn't make him feel inadequate it was an unnerving experience and the steep learning curve in his transition to manhood had begun.

He looked around. The huge bearded centre half Paul Bradshaw was sat opposite him in deep conversation with left back Roy *'animal'* Dickenson. To his right he was aware of his club hero, fellow striker Johnny Cleveland who, at thirty four, had proudly worn the number nine shirt for more seasons than Steve could remember.

For a brief second he wondered what he was doing there in such exalted company. Then Will Grealish walked in. Wearing a black track suit, training boots and a referees whistle around his neck, he oozed confidence and like an actor taking to the stage, he strode to the centre of the room. The place went quiet.

"We've got to crack on this week. Lynton Rovers on Saturday, never an easy derby. Big home crowd....good atmosphere. We need to do the business. We *must* win that......not let our fans down. Not let ourselves down. So....a good session this morning.....loads of hard work, no slacking or skiving by anyone.....got it?"

There were murmurs all around and the odd *'yes boss'* from some.

"As you can see, new lad here this morning, Steven Baker. Signed yesterday from Dunsbury Grammar."

All eyes *were* now on Steve and he suddenly felt uneasy and self conscious. The intimidating bearded centre half Paul Bradshaw couldn't resist coming in with a timely quip.

"Good looks now a condition of professional football status, boss?" he asked with the lucidity which belied his outward persona. Most were now laughing at Steve's expense. He didn't mind that. He knew he would have to take stick initially to gain any respect from his new set of team mates and smiled as the good humoured teasing continued.

"Or is it a ploy for the club to gain the support of the women of Southfields?" Bradshaw added glibly.

"If that *was* the case Paul," Will Grealish was quick to reply "Then you'd be banished immediately to the annals of the Sunday league, I can tell you now," he added amidst more laughter.

Bradshaw threw his towel at the man in the middle in a jocular manner of surrender but didn't say anymore.

"I'll tell you what," Grealish continued "This lad can play. I've seen him. He can also score goals, and he's been a passionate supporter of this club since he was a toddler, and probably knows more about its' history than you lot put together. Now I don't mind you making fun of our lily white new boy, but I also know you'll cut him a bit of slack along the way. Make myself clear? Now Steven, you got anything to say?"

Steve was taken aback but his answer was immediate.

"It's *Steve*, boss. I'd like it if everyone called me Steve," he said with aplomb.

"That's told you boss," Paul Bradshaw was quick to add. It was the perfect start to Steve's professional football career.

The home derby with Lynton drew a big crowd as expected and Southfields won the tense and sometimes bad tempered encounter by an only goal scored in the second half by Johnny Cleveland. The Southfields legend milked his celebration to such an extent he was booked for wasting time. He didn't care one iota though. He'd scored the winner and to him and seven thousand loyal, cheering fans, that's all that mattered.

Steve had impressed both his manager and team mates in the training sessions leading up to the match but he knew he wasn't ready to make his debut in such a demanding game. His manager agreed and he watched from the stands. He was introduced to the fans before the kick-off though and received rapturous applause from them. Even that was like a dream come true for the youngster with the blond crew-cut from Felgate Road. He was one of their own and they welcomed him accordingly.

The weekly Southfields Gazette had hit the streets the previous day and the back page headlines read *'Local young striker signs for the Hornets'* and the piece was accompanied by the photo of Steve holding up the team shirt. As a result, instant minor celebrity status was thrust upon him, albeit in a small and localised way. Nevertheless it was a massive boost to Steve's ego and he revelled in his new found prominence within the community.

It was also the big topic of conversation in the Barton Bridge flats with George and Mary Baker justifiably proud of their son. Steve hadn't forgotten Tommy either, giving him two match tickets and promising more in the future. Even Angelo and Freddie Mantovani couldn't help but notice the new found interest in the Baker household. They were keen not to miss an opportunity for their own personal gain and decided to keep a close, but discreet, eye on Steve's unfolding career.

His debut for the Hornets came even sooner than he expected. It was a Wednesday night league cup tie away to lowly, unfashionable northern outfit, Appleton United from the fourth division. Southfields were the clear favourites and were cruising at half time with a two goal lead courtesy of centre forward Johnny Cleveland, who finished off two classy moves with strikes of the same quality. It gave Will Grealish the ideal opportunity to bring Steve on as a substitute for the celebrated number nine.

Steve didn't disappoint his manager and matched his hero Cleveland with two opportunist headed goals in the second half to help his team to a deserved and comfortable four nil win. He would have loved to have opened his scoring at home in front of a big crowd instead of the two hundred or so Hornet's fans who'd made the long trip north but nothing was going to dampen his spirits on such an impressive and successful debut.

Normally after a midweek match the players would return on the team coach the same night but Will Grealish had decided to take the team up on the train to the seaside town of Appleton on the Wednesday and stay overnight in a hotel on the promenade. It was his way of rewarding the squad for their hard earned victory over their local rivals, Lynton Rovers.

It was a gesture not lost on the group of players and most headed off to the pubs and clubs of downtown Appleton after their cup win. Grealish made just two stipulations as he watched them all leave the football ground in a convoy of taxis. The first being a curfew at the hotel no later than one in the morning. The second, being sober enough to walk into the hotel foyer unaided.

The Flamingo Club on the sea front was the venue favoured by most of the players and Steve was happy to tag along. Clubbing was a new and exciting experience for the sixteen year old and he found the buzz and surroundings of the night spot both modish and exhilarating. He also found the atmosphere intoxicating in more ways than one, especially after some of his team mates had plied him with exotic sounding cocktails.

He'd never been happier though and revelled in the setting and the ambience of the club. The abundance of women also came as a big shock. Real women as opposed to the giggly teenage girls of Dunsbury Grammar's prom dances. It frightened him somewhat but he decided to be as cool, suave and sophisticated as he perceived the rest of the men there to be. But that was becoming harder the more alcohol he consumed.

He was standing at the bar when a particularly curvaceous and attractive woman came over to him.

"It *was* you, wasn't it?" she asked candidly. Steve was taken aback. He wasn't used to being approached by good looking, sexy women and looked at her blankly.

"At the match.....earlier," she continued.
Steve swallowed hard. "Yeah, I play for Southfields....the Hornets," he blurted out gawping

at the dark haired beauty in a shimmering, emerald green low cut mini dress, who had just invaded his space.

"I thought so," she replied, moving closer to him. She held out her hand.

"I'm Tanya, by the way," she said. He took her hand rather awkwardly.

"I'm Steve....Steve Baker," he replied, mesmerised by her big brown eyes and pouting lips. Tanya pushed out her cleavage and Steve found himself staring down at her voluptuous breasts.

"How about buying a lady a drink?" she asked well aware his gaze was centred on her bosom.

"Yeah....yeah....of course."

"Bacardi and coke then." Tanya replied slipping her arm through his. Just the smell of her womanly body so close to his made him go weak at the knees. He ordered her drink and noticed his team mates all around him had big grins on their faces. He handed her the drink.

"You were at the game?" he asked.
Tanya nodded and sipped her Bacardi and coke.

"Could have had a hat trick," Steve continued feeling a little more relaxed in her company. Her hand furtively yet purposefully touched his inner thigh and lingered there briefly. His erection was instantaneous. Tanya smiled knowingly as Steve blushed uncontrollably.

"You still can," she whispered into his ear. Steve's mind was elsewhere, desperately trying to control his excitement. It wasn't working.

"Can what?" is all he could utter. "I can still what?"

"You can still score.....tonight. Still get a hat trick....know what I'm saying?" she said quietly feeling for his hardness. Suddenly Steve knew exactly what she meant. He was completely flummoxed. Things were going too fast, moving too fast. He didn't know what to do or what to say. He was desperate to get to grips with the situation.

"What do you do?" he asked clumsily, trying to change the subject. It was Tanya who was in control and she knew it.

"I'm in customer services.....I'm an HCH," she said nonchalantly. "Anyway, what do you say?" her voice was now more provocative as she pulled him closer to her. The bulge in his slacks wasn't disappearing, it was getting bigger.

What was subsiding though was his puerile embarrassment. He couldn't beat it so he thought he had no option other than to go with the flow. He put his arm around her shoulder, much to the delight of his team mates looking on. It was them all along who had set up the impromptu liaison in the first place. They had procured, and paid for, Tanya's services earlier that evening without Steve's knowledge and were there to see the contrived relationship between the two of them blossom as quickly as possible.

She hadn't been to the match as she'd said. She

hated football and had never set foot in the town's football stadium. But she had a job to do and a little white lie here and there didn't seem to bother her. It *was* true, she was in customer services and she well and truly serviced her customers. The abbreviated job description HCH she gave Steve, meant *High Class Hooker* and summed up her profession perfectly.

"Come on, let's get out of here....come back to my place," Tanya urged continuing to take the initiative. Steve had no idea he was the centre of the devious set up and couldn't resist her charms and persuasive power over his sexual desire, and with his team mates looking on expectantly, she led him like a lamb to the slaughter away from the bar and out of the Flamingo Club.

She continued her amorous advances in the taxi, much to the cab driver's delight as he repositioned his rear view mirror to get a voyeuristic view of the action in the back. She kissed him so expertly Steve was left gasping for air as her tongue probed and explored, and the driver had a bird's-eye view of her hand homing in on the stiffness between his legs. The show was over far too quickly for the taxi driver though, as he reluctantly pulled over on Tanya's instructions a few minutes later.

Tanya's *place* was a swanky penthouse apartment in the new marina development in the seaside town. But even before Steve could admire the spectacular vista he found himself naked on her sumptuous, king-size bed. She'd stripped him of his clothing and was sitting on the bed beside him still fully dressed but minus her high-heeled shoes which she'd kicked off in the lounge.

She was almost twice his age and had come across the male anatomy in every size and shape but she never tired of the company of the virile younger man and the alluring and erotic bodies most of them proudly possessed and were keen to show off. She found Steve Baker no exception and he lay back expectantly as her eyes seduced him.

She took his penis between her thumb and forefinger and with the merest of touches, moved and caressed it gently. Steve closed his eyes and moaned. He was in seventh heaven. No one had ever done that to him before. Like most adolescent boys he'd experimented with masturbation but by its' very nature it was a secretive and solitary diversion carried out mainly in the privacy of his own bedroom and, although pleasurable, was dispensed with so much urgency, the enjoyment was tempered by the immediate need for self gratification and sexual satisfaction.

This was *so* different. It was an experience he could enjoy and savour beyond his wildest dreams. Or so he thought. What he didn't take into account was the physics of mind over matter, especially in one so young, and one who's sex drive was rising so rapidly it could easily catch him unawares. On this occasion that was exactly what was about to happen.

His erection was now enormous and Tanya could feel him throbbing under her expert touch. Steve found it sheer bliss and could have lay there forever. But something was happening deep within his sexual metabolism. Tanya's stroking had triggered the chemical and physiological chain of events that would inevitably lead to orgasm, and to Steve's greatest fear, premature ejaculation.

He was too embarrassed to say anything to the woman who was giving him so much pleasure, and for him the point of no return was fast approaching. He centred his mind on non sexual things, mundane run-of-the-mill chores like cleaning his mud caked football boots, opening his post office savings account, anything other than sex. But it wasn't working. He looked down at his erection which was now pointing straight up at him.

He caught Tanya's eye. She was smiling enigmatically and Steve was sure exactly what was happening inside both his body and his head. He was right. She watched intently as his moans turned to gasps. Her hand slipped down to his tight young balls and cupped them gently. He came instantly, crying out involuntarily as warm semen spurted out over his chest and stomach.

He was mortified. He'd shot his load all over himself on his very first sexual encounter with a real woman. It was a complete disaster. He felt humiliated and ashamed.

"It's alright," Tanya said quietly, reaching for a box of tissues. "It was my fault. I knew what I was doing. It' not your fault, honey, I wanted to watch you, that's all." She wiped his chest and abdomen with the tissues, "And besides....I wanted to get the first one out of the way so we could then enjoy ourselves." She also wiped away a tear on his cheek and kissed him lightly on the lips.

"I don't understand." Steve spoke at last.

"You will," Tanya replied as she stood up beside the bed. His erection had naturally subsided but was still semi-erect. Tanya wriggled out of her emerald mini dress, unclipped her bra and let it fall to the floor. Steve's eyes were like saucers as he ogled her large, well formed breasts. By the time she'd slipped off her knickers his penis was rock hard again. Tanya climbed onto the bed, straddled Steve's sizeable member and sunk down on it, enveloping it completely. She moved rhythmically up and down, her hands resting on chest.

"Now....had I done this earlier, you would have come by now.....not good that." She began to move quicker. "Come on....do your bit." Her voice was now more intense and her breathing quickened. Steve accepted her invitation and started to respond, slowly pushing up inside her. Tanya had been paid to take his virginity and was thoroughly enjoying the task. She moaned as Steve sensed her urgency and he thrust himself into her with such rhythmic fervour, he came again. Tanya encouraged him to continue and she reached her climax shortly after, crying out and throwing her head back in ecstasy as she did so.

Over the next hour Tanya's carnal instruction resulted in them trying various different coital positions and Steve reached two further orgasms before even his youthful sex drive waned, and he dozed off in the luxurious king-size bed next to the masterly seductress who had metaphorically just turned him from a boy into a man.

"Jesus Christ!" he exclaimed some time later, leaping out of the bed. "Is that the time?"
The red *led* numerals of the bedside clock-radio shone out like a warning beacon. It was two fifteen. Tanya stirred briefly, then turned over and went back to sleep. Steve was in a panic. He threw on his clothes and rushed out of the opulent apartment block into the deserted streets of Appleton's marina district. There were no taxis around. The cool breeze hit his face. He was completely lost and Grealish's words *"No later than one o'clock"* were ringing in his ears over and over again.

Only the night porter was around when Steve eventually made it back to the hotel. Or so he thought. Having got his room key with the minimum of noise and fuss, he tiptoed towards the elevator.

"One o'clock Baker....I said one o'clock." Will Grealish was sitting in the reception lounge adjacent to the foyer. Steve stopped in his tracks.

"My office, Friday morning, ten o'clock..savvy?" Steve looked across at him and nodded sheepishly.

"Savvy?" Grealish's impatient voice was markedly louder.

"Yes boss," Steve replied. The elevator came to his rescue and he breathed a sigh of relief as it whisked him up to his room. His thoughts were on Tanya, the *high class hooker*, as his head hit the pillow. He had no idea she was a prostitute, one who was paid to relive him of his virginity, and in that naive state, he slept soundly.

Later that day on the journey back to Southfields his team mates confessed all. The way he handled the revelation was a testament to his maturity, and he even went as far as thanking them for their consideration regarding his sexual needs *and* their generosity in paying for Tanya's services. It was all delivered in his best grammatical diction which his team mates found hilarious and Steve knew his social acceptance into the team was well on the way to being successful.

The biggest test was yet to come though. It was in Will Grealish's office on the Friday morning. Grealish, although not directly involved in the innocuous deception, knew all about it and in some ways was having *his* bit of fun at Steve's expense by having him report to his office to receive what Steve thought would be a mild admonishment at best and a bollocking at worst.

The test was whether he would drop his team mates in it by blaming them for setting him up resulting in his lateness back at the hotel, or whether he would be man enough to take responsibility for his own actions and blame no one but himself. He had no idea Grealish was in cahoots with his fellow players and admitted his culpability, much to Grealish's satisfaction. He still got a bollocking though, albeit tongue in cheek as Grealish was concerned. But Steve didn't know that!

Chapter 6

Steve's seemingly smooth transition from schoolboy to professional footballer was progressing beyond even his expectations, and he had settled into the club's routine without too many problems. The demanding training and fitness programme was having its effect on his developing body, and to Will Grealish's satisfaction his physique was beefing up as he'd hoped. The only part of his personality he wanted Steve to look towards was the passion within him, or lack of it as Grealish quite bluntly pointed out to him in the privacy of his office.

Steve was growing into a solid, dependable and organised young adult and his footballing skills and ability were unquestionable. Grealish told him those attributes alone weren't enough to achieve the success Steve craved, and if he wanted to ever play at the highest level he needed to become almost obsessively intense and zealous to the extreme in his commitment on the pitch.

Grealish never minced his words and described Steve's persona on the field of play as far too gentlemanly and sportsmanlike and urged him to regard every opponent and every defender that stood between him and the oppositions goal as the ultimate enemy, and be treated as such. It was something Steve knew would take considerable effort as he realised what his manager was getting at was alien to his way of thinking, but he was also conscious of his burning ambition to be the best, and that took precedence over everything else.

Away from football he was still happy living at home, although the need for a degree of independence inevitably caused friction between him and his father, George. But Mary was always there to act as an intermediary and the situation never got out of hand. There was one subject on which agreement between Steve and *both* his parents wasn't forthcoming and that was the means of transport he chose to spend his money on.

He was still too young to drive a car, yet he desperately wanted wheels of his own. The result was a brand new Lambretta motor scooter. It's red and silver livery and abundance of chrome possessed all the panache of Italian styling and features he was looking for. The mod craze was gaining momentum on a national basis and Steve didn't mind being part of it. He already had the crew-cut hairstyle synonymous with the trend, and his acquisition of a parka jacket, complete with its' compulsory fur around the hood, completed the unofficial mod uniform. The new Lambretta was both a means of transport and a fashion statement and Steve had loads of fun whizzing around the streets on it.

One person who didn't share either his taste or

enthusiasm for his new purchase was Tommy Nelson. He hated motor scooters and he'd voiced his opinion to Steve on more than the odd occasion. He was peeved that Steve's dumpy Lambretta was getting all the admiring glances and attention in and around the environs of Felgate Road, when his far superior and beautifully sleek Norton motorbike had been hidden away for months in a back street lock-up.

But all that was about to change. It was Wednesday, May 15th, Tommy's sixteenth birthday. He had a busy day planned and was up early determined to make the day special in every way. He'd waited patiently for this moment in his life and wanted to savour every minute. He left the Barton Bridge flats around eight thirty with his mum's birthday wishes happily ringing in his ears. His dad, Harry, had been chauffeuring until the early hours and had not surfaced from his slumbers. Tommy guessed he wouldn't have known what day it was anyway, and to be honest it didn't bother him either way. He was past caring what his dad was up to and more concerned about his own future.

His school uniform this particular morning consisted of a black leather jacket he'd picked up at the market and a pair of faded denim jeans. He was fully aware this attire was banned at Heathfield Secondary where he'd spent the past five years, but today he was going to wear what he pleased.

He looked lean and mean as he sauntered

casually out of the flats and noticed Steve over by his Lambretta. Tommy went straight over to him but Steve saw him coming and got the first quip in.

"Wow Tommy....thought you were James Dean for a minute."

"Ha ha, very good. Getting ready to milk the thing?" Tommy was quick to reply.

"Very droll Tommy....I like it," Steve laughed. Tommy had no intention of prolonging the obtuse banter.

"Great goal Saturday....a real cracker," he said changing the subject.

"Thanks mate.....just in the right place and all that. Oh.....while I remember......" he reached into his jacket pocket "A couple of tickets for next week's cup game.......and happy birthday," he beamed handing Tommy the tickets. Tommy would have put money on Steve *not* remembering his birthday and was completely taken aback.

"Thanks Steve......yeah thanks, it means a lot. And thanks for these," he said gleefully holding up the match tickets. "Anyway, I'm late for school. See you later," and he strolled off down Felgate Road. Steve gave him a sideways glance as he kick-started his Lambretta, he knew leather was banned at the comprehensive school.

Tommy wasn't going directly to school. He had something far more important to do. Today, being late for school didn't matter. Instead he made straight for Somerset Place market and the lock-up where his Norton was gathering dust. He got the key from Dennis at the record stall and couldn't get the machine out fast enough.

"What's going on?" Dennis asked when Tommy had dusted the motorbike off and wheeled it round to the stall. He knew Tommy should have been at school and would be in trouble if he was caught bunking off again.

"My birthday," Tommy said, "My *sixteenth* bloody birthday Denny. Know what that means?"

"You can ride the Norton?"

"And I can leave school."

"You can what?"

"Leave school Denny. I'm allowed to....I can....legally."

"Yeah?"

"Yeah Denny..and I'm leaving today, no sweat." Dennis broke off to serve a customer while Tommy gave the fuel tank a polish.

"And do what?" Dennis asked when he'd finished.

"Do *what*?" Tommy repeated, suddenly thrown by the concern Dennis was showing for his future. As far as he was aware, Dennis was very much like himself, happy-go-lucky and fearless and didn't give two hoots what tomorrow might bring. He shrugged.

"You must have some idea, Tommy?"

"Yeah I have, but can't say too much now. You free lunchtime?"

"Yeah, Slade's coming around one....why?"

"Fancy a little jaunt?"

"What.....on that?"

"Yeah, 'course."

"You legal....tax and everything?"

Tommy gave Dennis a look of incredulity.

"Do you want a ride or not? You're getting just like an old woman, do you know that?"

It was now Dennis's turn to shrug. He looked at the Norton sitting there ready for action.

"Yeah, let's do it Tommy. It'll be great....fucking great.....right on."

That was exactly what Tommy was waiting to hear.

"Right. Got to go to school first and I'll be back later."

"You riding the bike to school?"

"To damn right.....I'll show 'em."

He donned his crash helmet, started the powerful machine and with the briefest of waves to Dennis, he manoeuvred it carefully through the market towards the High Street.

It didn't take long to get to Heathfield Comprehensive and he proudly rode it up the school drive, revving the engine excessively before coming to a halt in the staff car park between the headmaster's impressive black Rover and the deputy head's less imposing Ford Popular.

Within seconds, inquisitive faces appeared at the classroom windows all around, eager to see what the commotion was all about. Tommy was in his element and gave the bike a final twist of the throttle which sent an ear splitting roar throughout the school complex. He then strode purposefully towards the school's main entrance, his black leather jacket flung nonchalantly over his shoulder.

His meeting with the headmaster was brief and to the point, and with the words *'You're making a huge mistake, Nelson, mark my words'* ringing in his ears, he turned his back on Heathfield Comprehensive forever.

It was just after one o'clock when he got to the market. The thirty six year old owner of Subway Records, Victor Slade, stared at him as he brought the machine to a halt by the stall. His attention then turned to Dennis Carter.

"Half an hour, Dennis....no more, do you hear?" Then he glanced back at Tommy.

"And don't think I didn't know who's bike it was cluttering up my fucking lock-up."
Tommy looked at his pale, gaunt face.

"My birthday today, mister Slade," he chirped, hoping the stall holder's mood might lighten a little. It didn't.

"I should be charging you rent, you young whipper-snapper," is all he said. Tommy wasn't finished though.

"Can I have a word later," he asked boldly.

"You can, but I'm not in a generous mood. So if it's a favour....or money you're after, you're out of luck. Get it?"

Tommy said no more. Dennis went to the bike and climbed on the pillion seat.

"Eh, I've got no helmet," he said as Tommy started the engine. Tommy saw one on a parked and unattended motorbike further along the street.

"We'll borrow that one....won't do any harm," he said reaching for it as he slowly rode by. He passed it back to Dennis.

"Stick this on and hold tight.....the thrills are about to begin," Tommy's voice mimicked that of a ringmaster at a circus and they were off. Tommy was right, the thrills *were* about to begin, in more ways than one. It was the open road Tommy was seeking and he found it on the dual carriageway heading west towards the racecourse and beyond to the chalk hills of the downs.

This was the exact environment the Norton Manx was designed and built for and Tommy's first ambition of becoming an unofficial member of the *'ton up gang'* was about to be realised. The bike's performance was superlative and effortless, and Dennis was holding on for dear life as the needle touched ninety. Tommy couldn't be happier. He pushed the machine even further and enjoyed every nerve tingling minute of the experience.

A roundabout loomed up ahead. Tommy's reaction was immediate. He shut the throttle down and gently applied the brakes and an impending disaster was averted. But the drama wasn't over. Approaching the roundabout they sped past the

Mill House Cafe's car park where a police car was waiting. Confrontation was inevitable and both Tommy and Dennis looked back as they reached the roundabout to see the vehicle was already on the move with its' blue light flashing ominously.

Tommy wasn't about to surrender at the first sign of trouble however, even when the law was involved. Nothing was going to spoil his special day and his quick thinking took them all the way around the roundabout and back the way they came along the dual carriageway. He knew beyond the roundabout the road narrowed prior to entering a village and evading the police would be almost impossible. Dennis shouted in his ear as he accelerated.

"What the fuck you doing, Tommy?" The excitement in his voice was unmistakable.

"Just trust me.....and hold on bloody tight," Tommy shouted back over his shoulder. The wind was buffeting his face as he struggled to keep the Norton's front wheel on the road as the machine accelerated fiercely under his strong, sinewy frame.

In all his life he'd never experienced such pleasure and danger all in one exciting episode. He was nervous and scared and even though he was being pursued by a police car, he refused to be intimidated and capitulation wasn't even considered. The blue flashing light had followed them and was on the carriageway not far behind. The car was a brand new Ford Escort with the distinctive light blue bodywork and white doors. It's engine had been tuned to police specifications and apart from the big motorway Rovers, was the fastest urban police vehicle on the British roads.

Tommy had seen them around , but had never been chased by one. It was the moment of truth. He crouched down over the handlebars and let the Norton go. Eighty five, ninety, ninety five, the acceleration was constant and the bike pulled like a mustang stallion on the Texas plains. As they hit one hundred miles an hour the souped up police Escort was a dot on the horizon behind them.

"Wowee!" Tommy screamed in a cry of unabashed jubilation. Dennis was still holding on for dear life but his contorted, wind ravaged face was beaming nevertheless. Tommy hadn't finished. The road was dry and the traffic, light. He'd seen off the chasing police car and Southfields was still a few miles away. He knew the Norton's top book speed was listed as 130mph and he fearlessly pushed it to its' limits. He was euphoric when the speedo reached 124mph and eased down on the throttle as they reached the western outskirts of their home town.

The pace was positively sedate by the time they reached the High Street and was down to a crawl when they entered the market where their momentous, but brief journey, had begun. Having deposited the borrowed helmet back on the parked motorcycle they went to face Victor Slade.

"Half an hour I said. Do I have the word *mug* written all over my fucking forehead? No, I bloody well don't. You're taking the piss, Dennis Carter." He made a point of looking at his watch. It was an exaggerated gesture. "Over an hour it's been and I'm a busy man."

"It's my fault," Tommy cut in.

"I don't care who's bloody fault it is. Now get back behind that counter, Dennis and don't say a fucking word. Now I've got to get on."

"You said I could have a word mister Slade," Tommy said impudently.

Victor Slade was a strange man. Everyone he knew or had dealings with thought him a bit odd and a little out of the ordinary. He even looked somewhat peculiar with his sharp features, thin face and wiry build. It made him seem quite angular and awkward in movement at times. His choice of clothing was also a tad eccentric. He was never seen wearing anything other than a brown serge, worsted suit popular just after the war, brown suede shoes and a matching brown trilby hat from the same era. His mop of untidy, mousy brown hair completed his rather bizarre appearance.

He called himself an entrepreneur, but to most he came across as a bit of a spiv. But for all his quirkiness he was a confident, self assured, streetwise individual who, despite his unconventional and money led approach to life, seemed very successful when it came to his business dealings within the community and beyond. This prosperity was reflected in the gleaming black, top of the range Ford Zodiac he owned and he was proud to drive the stylish vehicle and even more importantly, to be seen behind the wheel of the fashionable, slightly vulgar, expensive status symbol.

"What is it Tommy....and you can cut the *mister* crap. Victor will do. Now....out with it."
Tommy came straight to the point.

"I need a job."

"You've got one....every Saturday."

"I need a fulltime job."

"Why?"

"Because I've left school."

"And good old benevolent Victor bloody Slade will come to the rescue."

"It's not like that....honest," Tommy pleaded. Victor's glibness didn't last long when he realised, for once, Tommy wasn't being flippant.

"Look Tommy.....look around you. It's a record stall in a market......."

"But it could be so much more."

"What *are* you on about?"

"Expanding," Tommy replied tentatively. Victor was intrigued.

"My office....now," he said, "And you Dennis, make me some dosh for Christ's sake."
Victor's *'office'* was his black Ford Zodiac parked just around the corner. Many of his business dealings

were instigated in his car. They both got in the back.

"Go on then," Victor urged as Tommy sank back in the plush upholstery. He took a deep breath.

"Expand the business.....not here in the market, but in the High Street."

Victor's interest was growing. "I'm listening."

"Musical instruments....the future." Tommy was doing his best to sound as businesslike as he could. Victor glanced at him, his trilby pulled down over his forehead.

"All the youngsters are into music these days, and it's getting bigger. It's going to sweep through the whole world. Anyway, you open a High Street record shop and sell guitars and stuff as well, you'll make a fortune. And this is where I come in."

Tommy certainly had Victor's undivided attention. He felt a bit out of his depth but he couldn't quit now.

"Go on," is all Victor said, keen to find out more.

"Dennis can run the record side, he's good at that. You can have those new booth things, where you can listen in private. Get all the youngsters in....no sweat, and I can deal with the instruments. I know all about them. I can play the guitar an' all. You could have drum kits, trumpets....even organs."

"And a classical selection, possibly," Victor's interest was increasing by the second.

"I play the piano," he continued, flexing his long slender fingers.

"I never knew that," Tommy replied.

"There's a lot about me you know nothing about, laddie."

"And here's the best bit, Victor," Tommy chose his words very carefully, "There's a shop to rent in the High Street and it's just right. Just perfect."

"Come on....show me," Victor enthused, opening the car door and swinging his long thin legs out onto the pavement. Tommy couldn't believe how well his meeting with the idiosyncratic entrepreneur was progressing and was hard on his heels.

"There.....that one," Tommy pointed out the shop in question. It was right bang in the centre of the busy High Street.

"The business.....wouldn't you say?" Tommy's voice was gaining in confidence. Victor looked at the vacant premises and its' surroundings. Tommy was right, it was a prime location. He crossed over the road and studied the vista from there. Tommy followed him like a shadow. Victor smiled.

"I think I might be giving you a job, Tommy Nelson," he said with a look of satisfaction on his unusually elated face.

Tommy's birthday was going so well he didn't want to go home. Everything was going well. He'd left school, hit the open road on his Norton and had a thoroughly great time, and now it seemed he even had a job. When he did get home he saw the familiar limousine parked outside and his spirits were immediately dampened.

Dennis had given him a small amount of marijuana weed as a present. They had already shared a joint back at Subway Records earlier in the afternoon and Tommy was feeling suitably relaxed and at peace with the world. Confrontation with his family was the last thing he needed. From the hallway he could hear his dad talking in the kitchen.

"But we need the money and besides, I can't give it up."

The privacy of his bedroom beckoned and the prospect of chilling out smoking some of Dennis's grass was foremost in his mind but he lingered in the hallway all the same.

"But you could be in a lot of trouble," he heard his mum's worried voice, also from the kitchen. The conversation continued and Tommy listened.

"It's easy though....I'm out and about in the limo anyway."

"But what if they want more?" Silence followed June's question. Tommy made a move towards his room.

"I'll cross that bridge when the time comes," Harry replied. "And my life's not going to be bleedin' ruled by a couple of greasy fucking dagos who think they're Southfields answer to the fucking Krays, I'll tell you now."

Tommy had heard enough and sought sanctuary in his bedroom. He was halfway through rolling his joint when there was a tap on the door. To his relief it was his sister Emma

"Just wanted to give you these," she said, handing him a birthday card she'd made herself and a Crunchie bar.

"Oh Em......that's fantastic...thanks a million," Tommy replied grinning like a Cheshire cat. Emma didn't stay. She respected his privacy and left him to it. She was two years younger than him and quite shy. She was also small for her age and gawky. Puberty was still a little way off and she was yet to blossom as a young woman. But she had a pretty face, deep hazel eyes and long brown hair which she usually wore in a ponytail.

As brother and sister they were close, but not in a demonstrative or outward way. Tommy was very protective of her and she was happy to let him be that way. There were no dramas and their relationship was laid back yet loving and sincere.

Tommy heard the front door slam. He knew his dad was off out and he lay back contented on his bed slowly getting stoned on Dennis's excellent grass. His birthday was complete.

Chapter 7

Victor Slade's new High Street shop, Subway Music, was an instant success and Tommy, for the first time in his life, had some responsibility in the form of the day to day running of the musical instrument department within the store. He even suggested to Victor that he should take on a third member of staff, specifically, a young, sexy, leggy, blond female who would balance out the workforce on a gender basis, but principally to attract the young fellas into the shop. To both his and Dennis's surprise Victor was all for it and took on an eighteen year old girl possessing all the qualities Tommy had suggested.

It didn't take him long to try his luck with her, but she told him she wasn't interested. That didn't stop Dennis chatting her up though, but unfortunately for him, he got the same response. Getting the sexual aspect out of the way meant they were able to become plutonic friends and dependable, trustworthy workmates. Her name was Mandy, and Victor was delighted in both the way she attracted the male customers, even though she wasn't overly flirtatious with them, and most importantly, the ensuing rise in his profits.

Victor also realised he needed to appoint a

manager for the new enterprise and he found it in an ambitious Welshman he *poached* from Woolworth's along the High Street, where he was the assistant manager. He felt Tommy was just too young to take on the responsibility and he didn't believe Dennis had the qualities for such a demanding post.

Tommy enjoyed his job and got the chance to get his hands on some superb guitars, like the Gretsch Jazz and the Rickenbacker range, but his favourite was the Fender Stratocaster, and he showed off his playing skills on that particular model to many prospective customers and usually got a sale.

Another innovative idea he instigated was a large notice board within the store where anyone could post all sorts of things, from *'wanted'* and *'for sale'* ads to gig information. This had the effect of creating a muso community inside the shop and a meeting place for those interested in music generally. Initially Victor Slade wasn't sold on the idea, but sales went up and he soon changed his mind. He also recognised Tommy's imaginative dynamism and flair and promised himself he would reward him with a pay rise, but not immediately.

Tommy's mum, June, thought and hoped full time employment and the responsibility that went with it might have a calming influence on her son. But, if anything, it had the opposite effect. Tommy was not going to suddenly become a level headed, sensible teenager just because he'd got a job. His love of life combined with his overriding rebellious streak wouldn't allow it.

He approached the Barchester chapter of the Hells Angels to become a full member and was given a choice of tasks to complete in order to be inaugurated into the infamous motorcycle gang. He had to chose one of two options. The first was to have sex with *'Big Bertha'*, a blow up doll, with the whole chapter watching, and the second was to ride his trusty Norton Manx the wrong way down one of Barchester's busiest one way streets during the rush hour, wearing nothing but a jock strap. The decision was a hard one and in the end *'Big Bertha'* lost out. Tommy completed his task in the centre of Barchester without either crashing or being arrested and his initiation was complete. He could now wear his leather jacket with the Hells Angels logo emblazoned on the back without fear of repercussion and he was proud to do so.

There were other elements of his life that were leading him down the path of waywardness and they weren't about to be checked. His drug taking, for one, was on the increase. He thought smoking marijuana was merely a social pastime and could see no harm in it whatsoever. The trouble was, so did everyone else in his circle who dabbled in the illegal activity. The consequences of it becoming a habit and maybe escalating to the use of harder drugs like heroin and cocaine weren't even considered or discussed, such was their blinkered attitude on the subject. So long as they got their kicks they were happy.

Living at home was also becoming a bind for Tommy. He felt restricted and claustrophobic in what had become a discordant family environment. There was friction and conflict with his dad, Harry, and the more he did to pacify the situation the worse it seemed to get. As long as he could remember Harry had been a gambler. He'd bet on almost anything. Now it was mainly on the horses and greyhound racing. Tommy was also pretty sure his contribution to the family coffers from his mediocre weekly pay packet was also fuelling his passion for gambling.

His mood swings were a problem as well. On a good day, after winning big, he was the most jovial, charming man one could wish to meet. He would lavish gifts on June, Tommy and Emma and a party atmosphere would prevail. But usually, after losing heavily which was often the case, he was morose, bad tempered and despondent and itching for a fight, and his family were the poor unfortunates who took the brunt of it. Rows between Harry and June were now commonplace and ranged from the electric money in the jam jar on the kitchen shelf disappearing to the absence of funds to pay the monthly rent when it was due. amongst other finance related squabbles.

June lost every argument and Harry invariably

squirmed his way out of every conflict they had. Tommy would listen in and hope his mum would have the balls to tell him straight. But he was always disappointed and in the end even started blaming *her* for being so diffident and timid when he knew it was all his dad's fault.

What the family didn't know about was Harry's late night visits to the Lucky Seven Casino in Barchester when he was out chauffeuring. His losses in this establishment were beginning to make his flutters on the horses and dogs seem like mere trifling wagers in comparison. Tommy was also suspicious about his involvement with Angelo and Freddie Mantovani and that concerned him even more than his intensifying gambling habit. It all made for a tense and uncomfortable family environment and one he wished he could get away from.

Dennis suggested he move into the flat he shared with friends and Tommy was tempted to do just that, but he feared for his mum and sister Emma and couldn't just abandon them at the mercy of his father and the uncertain future they would probably have to face if *he* wasn't there.

*   *   *   *

Tommy had to wait until his seventeenth birthday before he got his long awaited pay rise from Victor Slade. Subway Music had been his most successful venture so far and was now a thriving business employing a staff of six. Tommy's contribution to that success was immense and although he was still happy working there he felt Victor had certainly taken advantage of him. For Victor's part, he'd had no qualms about using Tommy's naivety to the full, and he recognised the store's success was mainly due to the youngster's powerhouse approach and dedicated commitment as well as his own financial input.

One morning in the high street shop Mandy pointed out a slip of paper pinned to the notice board. Tommy was immediately drawn to it. It read *'singer/guitarist wanted for new group. gigs waiting'* with a telephone number scrawled underneath. Tommy wasted no time in 'phoning and arranged an informal audition with the band that very evening.

He'd never played with fellow musicians before and turned up at the pre-arranged meeting place, the scout's hut off Southfields Lane, not exactly nervous but with some trepidation nevertheless. Three guys were there to greet him and they'd assembled their kit on the small stage.

"Right, I'm Mitch..........this is Bomber, on bass....and Phil, on drums. I play lead. Plug your guitar in and we'll have a jam....see how we get on." Tommy nodded to each one in turn and set about preparing himself for what he hoped might be a life changing evening.

"Long Tall Sally," Mitch said "I take it you can play along on rhythm. We do it in E.....chords are E, A and B."

Tommy was keeping up so far.

"See how it goes," Mitch continued, "Then you can come in with your vocals. Looking forward to this, I am," he added enthusiastically.

He wasn't disappointed. After a shaky start the four gelled like they'd been playing together for some time. The drummer's precision, passion and zest drove the number along, complimented by the earthy, almost bottomless resonance of the electric bass guitar pounding along. Tommy's sense of timing was impeccable and his contribution on rhythm guitar was seamless, if a little unsure at times. Mitch's lead guitar, although sounding somewhat crude and distorted, added a new dimension that didn't exist on the original recording by the rock and roller Little Richard. The song did deteriorate into a three chord improvised jam session before Mitch brought it to an end.

"Brilliant!" he enthused, "Can't fault your playing, Tommy, but we *are* looking for a singer....a front man. Can you handle that?"

"I'll give it a try," Tommy replied, "I know the basic lyrics."

"We'll do it then," Mitch said, "Just sing the same verse over if you get lost.....yeah?"

Tommy nodded. He was keen to get going. "Shall we do it then?" he added taking the initiative. He stepped up to the microphone and the band struck up the intro. The result was pulsating and the look on Mitch, Phil and Bomber's faces when Tommy got to grips with the vocals said it all. Tommy was the guy they'd been searching for and Mitch was the first to say it when they brought the song to a close.

Bomber handed out cans of beer as the four sat on the stage to discuss their future. Tommy was ecstatic, but did his best to control his emotions at this time. He knew he could sing and play to a credible standard, but until he proved he could gel with others, the doubts within him as to his professional competence were there and very real. That evening his dreams of performing live on stage with a first rate band were one step closer to being realised, and although the name of the group, the Crimson Polka Dots, left a lot to be desired, their quality and potential didn't.

Mitch came into the shop the following day and asked Tommy to join the band. Tommy couldn't refuse and made a point of tearing the slip of paper on the notice board into tiny pieces before dropping them into the bin. An intense rehearsal schedule was discussed and planned with Mitch saying they had a wedding gig booked in a fortnights' time. He also said the scout hall was at their disposal as a practice venue and he was keen rehearsals should start that very evening. Tommy agreed. He couldn't be happier and it made the uncomfortable situation at home a little easier to bear, knowing he would be spending far less time there.

Tommy also found himself in demand when Dennis approached him seeking advice on a motorbike he was looking to buy. Tommy was delighted his opinion was valued, but concerned when Dennis told him he was funding the purchase with a loan. He went with Dennis anyway to view the Triumph Bonneville 650 his friend had fallen in love with. It was a fine and handsome machine and had a good pedigree and Tommy had to concede it was being sold for a bargain price and *he* would buy it if he got the chance.

A few days later Dennis was its' new proud owner and big plans were made for the two of them to explore the countryside together as soon as Dennis had mastered the art of riding the powerful machine. Tommy even suggested he joined the Hells Angels but after hearing the *'Big Bertha'* story he said he'd think about it for the future. Tommy laughed and called him a wuzz but inwardly he understood his reluctance to make a fool of himself in front of complete strangers and left it at that. At last Tommy could see some sort of future for himself and although the word *ambition* had never started a fire in his belly in the past, it was starting to mean something now, and certainly gave him plenty to contemplate on.

His passion for football in general and Southfields F.C. in particular remained and Steve Baker's continuing success was never far from his thoughts. His once best friend was still giving him match tickets when he could, and although their careers were taking different paths, the Barton Bridge flats was still the place where they both lived and they were invariably going to bump into each other occasionally.

Steve was now a regular in the third division club's team and his reputation as an up and coming striker, albeit in the lower leagues, wasn't going unnoticed by other, more distinguished, clubs. Near neighbours Barchester United, an established top first division side, was one who was keeping a close eye on him, a fact the local papers were keen to report on regularly. Steve knew it, and even at seventeen was mature enough to stay clear of any speculation and side stepped the probing after-match questions on the subject broached by some journalists hoping for a scoop.

Southfields had always been his club, but he also knew if he was to succeed he would have to move on sometime, but until that time arrived he was happy to play his football in the lower echelons and enjoy every minute of it. Will Grealish's exacting training regime had turned Steve's boyish physique into one of almost Adonis-like proportions. He was now over six feet and hadn't yet stopped growing. He was strong and muscular and was now a match for any bruiser of a centre half. His speed had significantly improved and he was feared by many defences in the third division.

His all round game was so complete he was now keeping his ageing hero Johnny Cleveland on the substitutes bench. Cleveland was not used to playing second fiddle and wanted to retire from the game, but Grealish persuaded him to stay at least to the end of the current season and the iconic number nine reluctantly agreed. Steve was worried about the repercussions of him being the preferred striker, but he needn't have been, because Johnny Cleveland was the supreme professional and bore no grudges whatsoever.

George and Mary Baker were delighted with their son's progress and did their bit by keeping his head firmly out of the clouds and on terra firma. At seventeen, it would have been so easy for Steve to lead the swanky lifestyle many young footballer's chose and to be led astray by the success of it all, but he was happy living at home and not tempted by the fast car brigade or the jet set lifestyle that was there for the taking. He knew one day he would leave home and hoped when that day came he would have the same support from his mum and dad that he'd enjoyed up to now and, more importantly, their blessing for whatever he did in the future.

His Lambretta was still his main passion outside football and he lavished his attention on it the same way Tommy did with his Norton. He'd added accessories to the Italian scooter, customising it to suit his stylish taste. Extra large sporty wing mirrors replaced the purely functional ones and more chrome was incorporated wherever possible.

The mod scene had grown at a phenomenal rate in Britain and Steve had flirted with the idea of becoming a fully fledged member of their trendy fraternity. Most thought he already was one, with his crew-cut hairstyle, Lambretta scooter and his fashionable ex U.S. army parka coat, but his inherent individuality combined with his increasing public persona as a professional footballer meant he didn't feel the need to belong to *any* organisation, especially one that potentially could damage his future, and he recognised the developing mod culture could have that negative effect.

Unlike most mods, he drew the line when it came to adorning his motor scooter with furry accessories, and he never wore their signature dress of Fred Perry shirts and sharp tailored mohair suits. The one aspect of their culture he *did* like was the jazz orientated music which had originated in the U.S.A.

All he was looking for was a bit of fun outside his demanding regime as a young, ambitious footballer and his Lambretta was the catalyst for that diversion. He was fully aware of the animosity between the up and coming mods and the motorbike riding rockers, as they were known, but as he wasn't directly involved, it didn't bother him. The fact that the mods thought rockers were old fashioned, dirty, greasy and uncouth and the rockers thought mods were effeminate, stuck up and snobbish was of no consequence to Steve and his lifestyle.

It was a beautiful Sunday morning. Southfields F.C. had won at home the previous afternoon and Steve was planning a day out at a mod's music event out in the country somewhere. His red and cream gleaming Lambretta looked stunning as he donned his parka and crash helmet prior to taking it out. He noticed Tommy's Norton wasn't there and came to the conclusion he must have had the same idea as him, to leave the metropolis behind and enjoy the beauty and thrill of the open road.

He met up with thirty or so mods outside the gates of Dunsbury Park and the group wasted no time in heading off westwards towards the downs in a blaze of colour and a cacophony of noise. Steve was right about Tommy. He'd left a lot earlier, planning a day out with the Barchester chapter of the Hells Angels and hoping to enjoy a stimulating day amongst the biking brotherhood he'd recently joined.

Their meeting place was the Mill House Cafe, a truckers' transport cafe also to the west of Southfields. It was renowned for its' excellent egg and bacon fry-ups and possessed the one ingredient every biker looked for in such an establishment, a noisy juke-box crammed with the latest rock and roll hits.

Dennis persuaded Tommy to take him along as

a guest and he was looking forward to his first experience among the infamous Hells Angels gang. There were only about twenty on this occasion, but it was special to Dennis and he was eagerly awaiting a memorable and exhilarating day's biking and a chance to see exactly what his Triumph Bonneville was capable of.

Being a Sunday there were hardly any trucks about and the group had the Mill House Cafe to themselves. The music was blaring and the coffees were flowing. The rockers of both sexes were having a ball. Tommy was the showman as usual and although he was new to the gang it didn't stop him putting himself about and singing along to the rock and roll hits emanating from the juke-box. He was happy amongst these likeminded people and could relax and be comfortable in their company.

Dennis quickly became part of the laid back scene as well, and was as chilled out as everyone else before too long. They had a full day planned though and their time at the transport cafe was limited. It didn't stop them lingering a little longer however, and savouring their coffees and the loud music before making the decision to hit the road.

The fifteen motorbikes clustered in the car park were easily visible from the road and didn't escape the attention of the approaching mods who left Dunsbury Park some time before. Steve was near the rear of the pack of Lambrettas and Vespas hogging the carriageway and he would have been happy just to ride on by, content feeling the wind in his face and enjoying the scenery. Those leading the convoy had other ideas though and slowed as they drew nearer to the cafe and saw the motorbikes parked outside it.

"Rockers!" One mod shouted, pointing to the bikes as he and those at the front of the pack turned off the road and into the car park. Even on such a lovely, balmy Sunday morning as this, confrontation was the overriding sentiment of the leading mod minority. The rest followed, including Steve.

"Fucking mods!" came the cry from within the cafe as one of the Hells Angels glanced out of the window and caught sight of the approaching cavalcade of motor scooters. Steve thought it was just a show of bravado from the bunch of mods around him. Just a bit of fun on the way to the music event, but others didn't share his view and it soon became apparent this was something more sinister.

They encircled the motorbikes, revving up their noisy engines as they did so. Every chapter member inside the cafe, including Tommy, made straight for the door. Dennis wasn't far behind. A twenty stone rocker the size of a bear was the first to step outside.

"Piss off you poncy fuckers," was his choice of words. But they fell on deaf ears. The scooters continued circling like Red Indians on the warpath around a wagon train encampment.

"Greasers......dirty rotten greaser rockers," one

of the mod's leaders shouted, provoking and antagonising the small group of bikers who only wanted to enjoy their day out. Confrontation wasn't the main topic on their agenda but they were not about to shy away from trouble if it was forced upon them.

The scooters all came to a halt the far side of the parked bikes, their engines still put-putting and spluttering away.

"Yeah....clear off....and take your poxy sewing machines with you," the huge rocker replied. It was a standoff, a war of words. The Hells Angels weren't looking for a fight, but the mods were itching for one. Inside the empty cafe the worried proprietor looked towards the telephone behind the counter. He didn't want to call the police, he didn't need the hassle. It was a Sunday morning, the weather was good. Why would he? *'Great Balls Of Fire'* had come to an end and the juke-box was silent.

Outside, the mod's leaders cut the engines on their scooters and the rest followed. Dennis whispered in Tommy's ear.

"Like the gunfight at the O.K. coral."

"Ssshh....." Tommy said impatiently. He was aware how serious things were and he considered flippant quips to be out of order. Dennis didn't say another word. The car park was now as quiet as a graveyard and the tension was mounting.

One of the mods placed his foot against a Norton 650.

"Don't you fucking dare," came the response from one of the rockers, thinking the bike was about to be kicked over. The foot remained there tantalisingly. A lone magpie swooped down and landed clumsily, hopping about in no man's land between the rival gangs. It squawked raucously then took flight.

The car park became eerily quiet once again. The mod's foot accidently slipped against the Norton, pushing it off its' stand and sending it crashing to the ground. The Hells Angels let out a battle cry of obscenities and charged. Initially, the mods were caught off guard, some of them still casually sitting astride their scooters, and they suffered as a result. Even though they were outnumbered the rockers were a formidable, well organised unit and their bravery more than matched their self belief. But the mods had numbers on *their* side and the rockers initial supremacy was short lived. It was all out war and no one was about to back down.

The cafe owner looked on from within the diner, grateful it had kicked off outside. The telephone was ready at his side but he refrained from calling the police preferring to wait and see if the brawl would fizzle out as it had on previous occasions. Tommy got the shock of his life when he suddenly found himself face to face with Steve.

"Lamp the ponce," a rocker to his right shouted. Tommy was momentarily thrown.

"Go on.....fucking hit 'im Tommy," the voice screamed. Tommy knew he had to react, to do something otherwise his credibility within the gang would have come under severe scrutiny. Quick as a flash he lunged at Steve throwing a left hook which landed plumb on his chin. Tommy was all over him, arms flailing wildly.

"Go down," he whispered, the urgency in his voice overwhelming. Steve realised what was going on and fell to the ground clutching his jaw. Tommy jumped on him.

"What the fuck you doing here?" Tommy said, but didn't wait for a reply, "Just trust me....play along....got it?"

Steve nodded and Tommy pretended to lay into him. The rocker near him was ecstatic.

"Fucking marvellous, Tommy....show the nancy boy who's boss," he said, seconds before he was felled by a mod grasping a coke bottle, which he duly smashed over his head.

"Stay down......whatever you do........just stay down," Tommy urged as he faked another punch into Steve's ribs before scrambling to his feet. All around fights and scuffles were escalating out of control. He feigned a couple of kicks into Steve's kidneys and midriff, whilst the Hornets' striker curled up in the foetal position and waited for more.

Just as Tommy was about to continue the pretence he heard a click. He knew exactly what it was and reeled around. He was too late. The dreaded click was the sound of a flick knife springing open, and before he could react the small, thin blade plunged into his stomach. The mod wielding the deadly weapon coolly drew it out, flicked it closed and calmly put it in the pocket of his parka.

Tommy's blood spurted everywhere. He was stunned and in a daze. Everything and everyone around him slowed down. He was aware of Dennis screaming something at him but all he could make out were murmurs all around. His hand went involuntarily to the wound in his belly and felt the warmth and stickiness of his own blood. Everything seemed so surreal. Steve was up off the ground in a flash.

"He's been stabbed," he yelled out. Tommy saw his lips move and the anguish on his face, but the words didn't register. He couldn't hear, and slumped to his knees as the adrenalin within him ebbed away.

Everyone else in the car park heard Steve's piercing voice though, and the scene changed both dramatically and in an instant as the full horror of what had just happened became apparent. Fist fights between the two rival factions had become commonplace and were generally regarded as a bit of sport and recreation. Cut lips, a bruise or two, the odd bloody nose, these were all an accepted part of the challenge and the tussle for supremacy between the gangs. But knives of any kind, especially flick knives in particular, were regarded as the weapons of cowards and had no place in the skirmishes they were involved in, however fierce and aggressive they became.

The fighting in the car park came to an end almost immediately and everyone's attention was drawn to Tommy's dire plight as he lay fighting for his life on the ground. It was amazing how, in a split second, the animosity between the mods and the Hells Angels had been put aside because of the seriousness of the circumstances, and Tommy's well being was the overriding factor that had brought them temporarily together.

Steve tore off his parka jacket and wrapped it around Tommy's abdomen hoping it would act like a tourniquet and suppress the incessant flow of blood streaming out of the laceration.

"Somebody call an ambulance," he cried out, desperate to keep his friend alive. Dennis rushed towards the cafe.

"Tommy......can you hear me matey?" Steve said as he knelt down next to Tommy's shaking body. "Can you hear me?" he asked a second time, only louder. Tommy nodded.

"You're going to be okay. Trust me.......just hold in there," Steve's voice was hesitant.

"Get the fuck out of here....you don't need this," the muted words gushed from Tommy's mouth. Steve knew what Tommy was getting at but his football career didn't seem so important with

Tommy's life hanging in the balance. The dilemma was there all the same.

'Keep him talking' he thought to himself, *'Don't let him lose consciousness.'* Similar film scenarios flashed through his mind where a comatose state usually resulted in death. Some of the mods had seen enough and fearing the imminent arrival of the emergency services, including the police, opted to leave the scene as quickly as possible. This prompted the Hells Angels to do the same and there was a mass exodus from the Mill House Cafe car park.

Dennis got to the cafe entrance just as the owner was about to lock it from the inside. He put his shoulder to the door.

"Call an ambulance," he yelled, "My mate's been stabbed."

The owner shrugged and reluctantly went towards the telephone behind the counter. This was the last thing *he* needed on a quiet Sunday.

"Now....quick....He's fucking dying out there," Dennis was beside himself. He noticed a payphone on the far wall.

"And I need change....for the phone," he said marching over to the counter.

"Change....I need change....now, you fat slob."

The owner begrudgingly handed Dennis some coins from the till whilst he dialled the emergency services. Dennis quickly punched some numbers into the new style payphone and frantically fed it with coins when the beeps went.

"Victor...is that you, Victor?"

"Who else would it be?" Came the answer.

"It's Dennis."

"I know who it is. What do you want....it's Sunday for fuck sake?"

"Tommy's been knifed in a fight with a load of mods. He's dying.....I know it, Victor."

There was silence at the end of the 'phone.

"You still there?" Dennis was frantic.

"I was thinking. Where are you Dennis?"

"Transport cafe near Downham Common."

"Have you called an ambulance?"

"Yeah, yeah....done that. But they'll be ages and Tommy's not going to make it. He's in a bad way, Victor. You've gotta do something."

Again there was a few seconds silence.

"What's the name of the cafe?"

"What's this place called?" Dennis shouted across to the owner.

"Mill House Cafe," came the reply. Victor had heard the owners response.

"Right Dennis, you do what you can and I'll see what I can do. Can't promise anything, mind. Now I've gotta go."

The line went dead. Dennis ran towards the door.

"They're on their way....emergency services," the owner called out. The car park was almost empty when Dennis got to Tommy's side. Steve was still there.

"Ambulance's on its way," Dennis said to him. He'd met Steve once or twice but they weren't friends. He knew he played for the Hornets though.

"And the police.....no doubt," Steve replied. Tommy was still conscious but looked deathly pale, and the parka Steve had wrapped around his waist was crimson with blood.

"I've got to go," Steve blurted out suddenly, "You staying here....with Tommy?" he added.

"Someone's got to," Dennis replied. Steve nodded and moved in close to Tommy.

"Hang in there, Tommy," he urged and then ran to his scooter.

The remaining few mods and rockers, having heard the police were on their way, also left, and suddenly Dennis and Tommy were the only ones there. Dennis knelt down next to his bleeding friend and workmate. All around it was quiet, eerily quiet. The sun was warm and a light breeze wafted over them. Dennis didn't know what to say to Tommy. It wasn't a situation he'd been in before. The wait was interminable. Five minutes crept by. Then ten. He gripped Tommy's hand and made small talk. Tommy said nothing, but more importantly, didn't lose consciousness.

Dennis suddenly heard the unmistakeable sound of a helicopter approaching. He was up on his feet in a flash and waving his arms frantically as the small aircraft came into view.

"Helicopter Tommy, look at that.....a frigging

helicopter......you'll be okay now. I'm off.....good luck mate ..."

A few seconds later his Triumph Bonneville sped out of the car park. Tommy was alone. The helicopter landed nearby. It wasn't the usual emergency services rescue type, but a tiny two seater Hughes 269, an ex-USA police vehicle with black tinted cockpit glass. The pilot ran to Tommy and somehow half dragged, half carried his limp form across the tarmac and manhandled him into the passenger seat. The helicopter was up and away in seconds and heading for Barchester City Centre.

By the time the ambulance and the police arrived at the scene all they found was a solitary Norton Manx and a pool of blood. Minutes later the helicopter swooped down towards the towering Barchester General Hospital. Seconds before landing the pilot, without divulging his identity, radioed the hospital's control centre informing them of his intention to deliver a patient with life threatening injuries onto the roof of the building.

"Sorry buddy," is all he said as he pulled Tommy's lifeless, blood-soaked body out of the aircraft and onto the hospital roof. Tommy heard the whirring of the rotor blades as the mysterious helicopter lifted off before he lost consciousness.

Chapter 8

Angelo Mantovani was also at Barchester General that morning, but not as a patient. He'd been out celebrating on the Saturday night with his brother Freddie at a nightclub in the city centre. The rapidly expanding and successful company the Mantovani twins ran, the Zanetti Corporation, had just become the major shareholders in the Lucky Seven Casino in the west end of the city after an aggressive takeover bid was found irresistible by its board of directors.

After a few brandies in the nightclub he'd met an attractive but impressionable young student nurse who couldn't resist his charms and good looks, especially after he'd plied her with exotic alcoholic cocktails. She was soon in the mood for sex and quite brazenly invited him back to her room in the students quarters of Barchester General, with that carnal objective high on her list.

Angelo knew student nurses had a reputation for being oversexed, orgasm driven and insatiable, but although a philanderer himself, he was yet to experience the delights of Barchester's student nurse fraternity, and had never fucked one. He guessed he was in for a good night though when her hand slid up the inside of his thigh to his groin and sought out his semi-erection while he drove the short journey from the club to her digs at the hospital in his Jaguar. The fact men were banned from the nurses rooms at night didn't bother this student and she sneaked him in discreetly without being seen.

She told Angelo exactly what she wanted and he obliged, stripping her naked before lifting her onto the single bed. She was warm and wet when he fingered her. Then his tongue went down on her, flicking her clitoris and tasting the erotic saltiness of her sex. Silence was the order of the day in these student premises for obvious reasons and Angelo's excellent foreplay was testing that stipulation to the limit as his sexy, young student nurse moaned and groaned under his touch.

It wasn't long before she wanted more and tore his clothes off before taking his sizeable erection in both hands and guiding it between her legs. Angelo entered her and without making a sound, proceeded to move back and forth in a slow, rhythmical motion, until he felt her hips responding, rising up and thrusting towards him. They both came in a frantic, almost noiseless, steamy, sweaty climax accompanied by some hushed giggles and sighs.

Angelo was now spent and content but his student nurse hadn't yet finished. As he lay back she felt for his penis and coaxed more life back into it before climbing on top of him and sinking down onto his hardness. She rode him until she was ready again, and Angelo watched as her hand went down between her legs and within seconds, another orgasm shuddered through her. When she rolled off they were both satisfied and quite happy to rest for a while. Angelo wasn't sure if he'd had *her* or vice versa. He smiled to himself as she drifted off to sleep in his arms.

He was unable to doze off in the cramped single bed and besides, sleep wasn't his main priority when he was in the process of building a lucrative and prosperous business empire with Freddie. Angelo was undoubtedly the driving force within the Zanetti Corporation, but he also realised Freddie had his qualities. In his opinion, loyalty was Freddie's overriding attribute combined with his dependability and honesty within the company. Angelo made all the decisions and Freddie, aware of his limitations within the commercial environment, was happy to play a supporting role to his elder twin, and reap the financial benefits giving him the affluent lifestyle his peers could only dream about.

At the age of just twenty, they both now owned luxurious and spacey apartments in the new marina development in Barchester's canal basin, Fiddler's Wharf. Angelo, not surprisingly, had the penthouse suite with a fabulous roof terrace which overlooked the city, and Freddie's swanky pad was just as extravagantly plush and opulent even though it wasn't on the top floor like Angelo's.

Freddie had also upgraded his red MGB roadster to an infinitely more lavish and eye catching Cadillac Eldorado coupe convertible. It was big, brash, and the exact same colour film stars and celebrities chose, flashy flamingo pink. It was so huge Freddie had to reserve two spaces for it in the underground car park. He adored it and cruised the city's streets at every opportunity, showing off his new acquisition to anyone and everyone. This didn't please Angelo though, a certain degree of anonymity was what he would have preferred.

The Zanetti Corporation's commercial interests weren't exactly squeaky clean, and although the Mantovani twin's lifestyles reflected the success of the company, the last thing Angelo wanted was to draw unnecessary attention to themselves and invite scrutiny from the city police or any other organisation which could adversely affect their profits, and the way they conducted their business ventures.

There wasn't one aspect of any of their enterprises that was completely legal and above board. Drugs had been the key to their burgeoning affluence and it was whilst living at home at the Barton Bridge flats with their parents that they first started dealing locally in marijuana, and realised they could earn far more distributing dope than they ever would grafting in the family fish and chip shop.

Their first acquisition from their ill-gotten gains was Prestige Cars in Southfields Lane where they also became Harry Nelson's employer. This was bought under the guise of the newly formed Zanetti Corporation and at the time very few knew the link with Angelo and Freddie Mantovani. The fleet of hire cars were the obvious front to expand the drug distribution scheme and their markets soon grew into Barchester itself.

Even though Harry drove the limousines he wasn't exempt from making the occasional drugs drop to clubs, hotels and other establishments in and around the city centre. He knew what he was doing but had little choice because had he complained he also knew he'd be fired. As a result he became an unwilling accessory, but an accessory to a criminal act all the same.

The Mantovani's next venture was in the dubious money lending sector. The brothers had set their sights high and this was to be no small back street concern but a string of modern, brightly lit high street shops all complying with the law, offering a varied selection of loans to a wide range of customers within the community. They chose the trading name 'Trusty Loans' and their first shop was right in the city centre.

It was successful from the very first day it opened and Angelo envisaged a chain throughout the city and he had big plans to go nationwide in the longer term. He was quickly becoming a shrewd and astute businessman, and with Freddie's support, the pair were developing into a commercial force to be reckoned with in the Barchester and surrounding area and one not to be taken lightly.

The darker side of the business was never far away though, and if there was money to be made the Zanetti Corporation was invariably involved. Freddie was the risk taker of the pair and enjoyed a gamble more than his brother. It was his ambition to own a string of betting shops, and it was this quest which brought to the fore the ruthlessness of the brothers and the sinister way they conducted business when it suited them.

Their narcotics distribution operation also led them to the drug, Diomin. It had recently been developed in the veterinary field as a mild tranquiliser administered to mainly domestic animals prior to full anaesthesia during an operation. Freddie's passion was greyhound racing, and he was a regular visitor at the Barchester dog track.

It was there he met Terry Brown, the owner of 'Terry Brown Betting', a small bookmakers in Southfields. Terry was also a trackside bookie and handled bets at the evening greyhound meetings. Freddie always lost more than he won and as a result Terry was more than happy to accept his bets. Freddie found out the new drug, if given orally to a greyhound in tablet form, would act as a sedative which would last no longer than fifteen minutes and would be untraceable if the animal was subject to a drugs test after that short period.

He then put his plan into action, but purely as a

dummy run to start with. He chose a minor race at the track and paid a handler to secretly give five of the six runners a Diomin tablet each just before they were loaded into the traps. To Freddie's amazement the greyhound that hadn't been drugged won the race, with the other five trailing lethargically in its' wake.

At the next meeting, his ingenious and deceptive money making scheme would be fully realised. He studied the race card with care and precision and came across a no-hoper in the penultimate race of the evening. At 20-1, the dog's price reflected its chances of winning, the odds being ideal for Freddie's cunning plan. Shortly before the off he approached Terry Brown with three thousand pounds to put on the outsider to win. Terry, although initially stunned by the size of the wager, was only too aware of Freddie's poor luck in picking winners and accepted the bet without laying *any* of it off.

His greed was his downfall. The other five dogs were duly drugged with Diomin and Freddie's no-hoper romped home the winner. Terry Brown owed Freddie over sixty thousand pounds which he didn't have. He was ruined. Freddie took his betting shop in lieu of the debt and shortly afterwards the bookmaker's body was found in Downham Woods with a bullet through his head. He'd taken his own life.

Freddie was happy though. He now owned a

lucrative betting shop and even had the audacity to use the same trading name, 'Terry Brown Betting', and insisted the business was put under the umbrella of the Zanetti Corporation. Angelo wasn't happy with that but went along with his brother's wish all the same.

P.C. Derek Dooley investigated the bookie's death and his enquiries led him to the circumstances of the unfortunate man's demise, but at that time the twins involvement wasn't obvious and because the Coroner returned a verdict of suicide the case was closed and Derek Dooley's investigation went no further. Terry Brown was a well liked and respected local Southfields man and his death came as a shock and a worry to many in the community and P.C. Derek Dooley was no exception.

There was a large turnout at his funeral and many local people paid their respects. His widow Sharon was left penniless and Derek Dooley instigated a collection to help her through her financial crisis. The loss of her husband was hard to bear though and no amount of money could compensate for that.

Freddie Mantovani even had the gall to turn up at the crematorium and offer his condolences to Sharon, but he got short shrift and she told him exactly what she thought of him and the way he conducted his business ventures, and vowed to take revenge. He also contributed to her widow's fund without her knowledge. Had she known she would have thrown the cash right back in his face.

The Zanetti Corporation taking over the Lucky Seven Casino was their biggest and most adventurous coup so far and Angelo had major plans to turn it into *the* premier gambling establishment in Barchester. That distinction was currently held by the Platinum Casino Club not far away, but Angelo's determination was paramount and he would stop at nothing to achieve his goals and had that particular casino well and truly in his sights for the future.

Thoughts of business and conglomerates were cast aside though when his young student nurse stirred and reached for his balls. She was ready for more sex and with his erection growing rapidly to attention, so was he.

Chapter 9

Angelo had already left the hospital environs when Tommy was rushed straight to the operating theatre where he received emergency treatment for the deep knife wound in his stomach. Another half an hour and the massive blood loss would have resulted in death. The helicopter had saved his life. The surgeons noticed the blade's incision was only an inch from Tommy's spleen. If that small but vital organ had been punctured, the resulting internal bleeding would have certainly killed him, and probably as he lay in the Mill House Cafe car park.

Tommy cheated death that Sunday morning and after stemming the flow of blood from his ruptured stomach and receiving a sizeable blood transfusion, the surgeons were able to stitch the laceration in the stomach wall and transfer him to the intensive care department where his condition could be closely monitored around the clock. Being young, strong and healthy Tommy responded well to treatment in that high tech unit and within twenty four hours he was transferred to a side room adjacent to one of the surgical wards.

His identity wasn't known initially so his first visitor was Detective Constable Tim Sutherland from Barchester C.I.D. Tommy would have much rather seen someone a little closer, like his mum or his sister Emma. Even his dad would have been preferable to a policeman, but none of them even knew he was in hospital. The seriousness of his injury combined with his extraordinary arrival at Barchester General meant the hospital authorities had no choice other than to involve the police, and the tall twenty five year old detective stood beside Tommy's bed with a string of questions at the ready.

Tommy was in no mood for an inquisition from anyone, let alone a police detective, and pretended to be asleep. That didn't work however because D.C. Sutherland had pulled up a chair and was there for the duration. Tommy also needed to pee so he had to abandon that ploy in the end.

"Ah....back in the land of the living I see," the young detective mused as Tommy looked at him. Tommy said nothing.

"I'll introduce myself. I'm Detective Constable Tim Sutherland......Barchester C.I.D." he added, his tone quite informal. Tommy pointed to a papier-mâché urine bottle on his bedside unit.

"I need to go," he said. Sutherland nodded.

"I'll be outside the door," he replied, leaving Tommy to relieve himself in private.

He was uncomfortable and in pain but the detective wasn't going away and a couple of minutes later he was back in the room. He could see Tommy was in some distress.

"You can ring for a nurse," he said, pointing to a

red button on the wall near the bed.

"I'm okay," Tommy replied.

"I have to ask you these questions....and the first one is your name?"

Tommy was determined to only give the briefest of details to the officer.

"Tommy Nelson."

"Address?"

Tommy answered that question also, but refused to be grilled when it came to more pertinent enquiries as to the nature and circumstances of his injury. He just wouldn't budge. D.C. Sutherland didn't push it on this occasion but made it clear to Tommy there would be more questions to answer as his inquiry into the matter progressed.

"I'll let your parents know you're here. I take it that's okay?"

Tommy nodded. Sutherland put his card on the bedside unit as he was leaving.

"I can see you're not in the mood to talk at the moment, and I can understand that, but when you are.....give me a ring....anytime....and remember, I'm on your side, Tommy.....remember that," and he left.

Tommy was in pain and pushed the button on the wall. A nurse arrived and gave him a shot of morphine. Relaxation was instantaneous and before the drug could render him unconscious he reflected on one particular question D.C. Sutherland had asked him. It was whether he could remember anything about his attacker. He'd kept schtum about that moments earlier but suddenly something stirred in the recesses of his mind. Deep within his subconscious the vividness of the attack was rekindled. The sound of the flick knife springing into action. The faceless mod's fist thrusting the blade into his stomach. His fist. The back of his fist. The tattoo. Tommy desperately re-lived those dreadful few seconds. The tattoo. He could see it now. But what was it? It was slowly coming back to him. It was a playing card. The ace of spades. There was also a serpent. He could see it, the ace of spades with a serpent entwining itself around it. The morphine kicked in and he fell blissfully asleep.

"Oh Tommy, you gave us such a fright....me and your dad." It was his mum, June, who had arrived with his sister Emma. She fussed around him but didn't have much to say. Tommy couldn't tell her what happened and if he did, he knew she wouldn't understand and fret even more.

The main thing was he was alright and as far as his mum was concerned he felt ignorance of the circumstances and details was prudent on this occasion. He *could* talk to Emma though, but not in front of his mum, so their visit ended up more like a silent vigil at his bedside. Tommy asked if his dad would be coming to see him, but June evaded the question choosing instead to talk about *'that nice Tim Sutherland'*, the young detective and his exemplary manners and fine attitude. On their way out they passed someone Tommy *did* want to see. It was Steve Baker and Tommy's face lit up when he walked in.

"Am I glad I won't be going to your funeral, Tommy Nelson," Steve quipped.

"Where's my grapes?"

"Got you something better than grapes." He pulled a can of lager out of his pocket and tossed it to Tommy. "Nurses are a bit hot," he added plonking himself on the side of the bed.

"Great to see you Steve," Tommy beamed.

"And I've just passed your Emma....she's growing up a bit.....must say...."

"Don't you even think about it, she's only fifteen."

"Never stopped you, Tommy....eh?"

Tommy laughed, which sent pain right through his abdomen. The banter couldn't continue indefinitely though and it was Steve who broached more serious matters.

"I thought you were a gonna," he said awkwardly, "And I heard you were saved by some helicopter no one knows anything about."

"It was weird.....fucking weird, I tell you. Anyway....how did you know?"

"I saw it Tommy."

"No....you went off with the mods....I remember telling you."

"I left with them, you're right there. But I stopped in a lay-by, just down the road....on my own."

"You saw it.....straight up?"

"Yeah, went right over me. Strange it was...dark windows, the lot....and I saw the police and the ambulance as well."

"What ...you were still there?"

Steve nodded. "I didn't know what to do, I really thought you were going to die."

"Don't go all sentimental on me Steve.....don't. Anyway, you did the right thing getting the hell out of there......what with your football career and everything."

"I've thought about that, and I'm going to sell the scooter.....get out of this stupid mod thing. I was never one anyway."

"That's the best news I've heard all day," Tommy said sarcastically. "Seriously though, you need to get yourself a smart car....to go with your image and all that. What you thinking of getting?"

"Oh, I don't know."

"It's gotta be a sports car yeah?"

"I haven't really thought about it. I don't want anything too flash."

"Yeah, you do really...and I know just the right motor for you."

"Go on Tommy, surprise me."

"Triumph Spitfire. Not flashy at all. Pretty though.....two seater....hood and everything."

"Yeah?"

"Too fucking right. Suit you down to the ground."

Steve's visit did Tommy a power of good and he left him in high spirits, promising to get together for a few beers after he's discharged from hospital. Steve had it in mind to broach the subject of Tommy leaving the Hells Angels and moving on after what had just happened, but he knew how Tommy would react and wouldn't have thanked him for spoiling his visit with a lecture, so he thought better of it, for now at least.

The next afternoon he had a follow up visit from D.C. Sutherland, but Tommy kept his mouth firmly shut once again, much to the detective's disappointment. He was a clever man though and he saw patience as a virtue in his line of work, and was hopeful his softly-softly approach would get him results in the end.

Later that evening he had a surprise visitor. It was none other than his dad, Harry. Tommy was taken aback when he saw him but nevertheless he was pleased he'd taken the trouble to come. Harry was a genuinely likeable man and could certainly turn on the charm when it suited him. He pulled up a chair.

"Serious, this time," he said sitting down near the bed. Tommy shrugged.

"You going to tell me about it.....I think I've a right to know?"

Tommy could feel the hairs on the back of his neck rising and a red mist descending. He went straight on the offensive.

"Right to know. You've got a fucking....."

"Hold on, Tommy....I didn't come here for a row."

"What did you come for then?"

"I know things haven't been good between us, but you nearly died. Do you realise that? Has it sunk in? I'm still your dad."

Tommy didn't want a confrontation either, but he would never shirk away from one if it reared its ugly head.

"What happened son?"

"You really want to know, don't you?"

Harry nodded. He definitely wasn't looking for a fight.

"Tell you what, dad, I'll do a deal with you." He looked long and hard at Harry. He was curious.

"Go on," he said.

"I'll tell you what happened....and you tell *me* what the hell's going on with you. The gambling, nicking money at home....and don't look at me like that....I'm not stupid. And treating mum the way you do. All that......"

"Okay okay, I get the picture. You first," he retorted. Tommy realised his near death experience might just have been the wakeup call his dad needed. He sat up awkwardly in the bed trying to get as comfortable as possible.

"It was a mods and rockers thing, you know."

"When did you get mixed up with all that?"

"You do know I'm a Hells Angel, don't you?"

"You're what!?"

"You see dad.....you don't know what's going on, even in the family."

Harry was lost for words.

"I'm a member of the Barchester Hells Angels, and Sunday morning we planned a day in the country......that's all. The open road...our bikes...it was going to be great."

"And?"

"And a load of mods came looking for trouble, that's what."

"And you didn't?"

"No, we didn't." Tommy was irritated by his dad's assumption, "No, we were minding our own business and trouble found us. That's the way it was."

Harry nodded but said nothing. Tommy continued.

"Anyway, it was just a bundle.....a fight....no big deal.....until I got knifed."

"The copper said you'd been stabbed, but he didn't say any more than that."

"No dad, they don't say much when it suits them, do they?"

Tommy's attitude towards Harry was slowly mellowing. It had been a long time since they'd talked and the hospital environment seemed to be helping the situation. Tommy didn't mention the helicopter ride or Steve's involvement, but his dad seemed happy with the explanation so far, so he left it at that.

"Doctor says you were dead lucky."

"Said what?"

"Said if the knife wound had been an inch to the right it would have pierced your spleen and you'd have died."

"I didn't know that. He never told *me*."

"Perhaps he had his reasons," Harry replied. "Almost forgot......got you some grapes."

Tommy smiled to himself, "Thanks dad," he said.

"So, this Hells Angels thing.....you going to leave now?"

"Leave, why would I leave? Anyway, what's with you and everything? Your turn now."

Tommy was keen to get his dad to open up. Harry sighed. It was a long deep breath of resignation tinged with sadness.

"Where do I start?"

"You tell me," Tommy urged. He shifted uncomfortably in his hospital bed waiting for an answer.

"I'm in a spot of bother.....with the horses and dogs. Got in a bit deep," Harry finally confessed. Tommy listened.

"And there's work as well, that's even worse."

"Why?"

"Because Prestige Cars was taken over by the bloody Mantovani brothers, that's why.....and they're getting me doing their dirty work, and I've got no choice....no choice, Tommy lad."

"I said the Mantovani's' were trouble. Anyway,

what sort of dirty work?"

Harry looked behind him towards the door, making sure their conversation was private.

"I do the deliveries, drug deliveries...in the limo, all around the city. I'm driving around with thousands of their dirty bloody money....and I'm the one taking all the risks."

Tommy knew they dealt drugs but had no idea it was now on such a large scale.

"They're dangerous, son. Violent, bloody gangsters. I know you think they're just a couple of bullies, but they've got bigger....more powerful...and they scare me, I tell you."

Tommy's mind went back to the time the twins had just moved in to the Barton Bridge flats and he'd confronted them when they tried to intimidate him and Steve.

"I'm not scared of those greasy dagos."

"Then you should be," Harry replied.

"Why don't you leave?"

Harry sighed again, "Not as simple as that."

"Yeah....just leave."

"I can't."

"Why not?"

"There's something else. Its' Terry Brown's bookies I owe."

Tommy shrugged, "So?"

"They've taken over that as well. And Terry's done himself in. They're involved in everything....and they also had something to do with the poor sod's death, I just know it."

"How much do you owe?"

"Eight hundred."

"Jesus!.....eight hundred quid......eight hundred fucking quid?" Tommy was shaking his head in disbelief. "No wonder you were nicking the electric money.....and my money. Dad....how could you let it get to this state. How?"

Harry didn't answer that question. Instead, he went back to the hold the Mantovani's had over him.

"I can't leave 'cause I now owe them the money."

"You owe them eight hundred quid?"

"I'm in the shit, Tommy....I really am."

For once Tommy was lost for words. He stared out of the window at nothing in particular. Harry sat there forlornly, his chin in his hands. Tommy was deep in thought.

"I'll get the money for you, dad," he said, turning towards the pitiful figure sitting on the chair by his bed.

"I'll do it..... I'll fucking do it." He couldn't hide or disguise the emotion in his voice. "There's conditions, dad....you hear me?"

"I'll do whatever it takes."

"From this moment on, you don't go near *any* bookies, *any* dog tracks or fucking racecourses. Now I mean that. The gambling stops now....this minute....got it?"

He'd never spoken to his dad like that before and he

wasn't enjoying the experience.

"Got it dad?" he emphasised again.

"Yes, son," is all his dad said.

"There was something else," Tommy continued, "I was going to leave home, do my own thing...you know. But I'll put it off for six months....only six months....so we can sort everything. Mum and Emma don't need to know anything....not a dicky bird. You and me, we're the ones that have gotta fucking sort it. With me, dad?"

Harry wiped a solitary tear from his cheek. His only son had stepped up to the mark and he was one proud father.

"Now pass me those grapes and get out of here," Tommy joked. Harry stood up, leaned over the bed, gave him a clumsy sort of hug and left him to eat his grapes in peace.

The following day he was deemed well enough not to need the side room any longer and was transferred into the adjoining male surgical ward proper. Tommy wasn't impressed with his new surroundings. He'd lost his privacy and as he looked around every bed was occupied by what seemed to him to be decrepit geriatrics, not one under seventy. A slight exaggeration it might have been but it was a place Tommy didn't want to be.

As the 'new boy' he was bombarded with inane questions and never had a minute to himself. But although he couldn't see it, they were just ordinary folk who happened to be hospital patients and it wasn't their fault they were elderly. Tommy realised that eventually and although conversing wasn't his strongest point, he made an effort. All the old fellas liked him and as he was now on the mend, his bubbly personality came to the fore.

In the bed next to him was an elderly gent who was a yellowy orange colour. Tommy had never seen anyone looking like that before and when he asked the nurse, she told him it was jaundice. The man chatted enthusiastically to Tommy about his love of cars, but the following morning his bed had been stripped and there was no sign of the likeable character. He'd died in the night of cancer of the liver. That shook Tommy.

One advantage of being in the communal ward was the plethora of nurses who passed through, some of whom Tommy found quite alluring and sometimes arousing. Most of the time though it was just good to have young female company to chat with and share a laugh and a joke. They *were* nurses however, and he got his fair share of attention from them, both in a professional capacity and also socially.

There was one nurse related disappointment though, the bed bath. He was so looking forward to that ritual, but when the time came to expose himself the nurse merely tossed him a flannel and told him to wash himself. His rising erection shrank in seconds as the nurse disappeared through his privacy curtain with a smirk on her face and chuckling loudly.

There were a couple of memorable moments he found hilarious all the same. One warm night he couldn't sleep and a bat flew into the window at the far end. The subdued lighting had attracted it and it swooped around the ward unable to find its' way out. The two night duty nurses freaked out and were off like a shot. An elderly gentleman in the bed opposite was overjoyed and stared in wonder at the small furry mammal as it darted around. He called across to Tommy.

"The swallows are early this summer, laddie. I just love watching them on the wing." The enthusiasm in his voice Tommy found priceless, and he giggled away for ages, long after the frightened animal had found the open window and escaped into the dark night.

Another night an old fella had stripped naked and was sitting on his bed pretending to drive a car, creating all the relevant sound effects as he revved the engine and changed gear. It was three in the morning and the ward was as quiet as a graveyard. Yet this one octogenarian was noisily racing through imaginary streets without a care in the world and wearing nothing but a big grin on his face. The two nurses on duty were having trouble trying to subdue him and the other men in the ward were too well mannered to complain. Tommy wasn't though. He sat up in bed and shouted across.

"You senile old sod, put a sock in it you silly

fucker and put the thing in the bloody garage so we can all get some shuteye."
All the men concurred vociferously and shouted their own obscenities towards the poor guy who was obviously suffering from Alzheimer's or a similar disease of the mind.

Tommy was the hero and it all went very quiet shortly after that. He didn't want to stay longer than was necessary though, and soon began pressing the doctors to discharge him. Visitors were few and far between and he was bored. He hoped Dennis would come and see him, even Victor's company he could have endured for a short time, but both were conspicuous by their absence.

The band turned up one evening however, and Mitch, bomber and Phil took over the ward with their banter and high spirits, but they had an alternative motive for being there. The hugely important wedding gig was approaching and they needed Tommy as their lead singer and front man. Sitting up in his hospital bed he looked fit and well and in their eyes they couldn't understand why he was still there. The fact that his abdominal wall was still in the process of healing hadn't occurred to them. Music and the band were of prime importance and to them, everything else was secondary.

It played on Tommy's mind when they'd gone and after a lot of deliberating and soul searching he decided, if it was possible, he'd do the gig. His surgeon was doing his rounds the following morning and Tommy raised the subject of his discharge. The surgeon was sympathetic in his own straightforward, matter-of-fact way and was pleased with the speed of Tommy's recovery, but he stressed the seriousness of the injury and for Tommy not to rush the healing process, before moving swiftly on to his next patient.

Tommy realised the surgeon had cleverly sidestepped his question and his thoughts remained on his dilemma with the band. It was no surprise to either the nurses or the ward doctor when, the following day, Tommy discharged himself. He left Barchester General with a bag full of bandages and dressings under his arm, confidant in the knowledge his mum would look after him at home in the Barton Bridge flats.

Chapter 10

Tommy only had a few days to prepare both mentally and physically for the Crimson Polka Dots first major gig, the wedding reception in the upstairs function room of the Blue Boar Inn on the High Street. Physically, and not surprisingly, he wasn't in a particularly good condition and was surviving on pain killers. But mentally he was prepared and looking forward to the challenge. He knew his performance was crucial to his ambition of becoming a star and was under no illusions that if he fell short, his goal could become an uphill struggle.

He caught up with Dennis in Subway Music. He was on sick leave from work and the first thing Dennis did was apologise for not having the guts to visit him in hospital. Tommy wasn't bothered about that, he was just keen to get him to help out at the wedding gig in an unpaid roadie and sound man capacity. Tommy knew he had good *ears* for music and Dennis jumped at the chance of being part of the action. He didn't stay long at the shop fearing he'd see Victor and have to explain in some detail the events of the last week or so. He needn't have worried though because Victor was otherwise engaged in business matters elsewhere and their paths didn't cross.

The big night arrived and the Crimson Polka Dots took to the small stage at the Blue Boar to entertain the wedding party and their hundred or so guests. The venue was intimate and atmospheric and Tommy made the stage his own from the very first number. Space was limited there, which did him a favour in his restrictive condition, and his intake of pain killers completely alleviated his abdominal soreness and discomfort.

Sensational he wasn't, but competent and talented he most certainly was, and as the evening progressed the better his performance became. He could see Dennis was impressed, so much so he'd forgotten his duties as sound engineer and was dancing and enjoying the evening with all the other guests.

Halfway through the first set Tommy noticed an impeccably dressed man around forty sitting on his own at the back of the room. He was sipping champagne and watching the band intently. Tommy thought he looked just like Victor Slade. He caught sight of him again during the next song but he noticed the man was completely bald and his posture, even though he was sitting down, was more upright than Victor's. He thought the resemblance was uncanny all the same.

He looked for him later during the final set but there was no sign of the dapper individual. Tommy gave it his all and by the end of the evening he was shattered. After a couple of encores he signalled to the others in the band that he'd had enough and the performance came to an end.

"Terrific," Mitch said as he unplugged his guitar. Bomber and Phil were just as enthusiastic with their summing up of the evening and Tommy knew it had all been worth it.

Dennis was still on the dance floor, trying to extricate himself from the clutches of one of the bridesmaids he'd been snogging. Tommy was sitting on the stage enjoying a beer.

"What do you reckon, Denny?" he called across to him. Dennis came over.

"What was that?" he said.

"What did you think....us.....the band?"

Dennis helped himself to a bottle of beer from a crate at the side of the stage.

"Bloody good Tommy, it was bloody good."

"And me....?" Tommy couldn't resist asking, even though he knew his friend would tell him the truth whether he liked it or not.

"You were ace, Tommy....and the energy, don't know how you kept it up in your state."

"And the sound?"

"I played a blinder with that," Dennis joked, "Sound was terrific," he added.

Dennis hadn't finished summarising the Crimson Polka Dots performance and he sat down next to Tommy.

"Look.....I know I've had a few, but do you want

my honest opinion?"

Tommy was taken aback. "Course, Denny," he said. There was uncertainty in his voice but he respected the musical nous Dennis had accumulated in his time both at the record stall and in the new shop.

"Doing weddings.....not the way forward," he said frankly.

"I know that," Tommy replied sounding a little indignant.

"No, I mean musically. There's something there....can't put my finger on it. Powerful....but it's sort of rough.........raunchy, defiant. The whole sound....fuck......I'm useless with words."

"I know what you mean, Denny. I can feel it. That energy dying to get out."

"Weddings aren't the right place for it. You need to write your own stuff, Tommy."

"We've only just got together.......give us a chance."

"Well that's what you've gotta do.... I reckon, anyway."

"Rebellious rock," Tommy suddenly blurted out.

"Got it in one, Tommy. Couldn't put it fucking better myself. Rebellious rock......brilliant."

"Thanks for that, Denny, and for everything you've done tonight, mate."

"Yeah.....no problems. Is that it then.......'cause I've got a bridesmaid over there who's champing at the bit?"

"Yeah. One last thing. I saw this geezer earlier, bald....sharp suit...spitting image of Victor."

"Oh.....you saw him did you?"

"Yeah, he was staring at us."

"That, Tommy lad.....is the owner of this pub. James Slade. Victor's brother."

"Victor's brother?"

"Yep. *He* is mister big. Got a fucking great gaff in Dene Park and drives a flash Bentley. You must have seen him around?"

Tommy shook his head.

"They don't get on, Victor and him. He's got the lot.....and Victor ain't. Simple as that really. Oh....and a word of advice, don't *ever* mention him to Victor....he'll do his nut."

Tommy glanced at the bridesmaid standing impatiently by the door.

"Duty calls," Dennis said, pointing to her.

"I think your performance might just be beginning," Tommy said, laughing.

"Hope so," Dennis replied, and left Tommy sitting on the stage.

Mitch handed Tommy three crisp five pound notes, his share of the fee for the gig, which he gratefully stuffed into his pocket. It was earmarked for his dad's debt and he hoped there would be plenty more to come.

A few days later Tommy called on Dennis for another favour. It was to collect his motorbike from Mill House Cafe. The cafe owner had moved it into an outhouse after the police had left the scene on the Sunday, and he'd been safely looking after it since then. Tommy had already spoken to him on the 'phone so he knew his bike had been well looked after.

When he arrived with Dennis the owner was amazed to see the recovery Tommy had made, and was yet another who thought he wasn't going to survive. Tommy thanked him for his trouble and was also pleased when the owner told him he hadn't told the police anything about the incident, saying he saw nothing. He did ask about the mysterious helicopter but Tommy could truthfully say he was also baffled, and knew no more than him, except that it saved his life. He followed Dennis out of the car park on his prized Norton Manx, and although his riding position wasn't conducive to a pain free ride, the discomfort was worth every second and with the open road ahead and the wind in his face, he was glad to be alive.

That was almost the last time he rode the powerful machine. His promise to his dad that he would deal with his debt problem was with him constantly. The thought of the Mantovani twins having such an enormous hold over his father was abhorrent to him and filled him with disgust. He was also completely mystified as to how a couple of lazy yobs were able to get such a foothold on the ladder to wealth and affluence, and be so influential and dominant within Barchester's commercial environs and the community as a whole.

He searched his soul exhaustively and concluded his family meant more than any object or possession he had, however dear to his heart. He sold the motorbike back to the dealer he'd bought it from and although he lost out financially on the deal, he had a substantial amount to put towards his father's plight. He was still some way short of the eight hundred pounds required though but he was making significant headway and was confident the sum would be reached in the not too distant future.

There was another two wheeler absent from outside the Barton Bridge flats. Steve's Lambretta had gone. He'd sold it as he told Tommy he would. As Tommy looked wistfully at the empty space where his Norton had proudly stood next to Steve's garish fashion statement of a machine, a shiny, bright yellow Triumph Spitfire convertible came whizzing around the corner and screeched to a halt inches from him. It was Steve. He leaned across and pushed open the passenger door.

"Jump in, Tommy....I'll take you for a spin round the block." He was grinning like a Cheshire cat. Tommy couldn't refuse.

"I can see the papers now," he said sliding into the cockpit of the compact two seater, "Hornet's striker scores with team colour-coded supercar."
Steve laughed, "Hardly a supercar," he replied, sticking the gear lever into first and speeding off. The ride was exhilarating and fun.

"Where's your L-plates then?" Tommy asked as they headed towards the High Street.

"Took a leaf out of your book, Tommy. I'm flouting the law."

"Good for you," Tommy replied, sitting back in the bucket seat which wrapped around him. The admiring glances were coming from every direction.

As one of Southfields Football Club's most recognisable players, he was a familiar sight in and around the locality. His career was continuing to flourish and he was maturing into a muscular sportsman of the highest calibre. Gone was the plumpness that accompanied his boyhood, and his light, almost golden blond hair was inevitably darkening and would probably continue to do so until he reached maturity, and at nearly six foot two he was an imposing, handsome figure.

His prowess on the football field hadn't escaped the attention of some of the bigger clubs, and Will Grealish knew Steve would move on one day. He thought it inevitable given the quality and standard of his game coupled with the driving ambition he possessed. As his manager, Grealish was happy to get the best out of him and face the future when it arrived. Steve was also aware of the growing interest in him, both on and off the pitch, especially from the media, who sensed he could easily ascend to celebrity status within the footballing world, and become a money making machine for everyone in the industry, including the media.

Tommy also couldn't fail to notice the popularity Steve was gaining from young and old alike, and his good looks also enamoured him to the fairer sex, which Tommy found especially amusing and absorbing. He hoped one day he would reach his own iconic status within the music world, but until that happened he was content and happy to revel in, and be a part of, Steve's developing prominence on *his* way to fame and fortune.

He realised they had drifted apart. Had they both gone to the same school when they were eleven, it might have been a different story and their friendship could possibly have now been a formidable one which would last throughout their lives. They weren't bosom buddies anymore though, and although they enjoyed each other's company, and there was a natural affinity between them, the way their lives were panning out made it hard to envisage them being best friends in the years to come.

"You were right, Tommy," Steve remarked as he swung the Triumph into Felgate Road and pulled up outside the flats. "This little baby *is* something else," Steve enthused.

"Told you," Tommy replied, pleased Steve had listened to and taken his advice. Just then uniformed constable Derek Dooley walked by on his way to the flats. He looked long and hard at both Steve and Tommy and raised his eyebrows as he gave the gleaming sports car the once over, but he didn't stop and said nothing. There was a welcoming cup of coffee and a doughnut waiting in his flat, and although he noticed the absence of learner plates on the car, he had no inclination to challenge Steve on this occasion. The two youngsters waited for their neighbour to disappear inside the entrance to the flats before continuing their conversation.

"Must pass my test," Steve said leaning across to open the glove compartment. He grabbed two plastic stick-on L-plates, "And put these on the car," he laughed.

The engine was still ticking over.

"Where's your bike....I saw you got it back from the cafe?"

"Gone," Tommy replied. "Sold it."

"What?"

"Needed the money for something else."

"You're not in trouble?"

Tommy shook his head.

"You can always come to me.....if you are in trouble. Know what I mean?"

Tommy knew what he meant.

"I mean it. I'm on good money. I can help if you're short."

"No, I'm not in trouble....and yeah, thanks....I know where to come if I am." He suddenly felt awkward and a little irritated and was keen to change the subject.

"Tell you what......there's a big party up at Dene

Park tonight. Should be a good do. Women, wine....the lot. Why don't you come along?" Tommy said, sounding far more enthusiastic. Steve thought for a few seconds.

"And marijuana no doubt. I'd love to Tommy....but I can't, the football and everything."
Tommy wasn't surprised he'd declined. Steve's character was strong and unmoving as far as his football career was concerned, and in a way Tommy was envious of his steadfastness and inner strength.

"Thought you'd say that. You'll probably end up living there in some bloody great Dene Park mansion one day.....and be having your own swanky shindigs, the way things are going."
Steve laughed, "We might *both* end up there....when you become a pop star."

"Rock star," Tommy laughed, correcting him.

"Wouldn't that be great though, both of us lording it in Dene Park one day.... You never know," Steve said, keen to keep Tommy's spirits up and not make him feel in any way inferior. "If you do make it big, you'll have to change your name," he added.

"Why?"

"Tommy's not right."

"What you on about?"

"Too British......Tommy's far too British. You want a name that conjures up superstar status, like....Gene Pitney. Imagine if he was Tommy Pitney. Doesn't sound right. Doesn't quite have that....I don't know. You know what I mean. Just doesn't go, does it?"

Tommy could see his point.

"It doesn't have to be anything drastic. I'm not saying you should call yourself Elvis Nelson. Actually...that sounds good though."

Tommy couldn't help laughing.

"That *does* sound fucking good, Steve," he replied.

"No, I was thinking more like.....like Bobby. Bobby Nelson. Sums up that cheeky chappy, Anglo-American heart-throb. Bobby Nelson.....what do you think?"

Tommy had to agree, "Yeah, does sound good....must say."

"Anyway Tommy, I must be off."

Tommy climbed out of the car.

"Hope the party goes okay....tell us all about it...don't forget."

"You'll be jealous when I tell you," Tommy called out as Steve hit the throttle and the Triumph Spitfire accelerated swiftly away.

The party Tommy was going to that night was at one of Dennis's friends parents house on the Dene Park estate, and Dennis gave Tommy a lift there on his motorbike. Dennis was even more shocked than Steve to hear he'd sold his Norton, but when he pressed Tommy for a reason why he'd sold it so suddenly after the events at the Mill House Cafe, Tommy was just as non committal as he was with Steve and didn't tell him the real reason.

"Wow....what a place," Tommy enthused as Dennis's Bonneville came up the drive. It was a large Edwardian detached house oozing charm and character and Tommy was equally impressed with the array of expensive vehicles in the driveway. Dennis parked the motorbike and they headed towards the imposing front door. The house looked splendid all lit up, surrounded by its own well tended gardens.

"What do they do, your mate's mum and dad?" Dennis shrugged, "Not sure. I think he's a lawyer or something. They're away anyway. Come on......let's have a ball."

Inside, the unmistakeable aroma of marijuana hit them. Dennis filled his lungs with the heady atmosphere.

"Got any dope?" he asked Tommy. Tommy shook his head.

"Just some baccy," he replied.

"Take these and roll yourself a joint or two. I've got a few people to see and I'll catch you later....yeah?"

He handed Tommy a small packet of grass and some liquorice rolling papers.

"And help yourself to booze. It's all here....and it's all free," Dennis added and left Tommy in one of the huge reception rooms downstairs. He looked around. The lighting everywhere was soft, subdued and sexy. Joss sticks were burning and Indian sitar music was emanating from the state-of-the-art stereo system. Tommy sat down on the deep pile carpet and did exactly what Dennis had suggested, rolling himself a reefer with the intention of getting blissfully stoned. There were people everywhere, all doing their own thing. Some were sitting chatting, others dancing, but most were partaking in the mixture of soft drugs and alcohol. Tommy guessed some would probably be on amphetamines or even cocaine and heroin, but Dennis's weed he was smoking was strong enough for him and he was soon relaxed and chilled out just like everyone else in the room.

He wasn't mad on the Bangla style of music, but after a couple of joints even that didn't seem to matter to him. After a while he decided to go exploring. Dennis hadn't returned so he made his way upstairs to have a look around. The staircase was an obstacle course of snogging couples through which he picked his way carefully. The quality Algerian grass was having its effect and he pushed open a door on the landing, hoping to find a bed he could flop down on for a few minutes.

The first sight that greeted him was a semi-naked threesome on the floor in the corner. There were arms and legs everywhere and it was obvious they weren't in the middle of a game of dominoes. Then, in the semi-darkness, he noticed the bed, and on it there were two naked girls lying in the sixty nine position. Tommy's loins stirred. He stood motionless, watching as one girl's tongue flicked at the aroused and swollen clitoris of the other, licking and sucking at it intermittently.

Tommy was transfixed and his erection was pushing hard against his jeans. Amid the deep breathing the girl initiating the action lifted her head and looked towards him.

"Jesus bloody Christ!" Tommy exclaimed.

"Hell's bells!" the girl replied. It was Mandy from Subway Music.

"Jesus Mandy, what you doing here...with her?" Tommy's voice was hushed. Mandy couldn't help staring at the bulge in his jeans.

"Could ask you the same question," she replied. It suddenly dawned on him why both his and Dennis's advances didn't have the desired effect when Victor took her on at the shop. Her sexual preferences lay elsewhere. His hand went to his crotch. He was enjoying his impromptu voyeuristic encounter all the same, even though it was lesbian orientated. But Mandy wasn't giving a free show to anyone.

"Piss off, Tommy.....and go and have a wank somewhere else. Can't you see I'm busy. Or go and fuck someone.....I'm sure you'll find a willing partner. Go on, piss off....*now*.....and shut the door on your way out."

Tommy was disappointed she hadn't asked him to make it a threesome, and that particular fantasy, he contemplated, would have to remain one for the foreseeable future. He did as she asked and left.

Mandy was right, he didn't have to wait long for a willing partner. What he'd seen her doing had fuelled his appetite for sex and he found what he was looking for at the far end of the landing. A smallish, dark haired girl around his own age, wearing a tiny red miniskirt and a cream top, was leaning against the wall, smoking a joint. She looked vaguely familiar to him.

"Hi Tommy, sing us a song."

He looked at her diminutive yet nubile figure trying desperately to place her. It came to him when he noticed her cream skin-tight top harbouring a pair of extraordinarily large and voluptuous breasts. She was a regular visitor to Subway Music, hanging around the sound booths with her friends.

"It's Janice, isn't it?"

"Jackie.....it's Jackie. Here...." she handed him the joint. "You won't get better this side of Barchester."

Tommy took it and drew on it deeply.

"Wow," is all he could say as the pungent resin drug had its immediate effect.

"Best Marrakesh gold shit," Jackie remarked, keen to have it back. She couldn't fail to notice his state of arousal and pushed one knee gently against his stiffness.

"Well if you're not going to sing to me, make love to me instead."

Those were just the words Tommy wanted to hear.

It was the age of the permissive society. The

contraceptive pill for women was widely available and it liberated the female gender and suddenly their sexual desires and aspirations were equal to those of their male counterparts, and not surprisingly, promiscuity in women of all ages had increased significantly and a sexual revolution was inevitable.

Tommy put a hand under Jackie's top and found the softness of her huge breasts. She squirmed with delight.

"Wish we could go to my room......but here will do."

"Your room?" Tommy asked, homing in on a large erect nipple. "You live here?"

"Course I do. Me and my brother's party. Didn't you know? My room's the one at the top of the stairs.....the one you just came out of."

Tommy didn't have the heart, or the nerve, to tell her a couple of dykes were shagging on her bed. She took another drag on the joint and fixed her lips on his. Her tongue danced inside his mouth and they shared and inhaled the intoxicating vapour together.

Tommy's other hand went under her skirt and crept up the inside of her smooth, silky thigh. He smiled as he realised she wasn't wearing knickers, and his hand found her warm, moist sex. Jackie reached for his hardness. She stroked it and skilfully fondled his balls through the material of his jeans. His fingers caressed her sex and gently touched and rubbed her clitoris, while he continued stroking her breasts and bringing her inflamed nipples to new heights of sensitivity.

"You're a tease, Tommy," she whispered in his ear, "Stop messing about and do it."

He was as ready as she was and needed no further invitation. With the smouldering joint still in one hand she expertly unzipped him and released his rock hard penis. It stood up proudly, its end glistening with wetness.

Tommy lifted her bodily onto his throbbing erection and entered her. He thrust into her, lifting, sliding and pounding while she wrapped her legs around his waist. The pain from the healing wound in his abdomen was extreme, but it didn't matter. He had her against the wall and their intercourse was rigorous, passionate and relentless. The marijuana smoke wafted around them as the sweat broke out on their pulsating bodies. They were both gasping for air as the severity of their frantic lovemaking continued and they came in unison in an unrestrained, uncontrollable climax that Tommy thought only happened in films. It was wanton sex in the extreme and they both collapsed in a spent heap on the landing floor shortly afterwards.

Tommy caught up with Dennis a bit later but he wasn't his usual jovial self and when Tommy asked why, he clammed up, becoming even more morose, and left the party early insisting Tommy went with him. Tommy noticed a pink Cadillac convertible in the driveway as they left. Even he knew who that belonged to.

Chapter 11

Tommy's close encounter with death soon became a memory. All that remained physically was a small scar the size of a halfpenny just above his belly button. What stayed firmly in his mind though was the tattoo he'd seen on the back of his faceless attacker's hand. That vivid mental image of the grotesque serpent twisting itself around the ace of spades seconds before the blade was plunged into his stomach. That wasn't going away. Neither was the sinister helicopter that saved him from certain death.

It wasn't in his character to dwell on those things however. His music was far more important and clearing his dad's gambling debts was also a high priority. He realised doing the latter would only be possible from his earnings from music, and the success of the band became the single, most important aspect of his life from that moment on. Tommy's drive and commitment within the Crimson Polka Dots was also matched by lead guitarist Mitch and bassist Bomber, with drummer Phil not sure which way the band should go musically. Tommy and Mitch had the similar vision of a rock driven, rebellious style which was loud, brash and in your face. They both believed it should be non-compromising and reflect the passions within them as musicians and performers. Bomber was already a confident, intuitive bass guitarist and *felt* the music anyway. He was proficient in any genre and this new style suited him particularly well. Phil came round in the end though and the band, with Tommy's extravagant showmanship and nonconformist attitude combined with his highly original vocal talent, led the Crimson Polka Dots towards a style which was modern, innovative and contempary. Whether their targeted audience would agree was yet to be decided.

The scout's hut was still their practice venue and the band were doing their utmost to keep their new style under wraps until they were ready, but their rehearsals were getting so loud and raucous and sometimes purposefully discordant, complaints from local residents were becoming common and they were on a final warning from the scoutmaster to curb the noisy sessions.

Halfway through one lively rehearsal Mitch called everyone together.

"I've got some news," he said excitedly. "Was going to tell you at the end but I just can't wait any longer."

Tommy, Bomber and Phil looked on expectantly, sweat dripping from their faces.

"Saw the owner of the Blue Boar yesterday, had quite a chat....."

"And?" Bomber cut in impatiently.

"Told him about our new style and he sounded really interested. He's offered us a gig there next Tuesday night."

"What, upstairs in the room we played in at the wedding do?" Tommy asked.

"No Tommy.....in the bar, the *main* bar...in the pub itself. Not a lot of dosh unfortunately, but Slade, the owner, says he'll make it worth our while if he gets a good crowd in. Said he couldn't say fairer than that."

"Is that the bald geezer who was watching us at the wedding?" Tommy's questions were coming thick and fast.

"You saw him as well, did you Tommy?" Bomber came in.

"You couldn't miss him," Phil added.

"He's James Slade. He's got his finger in loads of pies round here.....and in Barchester," Mitch said "And he could do us a lot of good. He knows people.....and he's got a few quid himself," he added. Tommy had yet another question, "What did you tell him, Mitch?"

"Told him we'd do it....all our new stuff. We kick off at nine."

"That's fucking great," Tommy replied. Phil was the only one with any doubts, but the consensus was they'd give it their best shot and take it from there. Rehearsals took on a new urgency and the complaints grew as the noise levels increased and all four band members gave their full commitment.

By the Tuesday evening they were ready. Nervous, apprehensive and a little scared if the truth be known, but they *were* ready. Bomber had organised some posters and there was no one in Southfields who didn't know they were appearing at the Blue Boar Inn that evening once he'd publicised it. Nobody knew what to expect but the place was packed all the same. James Slade popped his head around the door of their tiny dressing room and sort of wished them luck, but his dead pan face and outward lack of enthusiasm did little to give the Crimson Polka Dots the pre-performance lift they'd hoped for, and their initial anxiety was now turning to outright fear.

As soon as they took to the stage their lack of confidence disappeared and they delivered. Their raw energy hit the unsuspecting audience like a thunderbolt. They'd never heard anything like it before. Kick drum driven rhythms, power chords, a thumping, stomach churning bass pounding out the low range energy, all topped off with Tommy's exceptional stage presence and unique vocal range delivered with almost dissonant perfection.

They were sensational and the Blue Boar Inn was witnessing a true musical revolution. Way over the far side James Slade looked on. Tommy saw him; saw his immaculate suit and shiny bald head. He looked unmoved, but was riveted to the band just like everyone else there that evening. The group's planned two sets with a break between them went out of the window and they played non-stop for an hour and a half giving the audience just what they wanted.

At the end Tommy was near to collapsing, but held it together and the four sought sanctuary in the dressing room amidst loud applause and chants for more. They had exhausted their repertoire though but did come back onto the small stage to briefly thank the audience both for their appreciation and also their enthusiastic involvement in the evening's event. The band were shattered and not a lot was said back in the dressing room afterwards. Ten minutes later one of the bar staff came in.

"Boss wants to see you lot in the back room," he said, "Oh....and by the way....terrific night, loved it...we all loved it," he added pulling the door to.

Mitch led the foursome into James Slade's 'office' shortly afterwards. It was a glorified tap room leading off the saloon bar. Inside it was small and pokey. A large desk dominated the space with two sofas next to each other against the wall. The bald headed landlord greeted them.

"Come in fellas, sit down....make yourselves at home."

Tommy thought his voice sounded similar to Victor's, but this was more refined than his boss's at Subway Music, and his delivery was more pronounced. Perched on the edge of the sofas the band looked far from at home.

"Drink everyone?" James Slade said filling four

glasses with whisky. It was a rhetorical question.

"No thanks.......not for me," Mitch replied. Tommy, Bomber and Phil weren't going to pass up the chance of a free drink and reached for theirs. James Slade refilled his glass and pushed the last remaining one towards Mitch.

"Have a drink my friend.....with me."
Mitch found his tone menacing. He glanced at Bomber, then at Tommy.

"Go on, Mitch," Tommy urged under his breath. James Slade's gaze was fixed on the young lead guitarist. The silence which followed, although brief, was edgy. Mitch leaned across, took the glass, put it to his lips and sipped.

"Great show fellas," James Slade said as he reached into his inside jacket pocket for his wallet and put eight ten pound notes on the table. "Bonus....twenty each....you did well."
The money disappeared off the table in a flash.

"Look, I'll come straight to the point. You've got something. Not sure if I like it, but that's beside the point. The kids loved it, they couldn't get enough. And I can get you more work, believe me."
The four looked on, keen to hear what the middle-aged businessman had to say. Tommy didn't stand on ceremony, he'd finished his scotch and James Slade happily refilled his glass before continuing.

"This type of music....what do you call it?" he threw the question to the room. Tommy and Phil shrugged. It was Bomber who replied.

"Doesn't have a name. It's new......it's just what we've come up with.....what we do. Names?...we're not into that."

"You've just said the word. *New*. Like rock and roll was new fifteen years ago and took the world by storm. This *could* do the same."

James Slade had the band's full attention.

"First, you've got to change your name. That's' a must. Crimson Polka Dots.....just doesn't do it. To me the music is darker...deeper, more sinister. What do you call your style....your gut feeling. Come on fellas."

"Rebellious," Tommy replied, "Rare and rebellious....anti society and all that."

That fuelled James Slade's thinking process. He took a swig of whisky and thought for a few seconds.

"Rebellious......I've got it. What about rebel rock......simple....makes a statement. Rebel rock?"

Tommy looked at Mitch, who then glanced at Bomber.

"I'm not sure," Phil came in. Out of the four he was always the more conservative. But the other three nodded enthusiastically.

"That's ace," Tommy said.

"And I've got a name for you," James Slade continued, "The Devil's Flock."

"The Devil's Flock?" Mitch exclaimed. He couldn't believe what he was hearing from a forty something square. Tommy got it straight away.

"That's brilliant mister........er.........The Devil's

Flock......we'll be banned," he started laughing, "We'll be bloody banned."

"Makes a statement," James Slade reiterated again, "And sums up the music perfectly," he added, "But you'll have to dress the part though."
The band were stunned.

"Look fellas, I know it's a lot to take in, but just hear me out. Then go away.....think about it, and then decide I'm right." He topped everyone's glass up except Mitch's and continued, "The Blue Boar's just the start. I can get you live performances in the Velvet club for starters, and the Starlight Palais in Barchester. Do you know what the audience capacity is there? I'll tell you.....over a thousand....."

"What's in it for you?" Tommy interrupted. He felt the question *was* pertinent given the circumstances, even though it came out sounding a tad disrespectful. But then Tommy wasn't one to stand on ceremony. What they didn't know was the owner of both those venues was none other than the man who was pouring their drinks, but he wasn't about to divulge that information to them, not just yet, anyway.

"Good question. It's Tommy isn't it?" James Slade replied. Tommy nodded and waited for the catch.

"I don't want a lot. I run Top Flight Entertainment, you may or may not have heard of it. I do the promotion and take my cut. Simple as that."

"You mean you want to sign us up?" Bomber

asked. James Slade shook his head.

"I'm not into management. You don't have to sign your lives away like some. No, fellas, we have a separate agreement for each performance. Anyway, we can discuss all this once you've got your heads around everything else we've talked about. Can't say fairer than that, can I? We can all make a great deal fellas, and this could just be the springboard to your success." He raised his glass, "The Devil's Flock.........plays rebel rock!"

"I'll drink to that," Tommy enthused. The others followed as well, raising their glasses to James Slade's clever toast.

That was the beginning of the band's success and Tommy's road to stardom. Their rise was phenomenal. The Velvet Club gig was the first, the publicity handled expertly by James Slade's organisation, Top Flight Entertainment. The posters for the event depicted Tommy, Mitch, Bomber and Phil regaled in black leather complete with hoods and blood red cloaks. The four ordinary working guys were transformed into dark, heretic, eccentric characters challenging the status quo and all it stood for. Tommy relished the part, throwing himself wholeheartedly into the make believe roll. He found it amusing and ironical that he'd done his best to live the part in his juvenile years, and now he could live out his dreams of nonconformity, on stage at least, and get paid handsomely for it.

The Starlight Palais in Barchester's west end

followed and the audience of nearly a thousand young people embraced the new craze of rebel rock with zealous intensity and, at times, frenzied eagerness. As lead singer and front man, Tommy's performances took on an almost mesmerising aspect, and he pranced and leapt around the stage like the Devil himself. His slim, wiry frame was also made to look larger than life under the powerful stage lighting.

The was one casualty however, Phil the drummer found the dedication needed too demanding, and was not comfortable with the paganistic part he had to play within the group. He left the Devil's Flock to join a twelve piece swing band where role playing wasn't part of the agenda. There followed a frantic search for an extrovert, virtuoso drummer who was willing to commit professionally and who's ambition was limitless. Mitch took control of the quest and found what the band was looking for in twenty year old Lennie. His exuberance and zest to spur the band on and take their initial style to new heights of proficiency and originality, combined with his off the wall approach to life generally ensured an almost seamless transition, and the Devil's Flock were ready to take on the world. James Slade was proving to be an impresario of the highest calibre and *his* objectives seemed to be purely money orientated.

He was just short of six foot, of medium build and shared the same sharp features as his brother

Victor. That's where the similarity ended however and in many other ways they were like chalk and cheese. James Slade owned a large detached house on the prestigious Dene Park estate on the outskirts of Southfields. The private estate was home to the rich and famous from the whole of Barchester and many aspired to live there.

It was only the wealthiest few who could afford such luxury surroundings though, and James Slade, whose nickname was 'Mr Big' to those around him who could only dream of such affluence and success, was one of those shrewd individuals whose business acumen was exceptional and everything he was involved in seemed to make him money. He drove a superb burgundy Bentley, his clothes were made by the finest bespoke tailors in town and he was never afraid to flaunt the trappings of his profitable business ventures.

To some, especially the gangster element in the city, his eminence was bordering on the infamous, and his name was often linked to the less salubrious side of commercial enterprise in Barchester centre. As a result he had his enemies and *was* known to Barchester C.I.D. but they had nothing on him, so they simply kept a watchful eye on his dealings.

Mitch and the band had no complaints though and to them James Slade was well on the way to bringing the riches and fame which seemed impossible just a short while ago.

Tommy's life was changing dramatically. For

the very first time he had money in his pocket and the future looked good. The gigs took the Devil's Flock further afield and the craze of rebel rock followed them everywhere. Television appearances followed and the band cut a single entitled 'Anarchy', written by Tommy, which was seized upon by the emerging independent radio stations, who played it constantly. But it was banned by the mainstream broadcasters, much to Tommy's delight. As the band's lead singer he was becoming the most recognisable member, and celebrity status was overtaking him quicker than he'd ever imagined. He was now more well known in the Southfields area than his footballing friend Steve Baker, and Steve was the first to point it out to him on one of the rare occasions they spent time together.

Tommy was now in the position financially to pay off his dad's gambling debt. For his part, Harry had kept his side of the bargain and hadn't bet on anything. He was like a new man and although still in the employ of the Mantovani twins, and still had to continue delivering drugs in the limo, there was light at the end of the tunnel and he stuck with it.

The biggest contrast though was in his mum's outlook on life. Tommy found the transformation in her was amazing. She was now running the home like she'd never done before and was a lot happier with life as a result of Harry kicking his gambling habit. Tommy even noticed his sister Emma spent more time with her mum and dad than ever before and wasn't forever in her room.

Harry was thrilled and a little embarrassed when Tommy handed him the cash to settle his debts and promised Tommy he'd do so that very week. He was again true to his word. The following day he called into Terry Brown Betting and handed over nearly nine hundred pounds in cash to the manager there.

"Have a big win in the casino then?" he asked, checking the money against Harry's account.

"Something like that," Harry replied. In the past he'd chat all day to everyone and anyone, but now his business wasn't going to be commonplace anymore and would only be shared with a handful of friends and acquaintances he knew he could trust.

"Your slate's clean," the manager said, "And you have a hundred credit limit."

"Signed receipt if you don't mind," Harry demanded, reaching out with an open hand, surprising the bookie, who raised his eyebrows.

"No problem," he said and duly gave Harry the proof of payment he asked for. He stuffed it into his pocket and triumphantly walked out of the betting shop.

He turned up that evening for his usual shift at Prestige Cars and promptly gave the supervising controller a weeks' notice. His limousine was at the Mayor's disposal all evening so there were no planned drug deliveries for him to carry out. He knew Angelo Mantovani would show his face some time though, so he also knew it wouldn't all be plain sailing at work that night. He was right. Angelo visited the office around one in the morning.

Just because Harry wasn't involved in the illegal side of the business that evening didn't mean no one else was and Angelo had a considerable amount of money to collect as a result. He quite happily handled the money but was never seen anywhere near the narcotics he dealt in. He wasn't at all happy with Harry handing in his resignation and because of the late hour he couldn't verify Harry's account at the betting shop had been cleared.

Harry was ready for a verbal assault when he came face to face with the boss, but Angelo said nothing, choosing to bide his time and stay, as always, one step ahead. His stony glare said it all though and Harry was relieved when the call came in to collect the Mayor and his party from the Guildhall in Barchester.

The following day he pondered on what Angelo might have in store for him before he could finally leave, and his apprehension turned to genuine concern and unease the more he thought about it. He knew only too well what Angelo and Freddie were capable of and he wasn't going to underestimate either of them. What to do in the circumstances though was a different matter.

He had no intention of involving Tommy this

time, but there was someone he could approach and share his anxiety with, his neighbour and friend Derek Dooley. The fact that he was a police constable almost deterred him, but he realised the scenario in question affected not only himself, but also his family, and after all they'd been through he wasn't going to jeopardise their future happiness together because of his pride in not seeking help from a trusted confidant.

Luigi and Chiara Mantovani still lived in the flats so Harry had to be extra careful not to be seen knocking on the police constable's door, just in case Angelo got to hear via his parents. He explained the situation to Derek, choosing exactly what he thought his neighbour should hear. He mentioned about his gambling debt even though his pride told him to do otherwise. Derek's respect was far more important to him than his own dignity and self esteem in the matter and Derek knew about his habit anyway. The euphoria when winning and the despair when he didn't was obvious for all those around him to see.

He didn't tell him Tommy had paid it off though, his pride wouldn't stretch that far. It wasn't until he'd told Derek about the drugs operation, and the compulsory part he was obliged to play in it that the conversation took on a different slant and inwardly Harry seriously questioned whether he was doing the right thing. Derek was understanding and diplomatic though which put him somewhat at ease.

"I knew they were into drugs, everyone at the station knew that, but we had no idea how," Derek said.

"I'm scared, Derek, otherwise I wouldn't be here. I reckon they're going to stitch me up.....with the law I mean.....before I go. They're clever bastards ...... they'll have me....I'm sure of it."

"But what can I do?" Derek asked.

"Alright, listen to this. Let's say on my last night I have a delivery to make......just a small one......a few quid's worth let's say.... and Angelo Mantovani tips off the drugs squad. I get done, Derek...don't I? Fucked up good and proper. It'll be my word against the might of the Zanetti outfit. I wouldn't stand a chance. I'd be down the nick as fast as you could say Jack Robinson...and I'll do a stretch for it."

"Hold on Harry. I can certainly see your point. But I'm a uniformed constable, that's all. I don't have the clout."

"So you can't help me?"

"No, I didn't say that. It's very delicate....you coming here when I'm off duty and everything. Very tricky."

"You wish I hadn't?"

"No, not at all. First and foremost I'm your friend.....but I'm still a copper."

Harry was losing patience. He needed to know what Derek could or couldn't do.

"Come on, Derek, surely you can do something?"

Derek Dooley was also in a quandary. He'd been a police constable for a long time, far too long in his opinion. He was still ambitious within the force and sergeant status was within his grasp. Harry knew that and was also aware how important promotion was to Derek's career.

"Sergeant Dooley does have a fine ring to it, Derek.....if you know what I mean."

Derek smiled, "You *won't* go to prison, Harry, trust me on that. But be prepared for a bumpy ride.....get my drift?"

"I do, Derek.....and thanks for this....I mean it."

They shook hands at the door rather formally and Harry sneaked out of the flat under cover of darkness still fearful of being seen. He had work to go to though and didn't hang around.

Chapter 12

Tommy waited for confirmation from his dad that he'd cleared his gambling debt before telling the family he was leaving home. He was now eighteen and the time was right. The Devil's Flock were riding high in the charts and gigs were coming thick and fast. Dennis had also been pestering him to come and live in the shared flat in town. Tommy was satisfied knowing his mum and Emma would be fine now his dad was on the straight and narrow and everyone was happy.

Dennis was thrilled when Tommy moved into the maisonette above the greengrocers in the High Street and had even spent time cleaning his room. Tommy had noticed he'd changed over the last few months and seemed to have the weight of the world on his shoulders, which was very unlike the Dennis Tommy had grown to know and like. Even at work in Subway Music he was morose and his usual ebullience wasn't there. He still chatted up the girls though so Tommy wasn't that concerned.

His room at the top of the maisonette was just right and he and Dennis celebrated with a couple of joints. Dennis wasn't content with just a couple however, and the evening turned into one Tommy didn't much care for. They *both* ended up stoned out of their heads and although Dennis was having the time of his life and enjoying every minute, Tommy realised he was no longer in control of his own actions and that scared him. In the end he fell into a drug induced stupor and drifted into a deep sleep.

It was work as usual the following morning though and miraculously they were both up and , if not exactly raring to go, they were in the shop at opening time. Things had moved so quickly for Tommy over the last few months. The band were monopolising most of his time and although he'd considered leaving work and becoming a full time performer and musician, he wanted to stay in the High Street shop and was happy there.

A few days later he was tidying up in the shop prior to closing time. It was after five thirty and Dennis, Mandy and the other staff had already left, putting the closed sign on the door as they did so. The manager, who normally locked up, was nowhere to be seen. Tommy was in no rush, the evening was his for a change, and a new stock item had arrived, a superb Les Paul custom guitar, that he was itching to get his hands on.

Before he had the chance though he heard music coming from upstairs in the classical instrument department. He didn't venture into that area very often but as there was no one else around he felt he'd better investigate. It was the sound of a piano and Tommy could only assume someone had left a record on the stereo system up there. As he neared the top of the stairs he was greeted by a familiar voice.

"Come up Tommy, I've been expecting you."

There was a figure sitting with his back to him over the far side playing a Steinway grand piano. It was Victor Slade. The dark suit, two sizes too big, the straggly brown hair stuffed under the angled trilby, everything about the man wasn't quite right, didn't quite fit. But the music was remarkable, and brilliant.

"Come....." Victor gestured him over with a nod of his head, "But don't say a word."

Tommy was mesmerised by the wonderful sound coming from the Steinway, and couldn't believe the maestro performing was none other than the awkward, clumsy and uncoordinated Victor Slade.

He stood at his side and watched. The piece of music sounded vaguely familiar and nostalgic, with romantic melodies and huge crescendos making the hairs on the back of his head stand up. Victor's face showed no emotion, his sharp features unmoving as his eyes stared across towards the window overlooking the High Street. There was no sheet music. Victor was playing from memory. Tommy's gaze centred on his pale, slender hands and extraordinarily long fingers as he skilfully made the instrument his own. There was no flamboyance, no grand gestures, no beaming smiles as he played out the finale giving Tommy goose bumps all over his unsuspecting body. Victor sat back.

"The Warsaw Concerto," he said matter-of-factly. "Not really classical. Composed for a film about Nazi Germany's invasion of Poland during the war. Nice piece though. Did *you* like it, Tommy?"

Tommy was lost for words. The upstairs department, which had been filled with Victor's virtuoso performance, was now silent. Victor spread his arms, "And this magnificent Steinway.....the resonance....the tone....and don't you start fu...... swearing, not up here....or you're fired."

Victor's plain speaking put Tommy at ease.

"I never knew," he said, "Never knew you were an expert....makes me look like a novice, it really does."

Victor closed the lid of the piano.

"You can play like that....if you put your mind to it."

"You're joking, Victor?"

"I'm not. Anyone can, with the right guidance."

Tommy was lost for a reply.

"Anyway, I want to talk to you. Pull up a stool."

Tommy was still amazed at what he'd just seen.

"Why aren't you playing to thousands in concert halls?" he asked, fetching a piano stool from the Bechstein nearby.

"Can't stand the lights, the people, the travelling....the big venues. Answer your question?"

Tommy nodded. Victor had answered his question perfectly.

"Anyway, the manager's job's free here and I'm offering it to you."

"Where's Mr. Thomas?"

"He's gone. I got rid of him. Fiddling the books he was. Now....what do you say? You're eighteen now, good at the job and the important thing is, I trust you."

"I don't know what to say."

"Of course you don't Tommy, you've got a lot going on....I know that."

Had Tommy not been involved with the Devil's Flock phenomenon he would have jumped at the chance of becoming the manager of such an exciting enterprise as Subway Music, especially at his age. He knew he would have to broach that subject with Victor if he did take the job, but Dennis's warning regarding his involvement with Victor's brother James was firmly in the back of his mind. Tommy took a deep breath.

"It's about that, Victor. Music and playing has always been right up there for me, and the band has really taken off."

"I know that. Everyone knows that."

"And there's your brother......" Tommy decided he wasn't going to skirt around the issue. It wasn't his way. Victor went quiet momentarily.

"I didn't want to bring him up, but he's there, handling everything." Tommy didn't know what else to say. He was waiting for Victor to go on the offensive and denigrate his brother in no uncertain terms, which is what Dennis said his reaction would be. But to his surprise, Victor was more philosophical.

"I know he's there, Tommy. I'm well aware what he gets up to. His flash lifestyle.....and that's another reason I want to talk to you."

Tommy was finding it hard to keep up. He decided honesty was the best policy.

"You're losing me Victor. You offer me a job, and you go all.....all."

"Cryptic?"

Tommy nodded.

"Alright, forget about the job for the moment. Have a think and let me know in a few days, and come to me if there's anything you want to know.......okay?"

Tommy nodded again but didn't answer.

"Right then...your musical career, let's talk about that."

Tommy was listening.

"I think you're making a mistake going down that road.....a *big* mistake."

"Why?" Tommy could feel his hackles rising.

"As part of a band, front man to a band, whose music is a little.....let's say obscure and ambiguous to say the least. No, I can see you don't agree, but hear me out. Short term.....yeah, you'll sell a lot of records, make money.....even conquer the world! But I'm looking at long term, and what's right for you. Others may be able to make that happen, but as soon as the bubble bursts, and it will Tommy, you'll be pigeonholed into that unmistakeable style and your benefactor will pull the plug. Your career will plummet into oblivion."

Tommy couldn't believe what he was hearing.

"This isn't....now don't fly off the handle Victor."

"Isn't what?"

"Isn't sour grapes with your........"

"It's nothing of the sort. Now, let me finish?"

Tommy was now so confused he shut up.

"You're already banned by the BBC, on the radio and television, and ITV will follow. It's sensationalism, Tommy, and you're caught up in it. I have a way of giving your career the longevity it deserves and making you a worldwide star in the process."

There was a noise downstairs. Tommy leapt off the piano stool.

"The fucking front door's open," he whispered, and went towards the stairs.

"Careful Tommy," Victor's voice was also hushed as he followed not far behind. Tommy was down the stairs in a flash. He saw a youth wearing a dark tracksuit near the till.

"Oi!" he shouted at the top of his voice as he sprinted towards him. He had no thought for his own safety and rugby tackled the youth as he made a desperate bid to escape via the front door.

"Gotcha you fucker," Tommy exclaimed as they both careered across the shiny floor, sending a display rack full of sheet music flying everywhere. The youngster was no older than himself and just as slight. Tommy had his arms pinned to the floor above his head when Victor arrived, puffing and panting.

"Get him up, Tommy," he demanded.

Tommy struggled briefly before he manhandled the interloper to his feet, clipping him around the ear for good measure before securing him in a vice-like grip.

"Good work Tommy," Victor's praise was rare. He then turned his attention to the track suited young man. "So....you thought you'd have one over on Victor Slade, did you?"

"The.....the door was open. I didn't....."

"Smack him, Tommy," Victor cut in irritably. Tommy looked at his boss.

"Slap the bastard," Victor insisted.

Tommy obliged, throwing a decent left hook into the youth's midriff.

"The door was open was it, you young punk?.....and you thought you'd stroll in and rob me blind?"

Victor turned to Tommy, "Let him go," he said.

"Let him go....you sure?" Tommy replied.

"Yes....let him go," Victor reiterated, stepping towards the youth and placing a hand on his shoulder. Tommy released his grip. Victor felt for a specific pressure point on the intruder's neck. He found it and rendered the youth, who was now scared stiff, into a virtual paralytic state.

Victor marched him towards the door. Tommy looked on as the seemingly hypnotised figure moved like an automaton under Victor's control. Tommy ran ahead and opened the shop door and Victor escorted the youngster out onto the pavement. The High Street was busy and there were people everywhere. Tommy stood in the shop doorway and watched as Victor let go and stepped back. The intruder's trance-like state continued though and he walked on. Tommy glanced at Victor, whose eyes were fixed on the dazed track suited figure. He stepped off the kerb between two parked cars and Tommy watched in horror as he walked straight into an oncoming double-decker bus. He was killed instantly. Amidst the ensuing pandemonium, Victor, showing no emotion whatsoever, turned to Tommy, whose expression typified the shock and revulsion on the faces of everyone else who'd just witnessed the harrowing and gruesome scene, and took him to one side.

"Make yourself scarce.....go......*now*. I'll lock up. *Go*......right now," and he pushed Tommy away from the grisly action. "We'll continue our talk another time. Now piss off Tommy, get a grip and say nothing to no one."

The apparent suicide of someone so young in the normally uneventful suburb of Southfields was big news and fed the media for days afterwards. Not surprisingly, eye witness accounts varied. Some said the youth deliberately walked into the traffic, while others were of the opinion he wasn't looking where he was going, suggesting it was an unfortunate accident. There was even one woman who said it looked like he was high on drugs! Everyone, including the press, would just have to wait for the outcome of the Coroner's verdict at the inquest to find out if the truth was forthcoming.

Harry Nelson's mind was far from the High Street incident however. He had important matters of his own to bring to a conclusion. The week's notice he'd given Prestige Cars was well on the way to being completed, but the time was going painfully slowly for him and he was becoming more apprehensive the nearer he got to leaving the company and more specifically, freeing himself from the clutches of Angelo Mantovani.

His last night arrived and he turned up for work as usual, well dressed in his smart chauffer's uniform. He was given the black limousine for the evening and set out on his first run, collecting a hen party and driving them to one of Barchester's west end night clubs. The atmosphere in the seven seater luxury vehicle was bubbly and jovial even if the banter and girlie jokes were somewhat vulgar and bawdy.

Harry much preferred ferrying fellas on stag night parties to groups of raucous, giggly girls. He found they were better behaved and more generous with their tips, but having a plethora of horny women as passengers did have its benefits, and he was groped and had his private parts felt on several occasions. It was all done in the name of good fun though and that's as far as any sexual connotation went. Harry tried his best to enter into the spirit of things but he was on edge worrying about what the remainder of the evening might bring and, more precisely, what Angelo Mantovani had in store for him.

The time dragged and his mood deepened as his shift went slowly by. He saw Angelo around one thirty back at the office in Southfields.

"Got a little job for you. Special delivery," Angelo said as Harry went straight to the coffee machine.

"Your boy Tommy's doing well I see," he added as Harry busied himself at the machine. Harry didn't want to *chat* with Angelo. He wanted nothing to do with him.

"Me and Freddie saw them at the Velvet Club.......he's some performer."

"I've not seen them," Harry replied curtly. He realised he had to say something to the man.

"No, he's good, Harry.....fair play, and you should be proud."

Harry took his plastic cup of what looked like coffee, even if the taste bore no relation to the real thing, and thought he didn't need the likes of Angelo Mantovani telling him how proud he should be of his only son. He sipped his drink.

"Not my sort of music really. Freddie liked it, but then he's easily pleased. Prefer Latin American, me....something with a bit of style."

"Thought you would," Harry said under his breath."

"What?"

"I said *that's good*," Harry quipped.

Angelo nodded. "Anyway, take this and guard it with your life. Delivery to the Platinum Casino Club, to the manager there, Robert Pullen. This is for him personally. Give it to no one else. Clear?"

"Any money to collect?"

"No, not this time," Angelo replied and went off to the inner office. Harry took the small package, put it into the glove compartment of the limo and went on his way.

'The Platinum Club' he thought to himself, *'I'll be nicked before I get anywhere near there Angelo, and you bloody well know it. You must think I was born yesterday, you fucker'* he contemplated inwardly and headed towards Barchester city centre.

It was a twenty minute drive to the casino and the traffic on the streets at that late hour was pretty sparse. Harry was convinced he'd been set up. His eyes were everywhere. On the rear view mirror, the wing mirrors, on the road ahead, searching for the police who would undoubtedly catch him red handed with the drugs on him. He'd put his trust in Derek Dooley, but he had no idea if the constable would swing it for him.

The tension was almost tangible. He passed a dark coloured Ford Zephyr waiting at a junction. He half expected it to follow, but it didn't. What looked like a Jaguar came up behind him with its powerful, distinctive headlights.

'This was it' he thought. He knew the drugs squad often used unmarked Jaguars in their quest to beat the dealers. They were fast and their superb road holding capabilities at speed usually gave them the edge. Harry's speed was constant and sedate, but his hands were shaking on the steering wheel and his heart was pounding.

The Jaguar remained menacingly close behind him. His paranoia was now extreme and beads of sweat glistened on his forehead. It was when he saw the bright neon lights of the Platinum Casino Club ahead that the Jaguar made its move. It pulled out, overtook him and left him in its wake as the sleek vehicle accelerated away. Within seconds it was gone. Harry pulled up outside the casino and turned the engine off. He heaved a sigh of relief and composed himself, whilst simultaneously scanning the immediate area for signs of police presence. He could see none, so he took the package from the glove compartment, stepped out of the limo and made his way to the casino's main entrance. Some steps led up to the impressive Georgian portico where he was met by a burly doorman.

"I've got a delivery for a guy named Pullen," Harry said, still with one eye on the street behind him. It was now or never he felt, and held the small package out for the doorman to take.

"Which one?" the well built man asked.

"What do you mean?"

"Which Mr. Pullen. Robert, the manager, or his son John, who runs the bar?"

"The manager.....yeah.....it's for the manager." Suddenly he remembered Angelo saying he *must* give it to him personally. All he wanted to do was get shot of the package and finish his shift. The doorman went to take it.

"Just remembered, I've got to deliver it personally."

The doorman shook his head.

"My boss made it clear. I've got to give it to him in person."

"Not dressed like that you don't."

"This is my working uniform."

"Precisely. This is a high class establishment and you're not wandering around looking like that. Give it to me, I'll see Robert Pullen gets it......okay?" Harry shrugged. He wasn't going to argue with the huge man.

"Guess it'll be fine," he said and handed it over. His last task was to collect the hen party from the night club not far away and drive them back to Southfields. He was in a much more relaxed mood and now didn't care if he *was* stopped by the law. The girls were suitably inebriated but tiredness had tempered their high spirits, and Harry was able to enjoy their company on the trip back through the now deserted Barchester streets.

With the job done and feeling much better he parked up the limo around the back of Prestige Cars and handed the keys to the only person left there, the car controller.

"Everything okay?" he asked looking up from the paperwork on his desk. Harry nodded.

"Everything's fine......I'm off now."

"Good luck for the future then, Harry."

"Thanks," Harry replied and strolled out. It was a clear, cloudless night and dawn was hovering on the horizon ready to signal the start of another day. Harry's step on the ten minute walk back to the Barton Bridge flats was brisk and there was a spring in his gait as he looked towards a brighter future for himself and his family. Angelo Mantovani and the Zanetti Corporation were far from his mind as he had the radio on quietly in the kitchen and made himself a proper cup of coffee. His chilled out state didn't last long however as the five o'clock news came on the radio:

'We have reports of an explosion at the popular Platinum casino in the centre of Barchester. Emergency services are attending and it's not been confirmed if there are casualties at this stage We will bring you the full story as it unfolds, so stay tuned.'

Harry realised it wasn't drugs he was carrying, but something far worse. A bomb.

Chapter 13

The blast at the Platinum Casino was not surprisingly the main news event that morning, and conflicting bulletins were circulating almost on an hourly basis, such was their regularity. Reports were sketchy however, and there had been no official statements issued by the relevant authorities. Rumours regarding casualties, including possible fatalities, were rife though and the media were desperate to get information and details on the developing situation, however insignificant.

All this effectively overshadowed the big sports news of the day. For weeks Southfields F.C. manager Will Grealish had been holding talks with Barchester United's head coach Jock McFadden over the possible transfer of Steve Baker to the affluent first division club. Barchester's scouts had been keeping a close eye on him for a lot longer than that and now Steve was eighteen and not considered a minor in the legal sense, the Barchester coach thought the time was right to make his move.

Everyone, including Grealish, knew Steve was now far too good for third division Southfields, and Grealish wasn't going to hold him back or stand in the way of his burgeoning career. There was also the financial position for the small club to consider and a huge transfer fee had already been discussed in the lead up talks between the two clubs. Once that had been agreed on it was down to Steve to accept the personal terms of the contract Barchester Utd. were offering him.

His dad was on hand to guide him through the legalities of the agreement, and once he'd given Steve his opinion that there was nothing irregular or untoward in the contract, and the deal was a once in a lifetime opportunity for his son to play in the top league, he stepped back telling Steve he was now master of his own future. He also reiterated he would always be there for him whenever he needed help or guidance. To have the blessing and support of his dad meant so much to Steve and gave him the inner confidence to be his own man.

This particular morning as he walked into Barchester Utd's reception area adorned with trophies spanning nearly a century, *that* opportunity was his and he was going to enjoy it to the full. He duly signed for the club in Jock McFadden's plush office in the company of Will Grealish, three executive members of the Barchester club's board of directors and a handful of reporters from both the local and national press.

It was all very low key but Jock McFadden told Steve the razzmatazz would surely follow and urged him to take it in his stride, enjoy and embrace the occasion over the next few days, then set his mind totally to his new club, Barchester United. It was a record transfer fee for the third division club and Will Grealish, although losing his best player, was happy in the knowledge the resulting funds would keep Southfields F.C. solvent for the foreseeable future.

Tommy heard the news from a customer in Subway Music later that morning. It took him by surprise even though he knew Steve was destined to play top flight football. He thought perhaps Steve might have chosen a club away from his home city and begin a new and exciting stage of his life in another part of the country. Barchester Utd. had pursued and chosen *him* though, but Tommy didn't know that. He did feel a bit disappointed Steve hadn't mentioned anything about the move, but he was also aware they were no longer bosom buddies and he probably would have acted the same way had he been in Steve's shoes.

The main story on the lunchtime news was the explosion at the Platinum Casino and a police spokesman confirmed the blast was caused by a bomb in the basement of the club. Details of two fatalities emerged. The first was a woman cloakroom attendant and the second being the club's doorman. No names were forthcoming. The bulletin stated there were no other casualties and the building was being made safe by fire-fighters at the scene, although the damage was confined to the lower ground floor level. The news message also said the casino would remain closed for safety reasons and the owner of the establishment had been informed. The owner was James Slade, but that information wasn't given out over the air waves. He'd spent all morning at the scene and was doing his utmost to give the police all the help he could in their quest to piece together the details of the unusual crime.

Tommy was about to take his lunch break when his dad walked into the shop. He looked anxious and tired. Tommy saw him coming.

"Hi dad, Steve's signed for United.....what a turn up. Didn't see that coming, did we? You look awful....what's up?"

"Had a long night," is all Harry said.

"Oh yeah......your last night. Hey, how about I treat you to a Wimpy. My lunch break now....you can tell me all about it?"

"Yeah, I need to talk to you anyway," Harry replied.

"I'm off now," Tommy called across to Mandy. She nodded and Tommy and his dad walked out into the High Street.

"Terrible about that bomb in the casino, eh dad. Two dead they say." The Wimpy bar was about a hundred yards up the street. Harry stopped abruptly.

"Two dead. When did you hear that?"

"Just now....on the news. The doorman apparently, poor sod, and a woman."

Harry was stunned. "The doorman?"

"Yeah....didn't you hear me?"

"I've gotta go."

"What? What you on about, dad. The Wimpy's just here."

"I can't. Sorry Tommy........some other time."

He turned and hurried off leaving Tommy flabbergasted. Harry got as far as the churchyard at the top of the High Street and made his way to a wrought iron bench under a huge yew tree. He slumped down and put his head in his hands. He was utterly distraught. So much was flooding his confused head. The doorman, dead. The burly guy he'd spoken to only a few hours ago. He'd given *him* the package, the bomb. He'd handed him the bomb and now he was dead.

The wind rustled the new bright green leaves on a handsome horse chestnut nearby. The churchyard looked serene and beautiful. Harry's mind was racing. It suddenly hit him that the bomb was meant for the manager, and he was supposed to give it to him personally. To him, Angelo had said. Angelo's orders, give the package specifically to the manager, no one else.

His chain of thought remained with Angelo Mantovani, who was rapidly becoming his fearful nemesis and it made his blood run cold. He *had* well and truly stitched him up. Harry knew he was now an unwitting accessory to murder and his complicity would surely land him in big trouble with the police. He wished now he'd been a simple, uncomplicated drugs courier and not an envoy of death.

The more he contemplated on the situation the more complicated it became. He'd involved Derek Dooley, a uniformed police constable, and confided in him. Why on earth did he do that? he reflected solemnly. He was alone in that churchyard, more alone than he'd ever been in his life. His melancholic thoughts turned to Tommy, his so called *wayward* son, who had already sacrificed so much for him in recent months, and had tirelessly got his life back together. How could he possibly burden him with these new problems and the predicament he was now in.

He thought about his long suffering wife June, who was only now starting to enjoy life having lived with a moody gambler for so long, and young Emma, who deserved a better father than the one she'd had to put up with since she was a child. In Harry's depressed state the list seemed endless. The breeze swept through the churchyard once again. Harry, with his head bowed, sobbed quietly. His life was a real mess and he cut a lonely figure in the sobering environs of All Saints Church's consecrated grounds that lunchtime.

Tommy went to the Wimpy bar alone, his lunch consisting of a burger and coke. He would have much preferred a couple of pints in the Crown opposite, but lunchtime drinking was banned by Victor and was a sackable offence, so he refrained.

He hadn't seen Victor all morning and was wondering when he would resume the conversation he was so keen to have when it was cut short by the unfortunate intruder.

Tommy was also pensive that lunchtime. His life, although exciting and quite extraordinary for one so young, was becoming complicated in ways he found hard to deal with. Entrepreneur James Slade was pulling him in one direction and Victor seemed to be doing the same in another. His dad was becoming an enigma and Dennis Carter, his flatmate, colleague and friend, was rapidly turning into a morose, almost morbid individual and Tommy had no idea why. That became clearer to him however, back in the shop later that afternoon.

Freddie Mantovani's extravagant pink Cadillac pulled up outside Subway Music around four o'clock. Tommy saw it first and although it put the wind up him he nonchalantly carried on as if he hadn't seen it. He watched as Freddie walked in. Well dressed in a grey mohair suit and white open necked shirt, his walk was more of a swagger and his broad muscular frame gave the impression he was a lot taller than his five foot nine inches. His short dark brown hair was immaculate and he looked very distinctive.

He didn't even look at Tommy as he headed towards the customer services area where Dennis was.

"Boss wants a word," he said curtly. He

dwarfed Dennis, even though he was only slightly taller than the slim twenty one year old.

"I'm busy," Dennis replied cheekily.

Freddie smiled menacingly. "Mouthy as usual, eh? Angelo wants to see you....now....right now. I won't ask again."

Dennis held his hands up in a mock gesture of surrender. "You have a way with words, Freddie."

"Mr Mantovani to you, punk. Now come on....we haven't got all day."

Tommy heard the brief conversation and looked on as Dennis followed Freddie out of the shop. The Cadillac's hood was down and Angelo was reclining on the sumptuous white leather seating in the back. Freddie casually slid into the driver's seat and Dennis went to open the front passenger door. Freddie scowled at him.

"In the back you fucking idiot," he sneered. Dennis duly got in the back and sat next to Angelo. Tommy watched from just inside the shop doorway as the huge car moved effortlessly away and out of his sight.

"We have a problem," Angelo said. He looked especially dapper in a navy, pin-striped three piece suit complete with a pair of stylish Italian black patent leather shoes. Dennis didn't reply.

"Our manager at Trusty Loans says you're in arrears," Angelo said taking a small notebook from his jacket pocket and flicking through some pages. "To the tune of two hundred and eleven pounds, fifteen shillings."

"Yeah.....I can explain that," Dennis replied defensively.

"I'm not interested in explanations, Carter, you're out of order......"

"I said I could explain....."

"Shut it," Freddie insisted gruffly as he drove the Cadillac sedately along Southfields High Street. Angelo waved and smiled at acquaintances he knew along the way. Dennis thought he looked pompous and ridiculous.

"We have a solution to the problem," he turned to Dennis for the first time since he'd got in. "We need you to do an errand for us.....and in return, if you complete the task to our satisfaction, we wipe out your debt."

Angelo suddenly had Dennis's undivided attention.

"Wipe out me debt, everything I owe?"

Angelo nodded, "You go on a short trip. You take a suitcase we give you, and you go to Morocco. You exchange the case with another and bring it back to us, here. That's it....couldn't be simpler."

"It could," Dennis said cynically, "For a start, I've never been further than the Isle Of Wight....let alone South America."

Freddie burst out laughing.

"I'm serious. Never been abroad, me. Never. Don't have a passport or anything."

"That's no problem," Angelo said as Freddie stopped the Cadillac outside Woolworths. Freddie tossed half a crown into Dennis's lap.

"Get your photo taken, pretty boy.....in there....in the booth. We'll wait."

"And don't be all day," Angelo added as Dennis took the money and disappeared into Woolworths. This interlude gave him valuable time to think about the predicament he now found himself in. Should he refuse to do it, he thought. But that idea was quickly discarded. He was neither brave nor completely stupid and realised the Mantovanis were ruthless adversaries who could cause him a lot of aggravation. He was also well aware he was spending far too much on drugs, although he was adamant his habit was purely social and not obsessive or addictive. Nevertheless it was money he should have earmarked for paying off the loan he took out to buy his Triumph Bonneville motorbike.

He was under no illusions about the *errand* he would be doing. He was fully aware it was probably drugs smuggling and, if caught, would mean a prison sentence, and a long one at that. But he'd owe the twins nothing, and that alone meant everything to him, and that swung it. He came out, got in the car and handed Angelo the strip of photos.

"I'll do it," he said confidently. Inwardly though, he was far from self assured.

"Thought you might," Angelo replied. It was hard to believe all three of them were the same age. Angelo and Freddie were self motivated and sophisticated, whilst Dennis was still rough around the edges. They went to the same school, Heathfield Secondary Modern in Southfields, but no one would have guessed that, such was the chasm between *their* general enlightenment and knowledge, and Dennis's streetwise but basic grasp of an average education.

"Right....now listen," Angelo continued, "You're to be at Prestige Cars in Southfields Lane, seven in the morning......that's tomorrow morning. You know it?"

Dennis nodded. The Cadillac headed up the High Street towards the church. Dennis started mimicking Angelo and waved in an overly genteel manner to complete strangers walking along the pavement. Freddie saw him in his rear view mirror and was incensed.

"Listen to my brother you fucking moron," he said, "And quit taking the piss....or I'll stop this motor and sort you out."

"You'll be given a suitcase and taken to the airport. You get the ten twenty flight to Marrakesh in Morocco, where you'll be met by a guy called Khalid Baba. With me so far?" Angelo asked. Again Dennis nodded.

"You'll be taken to an address in the city where you hand over the suitcase and you'll be given another. Then you'll be escorted back to the airport where you get the eight ten flight back here. You'll be met at the airport and driven back to Prestige Cars......oh...and your name's Keith Duncan. Now all this will be explained again in detail tomorrow morning. So is everything clear?"

Dennis knew when to draw the line between seriousness and frivolity and wasn't about to try Freddie's patience again at this crucial time.

"Yeah....I know what to do....and I won't owe you a penny, either of you....straight up?"

"So long as you don't get caught," Angelo quipped. Freddie laughed at his brother's quick witted comment as the Cadillac drew up outside Subway Music.

"Make it happen, Dennis Carter.....you make it happen. Seven o'clock, Prestige Cars....oh....and not a word to anyone. Now hop it."

Angelo's final comment couldn't be clearer and Dennis got out and watched as the pink American dream machine accelerated away.

Dennis was lucky Victor hadn't yet graced the shop with his presence as he wouldn't have taken kindly to one of his employees skipping off during working hours. Dennis said nothing to Tommy but he could see the concern on his face during the remainder of the afternoon. Tommy chose to bide his time and tackle his friend later, back at their flat. It made for an uncomfortable atmosphere which neither of them would address.

Victor turned up just before closing time. He'd offered Tommy the vacant manager's job and for the time being he was the key holder so had to be there to open and close the premises.

"I want to continue our conversation, Tommy.....about your future," he said as the last customers were leaving the shop.

"When?" Tommy asked.

"Now. We'll lock up and retire to my office." Tommy knew he meant his car, and agreed. Dennis left without saying a word to anyone and Victor and Tommy walked to the black Ford Zodiac parked around the back.

"Where were we?" Victor asked making himself comfortable in the driver's seat. Tommy noticed he still had his trilby on and wondered why, in the confines of the car's limited interior headroom.

"You were on about making me a star."

"That's right.....before that fucking low life got in the way."

"Yeah, I've been thinking about that and I still can't work out......"

"Nothing to work out, lad. Get it out your mind and say no more about it."

Tommy was fiddling with a mobile hanging from the rear view mirror. It was a glass disc with a gold, five point star in it. Victor continued. "You can make it on your own..... I know it."

"What....go solo?"

"That's exactly what I'm saying."

"What about the band?"

"Dump the band, Tommy, for your own sake."

"But they're part of......"

"Dump the fucking band. You're the star...and

with me behind you, the world's your stage."
Tommy flicked at the mobile and it spun around.

"How?" Tommy wanted to know more but was sceptical. James Slade was the one who'd catapulted him and the band into the limelight, and he couldn't help feeling Victor was trying to outdo his brother. He knew how tetchy Victor could be on the subject though, and was loathe to bring it up there and then.

"Now listen very carefully, Tommy and I'll tell you *how*........and stop fiddling with that bloody pentagram."
Tommy sat back and folded his arms. He decided to listen even though he wasn't convinced Victor could further his musical career.

"I've been waiting so long for someone with your talent to come along and this is a big chance for both of us. I *can* launch your solo career....but in the mainstream.....pop, if you want to call it. You change your style to suit the main markets both here and in America. Even throw in the odd ballad, a love song. You'd have to change your name though."

"What?" Tommy said, he remembered a similar conversation a while ago on the same subject.

"Your name...at least your first name."

"Go on....tell me it's too British, and not sophisticated enough."

"That's exactly it. Uncanny, that."

"And what do you say to Bobby.....Bobby

Nelson?"

Victor hesitated for a few seconds.

"Fucking perfect," he replied. "This is going better than I thought. So......interested?" Victor certainly had Tommy's interest.

"In a way, yeah....I am. I'm curious how you could do it, make me successful and all that. What about a girl singer....easier that, if you ask me?"

"No chance."

"Why?"

"Women, they're temperamental, fickle, indecisive. Then they go and have a baby. No, I can't be having with all that. My protégé will be male....end of story."

Tommy laughed. He knew Victor was eccentric, even a bit strange, and he hadn't yet been able to fathom him out, but he had no reason not to trust the man.

"Alright, you've got my attention, Victor. Convince me. Convince me I should leave the Devil's Flock and get rid of someone who'll remain nameless. Go on, Victor.....I'm listening."

Tommy had laid down the gauntlet and that was exactly what Victor was banking on. He was in his element. His usual pale, thin face was flushed with enthusiasm and his deep set brown eyes bore a twinkle that was rarely seen. His long, slim fingers drummed rhythmically on the steering wheel.

"I can make it happen, Tommy. High class gigs. Television appearances. A guaranteed recording contract. Tours of both Europe and the States......"

"How.....how can you do that?"

"You've seen me play the piano. You said I was world class. Well Tommy, I am...."

"But?"

"Let me continue. I *could* be a maestro playing concerts worldwide. But I don't fucking want to. I've got no interest in being famous. Rich.....yes. I want to be the richest man on earth. But fame....no. Look at me....do you see a famous celebrity, honestly?"
Tommy laughed. Victor's wiry, angular disposition and sharp features weren't akin to handsome good looks.

"No, didn't think so. Now, back to the important matter of your success. I'll spell it out. I'll advance you twenty thousand pounds, up front, and we start immediately on your solo career. I will be your manager and agent and we will sign a legally binding contract to that effect. I'll take ten percent of your earnings as your personal manager, and another ten percent as your agent. Twenty percent in total...."

"Shouldn't that be fifteen percent if you're doing both?" Tommy interrupted pertinently.

"Should it fuck. No....it might be the done thing in the industry but not in this deal. I take twenty percent, non negotiable. You get fame and fortune.....and I just make a fortune. What do you say?"

"Twenty thousand up front?"

Victor nodded. "Conditions are these," he continued. "You stay at Subway Music, for the time being at least, even if it means part time. I'll get someone else to manage the place, don't worry about that. And you tell the band...and my brother....your decision to go solo. You tell them personally. Got that?"

Tommy was wondering when James Slade would come into the equation.

"Where's the catch?" he asked.

"No catch, Tommy. A business deal, pure and simple. I know you've got the talent to go all the way and make me a lot of money, and that's what I'll be investing in. That's it. I *could* talk all day weighing up the pros and cons and praising you to the hilt, but that's not my way, and I think you know that. I'll give you time.....time to think it over, but I can't give a lot. Understand?"

Tommy flicked at the pentagram mobile, sending it spinning. He didn't need time. It *was* great being the lead singer and front man of the Devil's Flock and Mitch and the boys were excellent musicians and fun to be with. But he wanted more. He craved superstardom and he would do whatever it took to achieve that pinnacle of success.

He looked at Victor and James Slade jumped out at him. For some unknown and inexplicable reason he trusted Victor but not his brother, James.

"I'll do it Victor.......I'll fucking well do it," he said, unable to stifle a laugh. Victor wasn't laughing. He sat motionless in his worn and shabby brown suit and matching trilby.

"Think it over, Tommy....please."

Tommy shook his head.

"Bobby Nelson, here I am. Make me a star, Victor. I'm ready," he beamed. Victor smiled.

"I think you are. I'll get the ball rolling......and you do what you have to do, yeah?"

Tommy nodded slowly and thoughtfully. Victor reached forward and turned the key in the ignition.

"Now piss off." he said dryly, "I'm going home."

Chapter 14

After Harry Nelson's sobering lunchtime experience in All Saint's churchyard he stopped off at the Crown further down the High Street for a consoling pint, and proceeded to get well and truly drunk in the relaxing, homely atmosphere of the seventeenth century hostelry.

It was late afternoon when he got back to the Barton Bridge flats and spent the next few hours flaked out on the sofa in the lounge. His peace was shattered however around eight in the evening when he had a visit from D.C. Tim Sutherland from Barchester C.I.D. To Harry's astonishment and dismay the detective had some questions for him relating to the bombing at the Platinum Casino, and Harry was caught completely off guard, which was exactly why the ambitious young detective chose to visit at that time and at his home.

He politely accepted a cup of tea offered by June, whilst Harry took a couple of pain killers for an approaching, niggling hangover, before beginning his line of questions. Harry was filled with trepidation as those questions became more pertinent.

"The pictures from the surveillance camera at the club show a dark Humber car, registration number CXL33, arriving at the club just after two on that morning. Our enquiries show the registered owner to be Prestige Cars here in Southfields." D.C. Sutherland could plainly see the look of horror on Harry's face even though he was doing his best to disguise it.

He had no idea he was being filmed. Cutting edge technology was now being used to provide places like banks, casinos and other related businesses with the means to monitor their premises, both inside and out, on a twenty four hour basis. Time delay, monochrome still photography was now in production and James Slade had embraced the new technology and installed the equipment a few months previously. It was now proving invaluable in the search for those responsible for bombing his club.

"What's that got to do with me?" Harry asked naively.

"We've already been to Prestige Cars, Mr Nelson, and they told us you were driving the car that evening, and they also said you no longer work for them, that you left their employ that very night." Harry was furious. He thought the time and effort he'd put into the company would have counted for something, but the implication that he'd left suddenly on the night of the bombing made him realise it meant nothing.

"Fucking right," Harry fumed. "I drove that car that night.....sure I did, and yeah, it *was* my last night. I'd given a week's notice seven days before that.....did they fucking tell you that....you satisfied now?"

D.C. Sutherland had no intention of continuing the interview on a confrontational basis and eased the tension by requesting another cup of tea.

"We're talking to everyone we can to ascertain why those two people at the club lost their lives, Mr Nelson. I'm only doing my job."

Harry nodded. He realised belatedly the last thing he wanted to do was incriminate himself by talking too much. "I understand. Is that it then?" he asked.

"Not quite," D.C. Sutherland replied. Harry was starting to feel very uneasy.

"We noticed you didn't drop anyone off at the casino," the detective continued, "Or didn't pick anyone up for that matter."

"What you getting at?"

"Nothing. Nothing at all. What were you doing there?"

Harry was in a quandary and needed valuable time to think. He didn't reply.

"Because the camera shows you out of the car talking to the doorman, and giving him something. Now, Mr Nelson.....talk to me."

Harry knew he should tell the truth. He was no murderer. He had nothing to hide. It was Angelo Mantovani the detective should be talking to, he thought. He couldn't implicate a dangerous gangster like Mantovani. There was no knowing what the repercussions might be for himself, and more importantly, for his family. He chose to say nothing more to D.C. Sutherland. The detective did push for an answer making it very clear to Harry the police *would* get the perpetrator of the crime and warned him their next interview could well be in the less salubrious surroundings of Barchester Police Station. Fear had determined Harry's stubbornness in not being forthcoming however, and Tim Sutherland guessed that was probably the reason, and didn't pursue the questioning further.

Harry didn't get much sleep that night. Neither did Dennis Carter. He also had an errand to do for Angelo and Freddie Mantovani and by the early morning his anxiety was bordering on fear as he contemplated what the day ahead would have in store for him. He'd never been abroad. Neither had he flown in an aeroplane. That alone would have given a lot of people cause for concern, but he had the added burden knowing his mission was illegal and should he be caught, would undoubtedly face a hefty prison sentence.

The outward journey was fine and the sheer exhilaration as the plane lifted off the runway and soared into the air took his mind briefly off his illicit assignment, and the suitcase in the aircraft's cargo hold he believed was full of cash. The hot, humid Moroccan air hit him as he stepped off the plane and onto the tarmac in Marrakesh. It was stifling, and dressed in sweat top and jeans Dennis soon found the sweltering heat uncomfortable and almost unbearable, the consoling factor being he only had to spend a few hours there, and would soon be back on the plane and on his way back to the cooler climes of Britain.

He picked the suitcase off the carousel and walked unchallenged through security and customs and out into the airport's concourse, where he was met by Khalid Baba as planned. Not a lot was said on the short trip into town, Dennis keeping the suitcase by his side the whole time. Everything about the place was alien to him. The heat, the busy, dusty streets, the dirty surroundings and the crumbling, neglected buildings.

To him the people all looked the same. Dark skinned, swarthy and shifty looking. It scared him. He was out of his comfort zone and with his lily white skin and blond hair, he stood out a mile. The pick-up truck they were in pulled into a shady courtyard surrounded by high whitewashed buildings. Khalid Baba waited some time before getting out of the vehicle, looking around as if he was expecting company. Dennis noticed his right hand shoved down inside a leather bag which was slung loosely over his shoulder. He could only assume the Moroccan was armed and that didn't help his overall sense of foreboding and uneasiness.

"Come........come," Khalid Baba said suddenly, and stepped out of the truck. Dennis was petrified, but followed, clasping the suitcase to his chest. The truck driver stayed in the vehicle. He too was constantly looking around and lit a cigarette. Dennis glanced back. He was sure he was also carrying a weapon.

The building he followed Khalid Baba into was surprisingly modern and clean, with marble floors and ornate plasterwork on the walls and ceilings. He was taken upstairs to an empty room overlooking the courtyard.

"The case.....the case. I will have it now," Khalid Baba said. Dennis's mind was racing. Why didn't they just shoot him there and then, he thought to himself. He handed over the suitcase. He was completely at the Moroccan's mercy and could only assume repeat business with the Mantovanis was good, whether it was drugs related or any other illegal trade, and considerable profits were being made by everyone concerned, and all parties wished to keep it that way. The wellbeing of the courier, Dennis surmised, was therefore crucial to their continued success. That gave him solace and hope that he might just be back on the plane later that day alive, and not be shipped back to Britain in a wooden box , or be found with a bullet in his skull, floating in the Mediterranean Sea.

Khalid Baba smiled for the first time since he met Dennis at the airport.

"I get you food...........chicken kebab............and drinks...yes?"

Dennis nodded.

"Over here," he pointed to a door in the corner of the room. "Washroom......for you. I must go now. I lock you in and I am sorry. That is the way it is......yes?"

Dennis shrugged. He had nothing against talking to the man, he just didn't know what to say. Khalid Baba carried the suitcase to the door.

"You will be safe here....I will be back soon."

Dennis heard the key turn in the lock as he left. He was alone. Alone in what he considered to be some Godforsaken hell hole on the northern tip of Africa.

He cast an eye over his sparse surroundings. What he'd give for a big, fat, calming and relaxing joint right there and then. He couldn't suppress a half smile though as the irony of his reflection dawned on him. The Moroccan was true to his word and was back within the hour with a late takeaway lunch of spicy, barbecued chicken kebabs and a big bottle of cherryade.

"I hope you enjoy the food," is all he said and left, locking the door again as he did so. Dennis tried the chicken. It was hot and piquant and he thought it tasted better than it looked. The fizzy pop quelled the resulting fire in his mouth and throat, and although he didn't finish the meal, it was adequate and kept the hunger pangs away.

He was now feeling a little less stressed and came to the conclusion he would have been killed by now if that's what his hosts had in mind. He stared out of the window and wished away the hours until he would hopefully be taken back to the airport. It was early evening when Khalid Baba returned. The sun was setting but the humidity hadn't decreased. Dennis was handed the same suitcase he'd brought out.

"Our business is complete, my friend. I will take you to the airport," the olive skinned Moroccan said in his best English, and escorted Dennis down the stairs and out into the courtyard. He could see the Moroccan was still armed, as was the truck driver and again he clutched the suitcase to his chest as he climbed into the pick-up truck. It got dark very quickly and nightfall was upon them as they approached the airport's departure building.

"I hope you have a safe journey, my friend," Khalid Baba said as Dennis eagerly got out of the truck. "I have a message for you to give to mister Angelo. Please tell him we are now even."
With that the pick-up truck sped away.

Dennis breathed a huge sigh of relief. He now looked like any other traveller as he joined the throng of people in the busy departure concourse. He spent longer than he hoped in the check-in queue and he never once let go of the suitcase the whole time he was in it.

He'd smoked Moroccan black once. It was considered the *'foie grasse'* of cannabis resin with its powerful and long lasting hallucinatory attributes combined with a heady, pungent odour. Because of its superior quality it came with a hefty price tag which was out of his reach, and he could only hazard a guess at what the street value of a fifty pound suitcase full of the stuff might be worth on the open market. He breathed yet another sigh of relief as the check-in girl relieved him of it and he watched as it trundled along the conveyor with everyone else's luggage.

The return flight seemed longer and it was after midnight when the plane landed at Barchester Airport. As soon as he stepped off the plane his anxiety level and apprehension rose dramatically. He sailed through passport control, even with his dodgy passport, giving him a false sense of optimism and complacency, but by the time he spotted the suitcase heading his way on the luggage carousel he was a bundle of nerves.

His eyes darted everywhere believing he was under constant surveillance. He became so paranoid he didn't pick the case off the conveyor but instead, let it go around for a second time. He wished he hadn't though when he was almost the last one there when it came around again, and he felt even more conspicuous and culpable. With the suitcase firmly in his grip he headed for customs.

He took a deep breath and entered. This is it, he thought, composing himself and looking straight ahead. His walk was nonchalant, his demeanour calm and placid. He'd practiced this particular routine in his head so many times it was perfect. Don't smile. Don't look at anyone and don't look at the suitcase. His heart was thumping as he strolled through customs as if he'd done it a hundred times before. The neon exit sign was in his sight. There was more purpose in his stride. It was now or never. Keep walking. Don't look back. Stay focussed.

"Excuse me sir," The dreaded words hit him like a bombshell. He stopped.

"What have you got to declare?" The words were clear and terrifying. Dennis turned to face the customs official.

"Nothing," he blurted out. His inner being was pleading with him to remain cool, collected and level headed. The customs man scratched his head.

"Nothing to declare?" he asked again.

"No.....nothing," Dennis replied gripping the suitcase as if his life depended on it.

"Then why have you come through the red channel. The green channel's where you should be if you've nothing to declare."

Dennis swallowed hard, "How stupid," he replied, "I was miles away......I didn't notice."

"Easily done I suppose," the customs man said.

"Have I got to go back then and go through the green one......or can I get out this way?"

It was the sixty four thousand dollar question, and freedom was in sight. The exit sign was beckoning and he took half a step towards it.

"Might as well have a quick look while you're here. Come this way sir.....if you don't mind."

Dennis looked at the official as if he was from

another planet. The game was up and the adrenalin drained from his body just as sure as someone had pulled a plug. How could he have been so stupid, he thought, so fucking brainless.

"This way sir," the voice repeated. He was *so* close, so close to pulling it off. He trudged over to the counter at the side and dumped the case on it.

"Name?"

"Den.......Duncan. Keith Duncan," he remembered just in time.

"Passport, Mr Duncan, please."

Dennis obliged, handing over the fake passport. A prison sentence flashed through his mind.

"Where have you come from?"

Dennis knew the questions would come thick and fast now. He was distraught, but couldn't let it show. "Marrakesh," he mumbled.

"Was it business or pleasure?"

To Dennis this was now an interrogation. The man studied his passport closely. The situation was getting worse and he was digging himself deeper into the quagmire.

"Pleasure," he replied.

"When did you travel to Marrakesh, Mr Duncan?"

"This morning. Well, yesterday morning now." The customs official raised his eyebrows.

"A day trip to Morocco......for pleasure. Unusual that," he said, opening the unlocked suitcase.

"Did you pack this yourself, sir?"

Dennis nodded.

"Now....is there anything you wish to tell me?" Dennis looked at him blankly. He guessed the grilling would continue into the small hours and he was resigned to the fact.

"Anything else you want to tell me regarding the contents of this suitcase?" the official asked again. Dennis shook his head dejectedly. A colleague was called over who looked on as the top of the case was flipped back. The customs official took out a newspaper and placed it on the counter.

"The Telegraph," he said and proceeded to take out another, and another. Dennis thought they would find the Moroccan black any second.

"The Times," the official commented taking out yet another newspaper from the case.

"No Daily Mirror, sir. Put you down as a *'Mirror'* man myself."

"Very fucking funny," Dennis replied. He'd had enough and the sarcastic remarks were riling him.

"Just doing my job, sir," he said.

Dennis smirked at the cliché. He was rapidly losing it and he didn't really care anymore. He looked at the man as he continued to take out newspaper after newspaper. The stack on the counter was getting bigger. Dennis's curiosity was aroused and he peered into the half empty suitcase. All he could see were daily broadsheets. The case was full of newspapers. There was no sign of any drugs.

Both customs officials were completely

mystified and called over their supervisor. Dennis's hopelessness took a turn for the better. He was also baffled but a modicum of optimism was creeping slowly in. Where *was* the cannabis, he thought.

"Search the lining," the supervisor said sternly, "Every inch of it," he added and marched off looking perplexed and frustrated.

The lining was cut to shreds but nothing was found. Dennis was now laughing. He couldn't stop himself. Things were on the up. The customs official handed him back the false passport which was promptly shoved into the back pocket of his jeans.

"You are free to go, Mr Duncan," came the authoritive, yet slightly peeved voice of the customs official. Dennis spread his arms.

"My suitcase, what's left of it. Would you re-pack it, please." He was euphoric and was happy to now milk the situation. The suitcase was duly packed by the two officials and they crammed every last copy into it before ignominiously retreating to their office. Dennis whistled the rousing 'Dam busters march' as he left customs in his wake and headed for the nearest exit with a distinct spring in his step. He was free. What he didn't realise was he was about to jump from the frying pan into the fire.

Cannabis resin was never the choice of contraband the Mantovanis had in mind when they coerced Dennis into his hazardous excursion. The merchandise in question was far more intrinsically valuable than dope. It was diamonds. Stolen diamonds were the name of this particular game and Angelo was the mastermind behind it. A daring raid on a security van in broad daylight just to the west of the city centre was carried out by Freddie Mantovani and his gang, colloquially known as the Zanetti outfit, two days before, and the heist netted them an estimated one hundred thousand pounds worth of the precious stones. They had been cut ready for the lucrative jewellery market and were on their way to a wholesale diamond house in the city ready to be distributed to the trade.

Angelo had it all worked out. He had a buyer in Morocco who would then ship them to Amsterdam, the diamond capital of the world. But the police activity was so great he felt he had to shift them quickly. He knew security would be so high, he would have to outwit both the police and the customs authorities. He couldn't just courier them to Amsterdam, that was far too risky. His plan was to get the diamonds to his buyer in Morocco, Khalid Baba, who would then courier them on to Amsterdam under the guise of marijuana, a soft drug legal in the Netherlands.

Amsterdam customs, working closely with the British authorities, wouldn't suspect the stolen diamonds would come via a known cannabis producing country like Morocco and Angelo thought his strategy was foolproof. He even had the likes of Dennis and other members of his staff believing the stack of newspapers *he'd* put in the suitcase along with the stolen diamonds, to bring up the weight and make it seem plausible, were bundles of cash and they would seem to be bringing in a large amount of cannabis resin from Marrakesh on the return trip.

Khalid Baba was supposed to pay Angelo for the diamonds, sending the cash back with Dennis in the suitcase. He would then make his profit from the diamond merchant in Amsterdam when he sent the gemstones on. Khalid Baba had double crossed Angelo, however, and instead of replacing the newspapers in the suitcase with cash, he didn't, and having kept the consignment of stolen diamonds for himself, sent Angelo's worthless newspapers back instead.

Dennis obviously knew nothing of all this. He believed it was purely a drug smuggling mission although he now had a good idea Angelo had been cheated by Khalid Baba. He also remembered the slightly cryptic message the Moroccan gave him to pass on to Angelo. He remembered it word for word.

"Please tell him we are now even"

Those were the last words he'd said at the airport. Dennis had been so elated having not faced incarceration by British customs he'd forgotten all about having to face Angelo and explaining the tricky situation. He had no idea how he would react but he knew it wasn't going to be pleasant, and feelings of nervousness and apprehension soon replaced those of jubilation as he left the arrivals building and stepped outside into the cool night air.

He was met and driven back to Prestige Cars as planned. Angelo was waiting in the back office having left a charity function in the city to be there. He looked immaculate in a black dinner suit, white shirt and bow tie. Dennis handed him the case and explained everything, including his experience coming through customs.

Angelo was remarkably calm and listened intently to all Dennis had to say. The only outward sign of anger was when he ripped off his bow tie and threw it to the floor. Dennis wondered how Freddie would have reacted given the same circumstances and came to the conclusion it didn't bear thinking about, such was Freddie's reputation for violence when things weren't going his way.

Angelo was different. His emotions were still there, but were controlled and managed from within, and Dennis was aware he was just as dangerous as his volatile twin brother. He didn't even open the suitcase, he just sat back in his chair , his arms behind his head.

"Khalid Baba gave me a message to give to you," Dennis said reluctantly. He knew he had to say something.

"Go on," Angelo replied. Dennis relayed the words exactly as Khalid Baba had told him. Angelo's reaction surprised him. Again he was calm and composed.

"Shafted by a petty Arab. What's the world coming to. *His* days are numbered. Oh......and you still owe me and my brother."

"What?" Dennis couldn't believe what he was hearing after all he'd been through, but that was of no concern to Angelo.

"Your loan.....still outstanding....unfortunately."

"You bastard. After all I've done."

"That's business," Angelo replied. He was coolness personified. Dennis wasn't.

"You can fucking go to hell. I owe you nothing. I'm not paying you another fucking penny."

"Don't cross me. Please don't do that. Now....I'm busy."

"Don't you threaten me," Dennis couldn't resist retaliation. "I'll drop *you* in it.....and your fucking brother........if you stitch me up. I'll tell them all I know about your drug smuggling ring." He still knew nothing about the diamonds.

"You won't get the chance, Carter," Angelo sat forward, "You ever think about that and you're dead. Now....as I said, I'm busy."

Chapter 15

A few days later the inquest of Subway Music's track suited intruder was held at the Coroner's Court in Barchester. The Coroner heard eye witness accounts of how the young man inexplicably walked into the pathway of the oncoming bus in Southfields High Street which resulted in his death. The tragedy had attracted considerable interest both from local people and the media, but the two main anonymous witnesses, Tommy Nelson and Victor Slade, weren't there.

Victor's insistence that Tommy kept his mouth shut about the bizarre incident had struck home. and Tommy, although baffled by Victor's actions which led to the youngster's death, thought it best to concur with his boss's wishes on this occasion. He was also known for being the lead singer with the Devil's Flock and he knew impresario James Slade wouldn't thank him for being publicly involved in a Coroner's inquest. The proceedings didn't take long. The Coroner rejected suicide as the cause of death and his verdict of misadventure was the one expected by most. In his brief summing up he said it was probable no one would ever know what really happened during that rush hour period in Southfields, and brought the inquest to a close.

The bombing of the Platinum Casino Club was still big news, and media speculation over the motive for such an attack was rife. Journalistic opinion was split between international terrorism, with some suggesting involvement from the IRA freedom fighters, and others implying it was down to dissident action by militant factions from the Arab states.

The popular tabloids were convinced gang warfare within the city formed the basis for the attack and, not surprisingly, the sensationalism they whipped up added drama and scandal to the story which, in turn, helped sell their newspapers. Ironically, they were right. It was Angelo Mantovani's ruthless desire to make the Zanetti Corporation the most powerful company on the planet that led to the bombing.

Zanetti had already acquired the Lucky Seven Casino not far away, but Angelo craved the addition of the more prestigious Platinum Club to add to his ever increasing portfolio of profitable businesses. He was biding his time though and when he was ready, he planned to make the owner of the club, James Slade, an offer he couldn't refuse.

James Slade had his own agenda for his casino and used the press to his advantage, announcing the grand re-opening that very evening. He'd pulled out all the stops to repair the damaged basement area and the premises had been given the go ahead by the health and safety agency and could once again open to the public. James Slade had also revealed the Devil's Flock would be making a guest appearance there and he was confident the evening would be a resounding success.

Tommy only got to hear of the impending gig when Mitch came into Subway Music around lunchtime and told him. Tommy had been wondering how he was going to break the news to Victor's brother that he was leaving the band to pursue a solo career and decided a farewell performance at James Slade's Platinum Casino, followed by his resignation, would give him the ideal chance. He knew it wasn't going to be easy but he'd promised Victor he'd do it sooner rather than later, so he set his mind to the task, spending the afternoon in the shop psyching himself up for what he thought could turn out to be a tricky evening ahead.

James Slade never missed an opportunity to promote both himself and his many business interests, and his nickname of Mr Big was testament to the fact that, approaching forty, he was a self made millionaire with all the trappings of an affluent lifestyle, yet his appetite to flourish in the competitive world of corporate commerce wasn't wavering in the slightest.

He was a secretive man and a confirmed bachelor and his sexual orientation and preference, although open to discussion, had always been kept under wraps, which all added to his overall mysteriousness and sometimes unfathomable behaviour.

Barchester's very own town crier was hired to get the glitzy evening off to a rousing start, and his announcement informing the guests the roulette wheels, blackjack and crap tables were now open was handled with the medieval aplomb and ceremony that could only be achieved by that unique public speaker.

The place was full, much to Angelo and Freddie Mantovani's dismay. They'd made the decision to attend after it was clear the event wasn't invitation only, and had donned their best dinner jackets and bow ties for the occasion. Other celebrities had also turned up and Freddie remarked to his brother that the only thing missing from the flashy affair was a gaudy red carpet and Liberace greeting the guests with a showy performance on his candelabra bedecked grand piano.

The Mantovani twins and James Slade rarely mixed in the same circles and when they did, their conversation never got beyond small talk. Angelo Mantovani was innately jealous of James Slade, yet he had already amassed a small fortune at the tender age of just twenty one. He had the good looks, the smouldering eyes and the physique his counterpart had never possessed, even in his youth. Angelo still felt inadequate and insecure when he compared himself to the middle aged mogul and impresario, and until he was financially more successful, then his unfounded inferiority complex would continue.

He and Freddie did meet their adversary briefly and as usual the encounter was contrived cordiality in the extreme. The brothers made sure the paparazzi knew they were there and strolled around the casino sipping champagne and smiling to the clicking cameras at every opportunity. Angelo could plainly see *this* casino was far superior in every way to the Zanetti owned Lucky Seven establishment nearby and promised himself one day it would be his.

The musical entertainment for the evening, rebel rock, was a million light years from the flamboyant and ostentatious pianist Liberace, and the Devil's Flock took to the makeshift stage with their very own style of flair and arrogance. Tommy, as usual, was the consummate professional and pranced around as if he were under the spell of the Devil himself. Expletives were commonplace in the lyrics of many of the songs, and those in the audience either loved what was on offer, or hated it. Most loved it however and the band went down a storm finishing their short set to rapturous applause.

Angelo and Freddie had left by then, having accomplished their objective for the evening, and were on their way to another glamorous venue, a night club around the corner where they could be seen to be having a ball and thoroughly enjoying life in the fast lane.

James Slade, being the band's unofficial manager, was there to greet them when they came off stage and ushered them to a table in the corner where he proceeded to open more champagne.

"Another fab performance, fellas," the casino owner enthused, popping open a bottle of bubbly.

"You've done this club proud....and me....thanks fellas.....and enjoy yourselves. Everything's on me tonight."

He sat back, satisfied his re-opening was going exactly to plan.

"I'm thinking about a tour of Germany for you boys. They'll lap it up over there, I just know it."

Tommy looked around him, at Mitch, Bomber, Lennie and the bald and dapper James Slade. He hadn't touched his champagne. Was he doing the right thing with the band on the cusp of possible international success, he pondered. Victor's words were tugging at his inner thoughts.

"Dump the band, Tommy.....you're the star....I can make it happen.....tours of Europe and the States."

The tantalising phrases were ringing in his ears. Then there was the advance, a whopping twenty thousand pounds, an absolute fortune for him.

"Tour of bloody Germany, Tommy," Mitch said, digging him in the ribs. "Rebel rock for the Krauts," he added, laughing loudly. Tommy was miles away in his own dream world of success and acclaim. His mind turned again to Victor Slade. Could he really make it happen, he thought. He took a deep breath.

"Look lads, I've got something to say," he blurted out. James Slade looked across at him, his deeply set brown eyes keen and inquisitive. All eyes were on Tommy. Could Victor pull it off. His mind was still racing.

"I'm leaving the band." Tommy's words were bold and decisive.

"What?" Mitch yelled.

"I'm going solo."

"You can't, your one of us," Mitch exclaimed.
Bomber came in, "You can't leave the band, Tommy. Mitch is right.....we're the band.....all of us. You can't be serious."
James Slade said nothing. Tommy glanced at him, waiting for him to explode.

"No, I'm sorry......I've made my mind up. I'm leaving.......been offered a deal I can't refuse, and to be honest I've gotta take it."
The words were now gushing and he needed to keep control of both his emotions and his dialogue. James Slade inadvertently came to his rescue.

"A deal you say, you've been offered a deal?"
The conversation was getting difficult and Tommy knew he had to be careful and watch what he said.

"Yeah......I can't go into details but I'm going solo and I've got a backer."

"Do we know this backer?" James Slade was quick to ask. It was the one question Tommy was fearing. Naming Victor as his prospective promoter was the last thing he wanted to divulge, especially to his brother.

"I can't say," Tommy replied.

"Come on, Tommy, I think you owe it to the fellas.....at least." James Slade's persistence was getting to Tommy. "You drop the bombshell, then you say no more on your future. Unfair that, I think." He continued, "They have a right to know....surely."

"Okay okay," Tommy said irritably, "It's my boss at Subway Music, Victor Slade. Now you know."

"My brother?"

Tommy didn't know what to say.

"My brother Victor?"

"Yeah.....your brother."

The ensuing silence around the table was embarrassing.

"I'll give you one word of advice, Tommy. If my brother's involved you make sure you get a signed contract from him. Understand? Don't let him fob you off with words and promises. A legally binding contract, that's what you want.....what you *must* have. I'll say no more on that. Now...I'm not a bitter man and I don't hold grudges. What you choose to do is up to you. I just hope you know what you're doing and I for one wish you every success. Now, I say we have a proper drink to drown our sorrows. You fellas agree?"

The other members of the Devil's Flock were

stunned by the unexpected news but nodded in agreement. James Slade called over to the bar.

"John......over here," he called out to the young bar manager, beckoning him over. John Pullen was the son of the casino's general manager, Robert Pullen. He was a couple of years older than Tommy and his dad had got him the job soon after he'd left school. He was a keen follower of the Devil's Flock and had seen them play live several times. He loved their music and was eager to meet them personally.

"It's great to meet you guys," he said enthusiastically. "Anarchy's fantastic....and done live....well...it just rocks."
He shook Mitch by the hand avidly. Then it was Bomber's turn. James Slade interrupted the barman's eager chatter.

"Twelve year old malts all round, John, if that's alright with you, fellas?"

"Yes boss....of course," John Pullen replied leaning over to shake drummer Lennie's hand.

Tommy was in no mood for idle banter with fans. He'd just quit the band and James Slade was acting like it was some sort of celebration, which he found decidedly odd. Then he realised he was so wrapped up in his own affairs he'd forgotten the Platinum Club had just been bombed and two staff had lost their lives. It also dawned on him that the man's business empire was far more important to him than being involved with a group of two bit musicians, however successful they might turn out to be.

"Now.....you're something else," John Pullen said facing Tommy. "The music....it gets me right here, in the pit of my stomach," he continued, "And your vocals.....wicked....just amazing."
Tommy nodded and half smiled.

"I wish I could sing like you," he added. It was obvious Tommy was his new found hero and he reached out to shake his hand.

Tommy sat forward. He saw the barman's outstretched hand. The back of his hand. His fist. The back of his fist. He shrunk back in horror. He never thought he'd ever see that tattoo again. But there it was, the dreaded ace of spades with the serpent entwining itself around it. Tommy's whole body recoiled in disgust. He recalled the click of the flick knife as it sprung open, and the blade, as it plunged silently into his abdomen.

The faceless, cowardly mod who didn't give two beans for somebody else's life. The spineless yob who almost took his. He had a face after all.

"Yeah.....the tattoo, has that effect on some people. Sorry about that." John Pullen was almost apologetic, but Tommy's revulsion for the man wasn't about to evaporate and he desperately tried to hold it together. He didn't shake John Pullen's hand. He stared into his face though, a long searching stare. But he found no answers. Tommy got up, and without saying another word to anyone, left the club

Chapter 16

There was also a celebratory mood that week in one of the households in the Barton Bridge flats, Southfields. Constable Derek Dooley had got his long awaited promotion to sergeant and had already taken up his new post in Barchester's Central Police Station. His dedication to the job had finally been acknowledged by his superiors and he was a proud and happy man.

Because he wanted to share his success and good fortune with his friends and neighbours, he organised an open evening in the flat. It was a gesture appreciated by many and the soiree was a great success. Even his neighbours from the top floor, Luigi and Chiara Mantovani, put in an appearance. Their stay was a brief one however, but most were there enjoying themselves to well after midnight.

Harry and June Nelson had also been invited round on another occasion a few days later. They were the only guests that evening and Harry, in particular, felt honoured that Derek Dooley considered him to be such a close friend. They'd been at the open house party and had a good time, but this get together seemed different and more special. Harry had been keeping a low profile since the bombing of the Platinum Club, and it was only through Derek's persistence that he decided to go.

The evening was relaxed and cordial, far removed from the last time Harry had visited his police constable friend. Their meeting then had been a much more clandestine affair when he'd sought Derek's help and advice regarding his involvement with the Mantovani brothers. A lot had happened since then and Harry was questioning whether he'd done the right thing in putting his trust in a policeman, even though he was a friend.

The conversation centred more on Tommy's exciting progress in the rock scene and the changing styles in popular music generally. The merits of the Devil's Flock were also discussed, but Harry and Derek both admitted they didn't really understand the genre and much preferred middle-aged crooners like Dean Martin and Frank Sinatra. The bottles of brown ale they consumed ensured the evening stayed convivial and uncontroversial and as a result their respective partners, June and Alice, could sip their glasses of Liebfraumilch confident the get together would continue to be a relaxing and chilled out one.

Harry was popular in more ways than one with the Barchester police fraternity that week. D.C. Sutherland also wanted a word with him, but their meeting wasn't a social one. The detective constable called at Harry's flat and insisted Harry accompanied him to Barchester Central for questioning. It was made clear he wasn't under arrest but the *invitation*, as the detective constable called it, was put in such a way Harry couldn't really refuse.

"I can't put this any other way, Harry Nelson, you're in big trouble," D.C. Sutherland said in the sparse interview room at the police headquarters.

"We've studied the Platinum Casino's time delay photographs on the night of the bombing and the only package delivered was the one you gave to the doorman just after one o'clock, and I believe that was the bomb. What can *you* tell me?"

"Am I being cautioned?" Harry asked tentatively. Sutherland shook his head.

"You're here under your own free will, helping us with our enquiries, you know that. There's no tape recorder. You're not under arrest. But for God's sake talk to me, Harry.....or I won't be in a position to help you. You know what I'm saying?"

Harry knew only too well. This wasn't the first time he'd sat in a police interview room. He knew the score. He looked across the desk at the young detective constable. This moment had been on his mind for days and he still didn't know what to say, if anything.

On the one hand the police were breathing down his neck and weren't going away, and on the other he was sure the Mantovani twins were watching his every move. He looked into Sutherland's eyes, but the young man gave nothing away. His dilemma was almost tangible. The police or the Mantovanis. *He* didn't bomb the casino, nor did he kill anyone. Sutherland said nothing.

Harry shifted uncomfortably in his chair. He decided he couldn't, and wouldn't, live his life scared witless by a couple of gangsters.

"I thought it was just drugs....not a bomb. I had no idea it was a bomb."

D.S. Sutherland sat there like a salesman closing a deal and knew when to say nothing.

"You've got to believe me, I was only delivering the bloody thing."

"On behalf of Angelo and Freddie Mantovani?" Sutherland asked, breaking his silence.

"It was given to me in the office."

"Who gave it to you?"

"It was just given to me."

"Who gave you the package, Harry......I won't ask again?"

Harry shifted in his chair. His uncertainty was still there. There was no tape recorder, no record of the interview, and no witnesses.

"Angelo gave it to me," he said finally.

"Angelo Mantovani?" Sutherland asked.

"Yeah."

"And would you give a statement to that effect?"

"Would I fuck!" Harry replied belligerently. Sutherland just nodded.

"It's a tricky situation, Harry.....this. Listen to

me. A little bird tells me you made quite a few *deliveries* when you worked for Prestige Cars. No, don't say anything....just listen for a minute. We *will* get to the bottom of this and if you refuse to co-operate you could find yourself serving a prison sentence....."

"For being in the wrong place at the wrong time?" Harry asked.

"Maybe.......but that's the truth of the matter........unless...."

"Unless I drop other people in it?"

"I knew you would understand."

"Why wasn't I stopped at the time then....by the drugs squad...if you knew what was going on?"

"It's only recently this information has surfaced," D.C. Sutherland replied.

Harry knew then Derek Dooley had betrayed his confidence in his search for promotion. It hit him hard knowing he'd trusted the man and put his faith in him as a law officer and friend only for that friendship to have meant nothing more than a stepping stone in his career.

"What do you say, Harry. Co-operation or...."

"Or what, copper?"

Harry was upset and it showed in his sudden change of attitude. D.C. Sutherland noticed it immediately.

"Vilification's *not* top of my list.....whatever you may think."

"I'm not saying anymore. I'm going. Charge me

if you bloody well want....I don't fucking care."

Tim Sutherland sat back in his chair. He knew his chance had gone.

"We'll talk again. You're free to leave," he said, successfully hiding his disappointment that Harry's co-operation hadn't been achieved.

*   *   *   *

Tommy's ordeal at the Platinum Casino Club had left him pensive and moody. He'd done what he had to though and realised he had nothing to reproach himself over regarding the band. It was coming face to face with the guy who'd stabbed him that had caused his dispirited state of mind. The flat in the High Street didn't help his melancholic inner self either. Dennis Carter was the main reason for that. From being a likeable, happy-go-lucky youngster who didn't seem to have a care in the world, Tommy watched him become a miserable, moody, paranoid drug addict who's attitude and behaviour affected everyone he came into contact with.

Tommy didn't know the reason behind his inexplicable change of character though and thought it was solely down to his ever increasing consumption of narcotics, but unbeknown to him and everyone else, his gambling addiction and involvement with the Mantovanis were the overriding causes of his condition, and the drugs were merely the means to escape the inner turmoil as a result.

Heroin was now his main stimulant and Tommy knew it. It kept him in a job, but only just. While he was at Subway Music the heroin did enough to get him through the day. But it was after work when he could no longer hold it together that his malaise came to the fore and Tommy bore the brunt of it back in the flat they shared. He tried his very best to get Dennis to open up and share the obvious burden of life that was prevalent within him, but it was to no avail and however hard he tried his efforts would inevitably end in a heated row. As a result, Tommy spent less and less time there and the only reason he didn't move out was because Dennis had been such a good friend and he was genuinely fond of the guy and cared about him. Tommy also had his own future to think about and having left the band, he was eager to get Victor to sign him up and get his solo career moving in the right direction.

He met him in his Ford Zodiac where Victor presented him with a four page contract. Victor told him to take it away and read it thoroughly prior to them both signing along the dotted line. Much to Victor's annoyance, Tommy decided to read it there and then. It all seemed very simple, uncomplicated and straightforward, but there was one clause he found hard to grasp. He pointed it out to Victor but was told the contract was a standard one within the industry for artist management. When Tommy pushed him to clarify that particular section, Victor did try but Tommy was none the wiser and still didn't understand it.

Victor stressed he should take the contract away and seek advice, be it legal or otherwise, and be fully aware of the terms and conditions before he committed his signature to it. Tommy was happy to do that. They were both keen to dispense with the legal formalities as quickly as possible so that Tommy, in his new role as *Bobby Nelson*, could pursue his dream of stardom with Victor backing him all the way.

There was only one person Tommy knew who had the nous and business acumen to advise him on the contract. That person was James Slade. But Tommy felt embarrassed seeking his guidance on the matter when he'd snubbed him in favour of his brother and quit the very band James Slade had supported and endorsed. The importance of his career outweighed any awkwardness and abasement however, and Tommy went in search of the influential entrepreneur determined to swallow his pride and further *his* future career.

He found him the following day in the Blue Boar Inn.

"You've got a nerve, Tommy Nelson, coming here. But as I said I don't hold grudges," James Slade said as he thumbed through the contract Tommy had impudently and boldly placed in front of him. "Don't you trust him?" he added.

"Nothing to do with trust," Tommy was quick to answer. "Your opinion matters to me.....and you did say I could come to you for advice."

"I said nothing of the kind."

"Well.....you know what I mean," Tommy said.

"Now, this agreement, it peeves me to have to say this, but I can find nothing untoward neither in it or with it."

Tommy looked at him blankly.

"Seems alright to me," James Slade added.

"What about this?" Tommy pointed to the clause he didn't understand. "What does it mean?"

"Could be construed as a little ambiguous, I suppose." James Slade admitted.

"But what does it mean........*the artist gives unequivocal authority to the management, both materially and spiritually, in its entirety and its fundamental nature.......*I don't get it."

James Slade read the relevant section again.

"It's like giving someone power of attorney....the legal authority to act for you....sign things for you on your behalf. That's what it means."

"Then why don't they just say that?"

"Jargon, Tommy....pure and simple."

"Nothing wrong with it then?"

"No. In your position, young and ambitious, I'd sign it. Perhaps not with Victor Slade, but then I'm biased."

"Everything else okay?"

"Seems to be." James Slade handed Tommy the

contract. "I've already wished you luck so I'll not do so again."

"Thanks Mr Slade, your honesty means a lot." Tommy took the contract and left the Blue Boar. His mind was at ease and he was ready for Victor to catapult him to stardom.

The signing of the contract the next day was a formality. Victor's black Ford Zodiac was again his preferred meeting place and although the actual signing was difficult and clumsy in such a confined space, they managed it. Tommy queried the blank spaces for witnesses to sign but Victor said he would sort all that out later.

Victor sat back. Tommy glanced across at him. He'd rarely seen him looking so pleased and relaxed. His pale complexion showed a hint of colour and even his sharp facial features seemed softer and less pronounced. Tommy thought it made him look younger than his thirty nine years.

"Something's been bothering me, Victor," Tommy said, changing the subject.

"Nothing should be bothering you, lad. I'm going to make you a star," Victor replied reaching into his jacket pocket for a small hip flask.

"Celebration brandy?"

"Not for me. You know when I got stabbed....."

"Chill out, Tommy.....I mean *Bobby*. Must call you that from now on. Very important, that. Come on....have a drink with your new manager."

Tommy shook his head. "A couple of days ago I saw

the fucker who stabbed me."

"Thought you didn't know who did it."

"I didn't. But the crazy mod who did it had a tattoo on his hand."

"I didn't know that."

"I never told anyone."

"Loads of people have tattoos. Here....have a drink."

"I don't want a bloody drink," Tommy said impatiently. "No, this tattoo was different to any I've seen.....definitely. There wouldn't be another one like it.....anywhere, I'm sure."

Victor could see how concerned Tommy was and decided to humour him for a while.

"Where did you see him?" he asked, taking a swig from the hip flask.

"Platinum Casino. We did a gig there the other night, when it re-opened after the bombing."

"Go on, I'm listening."

"I saw him....met him. Came face to face with the fucker."

"Calm down, Tommy, calm down. Would you recognise him again?"

"Too bloody right......he works there, Victor."

"Works there?" Suddenly Victor was showing more of an interest.

"He works behind the bar."

"Do you know his name?"

"Somebody said it, but I can't remember. Yeah...it's coming back now. He was in charge of the bar, I'm sure. Yeah....I remember now. The fucker was the manager's son, the bastard."

"The casino manager's son?"

"Yeah, I'm sure. That fucking tattoo....sent shivers down my spine, I'll tell you that."

"Forget it, Tommy. Just forget it. He'll get his comeuppance one day."

"But he's there, in my head.....and now I know who he is......"

"You've got more important things to fill your head with. Forget the barman, he's a loser."

"But I wanna get even."

"Forget it," Victor said, his voice becoming more forceful. Tommy had also noticed the colour had suddenly gone from his gaunt face. It took him by surprise.

"You're *Bobby Nelson*......the world's gonna love you. Focus on that. Stay focussed on that. And leave everything else to me, Tommy. Understand?"
Tommy nodded slowly but didn't reply. Victor held out the hip flask.

"Go on, have a drink with me, Tommy.....and let's toast the future."
This time Tommy didn't refuse.

*   *   *   *

A few days later Freddie Mantovani was driving the streets of Southfields, but not in his pink Cadillac. His mode of transport this particular evening was far less flamboyant and luxurious. He was at the wheel of a Commer van, utilitarian, dumpy and grey. His dress was also less sophisticated than usual. He had a job to do and jeans and a woolly jumper were adequate for the task in hand.

He was under instructions from Angelo to look out for one man, someone he was keen to have a private chat with. That man was Harry Nelson and Freddie concentrated his search around the Felgate Road area generally, and the Barton Bridge flats, where Harry lived, in particular. Freddie was parked not far away when he spotted Harry approaching the flats from Southfields Lane.

Freddie wasn't alone in the front of the van. He had muscle with him in the shape of two huge men dressed in black. He started the engine and the van sped towards the unsuspecting figure of Harry Nelson. The abduction was carried out with military precision and Harry was manhandled by the two big men and bundled unceremoniously into the back of the vehicle.

"Angelo wants a word," is all Freddie said as one of the heavies tied Harry's hands behind his back and taped over his mouth. The van headed towards Barchester. Their destination was to the east of the city centre and the Commer van came to a halt in a deserted, run down area alongside the Albert Canal. Harry was forcibly escorted across a dimly lit yard and into a vast disused warehouse.

Freddie followed.

"You're very elusive, Harry Nelson." The voice was Angelo Mantovani's, who was pacing up and down over the far side. Harry sniffed the air. The aroma was the distinctive smell of coal dust. The place was damp, unpleasant and uninviting. He was decidedly scared. Freddie pushed him in the back, urging him towards his twin brother.

"Very elusive indeed," Angelo said as Harry was shoved towards a chair near an old metal desk and made to sit on it. The two heavies stood nearby, looking on. Harry glanced around. The only concession he could see to the nineteen sixties was a modern black telephone, looking strangely out of place on the metal desk. Everything else seemed to be from a bygone age.

He noticed Angelo still looked smart, even in slacks and a roll neck sweater. He wondered why he was at the centre of such an elaborate, clandestine operation, but was in no position to demand an explanation, and because he was gagged he couldn't speak anyway. He didn't have to wait long for an answer. Angelo was in no mood to waste time.

"Get his attention, Freddie," he said to his brother. Freddie duly obliged and smacked Harry across the face with the palm of his hand. Harry winced.

"You've been....how can I put this.....chatty.... with, let's say.... the wrong type of people. Now I didn't have you down as talkative, but it seems you are.....and that gives us cause for concern." Angelo nodded to Freddie who slapped Harry's face again, only harder this time.

"Don't worry Harry," Angelo continued, patting him gently on the cheek, "You'll have your say, but for now....you just listen to me....okay?"
Angelo started to pace up and down once again.

"I know you're very friendly with the copper, Dooley. Yeah...he's a neighbour and all that, but my papa says suddenly you're like bosom buddies, you going round there all the time. And suddenly Dooley gets promotion. Funny that. Then there's the visits from a certain detective from the C.I.D.......A clever , ambitious young man.....a bit like me really. Following so far? Then you're invited to Barchester Police Station for a chat with the said detective. Cosy.......very cosy."
Angelo went down on his haunches directly in front of his seated captive, his face inches from Harry's.

"Then *I* start getting visits from the police....at my offices in the city, asking questions about you....and bombs." He slowly shook his head, "Embarrassing, that."
He got to his feet and walked around the desk. Harry knew he was in big trouble and he knew he was going to be hurt. His fear and apprehension was quickly turning to terror and he was powerless to do anything about it. Angelo turned to him.

"You can have your say now, but be quick.....I'm losing patience."

Freddie stepped forward and ripped the tape from his face. He couldn't resist another slap as he did so. Harry's head lurched to one side with the force of the blow.

"I'm waiting," Angelo said, his intolerance was beginning to show. Harry didn't know what to say. He recalled his recent interview with D.C. Sutherland and the fact that Angelo had featured in that tricky conversation. Angelo stared at him. He had to say something. Freddie made a move towards him.

"I didn't say a word....not to anyone," he blurted out. He knew he had to lie to save his skin. "Yeah, the coppers came round and they took me in. But I kept schtum.....I'd never drop you in it." Harry could see Angelo wasn't convinced.

"I like you, Harry.....I really do. I'm not just saying that. You were our neighbour after all. You paid back your debt.....don't know how....but that was an honourable thing to do. A fine gesture indeed. I wish I could just give you a warning, but there's more at stake than honour. There's the Zanetti Corporation, and I'm head of it. That company's integrity is in my hands. I must act.....surely you can see that....and understand my position? Don't worry Harry, we're not going to kill you," Angelo smirked. Freddie laughed. The two heavies looked on menacingly.

"Nothing more to say, Harry?" The smug hint of a smile had gone from Angelo's face. Harry felt it was pointless to say anymore. His thoughts were on his impending punishment. Knee capping went through his mind, but he could see no gun. Fingers smashed with a two pound club hammer was another option that terrified him, but he could see no such tool around.

"Do it, Freddie," Angelo said coldly, and turned his back on his helpless captive. Freddie took a suede glove from his jeans pocket and put it on his left hand, slowly and deliberately. Then to Harry's complete horror he produced a barber's cut-throat razor, opening it carefully and meticulously.

He went for Harry's face. Harry gripped his tied hands tightly together behind his back. He was petrified but ready for his features to be sliced apart. Freddie's gloved hand went to Harry's mouth, forcing it open. He grabbed Harry's tongue and pulled it out. Harry's eyes bulged in grim terror. He retched and gasped. One deft stroke of the razor's blade severed his tongue. Angelo was still looking the other way. Freddie held the bloody organ up for everyone to see, then threw it to the floor.

Harry screamed but only gasps came out of his mouth, along with a torrent of blood. His body was shaking uncontrollably.

"Never done that before.....chalk that up as a first, eh fellas," Freddie said to the two heavies, triumphantly. Harry's Head dropped onto his chest as he lost consciousness.

Angelo turned around. He didn't appreciate

Freddie's flippant comment and he was furious.

"That wasn't necessary....we're supposed to be professionals. This isn't a game.....and you two can wipe the smirks off your faces as well. Now get him out of here," he said, lifting the receiver from the telephone on the desk. The two big men carried Harry's limp, comatose body towards the door.
Angelo dialled 999.

"Ambulance.......injured man.......Butlers Wharf, Commercial Road, down by the canal. Me...?....just a friend.....doing his bit.
Angelo put the receiver down.

Chapter 17

Playing for Barchester United was worlds apart from stepping out, week in week out, for third division minnows, Southfields F.C. and Steve Baker's transition from being the small club's star player to a rookie striker for the prodigious top flight outfit was proving to be a huge learning curve for the young player.

The club's manager Jock McFadden's words of wisdom when Steve joined had been spot on, and he enjoyed the initial attention from the media, but it wasn't long before the extravagant publicity died down and within the club he was just another team member. The dressing room was studded with top class professionals, some who were regularly playing for their country and were well respected as a result. But Steve, to his credit, was modest in his outlook and showed enough humility to those more experienced players around him, which didn't go unnoticed by both the coaching staff and his footballing peers at the club.

He also showed great patience in not demanding a first team place, and outwardly he was content to bide his time in the reserves and wait for the opportunity to play on one of the biggest stages in English football. Inwardly though, success was never far from his mind. He also realised he was one of a new breed of footballers, one's who were clever, not just in their ball skills and understanding of the game, but clever intellectually.

Grammar schools had never produced the majority of the country's footballers. Traditionally they spawned top class rowers, cricketers and the occasional rugby international, but most of their pupils ended up in the commercial and business world, and those who were bright and fortunate enough to go on to university, usually became doctors, lawyers, accountants or similar vocational professionals and *not* sportsmen and women.

Steve knew he *had* to succeed. He'd given up his privileged position at Dunsbury Grammar before acquiring any qualifications. He probably could have gone to university and taken one of the many business opportunities on graduating as a result, but he'd left school and burnt his educational bridges at the tender age of sixteen to become a professional sportsman.

There was no going back and he was mature and smart enough to realise that. He was also mindful not to come across as someone superior in any way to his colleagues in the dressing room, and he was aware he could be ostracised if he did, and that would almost certainly end his burgeoning career with the club he was desperate to gain success with.

He'd seen that happen with an Italian

international signed from Juventus for a massive fee. He was a legend in Italy and although in the autumn of his career, he existed in an aura of his own greatness. That didn't go down too well in Barchester's more down to earth dressing room where some of the team looked upon themselves as merely jobbing professionals, and didn't aspire to gaining cult status in any way or form. The Italian superstar wasn't about to change his ostentatious ways though, and came across as flash and swanky as far as his team mates were concerned. He didn't last long at the club and returned home to finish his career in the lower leagues of Italian football, his self esteem intact if a little bruised by the experience.

Jock McFadden had been astute in nurturing Steve's talent from the moment he joined the club. He was now twenty and his place up front in attack was becoming more regular, although there were others always vying to fill the position of centre forward and keep Steve on the sidelines. The thrill of scoring in front of forty thousand fans was enough to keep him both focussed and hungry to play at every opportunity.

Fitness was also high on Jock McFadden's agenda and for someone so young, whose body was still maturing, the possibility of serious injury, given Steve's commitment on the pitch, was a major concern to the manager and he limited Steve's appearances because of that. McFadden was open and honest with the young striker however, and a place on the substitutes bench as a tactical solution, helped Steve to come to terms with his manager's regime. It was also a shrewd strategy as McFadden could bring on a quality player like Steve when necessary to bolster the attack if the team were struggling.

Steve was also a favourite with the fans, as he had been at Southfields and came across as a *'Roy of the Rovers'* type of character with a swashbuckling, never-say-die attitude to the game. His good looks also helped, especially on the pitch, and the club, always looking to recruit more female fans, used that to their advantage.

Off the pitch however, he was still very inexperienced in many ways and didn't seek the media's attention as much as they sought his. He sometimes thought how Tommy would cope in similar circumstances and the situations he found himself in, and it always brought a smile to his face knowing Tommy would probably have embraced the challenge, and his cheeky temperament and forthright manner would have come through and saved the day in any tricky situation.

He did meet up with his old school friend when Southfields invited Barchester to send over a team to play in a testimonial friendly for their long serving favourite, Johnny Cleveland. Tommy was known for his role as lead singer in the Devil's Flock and as a lifelong Southfields fan, was invited to the after match gathering at the ground's Hornets Nest

Social Club. Steve, having started his career with them, was still a big favourite with their supporters and was in demand. So was Tommy for his Devil's Flock fame, but they were able to share a drink and a brief chat between the speeches and other organised events throughout the evening.

Tommy couldn't believe it when Steve told him he still lived at home. Tommy told him in his own inimitable way, and in no uncertain terms, that he thought it was about time he got his own place and started living the life of a successful footballer. He said the Barton Bridge flats, although perfect for them both when they were growing up, wasn't appropriate anymore.

Steve listened with interest. He valued Tommy's opinion and had taken his advice in the past. Living at home had suited him, and his mum and dad were there whenever he needed them. Within days of seeing and talking with Tommy, he knew he was right. Subconsciously, he'd felt it himself, but hadn't realised how stifling and restricting it had become. His personality was developing faster than he imagined and he decided to take Tommy's advice yet again.

He found a beautiful apartment in a city centre mansion house. Security was excellent. It had a round the clock concierge service and designated underground parking. It suited him perfectly and he took it on lease. His decision to rent rather than buy was made in consideration of his parents future more than anything else, but he did have his own reasons as well. His dream location was the prestigious Dene Park estate. That's where he wanted to buy property for himself and he vowed one day to own a wonderful home there, where he could settle down and enjoy the fruits of his playing career and bring up a family in the environment of his choice.

Soon after moving into his city apartment he approached his parents with a view to buying them a house, giving them the security of their own home as opposed to a rented council flat. His proud father, George, initially refused Steve's offer. Having been promoted from assistant buyer to chief buyer at the engineering company, his financial status had improved and he almost had the cash deposit which would enable him, with a suitable mortgage, to buy a small house in the neighbourhood.

Steve's mother Mary was all for it though, and in the end she persuaded her stubborn husband to accept their son's offer and they found the semi-detached house of *their* dreams in the favourable Dunsbury Park area of Southfields.

The goings on and the increasing police presence at the Barton Bridge flats in recent times hadn't escaped Steve's attention either, and he was glad both he and his family were now well out of it. Tommy was right. The community spirit that had existed in their youth had gone from the place and it was becoming a more hostile and impersonal environment to call home and raise a family in.

Steve thought about Tommy's mum and dad still living there and the horrendous news surrounding Harry's recent incident, having his tongue cut out in a speculative gangland act of torture. Harry survived the ordeal but the neighbourhood were deeply shocked by the news. On his discharge from hospital he shunned everyone including D.C. Sutherland's constant questions. He could still communicate, even though he could no longer talk, but he refused to implicate the Mantovani twins in any way, shape or form.

Not surprisingly, Tommy was furious, but even he couldn't get through to his dad. June was there for him and helped his rehabilitation the best she could, but Harry was a changed man. He wouldn't accept psychiatric help or counselling and shut himself away. June was the only person who could give him solace but he wouldn't even let her get close.

The unfortunate casualty of the whole affair was Tommy's sister, Emma, who still lived at home. She was now eighteen and worked in Boots the chemist, in Southfields High Street. She had put up with so much grief in the family home from Harry over many years, and although her sympathies were with him on this occasion, the anguish of having to live through more troubled times left her distressed and at a loss as to what she should do.

Tommy came to her rescue. There was a room

free in the maisonette he shared in the High Street and he moved her into it. He gave her no choice and paid the rent in advance so she wouldn't have to. There was no resistance from her at all and she couldn't leave home quick enough. Her mum gave her blessing and Tommy arranged transport for her personal belongings. He did explain that Dennis Carter, who had the room above her, was having a few problems and was a little temperamental, but he didn't give the reasons why.

Emma had seen him around, with Tommy, but she didn't know him well and in any case she felt anything was better than living at home with her difficult, moody father, and it didn't put her off moving there. It was also handy for her job at Boots, as it was just along the High Street from the maisonette over the greengrocers, which was to be her new home.

She was maturing quickly from a gawky shy teen into a slim, attractive, curvaceous young woman. Her ponytail had gone, replaced with luxurious shoulder length brown hair, and her hazel eyes complimented her pretty face perfectly. Tommy was amazed at her transformation. His life had been so busy and eventful he hadn't found the time to involve his only sister in any part of it. He now felt distinctly guilty and promised himself he would do his utmost to make amends for his shortcomings and neglect, and having her living there with him would give him the ideal opportunity to get to know her again and hopefully cement their relationship as brother and sister.

He wasn't sure how Dennis would react to Emma moving in. He knew he should have discussed it with him, but in his present state he feared Dennis would be difficult and confrontational. Tommy knew for Emma's sake he had to act quickly and didn't want the hassle from Dennis. He needn't have worried. Dennis was thrilled. The room had recently been vacated by a God fearing, bible-bashing lay preacher who'd gone to the Outer Hebrides to join the Brethren of Jesus, a holy order on the fringe of Christianity. Dennis detested the man and all he stood for and when Tommy told him Emma was moving in because of troubles at home, he couldn't wait to welcome her and his mood took an immediate upturn.

How long it would last, Tommy mused, as Dennis chatted with Emma in the kitchen, was anybody's guess. He left them to it and went to his room. Dennis was gentlemanly and genuinely friendly towards his new flat mate over the next few days. Tommy was afraid his interest in his younger sister might be driven solely by sexual desire. He knew how shallow Dennis was in that respect as in the past, any introduction to an attractive woman would have fuelled his carnal yearning and seduction would have been his top priority.

Emma settled in well and Tommy was pleased his intervention was proving a success. It meant one less problem in his busy schedule Victor Slade was introducing to springboard his solo career, and the way Dennis had reacted to Emma moving in gave him hope that his friend's salvation, as far as his drug addiction and lifestyle was concerned, wasn't a hopeless cause and it gave him an idea, one that could benefit them both.

They rarely went out socially anymore and Tommy's suggestion they go for a drink in the Crown one evening was greeted by unusual enthusiasm by Dennis.

"I've been thinking Denny," Tommy said as they drank lager at a table in the corner, which Tommy had made for to give them privacy.

"Yeah, you're doing an awful lot of that, eh Tommy......not like the fella I used to know."

"Comes to us all," Tommy said philosophically.

"Yeah, but your only twenty for Christ's sake." Dennis was right and Tommy couldn't help laughing about his perceptive comment. Tommy noticed that for the first time in ages Dennis was almost back to his mouthy, likeable self. He could also see he'd made an effort to look presentable for the occasion, and at twenty three, still possessed the boyish good looks he had when he was sixteen.

His blond hair was a bit longer, and darker and with his steely blue eyes and fine features he still cut a handsome figure. Tommy thought it a shame his eagerness to sexually conquer the girls he met usually resulted in either a short lived liaison, or rejection before he even got his wicked way. Then again, Tommy reflected on his own personal life and *his* lack of meaningful relationships and came to the conclusion perhaps he was being overly critical.

"And you've not changed , then," Tommy asked candidly. It was a question Dennis wasn't expecting and Tommy could see the look of mistrust creeping back into his face. He'd seen that look many times over the past few months. Dennis didn't reply. Tommy changed the subject.

"You're okay then...with my Emma moving in?"

"Yeah, why not......you know me and the girls."

"Too right Denny."

"No Tommy...it's not like that. I like her......as a friend."

"You sure?"

"Come on Tommy.....credit me with some sense. She's your sister."

"You want me to buy that?"

"Yeah, definitely. I never had a sister. She's a good kid. I think we'd get on. I know she's a looker but I'd never......"

"Yeah, alright Denny. Anyway, I'm glad to hear that."

Dennis drank more lager, "So what do you want to see me for, it's been ages since we've been out?"

Tommy knew he'd arrived at the awkward and somewhat delicate part of the evening.

"How long have we known each other, Denny?" he asked, trying to make the question sound as nonchalant as he could.

"Five.....six years.....why?"

"And we've been pretty good friends, haven't we?"

"Yeah sure. Look for fuck sake Tommy, what's going on. Spit it out.....I'm not simple."

"Alright....you want it straight. Fine. You're not the Dennis Carter from the market stall that loved life and didn't give a fuck, that I met. You're not the happy-go-lucky so and so, the streetwise older guy I thought was *the* business."

Tommy stopped short fearing Dennis would just get up and leave. He didn't. Tommy didn't know Dennis's involvement with the Mantovani twins went back to when he borrowed the cash from Trusty Loans, *their* company, to buy his motorbike, just to keep up with him. He knew nothing of Dennis's trip to Morocco and the dangerous relationship he now had with the Mantovanis, and Dennis had no intention of telling him, just like Tommy wasn't about to enlighten Dennis about the fact he now knew the identity of the mod who stabbed him in the Mill House Cafe car park that Sunday morning, even though it was Dennis's 'phone call to Victor that probably saved his life.

Tommy changed track, "I need your help Dennis....I do, seriously."

Dennis looked at him in amazement.

"You what....you slag me off....and you haven't mentioned the 'H' word yet.....you're about to though. Come off it."

"No, Denny.....that's why I wanted to have this chat. Got a proposition for you, that's all."

"What's it gonna cost me?"

"It's gonna cost you fucking nothing....now just listen. I need someone to do stuff for me. Victor's got things planned, loads of things.....for me as *Bobby Nelson*."

Dennis immediately started to loosen up.

"Things are going fast....way too fast, and you're the *only* one I trust enough to do this job."

"A job?"

"Yeah...sort of."

"What was wrong with the Devil's Flock then?"

"I couldn't keep that up, night after night, and besides, Victor's got it all sorted. An album...TV shows....the States...."

"And you believe him?"

"Yeah, I fucking do, Denny. There's loads more to it but I can't say much at the moment."

"And what *job* you got for me?"

"I need a gofer, a personal assistant.....a roadie, I don't know. Someone to do the things I won't have time to do. I'm already going part time in the shop as from next week and I need someone. I can trust you Denny, I know that."

Dennis was interested and Tommy could see it.

"I'll just bung you some cash as we go, as I need you. You'll do alright...I can tell you that right now."

"Sounds easy enough."

"Who says it's gonna be fucking easy?"

"You know what I mean," Dennis replied smiling. He offered Tommy a cigarette. It was the first time Tommy had seen him smile for a long time.

"No....got to give those up now, especially those stinking French things you smoke."

"What about the odd joint?" Dennis asked.

"Ah...now that's different. And that brings me to this difficult bit."

"I just knew there was a catch."

"I'll lay it on the line, Denny....you've got to stop doing heroin."

"Don't beat about the fucking bush, Tommy," Dennis replied sarcastically. It wasn't the worst reaction Tommy expected so he continued.

"It's messing up your life. I know it....you know it and it won't be long before Victor knows it and you'll be out on your ear."

"You'd tell him?"

"Don't be so fucking stupid."

"It keeps me going, Tommy. I don't inject....I just snort it.....that's all."

"I know. And that's *why* you can do it. Dope's alright...the odd joint. I'm all for that. But knock the other stuff on the head." He pulled a wad of notes from his pocket. "I'm serious, Denny," he handed him the cash, "There's a hundred quid there. Take it.......and come and help me out. Could be like old times, you and me......yeah?"

"Hundred quid?" Dennis held the notes in his hand.

"Not for heroin.....for you to get your life together before it's too late."

So much suddenly flashed through Dennis's mind. He still owed the Mantovani's gambling money even though he'd told them to go to hell. He still had his job at Subway Music and now his best pal Tommy was offering him a lifeline.

"It'd be great, Denny....what do you say?"

Dennis looked into Tommy's eyes. He nodded slowly.

"Oh Denny.....that's fucking great. Get the beers in.....your shout," Tommy said laughing and pointing to the money he'd just given him.

Chapter 18

Tommy thought the way James Slade handled the Devil's Flock's exciting burst onto the rebel rock scene was impressive enough, but Victor's artiste management skills were about to make his brother's efforts pale into insignificance in comparison. It was true, James Slade was the supreme businessman and in most social and commercial circles Victor had always been considered inferior to his more flamboyant and charismatic sibling. James Slade was happy to mix in those circles and although he never flaunted the trappings of his success, modesty wasn't his greatest quality and he didn't shy away from showing off his affluence when he chose to.

Victor had no qualms however, when it came to Tommy's, or *Bobby's*, as he'd decided to call him, outward show of the future trappings of his success and encouraged him to behave financially as if he was already a big star and not be frugal in the way he spent *his* money. Tommy had Victor's twenty thousand pounds burning a hole in his bank account and Victor was keen for his protégé to spend some of it, but to spend it in public and have the media on hand to witness and report on it as if it were major news. He'd seen Brian Epstein adopt a similar policy where the Beatles were concerned, and he came to the conclusion it didn't do their public persona and profile any harm.

He knew the key to Tommy's success was in the marketing and he would pull no punches where that area was concerned. He didn't have to wait long for his first opportunity. Dennis suggested Tommy should buy a car. He knew he'd been given an advance, but Tommy didn't say exactly how much, just that it was a substantial amount. Since he sold his Norton to pay off his dad's debt he hadn't had wheels of his own, although his suggestion of the Triumph Spitfire to Steve was eagerly accepted when the young footballer was still riding around on a Lambretta scooter, when Tommy thought *his* rise to fame called for something more suitable.

Tommy chatted to Dennis one morning at work in Subway Music. He'd seen the new Range Rover being launched on the news and liked the look of it.

"You're having me on, Tommy.....surely? It's a bloody souped up van with windows."

"Some of the footballers are buying them."

"So what. They're for yuppies.....rich mums with kids.....to take to private school."

"The Queen's ordered one."

"Proves my point," Dennis replied quickly. "You need a sports car.....and I know just the one."

"Let's have it then, Denny," Tommy said, trying not to show too much interest.

"A Lotus Europa.....sex on wheels......just right for you."

"A Lotus Europa? You see me in one of those?"

"If I had the cash, that's what I'd go for. Two seater.....mid engined....sexy as hell."

"I see where you're coming from," Tommy replied. He thought again about his conversation with Steve on the same subject, "They do look the business," he added.

"They're sharp.....angular.....futuristic and *so* different," Dennis enthused. Tommy pondered for a few seconds.

"We could go in and see one," Tommy said tentatively.

"Yeah, now you're talking. Performance Cars....Barchester. They're the main dealers. We could go this lunchtime. I'll take you on the bike."

"Okay, we'll do that," Tommy replied, the excitement in his voice growing.

That lunchtime Tommy wasn't disappointed and a jet black model with dark tinted windows grabbed his attention.

"You can't afford a *new* one, can you?" Dennis asked looking on in disbelief at the sleekness and beauty of the brand, spanking new sports car. Tommy grinned and nodded. He'd made up his mind without even sliding into the cockpit.

The natty salesman in his Burton's suit was soon hovering around them.

"You ain't got a license, have you, Tommy?" Dennis whispered when the salesman suggested a test drive. He did have one, but it was fake. He'd bought it in his teens at a time when nothing he did was either legitimate or legal. It didn't stop him taking up the salesman's offer and Dennis watched as the two of them disappeared around the block in the fabulous motor.

Tommy knew he couldn't buy it there and then. There was certain protocol to be observed. Victor had to be informed so he could set the publicity wheels in motion and make the most of the event. Performance Cars were happy to go along with the ploy as any free publicity was welcomed by them, and the occasion was the first of many successful media led episodes in Victor's master plan to bring the name *Bobby Nelson* into every household in Britain.

Tommy was quite happy to be involved in the media circus and when all the hullabaloo was over he had what *he* wanted, his new supercar. Dennis was also satisfied with the part he played in suggesting the Lotus in the first place and Tommy gave him a cash bonus, recognising the fact.

Somehow Victor knew Tommy didn't have a lawful driving license and put him on an intensive course with an instructor whom he paid handsomely for secrecy in the matter. At the end of the lessons Tommy still had so many bad driving habits he was sure he would fail the test, and he felt the mistakes he'd made during it would end in the examiner failing him. But to his surprise he passed. His belief in Victor and what he could achieve was quickly gaining momentum.

His wardrobe had also been changed, in public at least. Victor wanted a clean cut image embracing the very best in haute couture and although Tommy wasn't so sure, Victor got his way and slowly but surely, he was creating that special person who would conquer the entertainment world. Tommy's cannabis smoking was next on Victor's agenda, but this time he knew he had to tread very carefully. He realised he wasn't going to change Tommy's inherent rebellious nature overnight so he cleverly sought mutual agreement whereby privately Tommy could continue with what he called his social smoking, but publicly his answer, if pushed on the subject, would be that he never touched the stuff. Compromise was the key word which both Tommy, and to a lesser degree, Victor, would have to embrace.

In some instances Tommy found it hard to come to terms with what was expected of him, but Victor's doctrine of global success for the raw talent he'd taken under his wing was enough to keep Tommy focussed on what he needed to do if he were to reap the massive rewards Victor had promised. Tommy was also aware he had to re-invent himself as *Bobby Nelson* and to *be* him in every way, even if it meant acting the part initially and growing into the character as if he were an actor in a play. Tommy had made his choice now though, and there was no going back. He looked good and felt good and his inner confidence was growing as rapidly as his targeted audience's perception of him grew.

Dennis was aware of the change almost straight away. Yet he was also becoming a changed man through Tommy's influence. As far as the heroin was concerned, he'd surpassed his own expectations and since his heart to heart with Tommy in the Crown he hadn't snorted any. He still found the withdrawal symptoms and cold turkey syndrome excruciatingly hard to cope with but he had Tommy's, and to a lesser extent, Emma's full support and encouragement and he was well on the way to breaking the habit and beating the life destroying drug for good.

He also kept his promise to Tommy regarding Emma and somehow refrained from making a pass at her. Dennis even joked to Tommy saying that was much harder than giving up heroin. The atmosphere in the maisonette was now so much better but Tommy knew it wouldn't be long before Victor would be suggesting he moved to somewhere more suited to an emerging superstar and Tommy, although resigned to do just that, for the moment was determined to enjoy the company of both his new found sister and his much changed friend.

Things were starting to move fast for Tommy and within weeks he was in Chapel Studios cutting a new album. Chapel Studios, as the name suggested, was housed in a converted nineteenth century Methodist chapel in the centre of Barchester. Victor chose it for its state-of-the-art facilities and the outstanding reputation of the in house producer and engineer for creating top class recordings.

The studios were one of the Zanetti Corporation's latest acquisitions but Victor didn't know that. Even so, the fact that the Mantovani twins were involved didn't bother him so long as he got value for money and the end product was of exceptional quality. The album was to be a mixture of timeless favourites and new material Victor had commissioned from several song writers. Tommy was a natural in the studio environment. He was cool, calm, patient and disciplined in his approach which the staff there appreciated, realising they had a super talent in their midst. It made the hard and sometimes repetitive work so much easier for all concerned and Tommy thoroughly enjoyed the experience.

It wasn't new to him though, having recorded lead vocals on the Devil's Flock single 'Anarchy', but the difference laying down one track with a band and a complete solo album of diverse material was huge. Tommy took it all in his stride and whilst Victor kept a very low profile and rarely visited the studios, he had his finger very much on the pulse during the whole process. The resulting album, simply entitled *'Bobby'* was both a triumph and a delight and showed Tommy's vocal range and versatility to its fullest. The cover depicted him walking barefoot on a windswept, deserted beach dressed in blue jeans and a loose white shirt that billowed in the sea breeze.

The record sold in huge numbers and *'Bobby Nelson's'* rise to fame was nothing short of phenomenal. Victor stayed in the background the best he could and orchestrated everything, from signing contracts on Tommy's behalf to arranging concerts and TV appearances. Tommy left the maisonette in the High Street and took a lease on a penthouse apartment in a city centre high rise development. He absolutely loved it and with his classy black Lotus Europa, he looked every bit the star Victor had planned all along.

Dennis played his part but he was much more than a gofer, and Tommy's reliance on him became so great, with Victor's permission, he left Subway Music and on the proviso that his wages would be bankrolled by Tommy, he became his personal assistant. Tommy had already left the shop to concentrate on his career. Victor suggested it when Tommy started working on the album and he knew he couldn't do both.

Dennis and Emma continued to share the flat above the greengrocers in Southfields. Their plutonic friendship had grown and Dennis was well on the way to looking upon her as the sister he never had. Emma was happy with that relationship and she could enjoy her new independence knowing she had two men in her life she could rely on if needed, Tommy and Dennis. Tommy was also happy with the situation knowing he didn't have the worry of his sister's wellbeing on either his conscience or constantly on his mind.

Tommy did make the effort to go back to the Barton Bridge flats to visit his mum and dad. He wasn't looking forward to the ordeal but he got a pleasant surprise when his mum told him Harry's convalescence had gone well and he had plans to go back to work chauffeuring, but she stressed it wouldn't be with Prestige Cars. He shared a beer with his dad but their conversation was limited to him writing down everything and although Tommy was patient, it was still laborious. Harry's vocal chords had been damaged beyond repair and he would never speak again. As Tommy was leaving he scribbled some words on his pad and handed it to Tommy. It read:

"I'm so proud of you, son. So.....so....proud."
Tommy smiled as he read it and gave his dad a big hug.

"Don't I get one then?" his mum asked.

"Course you do, mum. You're the reason.....and the *only* reason, he's turned the corner and looks like this." He gave her a cuddle, "And I'm *so* proud of you."

Harry hadn't heard from either Angelo or Freddie since his ordeal at Butlers Wharf and if he never saw them again it would suit him perfectly. D.C. Sutherland was a real worry to him though.

He'd said too much to him about the night of the bombing incriminating Angelo the way he did, and he knew that conversation, unofficial or not, would come back to haunt him one day. D.C. Sutherland wasn't about to give up on the case either. He owed it to the families of the two staff killed that night to bring the perpetrator to justice, and the amount of relevant paperwork piling up on his office desk regarding the case bore testament to that.

The Zanetti Corporation was also getting bigger and more powerful as each week passed and the Mantovani twins, especially Angelo, was becoming so dominant and influential within the city, he was well on the way to becoming untouchable by the authorities. D.C. Sutherland was very aware of that. He knew deep down Angelo *was* behind the bombing, even though his source, Harry Nelson, wasn't the most reliable and had been effectively silenced.

Time wasn't on his side if he wanted to put Angelo behind bars so when he received an anonymous telephone call suggesting the Platinum Casino Club's bar manager, John Pullen, knew more about that fateful night than his original police statement showed, the detective constable promptly arranged a visit there.

James Slade met him in the reception lounge and led him to the casino bar where John Pullen was slicing up lemons in readiness for the busy evening session ahead. He was bent over slightly and looked in some pain.

"What's up?" James Slade asked.

"Keep getting these stomach pains, boss."

"This is John Pullen, detective constable."

"Thank you Mr Slade. I remember him now."

D.C. Sutherland then gave the casino owner a look intimating he would prefer to speak to John Pullen in private, but James Slade didn't take the hint.

"Say what you have to say, detective constable.....I'm going nowhere," he said confidently.

"As you wish," D.C. Sutherland replied politely. "Mr Pullen, I'd like to ask you if you have anything to add to the statement you gave us regarding the night of the bombing?"

John Pullen continued slicing the lemons, but his movement was slow and ponderous. James Slade's eyes were fixed on the young man, his gaze deliberate and unerring.

"No, I told you all I know," Pullen replied.

"We have reason to believe there's something you're not telling us," D.C. Sutherland probed further. Pullen shook his head and put down the knife.

"Oh...this bloody pain...it's really getting to me."

"Mr Pullen?" D.C. Sutherland was waiting for an answer. James Slade looked on but didn't say a word.

"Every time I move....cough....anything....it's bloody crippling," Pullen lamented.

D.C. Sutherland could see the man was in so much

pain he was wasting his time. Pullen was now doubled over and unsteady on his feet. Sutherland could plainly see the anguish on his face and his inquisitiveness quickly turned to concern. James Slade didn't move. Pullen took a step towards Tim Sutherland.

"Jesus...." he wailed, "It's like I've been stabbed in the guts."

He collapsed on the floor in front of the detective constable.

"Call an ambulance," Sutherland barked to James Slade. John Pullen was unconscious when the medics arrived. His father Robert, the casino's general manager, went with him in the back of the ambulance on the short trip to Barchester General Hospital. John Pullen died there later that afternoon.

Chapter 19

Tommy's life was changing dramatically and faster than he'd ever imagined. Everyone wanted a piece of *Bobby Nelson* and Victor Slade was filling Tommy's diary to capacity. He was fit, strong and had bags of energy. He was still lean and mean as he was as a teenager but the moodiness had gone. Ambition had replaced capricious habits and Tommy was now reaping the benefits of his ability to change and go with the flow of the lifestyle he only dreamed about when he was singing along to the hits on a Saturday morning at the record stall in the market.

His fearless and belligerent attitude then had been tempered and honed to suit the character he was now, but his personality and nature wasn't that different from his youth. He was still errant and mischievous in his ways and the anxiety of what the future held was still there in the back of his mind. His *'live for today'* philosophy had mellowed somewhat and he now looked upon tomorrow as worth waiting for.

There was another trait to his disposition that had come to the fore as he reached adulthood. His selfish attitude had changed to one of helping others if he could. Members of his family had benefitted from his concern and involvement but others, like Dennis Carter, who he had no family responsibilities for, had also recently been on the receiving end of Tommy's new found benevolence.

Victor had managed to get hold of two tickets for Barchester United's annual player's dinner dance and had triumphantly handed them to Tommy so he could attend the glitzy evening. It was one of the most celebrated and prominent social events in the club's calendar, but Tommy wasn't so enthusiastic. Southfields F.C. was his team. It always had been and wasn't about to change. Barchester Utd, as big and successful as they were, didn't have the magic of the Hornets that he'd grown up with.

The tickets were like gold dust though and if it was Victor's intention for him to be there in a professional capacity, then he would go. He knew he couldn't go on his own, however. A female escort was imperative and for the occasion, when the press and media would be there in abundance, the more attractive his date was, the better. The trouble was, his relationships so far had been casual affairs. He had no one to accompany him who was either special enough, or someone he could rely on not to jeopardise his career in any way.

It was a dilemma he gave a lot of thought to and came to the conclusion his sister Emma was the ideal choice. Even he, as her brother, could see she was attractive and outgoing, and would be his perfect escort for the evening. She jumped at the chance when Tommy mentioned it to her and couldn't wait to go shopping for the right outfit.

They arrived at Barchester Utd's Stadium in a taxi. Tommy was proud of his younger sister, who looked stunning as she stepped out of the taxi to a plethora of flashing cameras all aimed at her.

She wore a low cut emerald green evening dress which accentuated her curvaceous proportions, silver high heeled shoes, and her long brown hair had been meticulously piled high on her head by the most fashionable hair stylists' in Southfields High Street. Dainty silver earrings complemented her pretty face and a silver necklace, a gift from her mum and dad on her sixteenth birthday, completed the look.

Tommy was at her side in seconds and put his arm reassuringly through hers. His dress was cool understatement personified. Not for him the starchy formality of a dinner jacket, waistcoat and dicky bow tie, even if James Bond did wear one. He was a pop singer, not an undertaker, and his contemporary look of vivid red jacket, black casual slacks, red patent leather shoes and an open necked white blouson style shirt was not only the height of fashion, but an outfit Tommy was totally comfortable in.

He had a big grin for the cameras as he strolled arm in arm with his little sister towards the entrance to the stadium's conference centre amidst shouts of *"Bobby.......Bobby.."* from some of his female fans in the sizeable crowd gathered there to greet everyone.

"Who's the young lady?" one journalist called out, but Tommy remained tight lipped and smiled profusely at everyone. He was in his element. Inside there were candlelit tables dotted around a small central dance floor and a stage to one side. Victor had secured a discreet table for two for Tommy and his guest. Little did he know the romantic setting would be wasted with Tommy bringing Emma along. Tommy however, was quite happy to be tucked away at the back and Emma didn't mind where she sat because she was enchanted by the occasion and was determined to have a good time.

There was one person Tommy knew would be there, Steve Baker. He caught a glimpse of him during the meal and waved, but Steve was on the other side of the player's table and didn't see him. There were a couple of speeches extolling the virtues of the football club, which was exactly what Tommy expected, before the evening's entertainment began. A ten piece swing band took to the stage but what drew Tommy's attention to them was the drummer who was none other than the original Devil's Flock drummer, Phil. It brought a smile to Tommy's face when they started their set with the classic *'Never on a Sunday'* and he thought it a far cry from Phil's thumping rhythms on their single *'Anarchy'*. He looked happy though and the band were excellent.

It didn't take long for the dance floor to fill up.

"No...I'm not dancing with you, Emma," Tommy said noticing his sister tapping her feet to the music and fidgeting in her seat. He knew she was itching to get on the dance floor.

"Oh...come on Tommy. We could just jig about a bit....it'll be fun." Her persuasive powers fell on deaf ears, "You've got to be seen in the thick of things. If your manager, Victor was here he'd make sure you......"

"Yeah....yeah....I know. Maybe later, okay. Now sup your champagne and don't spill it down your dress," he replied laughing. Even if she didn't get to dance, Emma was having the time of her life, and although the sparkling wine she was drinking wasn't quite the real thing, it was having its effect nevertheless and she was chilled out, relaxed and enjoying herself. Tommy felt a tap on his shoulder.

"Traitor!" the voice said, "Never thought I'd see the day when a Hornets stalwart deserted to the enemy."

Tommy turned around. It was Steve's familiar voice.

"Hi Tommy," he said.

Tommy put his finger to his lips.

"Shush.......it's *Bobby*.......I'm *Bobby Nelson*," he chuckled before standing up and shaking Steve's hand warmly. Steve Baker's huge frame dwarfed him. He was immaculately turned out in his club suit, cream shirt and matching club tie. His dark blond hair had been neatly cut and his smile filled his face. He took a step back.

"You look unbelievable.....er....*Bobby*. And those shoes! What you doing here anyway?"

"My manager's idea of exposure.....it's good to see you an' all, Steve."

"Ah...using big words now....and no swearing." Steve replied. The initial banter continued.

"*Bobby Nelson's* educated, and he never swears," Tommy said bursting into laughter. Steve looked at Emma.

"Aren't you going to introduce me to your......" He stopped in mid sentence.

"To my sister, Steve?" Tommy cut in.

"Oh my God!"

"Hello Steve," Emma said calmly.

"Emma....Emma Nelson. Well I'm....."

"Don't say it," Tommy again finished Steve's sentence. Emma stood up and Steve gave her a hug.

"Well I never," he said, looking at the beauty standing before him. "You look great. When was the last time we saw each other?"

"Three years ago, at the hospital....when Tommy was there." She knew exactly. She'd passed him in the corridor after visiting Tommy, and although they hadn't spoken she remembered it well.

"That long ago," Steve replied casually.

"Sit down," Tommy suddenly said, "Have a glass of...Asti....with us."

"Can't right now. Some club things to do, you know....and I'm needed over there right now."

Emma looked disappointed.

"Be back later though. Be good to have a chat," Steve added.

"And a dance maybe?" Emma asked tentatively.

"Maybe," Steve replied teasingly. Emma watched as he walked away. She really hoped he would come back.

During the band's break the grand raffle was drawn, then Steve went on stage to collect his award for the club's young player of the year. That surprised both Tommy and Emma because they knew nothing about it. The cameras flashed away and it was obvious Steve enjoyed the limelight. Fortunately for him, he didn't have to make a speech as he was still quite shy, and hadn't yet mastered the art of public speaking. Then there was a roll call of celebrities and famous sporting people attending and suddenly Tommy heard the MC call out the name, *Bobby Nelson*. He stood up and gave a modest wave to everyone. He was learning fast.

"Got some news for you," Steve said, grabbing a chair from the next table. Emma's face lit up. She wasn't sure if he'd come back.

"What....got yourself a new motor?" Tommy was quick to ask. He wondered how long the modest Triumph Spitfire would keep its appeal.

"Well....as a matter of fact......"

"Not a Range Rover......surely *not* a Range Rover?" Tommy interrupted.

"Ah...you haven't sold that pretty, yellow sports

car?" Emma said, "I used to watch you drive off in that sweet little car from my bedroom window back at the flats," she added.

"No Tommy, it's *not* a Range Rover. Mind you, a couple of the lads have got them."

"Go on then Steve, surprise me."

"It's a TVR Vixen soft top."

"Wow.......I underestimated your cracking taste....excellent," Tommy was genuinely surprised.

"What's a TVR?" Emma was nonplussed.

"Only one of the best British two seat racers you can get. It's awesome. What colour?" Tommy replied.

"Yellow," Steve said. They all burst out laughing, "But that's not the news I have," he continued.

"I've just got a Lotus Europa. Not quite a TVR, but....."

"I saw that on the local news. Good for you, Tommy," Steve said.

"What news you got then, Steve?" Emma asked, moving her chair a little closer to his. Just then Angelo Mantovani walked past. Self assured in his dark dinner suit, bow tie and immaculately slicked back hair he looked suave and sophisticated, oozing self esteem with every step he took.

"Cocky git," Tommy said, once Angelo was out of earshot.

"I agree," Steve replied.

Tommy watched him head towards a table where he

caught a glimpse of his brother Freddie.

"They're both here. What the hell they doing here?" he commented.

"They've probably got more right to be here than you......unfortunately," Steve replied.

"What you on about?" Tommy said. He was confused.

"They're the clubs newest shareholders, and directors."

"You're kidding me, Steve. They've got no interest in football at all....we all know that."

"They have now. Got a box on the halfway line and everything."

"It's wrong," Tommy curbed his wrath remembering where he was. "There's something wrong somewhere, Steve, when a couple of chancers with no talent can take over the city like they're doing."

Steve shrugged and turned to Emma.

"Got a little story for you," he said to her, "When we all lived in the flats, and the Mantovanis moved in, what were we Tommy.. fourteen...fifteen.. I can't remember exactly. Anyway, the two of us came up against their little gang one day outside the flats. They called us a couple of poofs....their very words, I remember that bit. They were real bullies, even then. But this bit, you'll love this bit Emma..."

Tommy said nothing. He remembered the incident like it happened only yesterday.

"Well....Tommy faced them up, there were at

least six of them...."

"Four," Tommy interrupted

"He took off his jacket and squared up to them. Fists raised, the lot."

Emma listened open mouthed.

"He said he'd fight them all, called Angelo a greasy dago, and do you know what he called Freddie?......Stupid he called him......priceless."

By this time Tommy was stifling a giggle.

"You weren't laughing at the time, Tommy," Steve said trying not to laugh himself.

"What happened?" Emma was eager to know the outcome.

"The gang lost their bottle...laughed it off. Tell you, Emma, your Tommy was just awesome."

"Didn't do much good, did it? Just look at them now," Tommy said. His smile had disappeared. Emma was enjoying Steve's company and was hanging on every word.

"I could write a book, Em....stuff I've done," Tommy remarked laughing again.

"You still haven't told us your news," Emma said.

"Right. Now I don't want anyone else to hear this," Steve's voice was hushed, "Nobody knows about this and I'm not supposed to tell anyone. Only my boss and the F.A. know....but I've got to tell someone. I can trust you two, I know that..."

"Get on with it, Steve," Tommy was intrigued but as usual, impatient.

"I'm being called up to play for my country... to play for England," he glanced around fearing he might be overheard. Tommy and Emma were lost for words.

"Next month.....friendly. Away in Poland I was told."

"Wow!" Tommy exclaimed, "Steve Baker, playing for England. Now that's what I call awesome," Tommy enthused.

"Doesn't mean I'll be playing, just that I'm in the squad. *They* don't even know," Steve gestured towards his team mates on the far side. "And if the papers get wind...."

"Well they won't from me and Em, that's a cert," Tommy assured him.

"Congratulations, Steve," Emma said.

"Yeah mate, I'll second that. You'll play...you wait and see," Tommy said filling their glasses with sparkling wine. "We'll drink to your international career," he whispered.

Just then the band came back on stage. Tommy thought he must go and say hello to Phil, the drummer before the evening came to a close.

"Fancy a dance, Emma?" Steve asked as the band kicked off their second set. Those were the four words Emma had been waiting for all evening.

"Yes, I'd like that," were the four words she had ready for her reply.

For a skilful, professional footballer Emma thought Steve was a bit wooden as he strutted his stuff and she thought his co-ordination and rhythm left a lot to be desired, but she didn't care. She was having a good time and as soon as the band slowed things down with a couple of ballads, Steve drew her to him and suddenly their bodies were as one on the crowded dance floor. Even in her heels she was still a lot shorter than him, but she felt special as his arms held her close and her body moulded itself against his.

Steve could feel her breath on his neck as she rested her head on his shoulder and snuggled up to him.

"What do you do then, Emma?" he asked quietly. Emma didn't want to talk. She was happy in his arms, moving to the music, and didn't want anything to spoil the moment.

"Emma?" Steve pressed her for an answer.

"I'm a beauty consultant to the rich and famous," she replied tongue in cheek.

"Wow....that sounds terrific."

"No, I'm joking. I'm a sales girl at Boots the chemist....but I am on the beauty counter."
Steve smiled, "What...the Boots here in town?"

"I wish. No....unfortunately Southfields High Street, so I don't see many rich and famous people."
He looked down into her big hazel eyes.

"You're very beautiful," his voice was still hushed but the words came out awkwardly. It took Emma by surprise.

"Only *great* you said I looked earlier," she said,

thinking Steve was being a bit patronising. He felt embarrassed and relaxed his hold on her.

"It came out wrong. I didn't mean.....well, you know...I'm sorry."

The band struck up the opening bars of *'Save The Last Dance For Me'*

"Ooh, I like this one," Emma said, reaching up and putting her arms around his neck. "Start again....shall we?" she added. Steve nodded and drew her close once again. Nothing was said for the duration of that song and the following half a dozen numbers.

It was now well after midnight and with the evening drawing to a close, people were starting to drift away. Emma caught sight of Tommy back at their table, pointing to his wrist. She didn't want to stop. She was happy in Steve's arms. Inevitably, the band played their finale, Elvis's *'The Wonder Of You'* and the house lights came on, bright and impersonal.

"Do you fancy....er....coming out one night?" Steve asked, still sounding a bit clumsy.

"What, on a date?" she could see Tommy out of the corner of her eye, looking impatient.

"Yeah....on a date. The pictures, a meal or something."

"You sure Steve, you're not just saying that?"

"I'm sure. I want to take you out."

"Then yes....I'd love to."

"I'll see you in Boots, and we can arrange it

then, okay?"

Emma nodded and gave him a peck on the cheek.

"I'll look forward to that, I really will," she said turning and heading towards her big brother. For her the evening couldn't have gone better.

Chapter 20

"Who told you that?" Tommy asked Victor candidly as they sat in the Wimpy Bar in Southfields High Street. Victor's Ford Zodiac, his preferred meeting place and unofficial office had, on this occasion. been forsaken in favour of his favourite frothy coffee only available in the popular burger bar chain.

"Pass the sugar, Tommy," is all Victor replied. He'd just told Tommy of the death of John Pullen. Victor's news had come as quite a shock and the details were sketchy and vague. Victor said Pullen had been taken ill with some sort of stomach disorder and had died in hospital. When Tommy pressed him for more details Victor told him as far as he knew, the condition was to do with the stomach membrane which had apparently ruptured.

Tommy was baffled. When he'd mentioned Pullen to Victor shortly after he'd signed contracts with him, Victor had seemed disinterested and was more intent on discussing his future than what had happened in the past, even though the Mill House Cafe car park affair had been a traumatic time for him and was still playing on his mind.

"How did you know about that?" Tommy demanded losing patience with his manager. Victor looked at Tommy, his deep set brown eyes giving nothing away. "And why don't you *ever* take that silly fucking hat off?" Tommy added.

Victor sipped his coffee.

"Now you're just being facetious," he replied. "If you must know.....I got it from the owner of the casino."

"But that's James, your......your brother, surely?"

Victor nodded, "That's right."

"But you never talk to him."

"Who said that?"

Tommy looked puzzled. He'd been led to believe they were arch enemies and had absolutely nothing to do with each other. He was delighted to hear of his tattooed assailant's demise though and didn't want to antagonise Victor further. Victor also had no intention of continuing the argument either.

"Let's move on, Tommy. The past's the past. I just thought you'd want to know, that's all. Anyway, the reason for this meeting.......America beckons."

Victor suddenly had Tommy's attention.

"What?" he said ineptly.

"Thought that might grab your interest, lad. America.....The States, next week. *Bobby Nelson* is appearing on the Don Lexton show, on IBC in New York."

Tommy grinned, "New York?"

Victor nodded, grabbing the attention of the waitress and gesticulating for another cup of his favourite beverage.

"What show again?"

"Don Lexton's."

"Never heard of him."

"Because you're a fucking Philistine, Tommy, that's why." He attracted unwelcomed attention from a couple on the next table who couldn't fail to overhear his swearing. He touched his trilby in response to their stares.

"So sorry." he said, sounding hypocritically apologetic, and turned to Tommy.

"Biggest talk show on the East Coast. Phenomenal for your career. You sing one song from the album.....and chat to the man. Up for it?"

"Well yeah.....of course."

"Got a passport....a *real* one?"

"Aah..."

"Didn't think so. I'll sort it. Get me some pics from that booth in Woolworths. I'll sort the rest. Now.....any other business?"

Tommy shook his head. His was still in shock. The waitress brought Victor another hot, fresh, frothy coffee.

"Then let me enjoy this in peace."

Tommy knew when not to outstay his welcome and left. He made straight for the library. It was a place he rarely visited but John Pullen was still on his mind. He went to the medical section and scoured the publications dealing with the abdomen and digestive system.

He was there longer than he anticipated, but

eventually found the probable cause of his adversary's death. Victor's words about the rupture of the stomach wall proved to be the key, and he found the rare condition of peritonitis, the inflammation of the peritoneum, the thin tissue membrane of the abdominal lining, which is often fatal if untreated, to be the most probable reason for his death. Tommy left the library knowing he *could* now move on, and went to the photo booth in Woolworths before seeking out Dennis to tell him Victor's fantastic news about America.

Emma didn't have to wait long for Steve to call into Boots to arrange their date as he said he would. Her rather plain staff uniform wasn't quite up to the stunning evening dress she'd worn at the football club dinner, and her hair and make-up were also less impressive and that made her feel apprehensive about meeting Steve again, and even feelings of inadequacy about herself generally were creeping in.

She was constantly looking towards the door of the shop hoping he wouldn't come in, take one surreptitious look at her in the cold light of day, and promptly walk out. Her fears were unfounded though and he caught her unawares parking around the back of the shop and coming in the rear entrance. He was casually dressed and was his usual ebullient self.

Emma thought he looked even taller as he reiterated what a great time he'd had in her company at the dance, but then she *was* minus her three inch high heels, and that had escaped her attention. She could see others in the shop glancing at him and trying to place where they'd seen him before, and in a way she found that exciting if a little distracting and unsettling. Steve was getting used to the recognition and realised it was all part and parcel of his prominent rise to success. As yet, the autograph hunters hadn't strayed far from the Barchester Stadium on match days, but Steve knew, with his pending international call up, that might not last long. It was something he'd embrace with a smile on his face when it did happen, and that's what he'd promised himself.

He didn't stay long in the shop, just long enough to arrange their date for the coming Saturday evening. Barchester were playing at home in the afternoon so he knew he would be free that evening and not be travelling back from an away match on the team coach.

As usual, Emma was working all day on the Saturday, but she was kept updated with the progress of the match during the afternoon by a young staff colleague and Barchester fan who worked in the storeroom, and who'd sneaked in a small transistor radio especially for the occasion. Whatever the score, Emma was determined to take an interest in the match and hoped her knowledge of it might enhance their evening together.

"We won," Steve said with a broad smile on his

face when he picked Emma up from the maisonette in Southfields High Street.

"I know.....and you scored," Emma replied, climbing into the passenger seat of Steve's yellow TVR.

"How do you know that?"

"Ah, my secret. It's not all perfume and paracetamols at Boots the chemist on a Saturday afternoon."

Steve pressed the starter button and the engine roared into action.

"Oh wow," Emma exclaimed as the throaty engine rumble went to the pit of her stomach.

"You wait and see what this beauty does," he said pushing the gear stick into first. "When did I get my goal then, first or second half.....see how much you *really* know?"

Emma was ready for the question. "Second half... and it was a lucky deflection, I heard."

Steve laughed as he hit the throttle pedal and the yellow sports car sped off, pushing Emma back in the leather bucket seat.

"Lucky deflection, eh?" he mused as they headed for the bright lights of Barchester.

The evening had got off to a good start for both of them, but especially for Emma, as her apprehension about the date had been building up all day. They were soon in the hustle and bustle of the Old Town district east of the city centre. Steve took Emma's hand, leading her through the maze of busy medieval back streets which made up the popular locality.

"Fancy Chinese?" Steve asked as they approached the *'Dragon's Kitchen'*.

"Yeah.....I like Chinese. Sounds good to me."
They stopped outside and peered in through the steamed up window. It was crowded.

"We go fifty-fifty on the bill mind," Emma said, looking at the menu on the door. "I pay my way, Steve.....okay with you?" She looked upon herself as a modern woman. She was working, had her own place and she was proud of her independence. That immediately fuelled Steve's mischievous side.

"Absolutely.....that's fine with me. Tell you what, it's packed in there. I know somewhere more.....more intimate. Food's good, not Chinese, though."

Emma liked the sound of *intimate* and nodded in agreement.

"It's not far, just round the corner."
They arrived at a small restaurant down an alleyway.

"Here we are.......Molly Maguire's.......this'll be perfect."

Emma couldn't see a menu anywhere on the outside.

"Normally have to book here, especially on a Saturday....but we'll try our luck."

He pushed open the door and Victorian Barchester greeted them. It was as if they had stepped back in time. Oil lamps, oak tables and chairs, dark crimson table cloths, everything was from the era. It was bijou and the atmosphere was cosy, snug and inviting. It looked full inside and Steve was about to turn and walk out, when a dark haired woman in a Victorian waitress costume greeted them.

"Mr Baker....good to see you this evening."

"We haven't booked."

"I have a table, here....in the corner....come this way."

Emma had never been in such a place before. All around people were chatting quietly and subdued laughter filled the room.

"You've been here before, then?" Emma asked looking around the tiny restaurant.

"Oh yes."

"I bet you bring all the......" she stopped in mid sentence, regretting what she'd just said, but Steve brushed it aside.

"No, I come here with some of the lads. It's a place we can relax after a match without the *'runners'* after us."

"Runners?"

"Chasers.....autograph hunters. We call them *'runners'*."

Emma nodded.

"*Then* we go clubbing, and pick up all the dolly birds," he said chuckling. The waitress brought the menus over. Emma took one look.

"You beast," she said. Bastard was the word she

had on her mind and would have used if they hadn't been in such fine surroundings. The cost of the main course alone was more than her weekly wage.

"We'll go Dutch, as you were so keen to do," he laughed.

"No wonder there's no menu in the window. I fell for that, Steve....good and proper."

"My treat." he said quietly. Emma smiled.

"You'll regret that," she said, her smile turning to a giggle as she buried her head in the menu.

They talked constantly throughout the superb meal. There were no embarrassing silences and their conversation flowed perfectly. They chatted at length about growing up in the Barton Bridge council flats and Emma was totally relaxed in Steve's company. That bothered her to some extent because it was like talking to an older brother. There was little mystery about the guy sitting opposite her on their first date. She already *had* an older brother. It was a lover she was after, a relationship with someone new and exciting. and the dream of being swept off her feet by a dark, handsome stranger. Handsome Steve most certainly was, but dark he wasn't and he was by no means a stranger. Emma found excitement in his company though and was more than happy to spend time with the guy she'd secretly fancied for some time.

Steve paid for the meal and they left the Victorian ambience with full stomachs. It wasn't the end of the evening however, and the pair ended up at the Top Rank Suite, a venue not far away renowned for its live music and late night dancing. Steve was up for a dance or two, even though he was physically tired after playing football, but he chose the slow smoochy numbers rather than jigging about to the up-tempo ones. Emma understood and was happy to dance cheek to cheek on this occasion.

Steve found her alluring and desirable and they moved as one, lost in their own utopian world on the crowded dance floor. Their closeness rekindled Emma's belief that Steve, far from being a brother figure, could well be the passionate, sexy man of her dreams after all. That opinion was further enhanced when he kissed her goodnight outside the maisonette in Southfields. He declined her offer of a coffee. It was late, he was tired and above all, it was only their first date.

Their kiss though was sensual, intense and fervent and Emma soon felt his desire rising in his nether regions, his growing hardness a pleasant surprise and one she was eager to prolong and enjoy. Her hand briefly and fleetingly touched him there before he made the tough decision to get in his car and drive away.

Emma watched as the yellow TVR drove off. She smiled, knowing *her* sexual desire had also increased and was on a par with his. Her frustration was only a slight inconvenience however, and she was more than happy with the way their first date had gone.

Steve's trip to Poland with the England squad was fast approaching and he was required to spend time at the training camp, be put through his paces, and assessed by the England coach. That, combined with his club commitments, meant his new found association with Emma was put on hold for a few weeks. That didn't mean they didn't see each other, just that their meetings were confined to lunchtime coffee bars or a walk in the park on a Sunday. Emma didn't mind though, she knew Steve's career was paramount and was happy to continue their relationship on that basis rather than risk jeopardising it completely.

*   *   *   *

Victor's arrangements for *Bobby Nelson's* venture across the Atlantic came to fruition and Tommy jetted off to New York full of enthusiasm and anticipation, and couldn't wait to experience the buzz of the city that never slept. He was also amazed at the way Victor had organised everything, including arranging his passport in such a short time.

All those thoughts he put to the back of his mind though as he landed at John F. Kennedy International Airport and was whisked into the city centre by an iconic yellow taxi cab. The smile on his face never wavered as the skyscrapers of Manhattan loomed up ahead. It was like a dream, but reality kicked in when the fat taxi driver, making his usual small talk, asked why he was visiting the city. Tommy's casual reply that he was appearing on the Don Lexton show was met with laughter and incredulity which bordered on derision by the gum chewing New Yorker. Tommy didn't have either the patience or the inclination to get the big man to take him seriously.

"We get loads of whipper snapper, wannabee Limeys coming here after fame and fortune.....what's your name, kid?"

Not so long ago Tommy would have given as good as he got but he wasn't going to take the bait this time.

"My name?....*Bobby*.....just watch the show tomorrow night, pal," he replied coolly as they arrived at the swanky hotel on Fifth Avenue Victor had booked him into.

"Thought you were joking when you said the Plaza."

Tommy smiled, gave him a tip, and told him to have a nice day before walking calmly into the world famous hotel.

The Big Apple lived up to his every expectation. He loved the noise, the hustle and bustle of the brash, everyday folk who lived and worked there. It was his type of town. Cosseted within the luxurious surroundings of the Plaza

Hotel he could have easily become blasé, but Victor's words of wisdom were constantly with him.

"It's not a holiday, it's work, Tommy." Victor had said, *"Enjoy yourself by all means but remember **why** you're there. Embrace it. Do it. You won't get another chance,"*

Jet lag was setting in and he needed to get his voice into good shape for his very first live performance in America in front of a television audience of millions. Tommy was determined Victor's words weren't going to fall on deaf ears and took a nap before going into his warm up vocal routine. The view of Central Park from his hotel room was enough to keep the smile on his face and he looked forward to the Don Lexton show with nerve jangling fearlessness, but nervous all the same.

He breezed through the show. Don Lexton was infinitely more famous than he was, yet the genial presenter treated him as though he was the star. His professional, friendly manner made sure Tommy stayed relaxed and focussed during both his performance and the ten minutes of chat which followed. His vocal presentation was superb and the trusty backing track, produced at Chapel Studios, sounded crisp and bright and was the perfect accompaniment to Tommy's live voice which gave him extra confidence to chat naturally with his host, which was also live on camera.

The result was sensational. The following

morning he couldn't even walk the streets without being recognised and approached. He was about to crack America and back in his hotel room he sipped Jack Daniels and pinched himself just to make sure the whole thing wasn't a dream. His thoughts again went back to Victor Slade, in his book, the genius who was making it all happen.

"To you, Victor, and to you *Bobby Nelson*," he declared in a loud voice, knocking back the legendary Stateside bourbon in a celebratory gesture of success. He spoke to Victor a couple of times on the telephone before flying back to Barchester. Each time Victor told him to savour the experience and enjoy it, but above all to stay out of trouble. For once in his life he was finding the latter easier to do and ended up having a fantastic few days in New York before returning to Britain.

*   *   *   *

Steve's trip to Poland, on the other hand, was much more of a learning curve for the young centre forward than even he imagined. Poland was an emerging football nation and were determined to show the rest of Europe they were no longer the proverbial whipping boys of the sport. England weren't the world champions anymore but were still right up there with the elite and Poland had something to prove, especially with their near neighbours West Germany doing so well in the recent Mexico World Cup. On that basis the scalp of England would give the nation a huge boost.

The National Stadium in Warsaw was the venue and the Wednesday night floodlit match was sold out. The Polish fans were exuberant, noisy and most definitely up for the encounter. There was a small pocket of die hard England supporters who'd made the long trip but they looked insignificant amongst the sea of red.

The tremendous noise from the partisan crowd could even be heard in the dressing rooms under the main stand, and Steve, although not in the starting eleven, was one of the substitutes and he found it intimidating even before he'd changed into his England strip. The match was a dour affair in the late evening drizzle with Poland using spoiling tactics right from the first whistle. The Italian referee was overly fussy, awarding the home team numerous petty fouls, much to the jubilation of the baying crowd. The result was a football match that didn't flow and for the neutral supporter, wasn't the spectacle of top class football they were promised.

It was invaluable experience for Steve however, as he sat in the dug-out and watched his team mates do their best to keep their discipline, retain possession of the ball and try to string a few passes together. Keeping the crowd quiet was the first priority and he knew an early England goal would have done just that. England didn't score and Poland were happy with a draw at half time. Steve was told if England failed to score by the hour mark, he would most probably be sent on to make his debut.

Being a friendly match, and of little consequence to the footballing world generally, the game wasn't being televised, although live radio commentary was being beamed back to Britain. The resulting lack of cameras fuelled the Polish players intent to do what they could, legally or otherwise, to get a favourable result.

It was still goalless after sixty minutes and Steve duly got his chance. He sprinted onto the pitch proudly wearing his country's white number twelve shirt. He wanted to score more than anything and was constantly a threat in the opposition's penalty area. Then *he* began to be subjected to the cheating tactics the rest of the England team had suffered throughout the match. Little tugs here, a discreet push there. He was bundled over in the box following a corner and got short shrift from the referee when he appealed for a penalty. That also drew a derisory reaction from the crowd and subsequently they jeered every time he touched the ball.

The spoiling tactics he was being subjected to were constant and alien to his perception of the game. Yet here he was, a professional, doing what he was paid to do. His inexperience was starting to show. Yet another corner floated in and as he rose to head the ball goal wards the big, opposing red shirted centre half grabbed him around the waist. Because the Polish defenders had got away with so much during the match, all thoughts of subtlety on their part had gone out of the window and it looked a clear penalty.

Steve instinctively tried to free himself from his opponent's grip and thrust an elbow into his shoulder. The centre half went down as if he'd been pole-axed, clutching his face. The crowd went berserk. The Polish player was still writhing on the ground when the Italian referee arrived on the scene. Steve was sent off. The red shirted centre half winked at him as he started the long walk off the pitch.

His naivety had been his downfall and the look on the England manager's face as he passed him on his way down the tunnel to the dressing room said it all. It was the first time in the history of the game an England player had been sent off on his debut. His ignominy was compounded even more when, sitting alone in the away dressing room, he heard the tumultuous roar of the crowd. Poland had scored. They went on to win the game one goal to nil and secured a famous victory.

Chapter 21

Tommy didn't have time to revel in his successful trip to New York when he got back to Barchester. Victor had been busy arranging for him to appear on 'The Groove', a live, early evening young people's music programme on the commercial channel. He needed a particular backing track for the show so he spent his first day back with the engineer in Chapel Studios creating the right sound for his performance the following evening.

He enjoyed the studio work. It was methodical, the atmosphere was relaxed yet productive, and his input was valued and appreciated by the demanding and professional staff there. They saw Tommy, with his lively sense of humour and infectious, bubbly personality, as a breath of fresh air compared to some of the fussy, miserable, egotistic prima donnas who recorded there and demanded perfection, when they were far from perfect themselves.

Two copies of Tommy's track were produced on cassette. One for him to take to the show, and the usual duplicate which was kept at the studio in case of emergency. Tommy spent the evening in a wine bar nearby with Victor, who outlined his plans for a major onslaught across the Atlantic. He stressed the successful taster, with Tommy only appearing on the Don Lexton show, was a precursor to a coast to coast tour he'd planned later in the year, and told Tommy to be ready for the challenge when it came. Tommy's penthouse flat was the ideal place for him to escape to later on when his return flight jet lag caught up with him, and he slept soundly in his plush new home that night.

He met up with Dennis prior to the TV show the following evening and was shocked to hear the news Steve had been sent off in his first game for England. Emma told him she'd listened to the whole match on the radio and heard the melodrama unfold. Dennis told Tommy she was astonished by what had happened, which prompted Tommy to say he would go and see her as soon as he got the chance.

He realised his life was becoming increasingly hectic as his rise to fame continued, and vowed to make the time for his family and friends whatever his future career had in store. Dennis was also leading a far more frenetic lifestyle in his new role as personal assistant to *Bobby Nelson* and his addiction to heroin and the morbid and depressed state his life was in as a result, was fast becoming a memory, and that pleased not only him, but everyone around him who knew of his past. His new found association with Tommy was also opening doors of opportunity in the glamorous music business and his social life, and more importantly, his romantic social life, was improving enormously. He was back in control of his own life and his future lay solely in *his* hands.

Dennis went with Tommy to the television studio and his services were soon called upon. Tommy's backing track was found to be faulty by the TV company's technical staff and Tommy was next up in the make-up room. He sent Dennis off to Chapel Studios to fetch the duplicate. It wasn't far but Dennis took a taxi to be on the safe side as Tommy had stressed the urgency of the mission.

He told the taxi driver to wait when he arrived and hurried into the reception area. He could hear the sound of drumming coming from studio one. It was early evening and not unusual for both recording and post production staff to continue until late, or sometimes right through the night if the project warranted it. The reception area was empty though and Dennis, aware of the no smoking rules in the building, stubbed out his aromatic French cigarette, respecting the studios rules as Tommy's ambassador, which in itself was indicative of his new, less rebellious attitude.

He found the duplicate cassette where Tommy said it would be and on his way out through reception he noticed a bag on the floor behind the desk. He stood and looked at it for a few seconds before his curiosity got the better of him and after glancing around, he pulled it out to have a closer look. It was a soft, black, leather holdall and felt plump and full under his touch. He could see the taxi waiting outside but he'd always been nosey by nature and thought it would do no harm to have a look inside. He slid the zip open and his eyes almost popped out of his head. The holdall was stuffed full of neatly bundled twenty pound notes.

He couldn't believe it and zipped the bag up again. The old Dennis would have grabbed it and scarpered. But this was the *new* Dennis Carter. Responsible, trustworthy, dependable and above all, sensible. His decision was taken in a split second. The old Dennis won the day and he legged it to the waiting taxi with the holdall held firmly under his arm.

On arriving at the TV studios he again asked the driver to wait, leaving the bag on the floor in the back, and went in search of Tommy.

"You've saved the day, Denny," he said as Dennis handed him the cassette.

"Look....something's come up. I can't stop. Be back in an hour...okay?"
Tommy noticed the excitement in his voice, "Yeah, sure...no problem. I'm on soon anyway."

"I'll see you later then," Dennis said and wasted no time hurrying back to the taxi.

"Southfields High Street, mate. Flat above the greengrocers......quick as you can," he said nervously, checking his booty was still there. It was.

*   *   *   *

"Tommy's on in a minute," Emma Nelson said enthusiastically. She was with Steve in the saloon bar of the Blue Boar Inn, Southfields. Steve wasn't very enthusiastic though. He was feeling sorry for himself and Emma knew it. She'd seen the back page pictures of his walk of shame in Poland's National Stadium plastered all over the daily papers and although sympathetic, she wasn't going to let it spoil the evening if she had anything to do with it.

It was their first meeting since Steve had got back and she'd missed him.

"I did nothing wrong," he groaned.

"Let's talk about it after Tommy's been on," Emma replied. She was glued to the television set in the far corner of the bar. Steve nodded and sipped his lager.

"Appearing for the very first time on The Groove," the vivaciously pretty girl presenter enthused, *"The gorgeous......the sensational.....Bobby Nelson."*

Tommy had never lacked confidence where performing was concerned and the bigger the audience, the more self assured and focussed he became. But doing it in front of live TV cameras was an art in itself and something most artists, including Tommy, had to work on to master. He hadn't perfected it yet but was a quick learner and would soon be using the cameras to his own advantage and not vice versa.

Emma was captivated and couldn't believe she

was watching her brother on national television. There was someone else that evening whose eyes were also fixed on the TV set. It was the landlord of the pub, James Slade. Dressed immaculately in a smart, fashionable suit, he looked distinguished yet somewhat out of place in the suburban, down to earth pub. But he was dressed for later, when he'd be rubbing shoulders with Barchester's more affluent clientele in his Platinum Casino Club. Along with the other establishments he owned, including the Velvet Club in Southfields, and the Starlight Palais in the centre of Barchester, he made a point of showing his face regularly and keeping each enterprise firmly in his control.

The bar wasn't very busy and he couldn't fail to notice Emma zealously watching Tommy's every move. He wandered over as soon as Tommy had finished.

"Fan of Bobby Nelson then?" he asked Emma. She looked round at the dapper, bald headed entrepreneur.

"You could say that," she replied.

"He's good. Local fella. Sang here once or twice, couple of years ago now."

Emma listened with interest but said nothing. Steve was in no mood for small talk with a complete stranger and ignored the Blue Boar's owner.

"I'm the landlord, by the way....and I've seen *you* somewhere, I'm sure," he said, looking towards Steve. He continued, "Yes, young Tommy Nelson, as he was then, sang here with the Polka dots. I remember it well."

Emma nodded. Steve drank his lager.

"And he was lead singer with the Devil's Flock. You must have seen them.....they weren't bad. Played their first gig here, in this bar. Packed it was. I knew he'd make it big one day, and look at the fella now. Anyway, I'll let you folks get on," and he started to walk away.

"Nice talking to you Mr........you're right, I knew he'd make it as well," Emma said. James Slade stopped and turned around.

"You know him then, Bobby Nelson?"

"Yes....he's my big brother," she replied, grinning. He was back at their table in a flash, much to Steve's disappointment, and he pulled up a chair.

The conversation between him and Emma centred on Tommy and his rise to fame, before James Slade had to go.

"Been nice talking to you," he looked intently into Emma's hazel eyes, "Perhaps we'll meet again," he added and glanced at Steve, "Oh, I remember *you* now. You're that footballer.....got sent off," he said as he left Emma and Steve to continue their evening together. Steve watched him go.

"Strange guy. Where do you want to go, Emma?" he asked now they were alone.

"Not sure really."

"I don't want to stay here all night," Steve said.

"I hope you're not going to be like this all

evening."

"Like what?"

"Like a bear with a sore head. Come on Steve, you'll get over it. Be old news soon."

"Will I ever get another chance?" he said wistfully.

"Of course you will. Anyway, I know where we can go. Chinese up the street. Buffet, I think tonight. All you can eat for a fiver. My treat tonight.......what do you say?"

Steve finished his pint. "Yeah, okay," he replied.

"And are you going to leave Mr Grumpy here?"

"I'll do my best," Steve said, smiling for the first time that evening.

Stuffing their faces in Southfields finest Chinese restaurant brought Steve out of his melancholic state and it was only a stroll back to the maisonette above the greengrocers later on. This time, when Emma invited Steve up for a coffee, he didn't refuse. They made love for the first time that night. The surroundings weren't quite the grandeur of Steve's mansion house flat in the city, but he didn't care. Having sex with Emma was the most fulfilling experience he'd ever had. She told him she was a virgin soon after they'd undressed each other and lay naked in bed prior to any foreplay.

She was pragmatic in her approach, and wisely didn't ask Steve if it was also his first time. His carnal initiation in the seaside town of Appleton under the expert guidance of the lovely Tanya was now only a memory. But what he learned from that high class hooker he was determined to use to give pleasure to the new woman in his life, and one who was fast becoming very special to him.

The events of the last couple of days were forgotten as he gently coaxed her to orgasm before entering her properly. Emma wasn't some subservient floozy though, and although it was her first time, her desire didn't stop her taking the initiative and straddling him once she'd got a little confidence. Passion inevitably gave way to exhaustion however, and the two young lovers succumbed to their mutual tiredness, falling asleep in each other's arms. They were blissfully unaware that in the room above them, hidden in the bottom of the wardrobe, was a black holdall containing many thousands of pounds.

*   *   *   *

It was two in the morning and the bag's disappearance from the reception area of Chapel Studios had already been discovered and was of major importance to one man in particular, Angelo Mantovani. Although the Zanetti Corporation was making huge profits from the ever increasing enterprises it owned, cash flow was particularly important in the day to day business dealings of the company and ready cash, and the desire for it, was something Angelo was still personally involved in.

That steady supply of untraceable funds had been the backbone to the organisation's rise to success under the personal influence of both Angelo and Freddie. It was drugs money and the brothers were now generating vast amounts of cash weekly with their heroin importation sideline. The money in the bag was payment for a consignment arriving imminently, and Chapel Studios, owned by the brothers, was the perfect rendezvous point to cement the deal with the suppliers, who were due to collect the cash that very evening, before Dennis intervened and walked off with it.

The wheels of the vast underworld intelligence service Angelo had instigated and cultivated over the past few years were set in motion that very night, and his thoroughness combined with his ruthless approach put the odds of recovering the stolen cash firmly in his favour.

Everyone who visited Chapel Studios that week were under suspicion, and that included Tommy, who'd used their services to produce the backing track for the show. As a result he was *invited* to a meeting with Angelo himself, but not at the studios, at the Zanetti Corporation's head office in the city. As Tommy had nothing to hide he agreed to the meeting, even though he didn't have a clue what it was about. The Zanetti offices were on the twenty second, and top floor, of the prestigious and futuristic glass building known as 'Excalibur', right in the heart of the city centre.

It was late morning when Tommy was whisked up in the elevator and he met Angelo in his fabulous glass clad office with spectacular and uninterrupted panoramic views over the city.

"Bobby Nelson.....it's a pleasure," Angelo said greeting him and sounding the perfect gentleman. He shook Tommy's hand and showed him to a sumptuous black leather sofa. Tommy smiled politely and sat down. Angelo had matured into a suave and articulate businessman. He was bright, quick witted, assured and confident. His dark Mediterranean good looks also added to the outward persona he'd created for himself and Tommy was impressed.

"We do know each other," Tommy said casually. Angelo sat down at his huge smoked glass desk.

"Of course we do, Tommy. I just wanted to welcome you with decorum and a modicum of respect, that's all."

Tommy laughed. He knew Angelo had taken both elocution and English language lessons privately whilst building his empire.

"You didn't learn those words at Heathfield Secondary Modern either," he said.

"We both grew up in.......let's say.....a testing environment, didn't we Tommy, and we've both done well."

"We're worlds apart," Tommy remarked candidly. Angelo shrugged.

"I admire you Tommy," he said, "And respect you......sort of."

"Why?" Tommy was quick to ask.

"I remember you standing toe to toe with me and Freddie when you were a kid."

"You remember that?"

"I do. And you had balls Tommy, I'll give you that.....and you probably still have, given your remarkable rise to fame recently."

"You and your brother were bullies." Tommy was choosing his words very carefully.

"And we're not now?" Angelo asked.

Tommy guessed that question was coming and merely shrugged.

"I remember you called me a dago," Angelo continued. Tommy was wondering where the conversation was going but wasn't about to back down.

"I called you a *greasy* dago, to be precise."

Angelo burst out laughing, "The good old days eh, Tommy.....the good old days. Do you like my office?" Angelo moved on.

"Very.....er.....snazzy," Tommy replied.

"Right, I'll get to the point. Had a spot of bother last night. Package went missing from the studios....Chapel Studios."

Tommy nodded.

"And I know you were on TV. And I also know you had a problem with your music, the backing track you did at the studios.....yes?"

Tommy nodded again.

"I want to know if you went there between six and eight last night, that's all?"

"Nope....at the TV station all that time. But my assistant went there to get the backing track you seem to know so much about."

"Zanetti owns the studios for Christ sake, I know what's going on, I make it my business to know. Now, who's your assistant?"

Tommy had no option other than to tell him.

"A guy called Dennis Carter, he's my P.A."

Angelo got up and went to the massive plate glass window behind his desk. He stared out.

"You telling me Dennis fucking Carter is your assistant?"

"I didn't know you knew him."

"I know him. The useless bloody druggie. You sent *him* to the studio to get your tape?"

"Yeah, why not....he works for me."

"More fool you then, Tommy Nelson. One more thing, we found a cigarette end in the reception, one of those French ones. Does he smoke them........I bet he does?"

"Yeah, he does. I've already told you I sent him there."

Angelo sat back down at his desk. Tommy continued, "You're sounding just like the bleedin' coppers......what's going on?" Tommy was genuinely mystified. If he'd inadvertently dropped Dennis in it, he didn't have a clue how.

"Alright Tommy, I'll spell it out. You have a word with Carter and tell him to return what's not his to the studios, same place he found it, seven thirty tonight. The place will be empty."

"And if he doesn't.....or didn't even take whatever it was ......"

Angelo looked Tommy in the eye. "I wouldn't even go there," he said menacingly.

"I'll tell him," Tommy replied.

Angelo got up to shake Tommy's hand but he was already on his way out. There was no love lost between the two of them and Tommy went off in search of Dennis.

He spent most of the afternoon looking for him in Southfields. He knew Dennis wouldn't venture much further, especially if he was in trouble. The truth was, Dennis didn't want to be found, by anyone. Tommy finally caught up with him in the Crown.

"You're in the shit, Denny, and it's all my fault," he said confronting him at the bar. He went on to relay the conversation he'd had earlier with Angelo. Dennis didn't deny anything.

"Didn't you know they own the studios?" Tommy asked trying desperately to get him to open up. He'd seen him moody in his heroin days, but this was different. It was an optimistic, stubborn frame of mind he'd never seen him in before.

"I'm going away for a bit. That's all I can say, Tommy. I'm sorry.....and I really mean that."

"You saved my life, Denny.....now what can *I* do in return?"

"I've made my mind up.....I'm going."

Tommy didn't know what to say. Dennis hugged him, "Don't make this any harder, mate.....you're a good friend, Tommy.....you've given me back my life. Now......walk away.....I'll be in touch."

Tommy sighed. His resolution had been broken and he had no choice other than do what his good friend asked. Nothing more was said and without looking back, Tommy trudged disconsolately towards the door and out into the High Street.

Another thought suddenly crossed his mind. The maisonette above the greengrocers wouldn't be at all safe now with the Mantovanis after Dennis and he suddenly realised it was also Emma's home. He made straight for the perfume counter in Boots.

"Hi sis," he said. Seeing Tommy at her place of work took her by surprise.

"What you doing here?" she blurted out.

"Can't explain now. When do you finish?"

"Half five....why?"

"I'll meet you then....here at the shop. Now whatever you do, *don't* go to the flat. Got me? I'll tell you why later."

Emma was bemused, "What's going on?" her surprise had turned to concern.

"Nothing to worry about. Just wait for me, that's all. You'll do that?"

"But why?"

"Just do it Emma.....yeah?"

"Okay Tommy, but I don't like it."

"As I said I'll explain later," he said and left the shop. He then went in search of Victor to tell him about the dire situation Dennis had got himself into.

Dennis stayed in the Crown as long as he could, as long as he felt it safe to do so. He was scared, infinitely more so than he'd let on to Tommy. It was dark when he finally ventured out into the High Street. He was also hungry. Going back to the flat was out of the question, he knew that. He stopped at the baker's and bought pasties, jam doughnuts and lemonade, sustenance that would have to suffice until the morning. He'd drunk more than he'd intended in the Crown and he needed to keep a clear head.

He had everything planned, but his crucial strategy didn't include the burden of coping with excess alcohol. He made for Somerset Place market. It was only a five minute walk away but it seemed like an eternity as he constantly looked around fearing the Mantovani gangster fraternity were following his every move. The beer he'd consumed only added to his paranoia and by the time he reached his destination he was a bundle of nerves.

He searched his pockets for the key to not only his possible salvation but also to Victor Slade's lock-up near the market, where he intended to spend the night. He found the key, unlocked the door and slipped inside the dark, damp, cell-like space which was to be his home until the morning. Victor was oblivious to him being there without either his knowledge or permission, and Dennis hoped it would remain that way overnight. Salubrious it wasn't, but he was jubilant in reaching the sanctuary he so desperately sought.

In the meantime, Tommy met Emma outside Boots and took her back to his penthouse flat in Barchester. He wouldn't tell her anything until he'd made them both a coffee and even then, the Mantovanis weren't mentioned by name and Tommy only briefly outlined the circumstances involving Dennis. Emma recognised the danger though. She'd grown up, just like Dennis, in an area where spivs and gangsters flourished and she understood the situation perfectly.

Dennis knew only too well the Mantovanis owned Chapel Studios, and when he took the holdall he had a good idea the money inside was linked to the brothers. He thought of it as payback time, for the long term grief they'd put him through, the danger he'd experienced on his forced trip to Morocco and the outstanding debt they still held over him, wrongly, in his view.

The holdall was already in Victor's lock-up. He'd removed it from the flat earlier before going to the Crown. From this moment on he was Keith Duncan, ironically the name in the false passport Angelo had given him when he went to Marrakesh. He'd also used the name earlier in the day to book a one way flight to Mexico City leaving Barchester airport the following morning. He wanted to fly to Acapulco but Mexico City was the only destination available so he took it.

He had the bag full of money, which although he hadn't counted he estimated to be around three hundred thousand pounds. He also had his false passport, the clothes he was wearing and that was it. The holdall would go as hand luggage, keeping everything simple with nothing to go in the hold. His plan seemed foolproof but until British Airlines flight BA286 to Mexico City lifted off and left Barchester in its wake, anything could happen and that's what Dennis realised and feared.

Proper sleep evaded him in the confines of the lock-up, although he dozed off intermittently. His anxiety was such he didn't even trust the comfort of candlelight, afraid his secret hiding place would be discovered. As a result it was a long and uncomfortable night. The following morning brought him renewed hope and confidence that a new life beckoned in more exotic climes and Dennis was ready for the most momentous day of his life.

A taxi to the airport was out of the question, he couldn't trust them. He got a bus and found himself in the concourse at Barchester Airport in good time. His dishevelled appearance combined with having no hold luggage for such a trip raised an eyebrow from the girl who checked him in, and customs, followed by security, which he was particularly worried about, were both a formality and he strode into the departure concourse still very edgy but with more conviction and optimism that he might just pull it off.

He never sat down for long, constantly moving from one seating area to the next, just in case he was being watched. It seemed an age before the gate number for his flight came up on the matrix. His heart was thumping and his stomach churning as he gripped the holdall and went in search of the aircraft's departure gate and his gateway to freedom.

He could see the jumbo jet regaled in its British Airways livery outside in the morning gloom when he arrived at the gate. He wasn't going to queue and risk being seen, so he kept on the move with frequent visits to the toilet as a result of his nervousness. Eventually the departure gate opened and a steady stream of passengers left the building to walk the short distance across to the aircraft. Dennis joined them, his clenched fist gripping the holdall as he stepped outside.

A comfortable, worry free life on the beach in Acapulco beckoned and had he believed in God he would have been praying his heart out that very moment. But he didn't and his anxiety and apprehension turned to unabated fear knowing that if anything went wrong Angelo would instruct his masochistic brother, Freddie, to do his worst, and he knew *that* would mean certain death. He kept walking, and the plane got bigger with every step. He looked around. The luggage buggy was returning empty back towards the main building. Two bright yellow tankers were completing the refuelling process. A solitary fire engine stood on standby and a small stationary helicopter sat not far away.

Something caught his eye in the distance. He quickened his step. Suddenly a black limousine swept across the tarmac heading straight for him. He was *so* close to freedom. The vehicle skidded to a halt and two burly, dark suited men got out and accosted him. The other passengers hurried by giving them a wide berth. The stockier of the two men grabbed Dennis's arm.

"Immigration, Mr Carter. We'd like you to come with us, if you don't mind," he said with authority. Dennis glanced at the jumbo jet. It was tantalisingly close, so much so he could almost reach out and touch it. He needed to act fast.

"No....you've got the wrong man, mate," he said as calmly as his situation would allow. The man wasn't impressed and held him even more firmly.

"Dennis Carter.....you're coming with us," he reiterated. Dennis went to the inside pocket of his jacket.

"I wouldn't do that, sir," the other man said, moving in close and shoving the barrel of a hand gun into his side.

"I'm Keith Duncan.....and I was only getting my

passport. Look, you've got the wrong man," he said holding up the false passport. The two big men looked at each other. Someone else was heading their way. Dennis had seen him climb out of the helicopter just after the black limo had arrived.

"Walk towards the car," the man holding the gun commanded, pushing the weapon even further into his midriff.

"Just walk towards the fucking motor," the other one hissed.

"Sorry guys," the third man interrupted, arriving on the scene. He pulled out a badge and held it up briefly. "M.I.5, narcotics division.....this one's ours. We've been waiting a long time for this." He quickly put the badge away, "Give him over lads, I'll take him from here," he said firmly. He was smaller than the dark-suited pair and had an American accent. The two big men stood their ground. Dennis didn't have a clue what was going on. He held on to the holdall as the drama unfolded.

"You guys, what....flying squad, customs, whatever. He's mine..........back off." He grabbed Dennis's other arm and frogmarched him towards the helicopter. The two burly men looked on perplexed, knowing their mission, under Angelo's specific instructions, had been thwarted, and to continue their abduction in such a public and security conscious place would be pointless.

"Get in, buddy," the man said. He was the helicopter pilot. Dennis had the chance to make a run for it but the two big men were still watching his every move.

"Or would you rather go for a ride with the Mantovani's gorillas over there?" he added. Dennis leapt into the small two seater helicopter.

"Who are you?" he asked.

"Who is that masked man?" the pilot replied as the rotor blades burst into life, "He's the Lone Ranger," he answered his own riddle. "Hi....ho Silver.....and away!" he exclaimed as the ex-American police helicopter lifted off the tarmac and soared into the air. Dennis held the holdall tightly in his lap and watched as the black limousine vacated the scene as quickly as it had arrived.

They flew over the jumbo jet and the main terminal building. Dennis looked back, dejection written all over his face as the British Airways aircraft he so desperately wanted to be aboard disappeared from sight.

"Hold on," the pilot said as the helicopter climbed sharply and banked, doing a complete acrobatic u-turn in the process. Dennis felt his stomach heave.

"Got to make it look good," is all the pilot said as the jumbo jet reappeared ahead. Dennis's despondency vanished in an instant. He remembered it was a helicopter which saved Tommy's life that Sunday morning at the Mill House Cafe, when everything seemed lost.

Seconds later they were back on the tarmac,

right next to the waiting aeroplane.

"Got your boarding pass? Have a safe trip buddy......wherever you're going," the pilot said, reaching across and offering Dennis his hand. Dennis shook it warmly. He could find no words that would do justice to the way he felt at that moment.

"Thanks," he said instead and climbed out of the tiny aircraft. He held the holdall tightly in his grasp and caught a glimpse of the mysterious pilot giving him a farewell wave through the tinted cockpit glass, before the machine took off, wheeled away and vanished in the dull, heavy skies.

He was the last passenger to board the massive plane and as it thundered down the runway and its nose lifted off terra firma, Dennis's freedom was guaranteed.

Chapter 22

The next few days held mixed emotions for Tommy. There was no news on Dennis, which on the one hand pleased him and gave him hope that his friend was okay and no harm had come to him. Yet he scoured the daily papers and watched the television news avidly fearing Dennis's body might be fished out of the Albert Canal or found dismembered in a skip somewhere.

He talked to Victor about it, having voiced his concerns when he found out Dennis was in trouble. He knew Victor had a soft spot for Dennis and under the surface really quite liked the mouthy, happy-go-lucky character. Victor would never admit to being fond of him though but he did trust him enough to firstly, employ him as a kid on his market stall, and then in his successful High Street music shop. Victor told Tommy he thought Dennis would be alright and was probably somewhere in the world keeping his head down for a while. Tommy wasn't so sure but Victor's sanguine words helped to allay his fears over Dennis's safety and whereabouts, and all he could do was wait and hope.

Emma was still staying with him in his penthouse flat. She was keen to go back to her own place but it had been ransacked on Angelo's instructions the very night Dennis was holed up in Victor's lock-up. The police had attended but as nobody was talking they had very little to go on. The landlord's insurance covered the damage and the maisonette was quickly made liveable again, but Tommy wouldn't let Emma go back there. He was adamant in his argument but didn't suggest *where* she should go. Boots was a half hour bus ride away and although Tommy's flat was luxurious and comfortable, she'd just got used to her independence and looking after herself in her own home. Tommy said he'd sort something out so she decided to give him a chance, bide her time, and wait and see how things went.

The events surrounding Steve Baker's unwanted newsworthy prominence had now subsided and Emma's consolatory words that the press would move on, the night they made love for the first time, had turned out to be spot on. A couple of weeks later they were out together in Barchester. Emma talked about the events involving Dennis and Steve chatted about his acceptance within the England team and the good news that he was in the squad for the forthcoming home internationals, and hoped to play a part in the first match against Wales in Cardiff.

After dancing the night away in a city centre nightclub they ended up in Steve's mansion house flat. It wasn't the first time she'd been there, or the first time they'd had sex there. But when Steve suggested she stay the night for the first time she was delighted and took no persuading whatsoever. Their lovemaking was exciting and prolonged and culminated in them both reaching lofty heights of sexual pleasure and satisfaction. Waking up in the morning in the same bed was again a new experience and signalled a further bout of energetic, erotic sexual intercourse before sharing yet another new experience, breakfast together.

"I love this flat," Emma said as she sat at the breakfast bar and looked up at the high Edwardian ceiling, with its ornate cornicing and plasterwork.

"I needed somewhere, near the stadium, where I could be myself. Mum and dad are fine, but.....but then you know all about that stuff."

Emma nodded, tucking into her toast and coffee Steve had rustled up.

Must find myself another place," she said, "Tommy's *so* good.....but I'm cramping his style....I know it."

"Has he got a girlfriend?" Steve asked.

"I don't know. Doesn't say much about that. His career's the most important thing in his life, and Victor , his manager. You know I've never met him. Tommy says he's strange and a lot of people don't get on with him, but Tommy seems to....funny that."

"Are you glad you stayed the night?" Steve suddenly asked, changing the subject. Emma smiled.

"Yes I am....really glad," she replied. She noticed his tousled, dark blond hair, his unassuming good looks. She was happy in his company yet she still doubted her own attractiveness and sexual desirability and even her own intellectual capacity.

"I like you a lot, Emma," he said, a little awkwardly. There was a brief silence. Emma thought he was about to ask her to move in with him.

"We get on well.....don't we?" He asked. Emma didn't answer. She was anticipating his next question and, more importantly, whether she was ready to move in with someone.

"You see...I don't want to spoil things, know what I mean?"

Again Emma remained silent. He took her hand and looked into her hazel eyes.

"Will you marry me Emma? There....I've said it now."

Emma almost fell off her stool in astonishment. She laughed, a short, stifled embarrassed laugh. It wasn't what she was expecting and needed to compose herself. Her confidence was sky high however and the moment was hers.

"Take me back to bed....and prove to me how much you want to marry me," she replied. Those were the most provocative and adventurous words she'd ever uttered. Steve duly obliged, his attention to detail in his subsequent lovemaking certainly giving her food for thought in seriously considering his marriage proposal.

Steve slept soundly for a while after his exertions and Emma snuggled up to him and thought about her options. He was young, handsome, rich and eligible and most importantly, she was in love with him and had been for some time.

There was no doubting her answer. The question was how long she should wait before telling him she would be delighted to become his wife. She decided just a few days would be long enough to keep him in suspense and prove she was no pushover. Any longer she thought would be both cruel and pointless. She waited until they were having lunch in a chic bistro a little later before telling him she needed time to think about his proposal. She wanted to gauge his reaction to determine whether he'd act like a spoilt child who couldn't get his way, or an unselfish, considerate and patient adult. Steve was naturally disappointed with her interim answer, but it didn't spoil either their lunch or their Sunday afternoon stroll along the Albert Canal, and in Emma's eyes, he'd passed her little test with flying colours.

Tommy's workload under Victor's demanding and sometimes strident regime was never ending and he found himself back in Chapel Studios putting vocal tracks down for his second album. His first was now selling well in the States and Victor was keen to flood the market on a worldwide basis to keep *Bobby Nelson's* name and products in the fore front of the music scene and to keep the substantial profits rolling in.

He was relaxing late one afternoon in the studio's lounge area after a particularly difficult session in front of the microphone when Angelo Mantovani walked in. He liked to keep a finger on the pulse of most of the Zanetti Corporation's subsidiaries and Chapel Studios was one of his favourites, and one he visited frequently. Angelo was rude and aggressive.

"I want a word with you, Nelson....in private," he said indicating Tommy should follow him into a side office. Tommy had a good idea it would be about Dennis and followed him in.

"Do you know how much your friend Carter fleeced me for?" Angelo said angrily. His words were music to Tommy's ears.

"He got away then?" Tommy said, smiling broadly.

"Got away?.....of course he fucking got away, and don't tell me you didn't know.....or didn't have *something* to do with it."

"Don't lay that one on me, pal," Tommy replied aggressively. Angelo was fuming.

"I'll tell you how much it was. three hundred grand.....but you know that."
Tommy didn't take the bait, "You must have pissed him off good and proper if it was that much."

"And he's made me look a right fool."

"As I said....I didn't know what he was up to."

"Come off it. His gambling....his debts.....the drugs.....Morocco?"

"All new to me," Tommy replied.

"And the helicopter stunt....."

"Helicopter?"

Angelo suddenly had Tommy's attention.

"A helicopter whisked him away....just when we had him. I've a good mind to hold you responsible."

"What, for the money he took?"

"Why not, someone's got to pay."

Tommy's hackles were rising fast. He'd heard enough. "Now you listen. I don't fucking care how bloody big and powerful you are, I will *never*, and I mean *never*.....be afraid of you, your halfwit brother, or your fucking organisation. When will you ever get that into your thick, bloody skull?" He walked out past the studio producer who'd come looking for him.

"I've had it for today," Tommy said to him, "Voice is shot.....see you in the morning."

"Yeah, that's fine, Bobby. No problem, good day's work," came the reply as Tommy left the studios.

It was good news all the way for the rest of the evening. Firstly, he met Victor in the wine bar they'd started to frequent near his flat. Victor caught him completely by surprise by handing him a cheque for mechanical and performance royalties for the initial sales of his first album. It was huge. Not as much as Dennis had stolen from the Mantovanis, but an amount that was beyond his wildest dreams. As he held the six figure cheque in his hand, and marvelled what he could do with it, Victor, as always, had more plans in the pipeline to keep the cash rolling in. This included tours of both Europe and America. But what pleased Tommy the most was Victor's intention of taking a full quota of backing musicians and singers on the tours, instead of him having to perform to backing tracks everywhere he went. That news, and a steady supply of quality red wine, eased his bad temper from earlier and he'd almost forgotten Emma was still staying with him when he eventually arrived home.

He was greeted by a wonderful aroma of rich, spicy food and welcoming ambient lighting when he got in the front door. Emma was relaxing on the sofa with a glass of white wine for company.

"Wondered what time you'd be back," she said as Tommy threw his jacket over an armchair.

"What's that smell?"

"Goulash......stuck it in the slow cooker this morning, before I went to work. Do you want some?"

"Oh yes.....I'm starving," Tommy replied with a big grin on his face. The goulash was superb, the beef tender and succulent. Tommy opened a bottle of red wine and offered some to Emma. She declined having her own white wine to savour.

"Red wine with red meat, Em," he said knowingly.

"We were both brought up in Felgate Road, Tommy. I'll stick with white," was her profound reply. After the meal they chilled out in the open plan sitting room. Tommy had half a bottle of red to get through and poured himself a large glass.

"Have you thought what you want to do, about where you want to live?" he asked Emma hesitantly, not wanting to sound like he was trying to get rid of her.

"Steve's asked me to marry him."

"What!....Jesus....break it gently why don't you,"

"I've been wondering how to tell you."

"You've certainly done that," he said, taking a large swig of wine.

"Well, what do you think?" Emma sounded apprehensive. She needn't have worried.

"Best news I've heard for ages."

"Do you mean that, Tommy?"

"Course I do. Steve's.....well.....he's the best guy in the world. You've said *yes* of course?"

"Not yet."

"Not yet? It's a no brainer, surely.....unless you know something I don't."

"No, he only asked me Sunday. I just needed a bit of time."

"Yeah, suppose you're right. But you're going to marry him?"

"I think so."

"Oh Emma , that's great news. What a turn up."

"I never knew he liked me so much."

"I'll let you into a little secret. Do you know when I was in hospital, Steve came to see me and he passed you in the corridor. He fancied you then....but I warned him off....you were only about fifteen. Don't say anything, mind. Big wedding I take it?"

"No idea.....but I never knew about Steve liking me back then. That's a complete surprise. Made my evening that, Tommy."

"Do you want a big do?"

"Not really. Just family and a few friends suits me. What about dad, do you think he'll give me away?"

"Come on Em, wild horses wouldn't stop him. He'll be chuffed......and mum too. No....it's great news....cheers," he lifted his glass to her.

"Oh thanks, Tommy. I just thought ....you might even be best man."

"If I get asked."

"Would you do it?"

"Yeah, 'course I would. When you going to tell Steve?"

"Soon," Emma replied, "Very soon."

Tommy sat back and rolled himself a joint. He had a big fat cheque in his pocket and his little sister was getting married to his lifelong friend. Life couldn't get much better than that, he thought.

Chapter 23

It was a crisp, sunny, autumn Sunday morning when the cream and black liveried vintage Rolls Royce arrived at All Saints Church in Southfields and for once in his life, Harry Nelson wasn't the chauffeur. He was the proud father of the bride and couldn't wait to walk his only daughter up the aisle on her special day.

Emma wore a fabulous pale primrose wedding dress and looked stunning as she entered the medieval church arm in arm with her dad. The church was full and all eyes were on her as the pair walked slowly towards the alter to the accompaniment of the rich, dignified sound of the pipe organ playing Mendelssohn's wedding march. Tommy was the only choice for Steve when it came to the best man and the two of them waited patiently, and nervously, for Emma to join them.

"Just a small do then, Em," Tommy whispered to her when she was stood next to them. He, as ever, was the joker and it brought a welcome smile to her face in the dignified surroundings as the rather solemn looking vicar got the wedding ceremony underway.

A short while later she walked back along the aisle as Mrs. Emma Baker, arm in arm with her new husband, Steve. The church bells were ringing out and all around was a sea of happy, smiling faces centred on the newly married couple. The Old Rectory in Dene Park was Steve's choice for the reception. The magnificent Jacobean hotel, surrounded by a lake and wonderful park-like gardens, had caught his eye when he and Emma were driving around the prestigious Dene Park private estate wistfully gazing up the drives of the fabulous homes there and hoping one day they might just own one of them.

It was the perfect setting for their wedding reception and although Emma would have settled for something less august and swanky, she was stepping into a new and glamorous life of a footballer's wife, whether she liked it or not. The occasion was also deemed socially important by the press and glossy magazine brigade who were there in considerable numbers, which wasn't surprising when the groom was an international footballer, the best man a pop star and virtually the whole of Barchester United's eminent team members were guests.

It was a proud day for both sets of parents, George and Mary Baker and Harry and June Nelson, but especially for George, who'd backed his son and given him every help and encouragement to fulfil his ambition as a top footballer, right from when he was a child. For obvious reasons, Harry Nelson was unable to deliver the customary bride's father's speech personally, but he'd prepared one on paper and Tommy read it out for him.

Tommy then had to say a few words as best man and couldn't resist an anecdote or two. He related the story of the race home from junior school that Friday afternoon when he and Steve were just eight years old. He said how a rather plump Steve had been handicapped by having to carry the school's pet hamster Goldie, in his cage, under his arm during the vital race between the two of them. Tommy won that race but for effect he embellished the yarn and told everyone Steve had powered past him on the home straight, subjecting Goldie to a near heart attack. He had everyone in stitches with his mannerisms and choice of language and it was hard for Steve to follow such a performance with his own groom's speech.

Emma had sent Victor an invitation to the wedding as he'd been pivotal in Tommy's rise to fame and also because she knew Tommy wouldn't want him to feel shunned or left out of the family celebrations being so much part of Tommy's life as he was. Victor replied to Emma saying he couldn't make it to the church, but would call in briefly at the reception. He did turn up at the Old Rectory but Tommy was disappointed he hadn't made the effort to really smarten himself up.

He was clean and tidy but still looked a little scruffy and out of place in the splendid surroundings, especially as he was wearing his trademark trilby hat. Tommy was embarrassed but he'd known Victor long enough not to be totally surprised and Victor was true to his word and didn't stay long. When Tommy introduced him to Emma she thought he looked vaguely familiar and although he was courteous and polite, she still thought him a bit strange.

The Barchester police were also represented at the reception, but only in the form of Sgt. Derek Dooley and his wife and daughter Carol who, being friends and neighbours of both the bride and groom, were invited guests. Tommy was completely taken aback when Carol Dooley came over to him and said hello. He didn't even recognise her. They'd been childhood sweethearts, but the tallish, blue-eyed eight year old with the short blond tom-boy haircut had changed into a slim, sexy looking, attractive young woman who's beauty took his breath away.

He was captivated by her and she knew it. their introductory small talk bordered on the embarrassing, and it was only when Emma intervened and suggested the two of them should get together, if only to talk about old times, that Tommy regained his composure and started acting like an adult again. They arranged their date there and then and the wedding reception celebrations continued with no further surprises.

Steve and Emma had discussed a honeymoon getaway and the Seychelles was top of Emma's list.

Steve's commitments within then club also had to be considered. The compromise was they'd stay the night in the Old Rectory and fly off to Paris for a few days in the morning. That way they'd have a honeymoon as such, and Steve would be back for the following Saturday's match, and the Seychelles would be pencilled in for the not too distant future.

The Old Rectory's sumptuous honeymoon suite in the ancient circular turret overlooking the lake was the perfect setting for the newlyweds to consummate their marriage which they did with passion, intensity and deep affection.

Chapter 24

As soon as the happy couple returned from Paris, Steve took his new bride back to Dene Park for some serious house hunting. His love affair with the esteemed and impressive private estate had increased and financially he was ready to buy there. Emma, on the other hand, was overjoyed moving into Steve's mansion house flat and was more than happy with life generally. For her, Dene Park was something wonderful for the future, but Steve set his heart on living there as soon as his football career started to gain momentum.

His dream was now a distinct possibility and although his substantial budget wouldn't get him the finest property there, he could certainly afford more modest, less expensive real estate, and if he took on a mortgage, his choice in Dene Park would stretch to something quite impressive. Steve's powerful TVR Vixen rumbled noisily through the wooded lanes and immaculately kept avenues as autumn cast its magic on the beautiful surroundings. Flaming red maples, rich yellow chestnuts and a myriad of distinct hues greeted the young couple as they drove to the property they were about to view, a Victorian family home on the fringes of the estate.

The dapper young negotiator from the estate agency was there to meet them.

"Welcome to Beechwood." he said shaking their hands, "And what a wicked car," he added enthusiastically. He was a Barchester Utd fan and certainly knew who Steve was. So much so, he found it hard to concentrate on showing the couple the house when all he really wanted to do was to talk football.

The detached four bedroomed Victorian home sold itself though. As its name suggested it was set amidst an area of beech woodland and was surrounded by its own large secluded gardens extending to an acre. The young negotiator pointed out it was private but not isolated, then showed them around the inside. It was full of charm and character and didn't disappoint in the slightest. They'd viewed another property with a different agent earlier but the art deco nineteen thirties styling did nothing for Steve. This one however, ticked all the boxes and he could certainly see himself living there with his new wife and hopefully, one day, a family of his own.

Emma was enchanted with the place. It was beyond her wildest dreams that she could ever aspire to live in such surroundings, but it was a fantasy that was about to come true.

"What do you think?" Steve asked her later having stopped at a country pub on their way back to Barchester. Emma sipped a glass of white wine whilst reading through 'Beechwood's' property details for the umpteenth time.

"It's wonderful Steve, just wonderful."

"Not too cut off?"

"No, it felt very safe....very homely. I'd have to learn to drive."

"Great place to bring up a family?"

Emma hadn't even thought about children. Everything in her life had changed for the better so quickly and dramatically she was finding it hard to keep her feet firmly on the ground.

"Could you live there," Steve continued, "I mean be happy there?"

"Oh yes. I'd still work though, for a time at least."

"Then we'll buy it, shall we?" Steve asked. Emma was lost for words.

"We'll buy it....make it our home....what do you say?"

" Yes Steve. Yes...yes...yes. I love it too."

*   *   *   *

Tommy chose Barchester ice skating rink for his date with Carol. Although it was a new experience for him he remembered she was lucky enough to be taken there by her parents when they were younger back at the Barton Bridge flats. Tommy was gripping on to the handrail at the side of the rink when Carol skated over, showering him with ice as she came to a sudden halt inches from him. She wasn't quite the proficient skater she'd been as a kid though and held on to Tommy for support, just in case her feet went from under her.

"This brings back memories, Tommy," she said as they both stepped off the ice onto the carpeted area around the rink. Tommy began to unlace his hired boots.

"These things are killing me," he said, pulling them off.

"I'll take you round later. See if we can get you away from the sides. You'll soon get the hang of it."
Tommy shrugged. Ice skating had never been top of his *must do* list but he chose this venue with Carol firmly in his mind.

"Wish you'd told me we were coming here....I would have dressed for it."

"Then it wouldn't be a surprise, would it?" Tommy was quick to reply.

It was chilly there, especially on the ice itself. But he was glad she was wearing a short skirt and a low cut top rather than the less alluring, but warmer, jeans and roll neck jumper she might have chosen had she known where they were going. They sat down. Carol was watching with interest all the different levels of skill on show out on the ice. Triple salko's and spins weren't Tommy's main concern. He was more interested in Carol.

"Funny I haven't seen you around," he said. Carol was mesmerised by one particular young girl who was gliding around the ice with consummate ease.

"Sorry, Tommy.....I was miles away. What did you say?"

"I said it's funny I've never seen you around."

"Work." she replied, "I'm away most of the time."

"What do you do?"

"Air stewardess....for B.O.A.C."

"Yeah? Wouldn't have you down as an air hostess."

"Air stewardess...*not* hostess."

"Sound a good job."

Carol loved her work and was only too happy to talk about it. "I enjoy it. Was in Singapore last week. Could be Los Angeles next.....or Barbados."

"Wow, what planes do you go in?"

Carol was in her element, "Boeing 747's mainly, jumbo jets to you, Tommy."

"I've been on a jumbo jet. Few weeks ago....to New York."

"Of course. Bobby Nelson's famous now. I forgot that, chatting here with you."

That remark was a breath of fresh air to Tommy, who was now acutely aware it was *who* he was that got most people's interest and not the real person behind the facade he and Victor had built to create the right image for his alter ego, *Bobby Nelson*. Carol continued with her passion for anything aeronautical.

"Nearly six hundred miles an hour we go in those aircraft. It never ceases to amaze me, Tommy, and five hundred passengers to look after. But I can't wait for Concorde to go into service. What a plane that is."

Tommy was happy to listen. There were still little mannerisms in both her body language and the way she spoke that had attracted him to her when he was a boy. He looked into her eyes as she talked enthusiastically about *her* career. He was relaxed in her company and didn't need to impress, and that made it easy for him to enjoy being with her.

"Have you got your own place now?" Tommy asked.

"No. Still with mum and dad at the flats. Dad's doing well, sergeant he is now, in Barchester. The place has changed though, it really has. Dad was pleased to get out of Southfields."

"Why?" Tommy asked, "I thought it suited him down to the ground."

"The trouble was he knew everyone, including the villains! And in the end it became a problem. He can do his job now and not be too personally involved.....if you know what I mean?"

Tommy knew exactly what Carol was saying and he lay the blame at the likes of the Mantovani brothers and other hoods who wanted to run the show and have the local constable just where they wanted him.

"Salt of the earth, your dad," he said.

"Trouble is, we still live there. It's not like when we grew up. Cor.....we had some laughs didn't we Tommy? Remember that time you and Steve threw wire onto the railway track. The flashes were awesome."

"How did you know about that.....and how did you know it was us?" Tommy was mortified. He was under the impression they'd got away with it.

"My dad knew it was you two, but you were kids. He understood that."

Tommy was almost speechless.

"What else do you know about me and Steve's antics back then?"

"Not saying," she teased. "Come on, put your skates back on and I'll take you out into the middle."

"Be gentle," he said, pulling on the uncomfortable boots once again, "Then we'll go to the bar....have a stiff drink. Somehow I think I'm going to need one," he laughed. Carol took his hand and Tommy was happy to let her take the initiative on this occasion.

*   *   *   *

Steve's offer for the purchase of 'Beechwood' in Dene Park was accepted by the vendors, and as a first time buyer the estate agency recommended the services of a local solicitor, Hill Associates, to carry out the conveyance. Their offices were based in nearby Southfields and the principal partner,

Quentin Hill, lived in an Edwardian house, also in Dene Park, so Steve decided to use them for the purchase. Life was going just as he planned. The added responsibility of marriage and home ownership he treated as stepping stones in his quest for a fulfilling and successful life. No one worked harder on the training ground and his desire to both further his club career and his international future, especially after his dismissal in Poland, had never been greater and he was slowly and surely developing into the complete player he'd set out to become.

Success and prominence at one of the country's leading clubs came with its problems however, and none of Barchester's players were immune from being caught up in trouble of one sort or another during their illustrious careers, and Steve was no exception. He, like many others across a wide spectrum of commercial business and entertainment, fell prey to the Mantovani twins. Their approach was very subtle. As directors of the football club he'd seen them around and one afternoon, just before he was leaving to join the England squad for the home international match in Cardiff, he was in the staff and players car park about to get into his car. He couldn't fail to notice the pink Cadillac parked nearby and the big man leaning nonchalantly against it.

"Steve....over here a minute." It was Freddie Mantovani and he had a big smile on his face. Steve duly went over. The last time he was confronted by Freddie was at the incident involving Tommy outside the flats some years before. It hadn't been a pleasant experience and as he approached he wondered if Freddie remembered him from back then.

"Off to Cardiff, eh?"

"Yes, it's going to be a tough one," Steve was polite and amiable.

"Well, I hope we stuff the Welsh. They hate us," Freddie said still grinning, "Look, we've got a match in a few weeks, home to Sandford. My brother Angelo wants to have a chat with you about that one. Anyway.....do your bit for England....and don't get sent off! Must go.....nice to chat with you."

He got into the Cadillac and left Steve standing there fuming. As a director of the club Steve thought his comment about him being sent off was totally uncalled for and unprofessional. Then he knew Freddie Mantovani had never remotely been interested in football and he put him firmly to the back of his mind.

*   *   *   *

Tommy saw Carol Dooley one more time before he set off on his tour of America. She'd just completed her long haul stint to Singapore and beyond and was keen to see Tommy again. He couldn't wait to spend time with her, either. It was a

Wednesday lunchtime and Tommy had planned a nostalgic afternoon and evening as a surprise for her. The Wimpy bar was their meeting place in Southfields High Street.

"This place hasn't changed for years," Tommy said as they sat down on the mock leather seating. The waitress put their coffees on the melamine table. Carol laughed, "Look, they've still got the pictures of the burgers and chips and the knickerbocker glories. What *are* we doing here, Tommy?"

"Magical mystery tour today," he said with a cheeky grin on his face.

"We eating here?" Carol asked.

"No Carol," Tommy laughed, "We'll have something later, okay?"

Carol nodded. Mixed grill in the Wimpy Bar wasn't her idea of a romantic dinner for two, which is what she hoped Tommy had planned.

"Anyway, how was Singapore?"

"Oh, it was fabulous. I've been there before. This time we went on to Melbourne, that's why the trip was longer than usual."

"Have you been there before.....Melbourne?"

"No, that wasn't on the original itinerary, it was a complete surprise. Nice and warm there. Late spring.....it was beautiful."

"I'm off to San Francisco, Friday."

"The big tour?"

"The biggest. I've got backing singers and my own band, with a stonking brass section, can you believe. Spending all day tomorrow with them.....final rehearsals and all that."

"What's it like, Tommy, walking out in front of all those people?"

"Scary.......really scary. I don't talk to anyone before I go on stage. I sort of psyche myself up, have my own little routine.....you know. But once I'm out there, boy.....is it an adrenalin rush. Then you go with the flow, hopefully. This time though, with all the live backing, I won't be on my own on stage. It should be fantastic."

"How long you away for?"

"Three weeks. Don't ask me where the gigs are. All I know is San Francisco, Los Angeles, a couple more down the west coast, then it's over to the east....New York and down there."

"How many?"

"Eight. Yeah...eight concerts and I'm back on the Don Lexton show before flying back."

"And your manager's arranged all that?" Carol asked, sipping her espresso coffee.

"Yeah, Victor. Don't know how he does it. He's more than just a manager really, more like a guru. To look at him you'd think he was a bank clerk or something pretty ordinary. And he's bit strange.....I tell everyone that....and he *looks* a bit weird as well. I wonder how he does it, to be honest."

"Is that the guy that runs the music shop along from here?"

"Yeah, how did you know that?"

"I saw you in there once. I knew you worked there."

"But you didn't come and say hi?"

"No.....I don't know why."

"Doesn't matter now, anyway," Tommy said, brushing it aside. The important thing was, he was with her *now* and he was determined to make the most of their time together.

"Right, you ready?" he asked, noticing quite a few glances and the odd stare from some of the other diners there. Carol was also aware they were becoming the centre of attention and was equally eager to leave. Tommy's Lotus Europa was parked discreetly around the back and they quickly made their way there.

"Don't know if I'd want people staring everywhere I go," Carol said as she squeezed into the passenger seat.

"One of the reasons I've got these tinted windows," he replied, pushing the starter button, "Goes with the job. I wouldn't have this motor if I didn't do what I do."

"I love this car, Tommy. But aren't you drawing attention to yourself by driving around in it?"
Tommy couldn't answer that one so he didn't even try. He knew she was right and put his foot on the accelerator pedal. They sped off in the direction of Dunsbury Park.

"I know where we're going," Carol said suddenly after they'd turned into Dunsbury

Avenue.

"We're going to the park....aren't we?"

"Thought it'd be nice to go back there," Tommy replied as they approached the wrought iron park gates. They drove into the car park passing the public toilets which were boarded up and no longer in use.

"This brings back memories," Carol said, peering through the Europa's tinted glass at the familiar museum and the refreshment kiosk next to it. The park looked a picture in the afternoon sunshine and the autumn colours all around were breathtaking in their splendour. Tommy took Carol's hand and they strolled off towards the boating lake.

"We're not going on a boat?" she asked sounding concerned. She was wearing a white mini dress and knee length white leather boots. Tommy looked at her. He thought she looked stunning.

"What....and get all your trendy gear messed up? No, not today....we're just going for a walk today.....and you're right, it brings back memories."

"Of us on our bikes...."

"And the ice cream parlour," Tommy added.
They sat down on a bench near the water's edge. There was hardly anyone around, and no rowing boats on the lake. A couple of moorhens were busy building a nest not far away and some mallard ducks were heading their way hoping for food.

"I've still got that bike," Carol said as Tommy

put his arm around her shoulder. She snuggled in to him.

"More than ten years ago now.....when we used to come here. I was madly in love with you," Tommy said, laughing.

"I know." came the instant reply, "You kissed me, over by the cemetery," she added.

Tommy's mind went back to when they'd played their little sex game and she'd seen his penis. He remembered it was a hot summer's day and they lay in the long grass together. Carol was also thinking of the same encounter in their halcyon, childish days. But they both felt uneasy about bringing the subject up and talking about it, especially as their relationship at this time was just blossoming. The moment passed.

"I remember you fancied Steve really, not me."

"No....that's not true. Anyway, everybody fancied Steve. He was just....fanciable. Now he's married to your little sister."

"Yeah, he's my brother-in-law. Funny how things turn out."

"That's right. And I'm glad we've met up again," Carol said taking his hand and stroking it. That gave Tommy the ideal opportunity to kiss her and he took it. Carol responded and what started out as a hesitant, slightly nervous gesture turned into a prolonged, passionate kiss fuelled by lust and desire.

Nothing was said afterwards, they were content

just to cherish the moment sitting in the park where they'd shared such fond and happy memories. Later they drove into Barchester and had a meal in the new Japanese tepanyaki restaurant, the Samisen. Tommy couldn't wait to try it out but it wasn't quite Carol's idea of a romantic, candlelit dinner for two, then she realised she should have expected that from Tommy, who she knew had never been an average sort of guy and was unconventional in many ways. The Japanese cuisine was fresh and delicious and was cooked in front of them in a flamboyant show of leaping flames and juggling utensils. It was the most entertaining meal she'd ever had and apart from the sushi starter which Tommy loved but didn't appeal to her, she enjoyed the experience immensely.

They ended up in Tommy's penthouse apartment. Carol was lost for words. The modernistic, open plan layout, the innovative simplicity and understated opulence, and the fabulous views over the city left her spellbound and open mouthed. She was starting to realise just how big a star Tommy was becoming and in a way it scared her and it made her wonder if she was out of her depth. Yet Tommy hadn't changed as far as she could see. His infectious enthusiasm for life was just the same and his rebellious nature was still apparent. Even his chat and witty remarks were still there. What had she to fear? she thought, before they ended up in bed.

There was no disappointment there either, for both of them. Tommy had it in mind to be the perfect gentleman and seduce Carol in the way he thought she might expect. But he hadn't bargained on her fervent sexual desire and their lovemaking was something he'd never experienced before. Her femininity never wavered but her intense passion and emotion took him completely by surprise.

For her part, she found Tommy just as unconventional between the sheets as in everyday life. His sheer enthusiasm and eagerness to please ensured her sexual pleasure was guaranteed, and that gave her even more incentive to bring Tommy to a height of gratification and fulfilment she hoped he'd never experienced before. It was late when he drove her back to Southfields and he knew a busy day lay ahead in the company of his band and backing singers in readiness for the most testing and possibly the most important three weeks of his life.

*　　　*　　　*　　　*

Thoughts of Carol kept him inwardly smiling on the long flight to San Francisco and he couldn't wait to feel her naked body next to his when he got back. But for the next three weeks he was superstar *Bobby Nelson* and he had a job to do.

The tour was fantastic. Big venues, huge audiences and a fabulous sound created by the travelling musicians and singers and *Bobby Nelson* delivered like he'd never done before. His voice was superb, his focus and mindset impeccable and the Americans lapped it up. The unmitigated west coast success was equalled by the concerts in New York and the east and *Bobby Nelson's* performances never once fell short of his own demanding standards. His relationship with the band grew and by the final concert in the Roosevelt Hall, Boston, a professional trust had grown between them all, which only enhanced an already successful show. The icing on the cake was appearing as Don Lexton's main guest on national television. He didn't even need to sing, just chat with the host about his phenomenal rise to fame, and his forthcoming second album, which Victor had stipulated in no uncertain terms that he *must* plug when he appeared on the show.

Filmed clips of the Los Angeles concert were shown at the end of the interview and his second appearance on the programme was again a triumph for *Bobby Nelson*, and he flew back to Britain the following day realising his three week tour of the States *had* proved to be momentous in his life and with thoughts of seeing Carol again firmly in his mind.

Chapter 25

Moving in day arrived for Steve and Emma while Tommy was on tour and they became the proud owners of 'Beechwood' in Dene Park. It was a dream come true for Steve, but the home internationals were approaching and he didn't have the time to fully appreciate his splendid new house or revel in the satisfaction of realising his ambition of one day living in Dene Park.

Emma was the more down to earth of the two and took control of the mundane aspects of the move, liaising with their solicitor, Hill Associates, so that completion day would present few problems. There was no removal van to book, because they had no furniture. Steve's mansion house flat was rented furnished, so the large Victorian house was empty the morning they took possession, and it was down to Emma to buy a simple camping bed and a few other essential items to start them off.

They had one visitor later that morning they weren't expecting. A shiny, burgundy Bentley swept up their drive and a smartly dressed man greeted them.

"I'm your neighbour, heard you'd bought the place." It was James Slade. He was carrying a bottle of champagne. Emma immediately recognised him as the owner of the Blue Boar, who'd introduced himself when she and Steve were there watching Tommy's television appearance.

"Yes, the pub landlord," she replied. The millionaire entrepreneur laughed.

"Yes, you could say that. Said we'd meet again though. Now we're neighbours."

Steve looked on. He remembered the sarcastic comment James Slade made that evening about his misdemeanour on the football field in Poland.

"Just brought you this.....to welcome you to our little community." He handed Emma the bottle, "Moet et Chandon's Dom Perignon........the best. I drink nothing else."

"We'll enjoy that Mr......?"

"Slade......James Slade. And remember, I'm only next door.....over there somewhere," and he pointed across their garden and the wooded copse beyond, then he got back in his Bentley and drove off.

"I still reckon he's a bit strange," Steve said, watching the luxury car making its way sedately down their driveway.

"Nice gesture though," Emma added, grasping the bottle of bubbly to her bosom.

Emma was also determined to continue working at Boots in Southfields and took the opportunity of a week's holiday so she could meet the initial demands of their new home and bring some semblance of normality back into their lives. She also considered cycling to work but Steve thought that a bit drastic. He was more interested in checking out Dene Park Golf Club nearby. He'd never actually played the game but he'd chatted to his solicitor, Quentin Hill, who was a member and he said he would sponsor Steve to get him into the exclusive golf club which would enable him to bypass the usual formality and uncertainty of joining a lengthy waiting list. Steve was keen to become part of the affluent community and he felt joining the golf club was the first logical step, and eagerly accepted Quentin Hill's proposition.

Emma didn't mind being the more practical of the partnership. Even as kids she could remember Steve having trouble with mundane tasks like repairing a puncture on his bike and invariably Tommy would come to the rescue to get the job done. She realised that was all part of his character and make up, and now they were married, she wanted to pull her weight and do her share and not be labelled a mere bimbo by the popular press, who used that terminology frequently when referring to the wives of high profile and highly paid footballers. She hoped to get the balance right so their married life would continue in the direction she wanted it to go, and she'd use all her feminine charms and acumen to that end.

* * * *

There was a postcard from Dennis waiting in

the mailbox at Tommy's apartment on his return from America. He took it to show Victor when he met him on his first day back, to brief him about the tour. Their meeting place, as usual, when Victor wanted to discuss anything in complete privacy, was the back seat of his Ford Zodiac. It irritated Tommy every time they met in such a confined, and what Tommy considered, a ridiculous setting to conduct business, but he wasn't going to let his exasperation show on such a triumphant day.

"Listen to this," he said, holding up the postcard.

"Hi Tommy. I'm fine. I'm rich. Working on my tan. Sent a card to you know who. Wish you were here. All the best. Denny. p.s. Saved by the lone ranger xx"

"Isn't that fucking marvellous, Victor. Don't get the Lone Ranger bit though." He turned the postcard over, "Acapulco beach, Mexico.....fantastic," He grinned.
Victor smiled, "I'm glad he's alive and well," he said refraining from swearing on this occasion. Tommy wondered how long it would last.

"Do you know how much he got away with?"

"I've a fucking good idea," Victor replied.

"Angelo collared me at the studios, like it was my fault. Told me it was three hundred grand. Imagine that. Bet Denny's in seventh heaven."

"He's very lucky," is all Victor added.

"I'm not going back to those studios, Victor, not with *him* running the show. I don't care how good they are. Find another one, would you.....please?"

Victor nodded, "Leave it with me. Now, let's discuss this tour of yours."

As Tommy recounted the highlights of his last three weeks, and there were many, Victor couldn't help but notice his exuberance was far greater than he'd ever seen before.

"Just wait 'til we reap the benefits of your little jaunt across the ocean," Victor said after patiently hanging on Tommy's every word. "This calls for a celebration, a fucking good *do*," he continued. Tommy was all ears.

"This Friday night.....you name the venue, Tommy."

"Velvet Club, and I thought you were calling me *Bobby* from now on?"

"What, that dump? No, somewhere in Barchester......and I'll call you what I fucking like."

"How about the Starlight?"

"Are you winding me up?"

Tommy suddenly realised both those night spots were owned by James Slade. He shook his head.

"It'll have to be the wine bar then," Victor said. His suggestion didn't surprise Tommy.

"Small place for a big *do*, Victor, surely there's somewhere else?"

Victor felt comfortable in smaller, less garish places where his privacy wouldn't be compromised.

"Who you going to invite?" Tommy asked. This was another question he knew he wouldn't get a straight answer to. He was also well aware Victor shunned the limelight.

"You ask me all these difficult fucking questions, Tommy."

Tommy couldn't help laughing. "It's going to be just you and me.....isn't it?"

Victor thought for a few seconds. "We can invite your sister Emma, and her new husband. I got on okay with them at the wedding."

"Yeah, I suppose so. And I've met someone I can bring along...."

"I didn't know you'd met someone."

"You don't know everything, Victor Slade. Mind you.....sometimes I think you do. No...her name's Carol. I can bring her...surely?"

"Can't see why not."

"That's five then," Tommy said knowing Victor would settle for that figure.

"Just right. We'll celebrate your fabulous, fucking tour then."

Their meeting went on for a while after that as Victor wanted to know every little detail about the trip before Tommy eventually excused himself needing desperately to have a pee.

Come Friday evening there was only four at Victor's soiree at the wine bar. Steve had left that morning to join the England squad in readiness for their match against Wales on the Saturday. Emma thought about not going and spoke to Tommy about it on the telephone, but he persuaded her she should get out and enjoy herself whether Steve was there or not. She got dressed up for the evening and booked a minicab to take her there, and bring her home at the end of Victor's little gathering.

It was a strange sort of party, starting as a low key affair which suited Victor's desire for anonymity but rather defeated his original intention to celebrate Tommy's success in America in a big way. As Tommy feared, the wine bar wasn't quite the right place. There was nothing wrong with the atmosphere, he just thought it lacked sparkle and the *joie de vivre* the occasion deserved, although he couldn't quite figure out why it didn't work for him. Carol, having met Victor for the first time, found him odd. His dress, his rough and ready outward persona, even his gravelly voice grated on her ears. But then he'd made Tommy a star and she couldn't fault his credentials on that score, and just like Tommy had done, she accepted him as *Bobby Nelson's* eccentric mentor.

Emma seemed the happiest of the four. She'd made the effort to look good and oozed radiance as a newlywed and someone who was happy with life. She'd known Carol from childhood, growing up in the Barton Bridge flats together. But they were never close friends although their respective families were. She was intrigued to hear how Carol had broken free from the shackles of a council flat upbringing and got herself an exciting and worthwhile occupation seeing the world within the aircraft industry, yet still lived at home in that council block. Carol told her it wouldn't be for much longer and Emma respected her for what she'd achieved and, not surprisingly, they got on well.

Much to Tommy's surprise, the evening was going better than he expected and Victor hadn't sworn once. As the alcohol flowed, so did the conversation, ranging from Victor's plans for *Bobby Nelson's* worldwide success to Emma's hopes and dreams that Steve's amazing rise to fame as a footballer would reach even new heights in the future. Tommy was happy for those around him to do the talking for once and for him not to be the centre of attention, and was content to chill out in the company of his personal manager, his sister, and the new love in his life, Carol Dooley.

Later on Victor ordered a bottle of Dom Perignon champagne for a celebratory toast to Tommy's triumphant tour of America, which was a fitting high point to the evening's get together. Not long after, Tommy noticed Emma looked a bit pale and withdrawn.

"You alright Em?" he asked.

"She doesn't look too well," Carol observed, "Thought she'd gone a bit quiet," she added.

"I'm f.....fine.....just feel a bit woozy," Emma replied, trying to put a brave face on her sudden malaise. Victor looked on. He didn't say a word.

"What time's your cab coming?" Tommy asked, putting a comforting arm around her shoulder. Emma's head dropped onto her chest.

"Not 'til twelve," she said, slurring her words. It had not long passed eleven.

"We need to get her out of here.....before she passes out," Tommy said, the concern in his voice was obvious.

"We can't wait for the minicab," Carol said.

"And my car's not suitable," Tommy cut in.

"I'll take her home," Victor spoke at last, "I've got the Zodiac outside. She'll be comfortable in that."

"You sure, Victor......you've had a few yourself?" Tommy said. He was pleased Victor had come to the rescue but was anxious about his ability to get Emma home safely considering the amount he'd drunk.

"I'll do it," Victor said.

"Come on, Em....we'll get you home," Tommy said helping her to her feet. It was obvious she couldn't walk so Tommy and Victor carried her outside to Victor's car.

"On the back seat," Victor said and they lay her down in the back of the Zodiac. Tommy could see she'd now passed out.

"Get her home safely, Victor.....I'm counting on you."

Victor said nothing and Tommy watched as the black Ford accelerated away. Victor didn't take

Emma directly home. He never intended to. He turned off the brightly lit city streets and headed towards the industrial estate. All around it was dark and deserted. Victor looked over his shoulder. Emma hadn't stirred. She was completely out of it.

The car park at Trevett's lock, on the Albert Canal, was his destination. It was a lonely, remote place that time of night, but that didn't unsettle Victor. He was on a mission and that dark and shadowy secluded spot suited his needs perfectly.

He wasted no time in joining Emma in the back of the car. She was oblivious to what was about to happen, which was exactly what Victor had planned. He'd secretly dropped a Ketamine sleeping pill into her glass of bubbly and her comatose state was assured once she'd drunk it.

Victor gently manoeuvred her into position, lifted her skirt and took down her knickers. Uncomfortable as it was on the back seat of his car, he unzipped his trousers and raped her there and then. There was no roughness, no severity. The act of sexual intercourse was neither relentless or merciless on his part and copulation was completed to his satisfaction within minutes.

He'd achieved what he'd intended and after pulling up Emma's underwear and rearranging her skirt, he was back in the driving seat and heading towards Southfields and Dene Park. He found the front door key to 'Beechwood' in Emma's handbag. He carried her in and up the stairs where he found the makeshift camp bed. He was fully aware of the medical properties of the strong Ketamine drug and knew he could leave Emma to sleep soundly under the influence of the medication, knowing there would be no side effects and she'd remember nothing when she came round. He laid her gently onto the bed, covered her with a duvet, and left.

Chapter 26

Saturday was the day of the big match, Wales versus England from Cardiff. Emma had already invited Tommy round to 'Beechwood' to watch it on their brand new TV set and have lunch beforehand. She knew he sometimes neglected his food intake and having lived with him for a short time after he'd insisted she vacated the maisonette in Southfields, she had firsthand experience of his *'eat when hungry'* philosophy. But then he'd always been a bit thin and scrawny looking, especially as a child, and his life had always been disorganised, so she knew he wasn't about to change his habits as far as his diet was concerned. She could also see he was fit, healthy and full of nervous energy and had no intention of interfering in his metabolism, or indeed, his life in any way.

She'd prepared one of his favourites for lunch, pepperoni pizza and salad, with the main event of the day, and with Steve hopefully playing a major role, to follow. After the episode in the wine bar the previous evening, Tommy was keen to make sure his sister was alright and his concern was still apparent when he arrived.

"Jees, you were in a state last night.....never seen you like that before," he said as soon as she greeted him at the front door.

"Must have been the bubbly," Emma replied, intent on shrugging off the inquisition she knew would follow.

"On top of all the other booze," Tommy quipped.

"I'm fine now though. Bit of a hangover, that's all," She replied, intent on steering the conversation away from what she believed to be her over indulgence the night before. "Anyway, got your favourite for lunch.....pizza," She said leading the way towards the kitchen. Tommy hadn't quite finished on the subject though.

"I was worried about Victor. No mishaps on the way home?"

"Don't remember."

"And another thing, how did he know where you lived?"

"How should I know. Now can we drop last night....please?"

"Sure, let's have some grub."
The pepperoni pizza went down a treat.

"Can't stay too long after the match......meeting Carol."

"Whirlwind romance, Tommy. You sure you're ready, with your career and everything?"

"Look who's talking,"

"Me and Steve are different. But yeah, I get your point."

"I'm *not* Bobby Nelson, Em. That's all an act. I'm

the same guy that grew up with people like Carol Dooley. I'm still a bit rough and ready. Always will be probably, whatever social circles I mix with. Steve's lucky, with grammar school and all that.....apart from having you as his wife," he laughed, realising he was getting too serious.

"He's who he is, Steve Baker. He hasn't had to pretend to be someone else to play football. Do you get my gist?"

"Yes, of course I do."

"Then you'll understand why I've no intention of getting hitched to a politician's daughter or someone like that....in high society."

"Hitched?" Emma exclaimed, "You getting married?"

"No...it was just the first word that came to me."

"But you're not ruling it out?"

"I'm not, Em. You know exactly what you get with Carol, and I tell you I get a real buzz when I'm with her."

"Yes, I can see that. I just want you to be as happy as me and Steve are."

"Yeah, thanks Em." It was Tommy who now wanted to change the subject.

"What do you think if I buy mum and dad a little place, away from Felgate Road?"

"Oh Tommy, be careful there. Dad's a real socialist. He'd stay there even if he hated it, principles and all that."

"But surely, if your son's successful, and wants

to spend money on you, that's different isn't it?"

"*We* know it is. But dad's from another generation. He won't accept charity, and I know this wouldn't be charity....you buying them a place, but in his mind it might seem to be. Oh, I don't know. Mum would go for it....she'd love it, but be careful with dad, that's all I'm saying."

"Yeah, I see what you mean."

"Do you want more salad?" Emma asked.

"I'll have more pizza," came Tommy's quick reply.

"Oh, I forgot to say, you'll never guess who our next door neighbour is?" Emma said. Tommy's mouth was full of pizza. "James Slade," she added. Tommy almost choked on his food.

"You having me on?"

"No, he drove up in his Bentley...bold as brass."

"How do *you* know him?"

"We met him at the Blue Boar, when we were watching you on TV. He came over and had a chat....he recognised Steve."

"Chat about what?"

"About you really. How you played there and all that. I also said I was your sister."

"Oh you didn't? Him and Victor don't get on. They're like chalk and cheese. I'd keep my distance if I were you. There's a hell of a lot of jealousy there. Be very careful what you say to the man. And tell Steve the same, yeah?"

Emma nodded. "I forgot he was Victor's brother,

anyway, almost time for the match," she said. "You go and turn the telly on and I'll clear this lot."

Kitchen chores were Tommy's pet hate and he made his escape to the living room in double quick time. The game from Cardiff was a fiercely contested affair and Steve was in the starting line up. He was too good for his Polish experience to hold him back and the England coaching staff realised that. He repaid their belief and confidence in his ability by scoring a terrific towering header from a corner which gave England the lead at half time.

Tommy and Emma's celebrations around the television set almost mirrored Steve's as he jumped up and down punching the air after he scored. He played well as a target man and kept the Welsh defenders busy, which resulted in their attacking prowess being limited. Steve also played his part in the second goal, laying on a lovely reverse pass to a team mate who coolly side footed it past the Welsh goalie. That second goal secured a deserved victory for England and gave the jubilant, travelling English fans plenty to celebrate.

*   *   *   *

It was a few days later when Angelo Mantovani caught up with Steve in the Barchester Stadium car park. This time Freddie's pink Cadillac was parked right next to Steve's TVR. Freddie approached Steve before he even got to his car.

"You can spare a few minutes, can't you, Steve?" he said, leading him to the Cadillac. He opened the rear passenger door. Angelo was sitting in the back.

"Jump in," Angelo said to him. Steve obliged and joined him in the back. Angelo waited until they were amongst the busy city traffic before continuing the conversation.

"As you know, we're home to Sandford in a couple of weeks, and you're one of our most influential players. The thing is, statistically, we're due to lose a home match." Angelo paused for a few seconds. Steve glanced at him. He didn't like what was being said.

"I'll get straight to the point, Steve. Our syndicate's had, let's say, a wager on the game, and we need you to......steer, I think that's the right word. Yes....steer the contest in our favour."

Steve could see Freddie's eyes watching him in the driver's rear view mirror.

"To be blunt, Barchester have to lose that match. We're going to win the league anyway, so one poor result's neither here nor there."

"What do you want me to do?" Steve asked, purposely sounding naive, but still taking in every word Angelo said.

"Do I have to spell it out?" Angelo replied.

"Quite frankly, I think you'd better." Steve said. Angelo stared out of the window at the passing traffic.

"One......you're in a position to score. You miss. Two......if you need to, you give away a penalty in the last few minutes. Is that clear enough?" Angelo was starting to lose patience. "There's a big bonus in it for you.....go towards your new home in the hills."

"And what if I don't want to do it?" Steve said tentatively.

"Ah, I think you'll do it. I think you'll do it for your new wife's sake.....for Emma's sake. Such a pretty girl.....and such a pretty face."

Steve tried to think what Tommy would say and do in the same situation. But he wasn't Tommy. He was scared. He knew these people meant business, and threats against his Emma terrified him. There was nothing he *could* say. Freddie drove them back to the stadium car park.

"You played a blinder on Saturday. Said we'd stuff the Welsh, didn't I?" Freddie said as he played the dutiful chauffeur and opened Steve's passenger door.

"Do the right thing, Steve," Angelo pressed home the point before the pink Cadillac drove off.

Over the next couple of weeks Steve tried not to think about the dilemma that lay ahead. His new home and recent marriage combined with his tough training schedule and his commitments to Barchester Utd. Football club, those were the things on his mind, not a couple of gangsters trying to fix a match. Those were his thoughts as he went about his daily life during that period.

He and Emma were settling into 'Beechwood' and one evening their conversation turned to the fact that it *was* a beautiful family home and perhaps they should think about starting a family. Steve instigated the conversation and they discussed it over a bottle of wine.

"I didn't think you were that bothered about having children," Emma said as they curled up on their new sofa together.

"Well, all this has made me think again. maybe I'm ready after all." he replied.

"You know my views, darling," Emma said snuggling up even closer, "We love each other, everything's going for us.....and what a great place to bring up a family," she added.

"Thought you wanted to carry on working,"

"I've been thinking about that. Knee jerk reaction I suppose that was, thinking my independence was at risk....and we'd just got married. And I was comparing me to my mum, and all she's been through raising a family. Silly really."

"So you'd be okay with a baby, and running the home?"

"Not really a hardship, is it ,Steve? I think we should. What do you think?"

"Yes, I see nothing wrong in planning for the future. Be strange though.... having a baby around. Do you think we'll cope.....not too young?"

"We'll be fine," Emma reassured him.
Steve chuckled, "Shall we start straight away then?"

Emma nodded and they finished the wine upstairs in their bedroom.

Steve toyed with the idea of telling someone about Angelo's latest money making scheme. He could have gone to his boss Jock McFadden, or even confided in Tommy. But he found the consequences too risky to seriously consider those options, and Angelo's threats regarding Emma had been made crystal clear that afternoon in the back of Freddie's Cadillac. He was resolved to deal with both the situation and the consequences himself, and carried on with his daily routine the best he could.

Match day against Sandford Rangers arrived quicker than he expected and even as he sat in the changing room Angelo Mantovani was dominating his thoughts. His glib remark about it being a foregone conclusion Barchester would win the league, even though the season was still in its infancy, was testament to the fact he, along with his brother, knew nothing about the game of football.

The ground was full, the crowd were expecting goals and Steve took to the pitch knowing on one hand he had a job to do, and on the other he had the safety of not only himself, but also the woman he loved weighing heavily on his conscience. The test was massive and after only ten minutes he had the opportunity to score the opening goal. The ball somehow arrived at his feet inside the six yard box and he only had the goalkeeper to beat. That split second was the most important in his life. Angelo and Freddie looked on with baited breath cosseted in their glass fronted, air conditioned director's box along with the other forty thousand fanatical Barchester fans inside the stadium.

The goalie rushed out. Steve tucked the ball into the corner of the net. The crowd went wild. One nil flashed up on the giant scoreboard. Angelo and Freddie sunk down into their plush seats. Steve couldn't do it. He couldn't throw a football match. He could never have lived with himself if he'd poked the ball past the post and missed. Whatever the consequences, he wasn't going to be intimidated or bullied by anyone, including gangsters, however powerful and violent they may be.

The prediction by most, of a heavy win for the home side against struggling opposition, didn't materialise however, and Sandford equalised just before half time. The second half was all Barchester but they couldn't score. Sandford *had* to win to satisfy the Mantovanis and their gambling syndicate and there were millions of pounds at stake.

The twins were on their feet waiting for Steve to concede the penalty that would guarantee their huge pay day. What happened next though, wasn't in their script. Instead, Barchester were awarded one when a Sandford defender handled the ball in his own penalty area. Steve pretended to go down with cramp. He was now the regular penalty taker for the team, and for obvious reasons, didn't want to take this one. His ploy didn't work though and the team captain handed him the ball after he'd received treatment for his non-existent condition.

He stepped up to take the spot kick and side footed it to the keeper's right. *He* dived to the left. Again the crowd roared and two goals to one flashed up on the scoreboard. He'd scored both goals and the big match rigging scam was in tatters. With just minutes to go Sandford made a surprising substitution. Instead of bringing on an attacker to salvage something from the game, they introduced a burly, defensive centre half. The reason why became obvious shortly afterwards.

Steve received the ball on the halfway line. He saw the challenge coming in from the opposition's new substitute, but he could do nothing about it. He was clattered by a thunderous, sickening sliding tackle just below the knee. He went down screaming. His leg was broken. Angelo and Freddie left the director's box as the trainer rushed on. The referee immediately gave the centre half his marching orders and he couldn't get off the pitch quick enough. Tears of pain rolled down Steve's cheeks as he was stretchered off amidst rapturous applause from the sympathetic and appreciative fans. The crowd of forty thousand then went silent and the siren of the ambulance could be heard by everyone as it whisked him away to Barchester General's accident and emergency department.

Chapter 27

After a three hour operation Steve's fractured tibia was pinned back into place and put in a plaster cast, and it was after ten o'clock when he was brought to the ward. His mum and dad were there, as was Emma and Tommy. The mood was sombre and downcast and Steve, having just come round from the anaesthetic, looked a sorry sight that evening. There was little anyone could say to lift him. Tommy tried his best but it was a futile effort.

To make matters worse, the place was inundated by the press, all vying to be the first to glean any sort of news. It was fortunate the surgeon made an appearance after he'd spoken to Steve's family and gave them enough information to send them scurrying away from the building. Retribution from Angelo Mantovani for Steve's disregard for his ultimatum had been swift and decisive, and the big question was, would he ever play football again?

No one, not even his surgeon, knew the answer to that question. Only time would tell, and Steve's inner strength and motivation to succeed plus, of course, the physical ability to do so. Emma stayed at his bedside that night. It was a mostly silent vigil with intravenous painkillers keeping Steve drifting in and out of consciousness throughout those difficult hours.

Jock McFadden and the whole Barchester team turned up *en-masse* later on the Sunday and it was touch and go whether the nursing staff would allow their visit. It was Emma who persuaded them Steve's morale desperately needed a lift and pandemonium reigned for a short time when their presence, albeit briefly, was sanctioned by the duty doctor. The press were milling around once again but Steve was oblivious to them and both welcomed and appreciated the club's support. To put on an outward show of anything approaching enthusiasm was extremely tough for him though, and Emma could see the deep down heartbreak in his eyes as he accepted his team mates condolences and best wishes for a speedy recovery, and she knew there would be problematic and testing times ahead.

The other major worry Steve faced was whether his punishment was deemed severe enough by the Mantovanis for the huge wager they'd lost, or whether their threats regarding Emma would come to anything, and until the initial trauma of his injuries and surroundings had passed, that was something which hadn't even crossed his mind. Late on Sunday evening he persuaded Emma that *she* needed rest also and she went home to 'Beechwood' shattered, both physically and mentally.

The incident brought home to Tommy the ability to enjoy life was a fragile commodity and one to be grasped and savoured at every opportunity, and he was determined not to waste his efforts and good fortune if he possibly could. This made his new found romance with Carol even more pivotal to his overall happiness and enjoyment of life and he met up with her at every opportunity he could.

She'd been away on a series of long haul flights to the southern hemisphere when Steve received his injuries and Tommy explained all to her over dinner at his place once she'd returned.

"That was a great meal, Carol," he enthused refilling their glasses with red wine.

"You should be cooking *our* dinner. I'm the one who's been slogging my guts out this past week."

"I can't cook.....you know that."

"Good excuse, Tommy."

He knew when she was joking but Steve's predicament wasn't the only serious topic he wanted to discuss. He waited until they were comfortably relaxed on the sofa before he broached the tricky subject he had on his mind.

"I'm so useless when it comes to saying how I feel. I can get up in front of thousands and think nothing of it."

Carol listened but said nothing.

"I can rave over a Norton Manx, or a Fender Strat, but the words dry up sitting here with you."

He paused, sipping his wine. "I'm in love with you Carol.....have been since I was ten. Move in with me....here in the apartment. I think we'd be great together."

"Are you asking me to marry you?"

"Well.....no..."

"No?...You cheeky monkey, Tommy Nelson."

"I just knew it would go wrong." Tommy sighed. Carol relieved him of his glass of wine, climbed all over him and gave him a big kiss.

"You're so cute when you're gullible," she giggled, "Of course I'll move in......been waiting for you to ask."

"You're not just saying that to get away from Felgate Road?" Tommy's confidence was quickly returning.

"Yeah....it's the swanky apartment, the stunning views over the city.....that's the draw."

"Thought so," Tommy replied pulling her to him. They made love there and then on the sofa. Then Tommy carried her into the bedroom and they did it again. Afterwards they languished in each other's arms, both sexually exhausted.

"When you moving in then?" Tommy asked. He was feeling a lot more self assured.

"The weekend?" Carol intimated.

"Yeah, the weekend. Like to be a fly on the wall when you tell your dad."

"You've got him all wrong, Tommy. He respects and admires you, although he'd never say that to your face."

"You *are* going to tell him?"

"I am. He'll be happy for me....I know it."

"What a great evening," Tommy said, letting his

hand caress her soft breasts. "And about the marriage thing, we can see how it goes.....yeah?"

"I'm not desperate to get married."

"I thought that. I can see that....the way you've stood on your own two feet and made something of your life."

"We're very similar, I think. Two peas in a pod," she replied stroking his chest. She was happy to stay the night and share the huge sumptuous bed with the man who'd just pledged his love for her, and they both slept soundly.

Tommy met Victor the following lunchtime in the city centre wine bar that had become Victor's favourite meeting place, almost taking precedence over his back seat office in the Zodiac. Their conversation was a lengthy one on Victor's proposed tour of Europe for Tommy. The band and backing singers had been kept on and Victor was keen to keep *Bobby Nelson* in the forefront of the music industry and, more importantly, to ensure the fortune he was making would continue for the foreseeable future.

The major points of discussion were the length of the tour and the number of countries involved. Victor, as usual, wanted to cram as many concerts in as many countries as humanly possible and in the end, compromise was reached and both he and Tommy were happy with the outcome. Tommy normally didn't stay in Victor's company once business matters had been dealt with but he had time to kill before an afternoon visit at the hospital to see Steve, and he accepted Victor's offer of a glass of wine and a roast beef sandwich.

"Carol's moving in with me," Tommy said, realising he'd have to tell him sometime and there was no time like the present.

"Is that wise.....with your career and everything going so well?" Victor asked. Tommy feared the conversation might go down that route.

"She'll be out of the public eye, Victor. I'm not planning on taking her on tour or anything like that. Anyway, she's got her own career, and she's independent."

"So long as the female fans think Bobby Nelson's free, single and available I suppose that's all that matters. But be careful, what you do and say in public.....especially what you say."

"We might get married even....if it...."

"Married?"

"Yeah, people get married."

"You can't get married."

"What do you mean?"

"Marriage is out of the question."

"What *are* you on about, Victor?"

"Down to me if you get married or not."

"Now you fucking listen here," Tommy couldn't believe Victor's sudden outburst.

"No, Tommy....you listen to me....and you listen carefully. We have a signed agreement....."

"You're my fucking manager, that's all. So stay

out of my private life."

"As I was saying, our agreement, which you signed, states that *any* legal contract you wish to enter into, and want to sign....goes through me. I say whether you sign it or not, as your personal manager and agent. You get married legally.....and I have the final say. It's a legal contract, Tommy, simple as that."

Tommy was stunned into silence. He couldn't believe what he was hearing from someone he'd grown to trust, if not respect. Had the words been spoken by his shrewd brother he would have understood, knowing James Slade to be the successful businessman he was.

"I'm not saying I'd veto any plans you have, but I have *my* interests to protect," Victor added. Tommy even thought he was starting to sound like James Slade.

Now this bombshell had been dropped he didn't want to say too much more without reading through the contract and he certainly wasn't going to create a scene in public. Not long ago he would have done just that, but he'd grown up fast and a part of that process had been as a result of Victor's influence and input in his life. He didn't finish either his wine or his sandwich and left the wine bar without saying much else, either.

He studied the relevant paragraph in his contract in the peace and quiet of his apartment. In fact, he read it three or four times, but the jargon and terminology he just couldn't grasp, and in the end set his mind to more productive matters, one of which was to prepare himself, both physically and vocally, for his busy European tour coming up.

*   *   *   *

Steve's hospitalisation prompted Emma to rethink her policy of continuing work and she quickly came to the conclusion Steve needed her time and support more than she needed her independence, so she left Boots the chemist the following week. A crash course in learning to drive was also imperative living in the seclusion of Dene Park , especially as it meant a taxi ride just to get a pint of milk and a loaf of bread.

Steve was in traction in a hospital bed in the city and was going nowhere for a while, which gave her the opportunity to play her part in Steve's recovery and running the home while he was indisposed. He was feeling more and more isolated confined to his hospital bed and as time went on he felt as if his club and team mates had forgotten him, such was his mental anguish. The events of that Saturday afternoon were still vivid in his mind, and on the one hand he desperately needed to confide in someone and tell them all about what happened on the pitch that day, and on the other hand, the Mantovanis hadn't followed up their threats regarding Emma, and that proved to be the overriding factor while he languished in his hospital bed and for the time being, he decided to tell no one.

*   *   *   *

Tommy's European series of concerts was yet another massive success. He named his backing band 'The Untouchables'. Victor liked the name, he thought it gave them a modern, yet retro, almost menacing slant and the billboards heralded *'Bobby Nelson and The Untouchables'* throughout the major cities of Europe. The monetary rewards from his American tour were now materialising and on his return to Britain, Tommy found himself a very wealthy man.

He went to see his mum and dad and broached the subject of buying them a house. What he thought would be a tricky situation and probably end in a row, didn't. Harry and June were both delighted and felt, just like Tommy had, that it was about time they moved on from the Barton Bridge flats. Tommy gave them a budget and told them to start looking for a suitable home. For the first time in his life he left that council flat with a warm glow and a satisfied feeling in his belly. For once, his was a proper family and he was chuffed to bits as he got in his Lotus and sped off down Felgate Road.

Tommy's buoyant mood continued over dinner when he told Carol about the visit. He'd also prepared the food and the fact that his chicken chasseur ready meal just needed heating in the microwave oven didn't matter to her at all. He contemplated discussing the anomalies of his contract with her afterwards, but there was another subject he was keen to discuss, and it wasn't marriage.

"How do you feel about us moving from here," he asked later.

"I love it here, Tommy, it's like a dream come true," Carol replied. He could see by the expression on her face she meant every word as well, which wasn't the reaction he was hoping for.

"I know it's a fantastic flat, but we only rent it....and I can't step outside anymore without being recognised and mobbed."

"You don't get mobbed....that's an exaggeration, Tommy.....come on."

"Well you know what I mean. I feel I don't have any privacy anymore, right in the middle of the city and all that."

Carol knew when Tommy was trying to tell her something important and gave him the opportunity.

"Where do you think we should move to, then?" she asked.

"I want to buy a place......our own place. Somewhere the two of us could grow into. Not a bachelor pad in Barchester."

"Alright, where?"

"Dene Park. We can afford to live there now."

"You sure you're not trying to keep up with

certain members of the family?"

"How can you say that, Carol. Look, this is me....Tommy Nelson. Keeping up with the Jones's, you know that's not me."

She knew he was right but wanted to see just how serious he was about wanting to live on the private estate.

"We could have our privacy....loads of space. A fabulous home, even a studio for me to record in. And you could still do *your* own thing.....flying around the world and all that. I'll never be a snob. You know that...... never ever."

She could see how excited he was and she also knew his sincerity was unquestionable.

"Who'll do the gardening?" she asked flippantly. Tommy knew then she was coming round to his way of thinking.

"We could go there and have a look, couldn't we. See what's on offer?" Tommy said.

"We could," carol replied, warming to his suggestion.

"Fabulous, we'll do that....that's fab. Oh, one more bit of good news," Tommy said, "Steve's leaving hospital next week, Emma told me. Isn't that wonderful?"

* * * *

Emma hadn't told Steve she'd taken driving lessons, passed her test and bought a car when she went to collect him from the hospital. It was his big day and the news hadn't escaped the sports media. Steve had the option of leaving in a wheelchair but chose to walk out of the main doors under his own volition aided by a pair of crutches.

The air felt fresh and intoxicating as he stepped out onto the pavement amidst the clicking of cameras and the cacophony all around. He found it overwhelming and didn't even realise Emma was his driver until they'd left the hospital behind and were amongst the busy city traffic.

To him, returning to 'Beechwood' was the perfect sanctuary where, with Emma's help and encouragement, he could begin his rehabilitation programme and with hard work, devoted commitment and a large slice of luck, he might just play football again. There was more good news when Emma's homely cooking replaced the bland hospital food at suppertime. She told him she was pregnant and they could look forward to being proud parents the following summer. Steve was overjoyed and it was the icing on the cake for what had turned out to be a momentous day for them both.

*   *   *   *

Tommy wasted no time in searching for his and Carol's dream home in Dene Park. Only a few years previously he would have given the prestigious estate a wide berth, calling everyone there toffee nosed and pretentious snobs. He almost believed he was still that same person. The rebellious, antagonistic, couldn't-give-a-damn individual who grew up with a chip on his shoulder. But now, due to his circumstances, he was growing accustomed to good food, fine wine, fast cars and an expensive lifestyle.

He was no longer that sixteen year old craving stardom and wealth. He was twenty three, he *was* a star and he was wealthy. He didn't *want* to change. He had no intention of forsaking all his youthful principles for the high life, but it was inevitable and with his heart and mind set on the auspicious surroundings of Dene Park, he had to concede within his subconscious that he should close that chapter on his boyhood, and move on to the better life he'd dreamt about and worked so hard to achieve.

It was different for Carol. Although she grew up on the same council estate there was love, encouragement and discipline in her home life, and attending Dunsbury Grammar was a major influence in shaping her future. Like Steve, she could have gone on to university but chose a job she loved doing. She still needed to study and gain exam passes but with stable surroundings and parents who cared for her, it wasn't surprising she'd matured into a level headed woman and if the chance of a better lifestyle was on offer, she wasn't going to turn it down.

They found what they were looking for, not in an austere Jacobean pile steeped in history, but an ultra modern, architect designed cubist property built from concrete and glass. The garden and grounds were landscaped to blend in perfectly, with large open lawns, symmetrical paths and walkways and a heated outdoor swimming pool surrounded by an entertainment area complete with its own bar.

It sat in two acres and was completely hidden from the road. Protection and security was ensured by high perimeter walls, and electric, remote controlled double gates. It's unassuming name 'Burnside' was chosen after the well known architect John Burn, who designed the unique and stunning contemporary home.

Tommy and Carol were both smitten by the place and although the price reflected it's exceptional quality and style, it was more than Tommy really wanted to pay for just a house. Carol's enthusiasm swayed it for him though and after they had wandered around on their own, discussing everything and taking it all in, Tommy told the estate agent if a deal could be done on the price, they'd have it.

Tommy was all for calling into 'Beechwood' and seeing Steve and Emma but Carol persuaded him the pair should be given time to settle back into a routine before being descended upon by the two of them, even if Tommy was family. Tommy protested but Carol got her way and they drove back to Barchester with visions of 'Burnside' filling their minds.

It was a good thing they hadn't stopped to visit, because Steve, although happy to be home, was plagued by the cruel events which led to his crippling condition. He needed to tell someone, to share the burden with someone, and Emma was the only person he could confide in. After a lot of deliberating and soul searching, he told her everything.

Chapter 28

Angelo and Freddie Mantovani had long since come to terms with their huge loss on the Sandford gamble. Freddie found it easy to put it out of his mind but then he didn't have the responsibility of running the business empire that was the Zanetti Corporation. Angelo had taken over that mantle when the twins first started the company, and since he was managing director, the burden of keeping Zanetti hugely profitable, yet somehow transparent as far as the authorities were concerned when it came to their more unscrupulous dealings within the business world, fell mainly to him.

Freddie enjoyed the trappings of success far more than Angelo but he was there any time his brother needed him and his dependability and loyalty was beyond question. It was two o'clock in the morning. He'd just returned from a Saturday night's clubbing and gambling, and the security barrier to the underground car park in his apartment block had just recognised the details on his personal card and allowed his pink Cadillac Eldorado to enter the subterranean environs.

As Freddie headed for his double parking space his path was lit by a series of motion sensor overhead strip lights. The rest of the area was in darkness. Freddie was on his own, even though it was a Saturday night. It wasn't through want of trying that he was alone however, as on this occasion he'd gambled all his cash away, so couldn't buy female company to entertain him in his bedroom until the early hours as he usually did.

He didn't attract the women like Angelo and even though his affluence could buy most things, his looks and especially his personality let him down, and even the gold digging female fraternity sometimes didn't want to be in his company. It was late though and on this occasion, having consumed a fair amount of expensive cognac, he was happy to settle for a good night's sleep.

The purr of the Cadillac's powerful motor stopped as Freddie cut the engine and stepped out. There wasn't a sound. The brief silence was broken by the cushioned clunk of the driver's door, and after locking the vehicle Freddie stepped away. Silence reigned once more. He heard a sound from the gloominess beyond his lit vicinity. The brandy had left him unsteady on his feet.

He wheeled around but could see nothing. Instead of making his way to the elevator he took the few steps to the rear of the car and peered into the shadowy darkness. He was armed. Everywhere he went he carried a gun. He *always* carried a gun. There seemed no reason for him to reach inside his jacket pocket and pull it out on this occasion though, or so he thought. He didn't scare easily and turned to go towards the elevator.

A shot rang out. Freddie looked over his shoulder. His legs went weak. He'd been hit in the lower back. He couldn't move. The second shot caught him higher up between the shoulder blades. Freddie was paralysed, powerless to reach for his gun. The third bullet missed him completely and ricocheted off the boot of the Cadillac, sending a pinging, metallic sound reverberating around the underground car park.

Suddenly the motion sensors caught the assailant's body movement and the area was bathed in harsh neon lighting. Freddie could see his attacker. He held on desperately to the extravagant rear fin of the American supercar, his pride and joy.

"You!" is all he could utter as his grip on the car began to wane. His assassin fired three more times and Freddie slumped over the back of the Cadillac. As the blood oozed from his body his attacker fled the scene, content in the knowledge Freddie Mantovani was dead.

Chapter 29

News of Freddie's death swept through the city. The sound of gunshot was reported to the police shortly after the incident occurred and the emergency services, including uniformed police, were on the scene promptly. Freddie was already dead and his killer had fled. A murder enquiry was up and running in no time and the whole area was cordoned off.

The media got wind of the action, as they normally did, and with Freddie's reputation, with him being a high profile figure, combined with the circumstances of his death, they quickly came to the assumption it was a mobster led assassination and the inevitable sensationalism began. Radio news bulletins were the first to report on the story, followed by the local television stations. Journalists from the daily newspapers were also there in numbers but their reports would have to wait for the following morning for publication.

Angelo Mantovani got to hear of his brother's death when the aftermath commotion woke him in the middle of the night. He went down to the car park and saw Freddie's body before it was taken to the mortuary. He was deeply shocked and went straight back up to his penthouse apartment and was neither answering his telephone, or accepting visitors, and even when the police tried to contact him to identify Freddie formally, he wouldn't respond to them and it was left to his father Luigi to do it.

It wasn't until the morning before Barchester C.I.D. got involved. Tim Sutherland had been promoted to detective sergeant and was heading the enquiry in its initial stages, and when he arrived there he already knew the identity of the dead man.

The crime scene was dominated by the pink Cadillac and that's where D.S. Sutherland began his cursory examination. A young uniformed constable was standing guard near the car.

"Have you been here all night?" Sutherland asked. The constable nodded, "I was one of the first on the scene. It's on my beat," he replied. Sutherland walked slowly around the car. A black felt pen had traced the outline and position Freddie was in when his body was found, slumped over the large rear fin of the vehicle. It didn't seem very accurate and it puzzled the detective sergeant.

"Did you see the way the man was, against the car?" he asked the constable.

"Yes, I saw him."

"Have forensics finished here, with fingerprints and everything?"

"Yes, they've done their job and gone," came the reply.

"Then would you lie over the back of the car in a

similar way the body was , just for me....as far as you can recall?"

The constable removed his helmet and did what D.S. Sutherland asked. He cut a strange figure slumped over the fin of the Cadillac.

"Hold it there for a bit," Sutherland said, looking at the pose from every angle. The constable also had an audience from the rest of the police presence there, who looked on perplexed.

"That's good. Thank you constable. That will be all."

"They'll have photos," the constable said putting his helmet back on.

"I know.....I just needed to get it into my head...you know?"

D.S. Sutherland's explanation wasn't convincing, but his methods within the force, although a tad unconventional, were leaving their mark on his fellow officers and they were beginning to come to terms with, and accept, his sometimes eccentric ways. He made a mental note of the bullet mark on the car's bodywork, which had also been circled with black felt pen, before leaving and heading back to Barchester Police headquarters not far away.

The forensic department's preliminary report was on his desk before lunchtime and he set about studying its every detail over the next hour or so. The local radio news was predicting all out gang warfare in the city, when D.S. Sutherland's superior, the Detective Inspector, walked into his office.

"What have got......anything?" he asked.

"I don't buy it sir.....the mafia stuff.....doesn't add up."

"Go on." the Detective Inspector urged.

"Professional assassins. One....maybe two bullets in the head. Our man was shot in the back, five times according to this," he pointed to the report.

"I'm beginning to agree," his boss remarked.

"And one shot even missed the target, by a couple of feet! No.....it's not a pro."

"Got any ideas?"

"I have, sir. I think it's revenge. He must have rubbed so many people up the wrong way in his short life, that's all I can say."

"Start delivering then, and let's nip this in the bud before the gangs *do* get involved." He didn't wait for his junior officer's reply and left his office.

Before the afternoon was over Harry Nelson was top of his list of suspects. He turned up unannounced at their new address, a smart semi-detached house in Southfields leafy suburbs. Harry wasn't pleased to see him.

"Can I come in, Harry?" he asked admiring the porch of the art deco styled house. "I *can* call you Harry....can't I? I feel we know each other quite well now." he added. Harry let him in. June offered him a cup of tea and , as usual, he accepted.

"Now let's keep this simple," Sutherland said reaching for a notepad and pen from his jacket pocket. He scribbled the word, *yes* on one sheet, *no* on the other and handed the pad and pen to Harry.

"Yes, no, answers will do, or you can write on the pad.....okay? Now, were you at home last night?"

Harry held up the *yes* paper.

"All night?"

He kept the *yes* in the air.

"You didn't go out at all?"

Harry signified with *no*.

"Do you know Freddie Mantovani has been killed?"

Harry held up the *yes* paper but wrote on the pad also. It read, *"We all know. I'm glad"*.

June brought in the tea, "He was here all night , I can vouch for that," she said.

"Thanks Mrs. Nelson," he took the cup from her, "very nice," he said looking around the tastefully furnished sitting room. Harry scribbled away on the notepad but June came to his rescue.

"It's a lovely house. We're very lucky, our son bought it for us."

Harry passed Sutherland his note, *"F off copper MYOB."*

"You weren't out driving then, last night?" D.S. Sutherland, if nothing else, was persistent. June also answered that question, "Harry doesn't work nights anymore."

"But he still drives?" Sutherland asked.

"Yes, but only during the day shift," June

replied.

"Do you own a gun, Harry?"

That question was answered with the shake of the head.

"Did Freddie cut your tongue out?" he asked abruptly, hoping to get a reaction. But Harry didn't respond.

"It's a while since we had our little chat about the casino bombing, and I'd just like to say that case is still open and we still haven't brought the killer of those two people to justice. Bear that in mind, Harry. Oh.....and my new card. I'm a D.S. now. Get in touch if you feel the need."

Harry didn't take the card but June did, before seeing him to the door.

He could plainly see Harry wasn't the chancer he used to be and came to the conclusion that if he intended killing Freddie, he would have done it long ago, especially if the Mantovani brother had violently mutilated him by cutting out his tongue and permanently damaging his vocal chords. He wasn't even sure if the man was capable of killing anyone, let alone shooting someone in the back, in cold blood.

Freddie's death was an eye opener for Angelo. He realised he'd become complacent and vulnerable as far as personal security was concerned, and went about hiring bodyguards for round the clock protection. He moved out of the penthouse apartment and sought seclusion and safety in a country house retreat and chartered a helicopter for his daily commute into the city.

Freddie's death also hit him hard but he couldn't let it show to those around him, and high on his agenda was his own private investigation to bring his brother's killer to his own kind of lawless justice. The Zanetti Corporation suffered as well, with its financial confidence taking a battering from the media's coverage of the homicide within the company's boardroom, but that only strengthened Angelo's resolve in his steadfastness towards the business he and his brother founded and nurtured, and he was even more determined to bring the name Zanetti to new heights and prove to himself that Freddie's death wasn't in vain.

* * * *

Tommy also moved out of his city penthouse flat but his circumstances were far removed from Angelo's. The beautiful, tranquil surroundings of Dene Park awaited him and Carol and they took possession of 'Burnside', their new avant-garde home in the country, looking forward to a new chapter in their lives.

This was the pinnacle of his success. He'd made it. All his dreams and aspirations had culminated in this moment. His single-mindedness and hard work had come to fruition and he surveyed his million pound estate with unpretentious satisfaction and joy. Yet everyday life was very much the same. His new surroundings made him consider marriage even more than before, but his thoughts were on the contract supposedly barring him from doing so.

Steve was also on his mind, battling to get his life back on course. It was at that point when he realised Utopia was unattainable, and it seriously made him think if it was, would he want it. His sister Emma, knowing their moving in day would be hectic and tiring, had invited them to 'Beechwood' for supper and he and Carol were more than happy to accept her offer. It was only two minutes away in the car and they couldn't wait to tuck into Emma's home cooking.

Tommy found Steve surprisingly upbeat and his awkwardness on the crutches when Tommy last saw him were gone and now he was quite adept on them.

"Come, Tommy, I want to show you the garden, before it gets dark," Emma said, taking his arm and leading him from the kitchen where the dinner was simmering nicely in the oven. The garden was the last thing on her mind, however, she just needed to talk privately with Tommy. Steve's revelation about his injury was playing on his mind and she had to tell someone. Steve hadn't sworn her to secrecy either and her brother was the ideal person to confide in.

She knew Freddie Mantovani was dead but they both had a good idea Angelo was probably the brains behind the speculative scam. Tommy was shocked but not surprised. He knew Angelo would stop at nothing to gain the Zanetti Corporation world supremacy, and the fixing of a mere football match he also believed was well within Angelo's self centred remit.

The simple hot-pot Emma had cooked for supper was appreciated and enjoyed by all and the talk in the comfortable surroundings of the sitting room over coffee was reminiscent and evocative.

"Remember I said we'd both end up in Dene Park," Steve remarked.

"No... what you said was, wouldn't it be funny if we did," Tommy corrected him. Steve couldn't help laughing. Emma was so pleased to see him beginning to enjoy life again. He'd turned one of the bedrooms into a personal gym and was disciplined enough to spend the time needed in there to get back to a fitness level the club would consider, before they would even start their exhaustive regime to get him match fit. That was still a long way off however, but it kept Steve focussed on what he needed to do.

He had no financial pressures as he was still being paid and he had a loyal and loving wife and a baby on the way, so he could count his blessings even though his future career was in jeopardy and him playing football again wasn't a certainty. His upbeat mood prompted Tommy's next question.

"Look Steve, don't know if you can help with

this, but there's bits of my contract with Victor I'm not happy with, and don't understand to be honest."

"I'm not the one to ask. My dad, maybe," Steve replied.

"No... I want to keep it, sort of impersonal.....not involve family."

"Mmm........I know what you mean. Hold on, there is someone I know. Solicitor....lives here on the estate."

"Solicitor eh?"

"Yeah, Quentin Hill, he's trying to get me into the golf club. You should join as well, Tommy, once you've settled in.....could be a laugh. He's got offices in Southfields....we used him to buy this place."

"I don't want to go to any offices. I need to keep it.....well.....sort of private."

"Tell you what. I'll have a word. He's a decent sort of guy. Maybe I can send him round to see you."

"Or I can go and see him."

"At his home you mean?" Steve asked. Tommy nodded.

"I'm not sure. But I'll find out. Now....who's for a drop of brandy?"

*   *   *   *

The following day D.S. Sutherland was ensconced in his office, checking the records of every known incident Freddie Mantovani had been involved in since he was sixteen. He'd discounted Harry as his killer and he knew his boss would be wanting answers. Papers were strewn all over his desk, but there was one episode going back five years that caused his gut instinct to home in on, and he decided to seek out and talk to the person who was closely involved with the incident concerned.

He had an address but it was in an area of Southfields he'd not visited before. He pulled up outside what could only be described as an old Victorian tenement block just off the Brook Road trading estate. Sutherland looked at the stark, uninviting building from inside his car. It made the Barton Bridge flats look palatial in comparison. He wasn't even sure whether to leave his police vehicle unattended in such a deprived and slum like area, but he had a job to do so he locked it and made his way to Bovington House, the address on his slip of paper.

He found flat forty seven on the third floor. There was no lift and the dingy stairwell stank of urine. He rapped on the steel clad front door with his knuckles and waited. Eventually the door opened and he was greeted by a rather large middle aged woman.

"Sharon Brown?" he asked.

"Who wants to know?" came the curt reply.
Sutherland held up his warrant card.

"Detective Sergeant Sutherland, Barchester C.I.D. Can I have a word....inside?"

She let him in. The flat was just as unwelcoming as the block itself. It was gloomy, damp feeling and cold.

"You know why I'm here, don't you?" D.S. Sutherland asked. They stood facing each other in the bare living room. Sharon Brown nodded.

"Freddie Mantovani's death. Do you want to tell me about it, Mrs. Brown?"

A solitary tear ran down her cheek. "Look at this....look around you. *He* was responsible. My poor Terry.....*he* might as well have pulled that trigger. Our lives were ruined by his greed.....his selfish ego and his greed. Even turned up at Terry's funeral, he did. Smarmy fucking git. Gave me nightmares that did. I couldn't take it anymore."

"You shot and killed Freddie Mantovani?"

She nodded. Tim Sutherland handed her his handkerchief as more tears ran down her face. She looked a pitiful sight.

"We had a good life.....the betting shop, everything. Now look what's left. I could easily have shot myself with that gun.....like poor Terry did." She went to a drawer in the sideboard and took out a pistol. "Same gun Terry used." She handed it to Sutherland who took a clear plastic specimen bag from his pocket and popped it in.

"I killed him officer. He saw me.....he looked around.....the lights came on. I knew I didn't have a choice then."

She put both hands out in front of her.

"I'm not going to use handcuffs, Mrs. Brown. But you're coming with me all the same."

D.S. Sutherland's instinct had been right. He'd got his killer, but he wasn't celebrating.

Chapter 30

Tommy had got into a regular routine of meeting Victor once a week to discuss everything and anything that involved *Bobby Nelson*. If something really important came up though, Victor would get in touch and they'd meet straight away. Their regular meeting place was the wine bar Victor was keen on and his Zodiac was only used occasionally when he needed to talk to Tommy in complete privacy.

Victor stressed in order to keep his finger on the pulse to maintain *Bobby Nelson's* successful career, he needed to know everything, and that included what the likes of Angelo Mantovani and his Zanetti Corporation were up to or had planned. As a result Tommy felt he had to tell Victor about the Sandford match fixing deception which had such serious consequences for Steve. When he mentioned it, Victor wanted to know every detail and Tommy had little choice other than to oblige. He also told Carol the truth later that day back at 'Burnside'. She was appalled but pleased Tommy had told her. It made her feel they were truly partners in every respect, even if they hadn't tied the marital knot.

News of Sharon Brown's arrest was seized

upon by the media, which left D.S. Sutherland no option other than to make public the fact that she'd been charged with Freddie Mantovani's murder. This dispelled the gangster led theories most newspapers had put out, but it didn't deter them, they simply looked towards the human angle with a seemingly innocuous, middle aged woman taking centre stage in a high profile murder enquiry.

Terry Brown's suicide *had* been reported on but it was never front page news and the circumstances of his death, and the part Freddie Mantovani played in it, wasn't known at the time by the press. Now, however, the unfolding story was full of intrigue and drama and the media couldn't wait to get their teeth into what they hoped would be another sensational story.

*   *   *   *

It was a few weeks before Steve managed to get Tommy a meeting with solicitor, Quentin Hill, at his Dene Park house. His business was usually carried out in his Southfields offices, and it was only because Tommy was a resident of the estate combined with his high public profile that he agreed to the informal get together in the sanctuary of his own home.

The large Edwardian house looked vaguely familiar when Tommy swept up the driveway in his Lotus. It was a Saturday lunchtime and the lawyer had just returned from a round of golf.

"You must join the club, Bobby," he said, greeting him cordially outside the front door. Quentin Hill was confident and assured and led Tommy through the house into the conservatory.

"Do you play?" he asked as they both sat down. The view looking out over the gardens was quintessentially what Tommy would have expected. They were mature and quite beautiful, even though the autumn colours had given way to the dull hues of winter.

"Not yet," Tommy replied.

"Good answer that. Just managed to get Steve Baker in the club. You should consider joining, if only for the social aspect. But I'm sure you'll make an excellent golfer."

The small talk didn't last long and Tommy handed the four page contract to Quentin.

"Is that it?" he said, surprised the document wasn't larger. It only took him a couple of minutes to scan through the paragraphs.

"And what's your concern?" he asked, beginning to sound more like a lawyer.

"Two points really. He says I can't get married without his written permission....and also paragraph four......I just don't understand that bit."

Quentin addressed his first point. "He's right, Bobby....on that. You signed this?"

Tommy nodded. Quentin was beginning to look concerned. "Mmm......look at this.....you see he's put here, *any legal contract.* Now.....this Victor Slade, what is he exactly?"

"My personal manager and agent."

"And you're happy with his professional competence?"

"Happy?...he's made me what I am. I owe my entire career to him and what he's done."

"Well, I can tell you now, a marriage certificate is a legal document and as such, you need *his* signature. So yes, he has to give you permission. I've never come across that before. *Never.* Are you thinking about marriage then?"

"Yes," Tommy was a little apprehensive in his answer.

"Does he know?"

"Yeah, I discussed it with him. That's why I'm here."

"Quite. And is he against you marrying?"

"He didn't say. I only said I was thinking about it, that's all."

"Do you think *he* thinks your career would suffer if you did?"

Tommy shook his head, "No...he hasn't said."

"Ah.....I see. Well, my advice is to persuade him you getting married *would* be beneficial to your musical success. I'm sure you could do that."

"Yeah, I could try that."

Their conversation was briefly halted when coffee was brought in. Tommy recognised the young lady carrying the tray. She also recognised him. He suddenly remembered where he was. It was the posh party venue Dennis had taken him to some years ago, when the smell of marijuana filled the air and Indian music wafted over the sex and drugs driven gathering of impressionable youngsters.

It was Jackie Hill, the lawyer's daughter. He remembered she was the willing, nubile, big breasted teenager he'd screwed on the upstairs landing that night. Now in her twenties, she looked just as sexy and even more attractive. She smiled enigmatically and knowingly as she handed Tommy his coffee. Quentin introduced her.

"My daughter Jackie," he said proudly, "Runs the Jacqueline Model Agency in Barchester."

"We've met," she said, "I knew Bobby when he was plain Tommy Nelson," she added evocatively. "Like the album, Bobby.....does things for me.....you know what I mean?" she added and Tommy watched her return to the kitchen. His train of thought had temporarily gone but Quentin brought him down to earth.

"Now this clause you say you don't understand. I think you've got trouble there."

"Trouble?" Tommy remarked, still trying hard to get Jackie out of his head.

"Tell me, did you get professional advice on this?" He held the contact up. Tommy remembered he took it to show James Slade and *he* could see nothing wrong with it.

"In a way," he replied, "I took it to someone I

know......a businessman."

"And he read it?"

Tommy nodded.

"Thoroughly?"

Tommy was worried. "Is it about giving power of attorney and all that?" he asked, fearing he was getting out of his depth.

"There's more to it than that, Bobby," Quentin was now sounding serious, "And to be honest this is out of my league."

Tommy couldn't believe what he was hearing.

"I know a man you should see, I'm sure he can explain everything to you."

"Everything. I don't understand."

Quentin Hill was saying no more on the subject. He handed the contract back to Tommy then scribbled a name and telephone number on a piece of paper.

"Imperative you see this man, William Seagram. Phone him. In the meantime I'll speak to him and tell him to expect your call."

Tommy took the slip of paper.

"What does he do?"

"He's a professor, an expert in the field of......of the human psyche," Quentin replied hesitantly.

Jackie was far from Tommy's thoughts as he drove away. The meeting with Quentin Hill had left him anxious, apprehensive and totally confused.

*   *   *   *

Sharon Brown's trial came up in the new year. Steve, Emma, Tommy and Carol spent Christmas in their respective new Dene Park homes. Tommy was thrilled to hear he was to be an uncle in July and Steve's physical progress was improving weekly. He could now drive, and walk unaided and was now spending considerable time at the club's treatment and training centre the other side of Barchester. He'd targeted the new season starting in late August for his return to match fitness and was on course to reach that objective and be selected for the first team once again.

Tommy had tried contacting William Seagram as Quentin Hill suggested, but his answer phone briefly stated he was in America on business and would get in touch with all those who'd left messages, on his return. Tommy duly left his message and contact details and waited.

Following Sharon Brown's confession she pleaded guilty to the murder of Freddie Mantovani. Her barrister tried to have the charge lessened to manslaughter prior to the court case, given the extenuating circumstances, but the Crown Prosecution argued she went to the underground car park armed and with the premeditated intention of killing, and from their point of view, that constituted murder.

Somehow the press got wind of the plea bargaining and tried to create a *crime of passion* scenario, but it never gained momentum. Sharon's barrister advised her, because Freddie was dead, it couldn't be proved he did anything illegal when he took ownership of the Brown's betting shop as a result of the debt Terry owed him, however that debt had come about, and her *only* course of action was to plead guilty to the murder charge and hope the judge would give her a more lenient sentence in court.

Angelo Mantovani breathed a sigh of relief knowing the skeletons of Freddie's dodgy dealings back then wouldn't be discovered and the integrity of his precious Zanetti Corporation remained relatively intact. He didn't even need to attend the court proceedings as Sharon Brown's guilty plea was accepted by the judge, and the case was a mere formality as a result. In his summing up he sympathised with Sharon's personal tragedy and circumstances, and sentenced her to the minimum allowed by law for murder involving a firearm, a life term of twenty five years. He qualified that prison term with the recommendation that parole be considered after she'd served half that sentence.

Sharon Brown looked a pitiful sight and a broken woman as she was led away, her only regret being she hadn't taken her own life after her revenge on Freddie Mantovani.

Chapter 31

When Tommy got the telephone call from Professor William Seagram he was in two minds whether to tell Carol. He decided it was something *he* had to deal with though and chose not to. He arrived at the professor's home, a basement flat in Barchester's Old Town, edgy and nervous. William Seagram was in his early sixties. He had a mop of grey hair and was well spoken. Tommy thought he resembled a nutty professor from a comic cartoon strip. After the introductory formalities Tommy handed him the contract.

"Sit down, please," Seagram said as he had a cursory look at the document. He then made himself comfortable on a leather armchair near the window. The room was quite dark and cluttered with all manner of books, mementoes and bric-a-brac.

"So.......you're a singer, and Quentin tells me your concerned with the contents of your contract with the man......Victor Slade?"
Tommy nodded.

"Knowing Quentin as I do, I shouldn't imagine he told you exactly what my field of knowledge embraces?"
Tommy realised he was a *learned* man, not only from his title, but from his choice of vocabulary.

"All he said was you were an expert on the psyche," Tommy replied. Seagram laughed.

"Quentin likes that word, expert. But.......down to business. I don't want what I have to say to frighten you, but it might come as a shock. So bear with me, hear me out and don't be too perturbed at what I have to say."

Tommy already had a disturbed look on his face but nodded all the same.

"I specialise in the study of Satanism, Devil worship."

A lump immediately came to Tommy's throat and the colour drained from his cheeks.

"At least you haven't passed out," Seagram said doing his best to make light of the matter, "Some do you know," he added.

Tommy was too astonished to reply with a quip of his own, which he would normally have done.

"Let me explain. Quite simply, Satan, or the Devil, or Beelzebub, whatever you want to call him, is *any* spirit blamed for evil. Devil worship is fundamentally the same as any other religion. There are fanatics of course, within it, the same as there are with Christians, Muslims, Sikhs and the rest, but generally those Devil worshippers who supposedly practice black magic and human sacrifice are a myth created by other religions to further their own ends, and to demonise, if you excuse the expression, the Satanic religion."

Tommy was perched on the edge of his armchair.

"What are you saying?" he asked pertinently.

"Most Devil worshippers are law abiding citizens who are rebelling against authoritarian creeds and dogmas. They *are* different from those who follow conventional religions and, as a result, they are hated, feared and misunderstood by them. It's a fact that more crimes have been committed in the name of Jesus, Allah and Jehovah than there have ever been in the name of Satan. If there's good......there must be evil. This balances the status quo."

"So they're harmless?" Tommy asked trying not to sound flippant.

"Ah.....I didn't say that. Knowledge is the key to power and a Satanist who *has* that knowledge, and also has a burning ambition to succeed, sorry about the pun, can be a very dangerous person. And that brings me to your Victor Slade."

Tommy was trying his hardest to take in what the professor was saying, but now he was linking Victor to the Devil, he was finding it hard to come to terms with.

"Do you know him well...........really well?" Seagram asked.

"I've known him about eight years, since I was sixteen. I always thought he was strange, but then that's Victor."

"Strange.....in what respect?"

"His looks, his dress.....mannerisms, you know, things like that. And there are things about him, things he's done, that I don't understand. But he's the one whose made me successful and I can't knock him for that."

"Precisely, and that's what the powerful, knowledgeable followers of the Devil aspire to. Does he seek public attention, they don't usually?"

"No, he stays out of it. I'm the one that's always in the limelight. And he said that's how it should be."

"Have you ever been to his house?"
That question took Tommy by surprise, "No, come to mention it, I haven't got a clue where he lives."

"And have you ever seen him with one of these?" he handed Tommy a picture of an inverted six pointed star within a circle, "It's the emblem of Baphomet, the pentagram. It symbolises goat head Satanism."

Tommy was gobsmacked.

"You have......haven't you?" Seagram said.

"He's got one in his car, hanging from the mirror. Little plastic thing. I've flicked it....spun it...you know....... What's going on?"

"I'm sure you must have heard the term, Devil's disciple? It's a name given by mainly Christians to certain, special, powerful followers of Satan. The real term is *Devil's actor*, those who act for the evil spirit. Now, look at Victor's name. Victor Slade. It's an anagram for *Devil's actor*. Can you see that? Victor Slade, I'm sorry to have to tell you, as far as I'm concerned, is a Devil worshipper, and seems to

be an important member of the creed's hierarchy."
Tommy shook his head in disbelief.

"And that brings me to the mark. The mark on those destined to serve him. Forget the physical sign, the '*666*' on a discreet and usually hidden part of the body. It was true centuries ago that if someone was thought to be a Satanist, or witch, the presence of a mole or other distinguishing feature was tantamount to their guilt. I don't hold with that opinion. As far as my research goes I think the mark is placed in one's spirit, an invisible indication of excellence in a particular field. I do hope I'm not going too fast for you?"

"No, I'll soon tell you if I get lost," Tommy replied.

"Good. Does he have a skill you are aware of that sets him apart from others you know?"
Tommy nodded, "He's an absolute genius on the piano. I heard him play once. World class. He had no idea I was there at first."

"But he continued?"

"Sure. Oh....it was just.....just wonderful. I asked him why he wasn't playing the concert halls around the world......but he pooh-poohed it."

"That's the mark, the mark of musical genius it seems in this case."

"What do I do?"

"That's the big question." He held up the contract," and this is typical, power and control over others......for life.....and legally."

"So he *can* stop me getting married? That's what Quentin Hill said when he read it."

"He's right. Victor Slade has you where he wants you I'm afraid."

"What about that clause four?"

"That sums it up for me. *The artist.....you.....gives unequivocal authority to the manager......him.......in its entirety etc*. You have signed your life away to the Devil. I'm sorry to put it bluntly like that, but that's my opinion I'm afraid."

"What can I do? He's made me a star. I've got a fabulous house, cash in the bank, a great lifestyle.....everything. What do I do?"

"There's one extremely important and significant point here. Even if he were the Devil himself, he couldn't make you a star. Only you can do that, my friend. With his help and guidance you may have succeeded, but it's down to you.....and *never* forget that. As far as what you can do, if your conscience is clear, and you're happy with Victor Slade's professional qualities and capabilities, which it seems you are, then go along with it. Oh....and that won't be his real name by the way. Don't rock the boat and get what *you* want by manipulation and ingenuity, and so long as he has no incline you know who he really is, you'll get your way."

"Don't tell him I know, you mean?"

"Under no circumstances. However difficult it may seem at the time, you must not tell him you are aware of his religious beliefs. However powerful and knowledgeable he is, he cannot read your mind. Remember that. I hope our meeting hasn't been too disturbing for you. I think you know what you're doing and if you stay on your guard, you'll do fine, I'm sure. Now....is there anything else? Oh....and by the way, I'm here if you need to talk again."

Tommy, although still very much in a state of shock, thanked William Seagram for his time, patience and sincerity and left the slightly eccentric professor's basement flat wondering if *he* was also a member of that spiritual creed. On his drive back to Dene Park he thought about the possibility that if he was, Victor would know soon enough and he would almost certainly have to face the repercussions.

The professor's words had made the act of Devil worship sound like any other religion and made it seem almost normal which, on reflection, worried him. Then again, it *was* his field of expertise and his matter-of-factness in discussing the subject seemed understandable. He also realised the consequences of his visit, if any, were out of his control.

He recounted in his mind how Victor dealt with the young intruder in Subway Music. The manner in which he used his knowledge of human pressure points to firstly disable the youth, then put him in a semi-hypnotic state so he wandered trance-like to his death, oblivious to anything or anyone around him. Victor didn't kill the poor guy but Tommy came to the conclusion his knowledge, and subsequently his power, probably did.

John Pullen's death, from peritonitis, was also a mystery to him yet he was sure Victor had something to do with it. Tommy also wondered if Victor was protecting him, and in the long term, his own interest. Many things, as far as Victor's involvement were concerned, didn't add up for Tommy but at least now he knew the reason why. There was no way he could tell Carol, Emma or Steve. He realised he could confide in no one, and that scared him.

He turned into his driveway, took a deep breath and did his best to clear his head before greeting Carol.

*   *   *   *

Victor had also been busy that day. He'd arranged a meeting with D.S. Sutherland at his favourite wine bar in the city. Normally Victor steered clear of the police but he had information he wanted to share with the authorities. It was the details about the match fixing episode Tommy had told him about. He told D.S. Sutherland all he knew but made it clear the particulars had come from a third party, so legally, his news was hearsay evidence.

Sutherland understood but listened with interest at what Victor had to divulge, and especially to the part Angelo Mantovani was said to have played in the clever plan. The detective sergeant was grateful for the information but wondered why Victor, who he'd never had dealings with before, should single him out to receive it. Sutherland knew it was his brother James Slade who was Angelo's adversary, after the bombing of his casino and the killing of his two staff. Through what Harry Nelson had unofficially told him he knew Angelo was implicated in that crime, but he still couldn't prove it and he left the wine bar happy Victor had confided in him but puzzled all the same.

A week went by before Tommy heard from Victor, and as far as he was concerned, no news was good news. He couldn't put off seeing his manager though and they met in the Ford Zodiac, which Tommy knew would be for a very private discussion. He sat next to Victor in the back of the car hoping his anxiety and trepidation wouldn't show.

"Got another royalty cheque for you......sign there," he said, handing Tommy another huge sum. Tommy put his signature to the chitty and Victor meticulously put it in his brief case.

"Want to check whether you're up for a tour of Australasia and Japan?"
That was music to Tommy's ears. There was no mention of Professor William Seagram. He sat back.

"When?" he asked, feeling a whole lot better.

"Couple of months. Be good for you."

"And the Untouchables?"

"Naturally," Victor replied.

Tommy had never been to those countries and to perform in Tokyo, with the band, would be another milestone in his extraordinary career. All thoughts of Victor being in cahoots with the Devil had vanished, at least for the time being.

"I'll get things moving. Oh....and don't forget the new studios are booked for next week."

Tommy noticed Victor wasn't swearing so much and was a lot easier to talk to.

"How's the new house?" Victor asked.

"Oh.....it's something else."

"I've not had an invite yet."

Tommy seized his moment. "Been busy, you know. Look Victor....I want to talk to you about Carol...."

"And I've only met *her* once," Victor cut in.

"Now we're living together and got the house and everything, I want to get married."

"Have you asked her?"

"Don't play games, Victor......you know I can't, not without your say so."

"Are you asking me then, for my consent?"

"Well yeah, if you put it like that."

"So long as marriage doesn't interfere with your career."

"Why should it?" Tommy was trying his hardest to stay cool, calm and collected. The professor's words about being clever when dealing with Victor came to his mind.

"If you're still as committed to a globetrotting

life of entertaining in the fast lane and making a shed load of money then I can't see any problem."

"You'll give me written permission?" Tommy said the words very slowly and deliberately.

"If she accepts your proposal......yeah.....I fucking will. Happy now?"
Tommy was ecstatic. So much so as soon as he got home he popped the question to Carol. She was leaving in the morning for another long haul stint to the far east and said she'd be delighted to be his wife.

Chapter 32

Victor spent the afternoon with Tommy a few days later on a photo shoot to promote the up and coming tour in the southern hemisphere, and he chose Barchester Zoo for the backdrop. Victor had the idea that *Bobby Nelson's* image could be enhanced with some danger, and introducing wild animals into the mix seemed the perfect answer.

Along with the caged beasts, he'd hired a tame tiger to bring drama and realism into the publicity photographs. Strategically positioned shots were taken of Tommy with caged lions, rhinos and leopards in the background, but the real action took place in an enclosure with just him, the tame tiger and its handler, plus a Land Rover, which housed Victor and the camera crew. The handler was under strict instructions to stay clear of the camera lens and the session began. Victor's ingenious stunt left Tommy scared witless.

The Bengal tiger was huge and padded around him as if it was contemplating a tea-time snack.

"Just be natural," Victor called from the safety of the Land Rover ten yards away. Tommy's mouth was so dry with fear he couldn't have replied even if he'd wanted to. He drew the line though when he was asked to put his arm around the majestic animal's head and give it a stroke.

The big cat was the undoubted star of the show and it would be the photographic director's job to turn the tables and make *Bobby Nelson* the centrepiece of the action. Tommy came through the experience unscathed however and it was yet another success for Victor and his inimitable entrepreneurial skills.

Victor had a busy evening ahead though and, happy with the way the session had gone, left the zoo early and headed into Barchester city centre. His Ford Zodiac drove around the back of the Starlight Palais night spot and approached the steel roller shuttered entrance to the basement area. Victor pushed a button on the dashboard and the automatic door opened. He wasted no time and drove the vehicle in and the electric roller shutter door closed silently behind him.

The underground hideaway was Victor's home. There was one other vehicle there and Victor parked next to it. The lighting was soft and subdued and he made his way to a solitary steel door on the far wall. Inside was a small, one bed-roomed apartment. It had been converted from the nightclub's basement store rooms into a secret living space. There were no windows, yet it was luxuriously appointed with modern state-of-the-art features including touch sensitive ambient lighting and air conditioning throughout.

It suited Victor perfectly. The connecting

staircase up to the club had been bricked up and concealed to such an extent even the Starlight Palais staff were unaware of its' existence. The espresso coffee machine was called into action and a delightful aroma soon filled the air. Victor kicked off his shoes and tossed his trilby onto the bed before pouring himself a hot cup of frothy coffee and sinking into the small but sumptuous sofa.

He was happy in his subterranean retreat although he used it mainly just for sleeping. His busy life had panned out perfectly and he had everything he could possibly wish for. He just needed to keep it that way and be one step ahead of everyone else, all the time. Next on his agenda was a shower and a change of clothes. One wall in the bedroom was given over to a substantial built in wardrobe and from it he selected an exquisitely tailored dark blue pin-stripe suit, white shirt and chose a pale blue matching tie from the hundreds on the rack. He settled on a pair of Italian black leather shoes before undressing for his shower.

As he entered the cubicle there was one last item to discard, his trademark mop of untidy brown hair. He removed the wig and dropped it on the bathroom floor. He emerged from the hidden sanctuary as James Slade and made his way to the vehicle parked next to the Ford Zodiac, his gleaming burgundy Bentley. He had a busy evening ahead running the Platinum Casino Club and ensuring his millionaire status and lifestyle remained intact.

Chapter 33

Things were moving fast again for Tommy. After a period when he could reflect on his success while he accumulated his fortune, and the revelations regarding Victor's unorthodox beliefs, he now had the tour of Australia, Japan and New Zealand to prepare for. His marriage to Carol was also high on his list of priorities.

He felt if their relationship was to have a lasting future it had to be based on trust, which meant there was absolutely no place for secrets. He thought long and hard about what he now knew about Victor, and his involvement with Satan, and he knew in his heart it was something he had to share with the woman he loved. He had no idea how she'd react of even if she'd want to share her life with someone involved in such complicated and possible dangerous liaisons with those who worship the Devil.

He had to take that gamble though, and if she chose to disappear from his life, he would live with that and wouldn't blame her. For the sake of his career he felt he needed to discuss the matter with her before he embarked on the approaching tour. He knew if he didn't, his performances would be compromised and the outcome of the tour would affect not just him, but his backing band and singers and everyone else involved in the series of concerts the other side of the world.

He decided to tell her as soon as she returned from the far east. When Carol did get back she was keen to talk about their marriage before Tommy left for Australia and that gave him the ideal opportunity to broach the delicate and sensitive subject of Victor's involvement with Satan.

Carol was astounded at what Tommy had to say and found it hard to believe that in modern day Britain, and in an ordinary place like Barchester, the occult could be so prevalent and hold such a firm grip on everyday people within the community. Summer was upon them and Tommy had chosen a sunny spot near the swimming pool to break the news to her over lunch. He hoped the bright surroundings might soften the graveness of the situation. He was wrong.

He told her everything from his initial meeting with Quentin Hill to his long conversation with Professor William Seagram at his basement flat. All thoughts of marriage had deserted Carol as she stared out across the pool to the trees in the distance. Tommy had never seen her like that.

"It really frightens me, Tommy. A part of me wishes you hadn't told me."

"That's how it hit me at first. It was like my whole world was crumbling around me."

"What are we going to do?" She was close to

tears and Tommy could see it.

"Exactly what the professor said. Now look at me, Carol......we can get through this. He said Victor can't *make* us do anything. He's just like you and me really, only cleverer. When I told him Victor had made me a star he put me straight and said I was the *only* one who could do that."

Tommy paused. He had to think, not ramble on. "If you want to call the wedding off I'll understand," he said bravely, giving her the opportunity to walk away and re-think her life.

"I needed to tell you, get it all out in the open before the tour," he added. Carol nodded and took a deep breath.

"I love you, Tommy Nelson. Let's get married. You've worked for all this. I'll get my head round it.....you wait and see."

Tommy took her in his arms and held her close. Nothing was said for what seemed an eternity for both of them. There was one more point Tommy needed to push home.

"You can't tell anyone , Carol. You mustn't. You know that, don't you?"

He was referring principally to her father and the fact he was a member of the police force.

"I know. My dad would go loopy if he found out." she laughed nervously.

"I can't tell anyone either....not even Em. Like the professor said, we've got to be just as smart as Victor bloody Slade, and never, ever, let *him* know we know."

"Right.....that's settled then," Carol said with renewed confidence and their embrace came to an end.

"Now, can we talk about our wedding, and where's my engagement ring?" she quipped. Tommy could plainly see she was putting on a brave face, and it was true, the events surrounding his marriage proposal meant thoughts of an engagement ring had completely slipped his mind.

"We'll go tomorrow.....you can pick one out....how's that?"

"Yes, I'd like that. We'll do that," she replied. Tommy could see the smile on her face this time was genuine. He was so glad he'd made the right decision in telling her and they could now both move on. They did discuss the wedding later and agreed they would arrange it for after the tour, and the arrival of Steve and Emma's baby, which would be due around that time.

*   *   *   *

The Australasia tour was yet another new experience for Tommy. *'Bobby Nelson and 'The Untouchables'* first concert was in Perth, Western Australia. It was winter out there but the weather was still mild and pleasant and Tommy found the conditions ideal for performing. It was the first of nine planned concerts over a period of four weeks, so the schedule, although still hectic, was manageable.

Then it was on to Adelaide, Melbourne, and the dramatic new Sydney Opera House. Everyone wanted to appear there, and although not the biggest venue on the tour, it possessed that certain kudos, similar to that of London's Royal Albert Hall, that attracted the top stars from around the world. Brisbane completed the Australia leg of the tour and it was on to New Zealand with concerts in Wellington, on the North Island and Christchurch in the south. Tommy loved New Zealand. The fans were more reserved but just as appreciative and the schedule gave him time for some relaxation and sightseeing.

He thought the place was just beautiful and was a little sad when they moved on to their last country, Japan. His disappointment leaving New Zealand was short lived though as the vibrant, intense Japanese took them to their hearts. Osaka was followed by the final concert in Tokyo, and the reception there was overwhelming. *'Bobby Nelson and The Untouchables'* gave it their all in front of forty thousand fervent fans, and that sensational concert brought to an end an ambitious tour that turned out to be an unmitigated, resounding triumph for everyone involved.

Carol had been busy arranging the wedding and had all the details to tell Tommy when he got back. Emma's baby was also due and Carol just hoped her All Saints Church wedding booking wouldn't coincide with the birth, as Steve had agreed to be best man and Emma was the maid of honour amongst the bridesmaids. With all that to consider plus her busy work schedule it kept her mind from dwelling on the subject of the Devil, which Tommy had left her to contemplate on.

Tommy met Victor in the wine bar for what was becoming his customary debriefing session following a concert tour. James Slade's alter ego was keen to know every little detail as usual and it turned into a long meeting. James Slade had invented Victor some twenty years previously, initially to close a particularly tricky business deal and had kept him on ever since. It was James's involvement in Satanism which brought about the anagram name he gave to his contrived side-kick and it was having him as his fabricated brother that had enabled him to accumulate the wealth and business assets he now enjoyed. It was hard work though, constantly changing from his normal self to the somewhat fascinating eccentric he'd made Victor. The monetary gain had outweighed the hardship and difficulty however, and Victor had become an integral part of his life and success.

Tommy was looking at him in a new light now after his meeting with Professor Seagram. A part of him wanted answers but there was another area of his subconscious that was desperate to keep everything on an even keel, especially now Carol was in his life. Knowing what he did though, he was finding it increasingly difficult not to quiz the man at every opportunity. In the end he couldn't resist the odd question.

"Where do you live, Victor. That's one thing you've never said?" he asked.

"It's never come up," Victor replied.

Little did Tommy know his home was a secret underground apartment in the bowels of James's Starlight Palais night spot not far away.

"There's a lot I don't know about your life, yet you know all about mine." Tommy knew he was pushing his luck.

"That's because I'm your personal manager and I'm making you all the money. I *need* to know."

"And I don't?"

"No, you fucking don't. You've got the home of your dreams, I'm allowing you to get married. You're rich......why on earth do you want to know about me. It's fucking irrelevant, surely?"

Tommy knew he had to be very careful and changed tack.

"Now I'm rich.....as you keep pointing out, let's say I fancied managing myself." He paused briefly, unsure whether he should pursue another contentious subject.

"Go on, Tommy....spit it out, if you're going to."

Tommy decided to continue, "Would you think about me buying you out?"

"So you could tear up the contact we have?"

"I didn't mean it like that. So I could manage my own affairs, now I'm older."

"I'd think about it, Tommy.....for precisely five seconds, then I'd reject your offer. You're signed up with me for life, matey.....and don't you fucking forget it."

Tommy knew that was the end of that conversation, and as far as he was concerned, the meeting as a whole.

"We're a good team, you and me," Victor's uptight stance had mellowed, "There's a hell of a lot of fucking dosh still out there with your name, and mine, stamped all over it. Relax.....enjoy your life, and stop questioning everything....yeah Tommy? Let me do the worrying, that's what you pay me for. Now, do I get an invite to Bobby Nelson's big wedding?"

Tommy didn't know what to say. The last thing he wanted was for his and Carol's special day to be turned into a publicity stunt for the promotion of *his* alter ego.

"We'll see," he replied with a contrived, cheeky smile, and left the wine bar.

*   *   *   *

Emma gave birth to a baby boy, Aaron, in Barchester General a week later. Steve, realising his prized TVR Vixen just wasn't a family car, confined it to the garage at 'Beechwood' and bought a big

Mercedes saloon to compliment the small runaround Emma had got after she'd passed her test whilst Steve was in hospital.

Her labour was short and the Mercedes came into its own as Steve drove her to the hospital just in time and proudly witnessed the delivery, giving Emma much needed support and encouragement. Gone were the days of a week's confinement in the post-natal ward after the birth of a first child, and within a couple of days the Bakers' had soon settled back in 'Beechwood' with their new family edition.

One of their first visitors was their neighbour from 'Hazeldene' next door, James Slade. He came bearing gifts for baby Aaron, one of them being a brightly coloured pentagram similar to the one in the Ford Zodiac, which he said would be ideal hung in the baby's nursery as a mobile to keep him amused. He turned up uninvited when Steve was out and that unsettled Emma. But he did live next door so she acted neighbourly and invited him in for a coffee and to let him see baby Aaron, who was fast asleep in a carrycot in the kitchen.

"He's beautiful," James said, peering at the sleeping infant, "He's got hands just like mine," he added noticing Aaron's long fingers. "Sign of artistic promise, that."

He placed another of his gifts, a small furry toy, in the carrycot next to the child.

"What's that?" Emma asked as he did so.

"Don't know really, just a little toy. A bear, a

lamb.....who knows. He *can* have it, can't he, it's perfectly safe?"

Emma could see no reason why the cuddly toy wasn't acceptable and nodded. James smiled. He knew exactly what it was, a caricature of a furry goat kid.

"Is it right you've named him Aaron?" he remarked, sipping the coffee Emma had just brought him. She nodded, "We like it, it's different."

"Goes back a long way, that name. To the Hebrew bible, in fact. In the old testament Aaron was the older brother of Moses. He was descended from Abraham and Jacob. He was a prophet of God and very important he was."

He drank more coffee. Emma, although not really enjoying his company, was intrigued with his knowledge, especially as it was her new born baby he was taking an interest in.

"He became the first High Priest of the Israelites, a leading figure back then," James added.

"I'd heard about the name, from the bible, but I didn't know all that," Emma said.

"An interesting subject," he replied.

"I take it you're a religious man then, with your knowledge and everything?"

"Yes, you could say that," he replied, smiling enigmatically. "Anyway.....must go, busy schedule and all that. Thanks for the coffee and I'm glad I got the chance to meet baby Aaron."

He hadn't outstayed his welcome and Emma was

thankful for that and watched his Bentley sweep down the driveway.

*   *   *   *

Carol's timing for her and Tommy's wedding day was perfect, being a fortnight later than the birth of the baby, and the environs of All Saints Church looked a picture in the Saturday morning summer sunshine. Derek Dooley proudly escorted his daughter up the aisle in what was a far more private affair than Steve and Emma's wedding. Tommy got his way with Victor who respected his wishes for once, not turning the occasion into the media circus Tommy had feared. He guessed the reason being that *Bobby Nelson* was already high in the public profile and perhaps his single status being curtailed wasn't the best news to publicise as far as his female fans were concerned. He'd also procured a signed statement from the man giving his legal permission for him to marry.

The reception was also low key in comparison to his sister's extravagant, formal venue at the Old Rectory Hotel. Tommy and Carol chose to use their home to entertain their guests after the church service and 'Burnside' proved to be the ideal mix of luxury and privacy. The weather was kind to them and the gardens, especially the area around the swimming pool, was the ideal place to celebrate their wedding with family and friends, in a lovely relaxed setting.

There was one noticeable absentee from the festivities, however. James Slade's alter ego, although invited to the wedding, didn't make an appearance. Tommy could understand him not attending the church service given his religious beliefs, but felt certain he'd show his face at the reception, as he had done at Emma and Steve's wedding. The truth was, James Slade had heard via the underworld grapevine, that Angelo Mantovani had found out he'd been implicated in the Sandford match fixing deception as a result of Victor's little chat with D.S. Sutherland and James thought it wise not to provoke Angelo further and keep a low profile for a while. A high society wedding was the last place he wanted to be seen and both Tommy and Carol were relieved he didn't turn up knowing what they did about the man. For them, it made for a more chilled out occasion and everyone had a good time.

Later on, Tommy made a surprise announcement which caught Carol completely unawares. Without her knowledge he'd booked a honeymoon for them both. The destination she also found unexpected. They were flying off to Acapulco the following day for the honeymoon of their dreams, and there was one person living there Tommy hoped to re-acquaint himself with, his good friend Dennis Carter.

Chapter 34

Angelo Mantovani's surveillance team of trained professionals had been keeping a close eye on Victor Slade and his Ford Zodiac for nearly a week when Angelo lost his patience after yet another visit from the ever inquisitive D.S. Sutherland. He was very clear in his own mind it was Victor who was responsible for the detective sergeant's persistence in the Sandford matter and it was becoming a concern to him, especially as Sutherland had now shown his face in the Zanetti Corporation's main offices on a number of occasions.

That was unacceptable to Angelo and he ordered his three man observation team to seize Victor and take him to their disused warehouse at Butlers Wharf, by the Albert Canal. What Angelo didn't know was that D.S. Sutherland had also arranged round the clock surveillance on *his* trio of heavies, who were now following Victor's every move in their Daimler.

James Slade was becoming increasingly concerned about the situation. His alter ego, Victor, was being constantly followed and his hidden apartment below the Starlight Palais was now under threat of being exposed. James knew it was Victor they were following because they'd tailed the Zodiac there and were still waiting outside the roller shuttered entrance when he drove out in his Bentley as James, and *wasn't* followed. He guessed Angelo was behind it and was extra vigilant wherever he went, either as himself, or Victor. He'd also made plans of his own should the circumstances get beyond his control and if the situation escalated in Angelo's favour.

It was a thundery summer's evening when Angelo gave the go ahead for the abduction, and James, in the guise of Victor, was in his favourite wine bar enjoying a bottle of red wine on his own. He chose to sit near the window to keep an eye on the Daimler with its three occupants which was parked right behind his Zodiac outside in the street.

The heavens had just opened and it was pouring with rain. The deluge, following a loud crack of thunder, was so sudden the street outside briefly turned into a river, and nobody was going anywhere. James thought he'd wait for the rain to ease before making his move. As it did so, it was the three in the Daimler who made theirs, much to James's surprise, and he was almost caught off guard.

The three big men got out of the car in unison and rushed towards the door of the wine bar. James was up and away and slipped out the back as they came in the front.

"Where's the guy in the trilby?" one shouted to

the barman. He got no answer. James was seen though as he clambered into his Zodiac and the men were hard on his heels.

James sped off, the Zodiac's wheels spinning violently, but the Daimler was a powerful car and he soon saw its vivid headlights dazzling him in his rear view mirror. A third vehicle joined the chase. It was a black, unmarked police Jaguar carrying four plain-clothed officers, including D.S. Sutherland. Two of the detectives were armed and the Jaguar had both vehicles in its' sights as the mini cavalcade accelerated through Barchester's wet city streets.

James was unaware the third vehicle had joined them but Angelo's heavies couldn't fail to notice and although they guessed it was the C.I.D. they were under orders, and the man in the trilby was *their* target and to those three hardened criminals, the police presence was merely an inconvenience. The Zodiac didn't possess the best road holding though and on the wet, slippery surface James found it a handful. It was rolling into corners and it took all his experience to keep the big saloon from careering off and crashing.

Both the Jaguar and the Daimler were renowned for their race-like grip on the road and James's Zodiac was no match for them. His Bentley might have outrun them, but on the corners even that was like driving a bus in comparison to the two classic marques following him. Angelo's men couldn't help but think it was going to be their night when James seemed to be heading towards the open spaces surrounding the Albert Canal. Their destination was Butlers Wharf, and that was the exact route James was taking.

The police following them had to be dealt with first though before they got their man and two sawn off shotguns were loaded in readiness for the onslaught on the black Jaguar trailing them. The rain had eased and the shotguns were trained on the police car behind them. The police driver immediately backed off, but it was too late. The sharp shooter gangsters took out both front tyres and in a shower of flying sparks, as the rubber flew off the wheels, the police Jaguar ended up in a ditch. D.S. Sutherland and the three other officers were shaken but in one piece, but their involvement in the night's action was over.

With that unexpected mission accomplished the gang then turned their attention to delivering, who they thought was Victor Slade, alive if possible, to the disused warehouse at Butlers Wharf. Within minutes, the gang were aware of a familiar sound above them. The whirring noise of rotor blades overhead meant only one thing for them, a police helicopter. They weren't going to outrun that, or shoot it down with a couple of sawn off shotguns, so plan 'B' came into operation and Angelo's words of *'alive if possible'* came to their minds.

Victor Slade, as they knew him to be, would have to be eliminated. The speed of the two cars had gradually increased and at one point James's Zodiac lifted off the road as it powered over a humpback bridge over the canal, but landed safely the other side with the Daimler right behind. The sound of the helicopter could still be heard as it tracked both vehicles over the open marshlands surrounding the canal area.

James turned sharply off the main highway onto a side road which ran adjacent to the canal. The Daimler was still there, it's headlights right up the Zodiacs backside, and so was the helicopter. The lane they were on ran parallel with the canal all the way to Trevett's Lock, where a sharp left hand bend took it the other side of the lock-keeper's cottage. It was an isolated spot and James's speed in the Zodiac along the wet and bumpy road surface was bordering on recklessness, but he was still in control and was going to give the Daimler a run for its money.

He pulled off his trilby, stuffed it down between the seats and wound down his window. Angelo's men weren't about to give up the chase, although their driver eased back on the throttle fearing the conditions were becoming perilous, even for their daredevil endeavours. James saw the bend loom up ahead and took his foot off the throttle, but he didn't brake. The Zodiac left the road, slid out of control across a rough, waterlogged meadow and plummeted into the canal beyond.

The Daimler came to a halt on the crown of the

bend, the three men having witnessed the sudden drama in front of them. Following the huge splash, as the Zodiac nosedived into the murky waterway, the only sound came from the helicopter above. Slowly the vehicle began to sink. Angelo's men watched as it disappeared under the water. A flash of lightning momentarily lit the scene as clusters of air bubbles rose to the surface.

With their mission accomplished, and with a final cursory glance towards the canal, the three men left in the Daimler, satisfied with their night's work and eager to shake off the helicopter which was still circling menacingly overhead. The aircraft didn't give chase however, but sought a safe place to land nearby. The pilot's orders hadn't come from police headquarters but from James Slade himself. His small Hughes 269 two seater aircraft with its tinted windows put down in a paddock nearby and the pilot dashed towards the canal.

He saw James's sodden, bedraggled figure kneeling on the bank. He was in a bad way, retching and gasping for air. In his left hand he held Victor's saturated brown wig and as the pilot reached him he slumped to the ground.

"Come on boss," he said, sitting him up and checking him over, "Let's get you home."

Ten minutes later the helicopter landed at 'Hazeldene' in Dene Park and James, still soaked through and shivering uncontrollably, had arrived home. Victor had been sacrificed to save both his life and his empire. He'd planned it all. Immediately after making his getaway from the wine bar he'd used his car phone to give the order to the pilot to go to Trevett's Lock where he planned all along to ditch the Zodiac in the canal and kill off his other half. It was purely coincidental the pilot had seen him on his way there, and with the villains thinking it was a police chopper following *them*, it had added even more credence to the sequence of events they'd no doubt be relaying to Angelo Mantovani.

James had been under no illusions how dangerous his daring stunt was and realised he could have drowned, but by opening his window fully, a vacuum didn't build up within the vehicle, and he was able to open his driver's door to escape his watery grave. Making sure Victor's trilby would be found in the car when it was lifted out, but *not* his wig, was a further stroke of genius that set him apart from most.

James had also used another clever ploy by getting his pilot to report the incident to the police, pretending to be the lock-keeper, and by the morning, Trevett's Lock was a hive of police activity. The lock-keeper, when questioned, said he hadn't witnessed or reported anything during the night, which left D.S. Sutherland, who was one of the first on the scene, somewhat bemused. Police divers were sent in to search the canal and it was lunchtime when the Zodiac was lifted out. The search for a body continued until dusk though when

Sutherland called it off. Having been involved in the chase the previous night he was pretty sure it was Angelo's men who were involved, but before any homicide had been committed he needed a body, and he wasn't about to find one. He did find the trilby hat though, and was convinced Victor Slade had not only drowned, but Angelo Mantovani's henchmen were responsible for his death.

*   *   *   *

Tommy and Carol were shocked when they heard the news about Victor on their return from their honeymoon. Neither of them had been to Mexico before and they found Acapulco a vibrant and stunning holiday destination. Prior to their trip Tommy had put an advertisement in Acapulco's local paper. It simply read:

"To Denny Carter. Staying at the Hilton, Acapulco. August 3-16. Get in touch. Tommy Nelson."

It worked a treat and the two met up several times during the trip. Dennis had never met Carol but they got on well and Tommy was delighted to hear he'd invested some of his ill-gotten cash in a motorcycle dealership in the city and was the proud owner of 'Duncan Superbikes'. He'd kept his false name, Keith Duncan and that's what everyone knew him by. Both Carol and Tommy were smitten by his beach front villa and Dennis was able to tell Tommy for the first time about his escape from the Mantovanis clutches and leaving Britain behind in the most dramatic of circumstances, including the role the mysterious helicopter played in the events of the most momentous day of his life.

He was still off the drugs and looked tanned, fit and healthy in his new life. The right woman had still eluded him though but he was confident love would come along before too long. He'd followed avidly *Bobby Nelson's* continued rise to fame and was thrilled his pal had made superstar status on the world stage and vowed to keep in touch, forever.

On their return, Tommy and Carol caught up briefly with Emma and Steve. At long last, with Steve virtually match fit and baby Aaron old enough to travel, they were off on their honeymoon to the Seychelles before the new football season began. The talk though, on their get together at 'Beechwood' was of Victor's drowning. The media had reported it as a tragic accident, but D.S. Sutherland knew there was more to it than that and he was sure Angelo Mantovani was the instigator, but as usual he had no proof and he still had no body so Angelo remained seemingly, and typically, above the law.

Emma called at 'Hazeldene' next door to offer her condolences to James Slade. He thanked her and told her he'd come to terms with his loss but because his brother's body hadn't been found, he was organising a memorial service for him at All Saints Church in Southfields and hoped she would attend. When Emma related the news to Tommy he was flabbergasted. Both Emma and Steve had no knowledge of the Slade's Devil connection and Tommy wasn't about to enlighten them, so his surprise had to be contained, which he managed to do. Nevertheless, inwardly, he thought it the height of hypocrisy that a follower of Satan would have anything to do with a Christian place of worship, whether they were alive or dead. but then Tommy had no idea if James knew of Victor's Satanism or not.

Tommy could talk about Dennis though, and he was in his element as he relayed the story of his new life in Mexico and the circumstances which led to him fleeing Britain. Everyone at 'Beechwood' that evening was jubilant knowing at least someone had got one over on Angelo Mantovani, and the Baker family flew out to the Seychelles the following day.

The memorial service went ahead as James planned but Emma and Steve were still on honeymoon so weren't there. Emma's absence disappointed James but Tommy and Carol turned up and most of the band and backing singers were there which boosted the meagre turnout in All Saints Church that Thursday morning. James had written a simple eulogy extolling the virtues of his brother's entertainment and entrepreneurial skills, which the vicar read out. But there was nothing on a personal level in the short speech that said anything about the man, and Tommy listened to what he thought was sanctimonious insincerity in the extreme. Not from the vicar himself but for the phoney drivel James had penned for him to read out. It made Tommy seriously question whether James knew of Victor's involvement with the Devil and whether he was doing James an injustice as a result. Then he didn't know they were one and the same person and refrained from passing judgement on that austere occasion.

Chapter 35

Not long after the memorial service Tommy received a telephone call from James Slade asking to meet him. Tommy was half expecting he'd get in touch and agreed. James stressed the meeting would be informal and as they both lived on the Dene Park estate, James invited him to his home. Tommy knew he lived next door to Emma but had never been there. He also decided he wouldn't mention it to his sister as he didn't know if it would concern her.

He drove into 'Hazeldene' expecting it to be akin to a fortress with high entrance gates and an intercom system linked to the house. But there weren't any. What he couldn't see were the hidden surveillance cameras and the high tech infra red beams strategically criss-crossing the driveway and park-like gardens. It was a modern, hi-tech security system which did the job perfectly and as Tommy approached the house, James was already aware of his arrival and was at the front door ready to greet him.

As he climbed out of his Lotus he noticed a helicopter parked to the side of the garage block. The house was beautiful, but far removed from the style of Tommy's ultra modern cubist property. It was late Victorian and built of brick with turrets and spires and there was an air of peace and tranquillity all around.

"Come in the house, Tommy.....far too warm out here for me," James said, leading the way. The late August sun was beating down and it suited Tommy perfectly, but he followed the smartly dressed millionaire businessman into his opulent home. James took Tommy into the library. Tommy had never seen so many books before in someone's house.

"I suppose you're wondering why I've asked you her?" he said gesturing for Tommy to sit down.

"I take it it's to do with Victor?" Tommy replied settling into a large leather captain's chair. James remained standing.

"Your Emma's back.....heard the baby crying this morning."

"What.....from here?"

"I've good ears, Tommy....you should know that. Saw the potential in you when you were just a raw singer in a band, didn't I?"

As far as Tommy was concerned that was water under the bridge. It was the present he was interested in.

"It must be pretty important to meet me here, and not in the Blue Boar."

"It is...... It's *very* important for both of us."

Tommy noticed the hesitancy in his voice, and he knew his business empire hadn't been built on indecision or uncertainty and waited for James to enlighten him as to why he'd been invited there.

"What I'm about to say will come as a shock.....a big shock. So don't fly off the handle, okay?"

"Depends what it is," Tommy replied.

"I don't have a brother, Tommy. I've *never* had a brother. *I'm* Victor....and I'm James Slade. I always have been."

Tommy laughed, "You're joking?" he uttered. He knew he wasn't joking. In all the years he'd known James he'd never joked about anything.

"Tell me you're joking?" Tommy pleaded. James was straight-faced.

"I invented Victor years ago. I've led a double life, Tommy, and it's given me all this," he spread his arms wide. Tommy couldn't believe what he was hearing.

"Have you ever seen James and Victor together?"

"They don't get on. They've never got on....come on...you're winding me up."

"That's what I led people to believe."

Tommy was perched on the edge of the captain's chair. He was speechless. James pulled out Victor's wig from the drawer.

"I'm James Slade. Suave, cool, calm and collected. I never swear, I like fine clothes, drive a Bentley. I live here in the splendour of 'Hazeldene'. I'm also bald as a coot. Now watch this."

He put the wig on.

"Now Bobby, you fucking tell me I'm not

bloody Victor fucking Slade, and you tell me I haven't made you a fucking shed load of dosh, Bobby Nelson?"

Tommy was astonished. Victor was talking to him. James pulled the wig off.

"I never intended things to turn out like this, but I *had* to kill him off. My life....all my hard work....this...everything would have been in vain. You are the only person on this earth that knows."

So many things were now flooding Tommy's muddled mind. He thought back to the Mill House Cafe.

"You saved my life....with that helicopter out there, when I got stabbed."

James chose that moment to sit down at his desk.

"You could say that," he replied calmly.

"And Denny, you came to his rescue...at the airport?"

James nodded, "I like Dennis....always have. Couldn't have him getting caught now, could we, especially when he had all that money belonging to certain individuals of Italian descent."

There were so many unanswered questions racing through Tommy's subconscious.

"And the piano?"

James flexed his long fingers and smiled.

"Ah.....the piano. The Warsaw Concerto, one of my favourites."

Things were moving too fast for Tommy now. He knew James was telling the truth.

"I need some air," he said clumsily and got up from the chair. James pointed to the door.

"Be my guest. Have a walk in the garden. Clear your head. When you're ready, we'll talk......and I'll have a brandy waiting."

Tommy's legs felt like jelly as he sought solace in the open spaces and filled his lungs with the fresh summer air. He thought about the night Victor took Emma home from the wine bar. It was no wonder he knew where she lived, because he lived next door. The Platinum Casino sprang to his mind, and Pullen, who'd stabbed him, and was now dead. He worked for James. Coincidences were mounting. His contract with Victor, who he took to James, who said there was nothing wrong with it and urged him to sign. He suddenly felt duped, conned by someone *so* clever it was beyond his comprehension.

Then the bombshell hit him. If they were one and the same person then James was the Devil's actor, the Satan worshipper who filled him with fear and dread, who'd used his supreme and ultimate knowledge to make him the star he now was and the fortune he now possessed. He felt sick. All he wanted to do was get in his car and drive away, to pretend it wasn't happening and hope it was all just a bad dream.

But all his life he'd never done that, never run away from anything. Should he run now, to live a life of torment and despair. In his head the answer was a resounding '***no***'. Tommy was a fighter and he wasn't about to give up now. He now had responsibilities, to Carol his new wife and the woman he loved. To his mum and dad. To Emma and Steve and not least to his millions of fans worldwide. He *couldn't* let all those people down.

He remembered the eccentric professor's words, *"He couldn't make you a star, only you can do that"* and *"However powerful and knowledgeable he is he cannot read your mind,"* and the most important piece of advice Seagram gave him, *"Get what **you** want by manipulation and ingenuity."*

Tommy was feeling better now and was ready to face his nemesis in the form of Devil worshipper, James Slade.

Tommy felt he now held the upper hand and so long as James wasn't aware he knew his secret he could face the man and perhaps even come out on top. That was the ace up his sleeve and he rejoined James with renewed confidence.

"Brandy?" James asked, pouring himself one.

"Too early for me," came the self assured reply.

"As you wish. Now we've got my....my double identity out of the way let's talk about your career." Tommy was prepared to listen and said nothing.

"You've done well under Victor's, and therefore, my management, very well indeed, and let's face it, you wouldn't have reached the heights you have without me behind you."

Tommy remained silent. What he didn't know was the companies James owned had got him to millionaire status, but to secure that standard of living for the foreseeable future he needed the twenty percent commission from every penny *Bobby Nelson* earned worldwide. James sipped his brandy.

"What I'm willing to do is this. I'll continue being your personal manager and agent. You can then relax in the knowledge your career will be in safe hands, the best hands I might add, and your income will not only be protected as a result, but would increase significantly under my continued involvement. And that brings me to your contract." Tommy knew then James had arrived at the reason he'd invited him there.

"You're not saying much, Tommy?"

"I'm listening," is all Tommy said. He realised he needed to stay calm at all costs. James poured himself another brandy and once again offered Tommy a glass. Once again he declined. James continued.

"Victor never existed and my take on that is the contract you have with me still stands, you agree?" Tommy wasn't expecting that. He didn't agree and his hackles were rising fast. But he needed to reply intelligently and cunningly and without losing his temper, that's what was crucial, not the immediate answer to James's question.

"I agree it's something we can discuss sometime," he said calmly. It was a masterly stroke and not only put the onus back on James, it gave Tommy the time to concentrate on the unfolding conversation rather than his own unruly temperament.

"What do you mean.....discuss sometime. We have a contract, Tommy......"

"Yeah, and I just happen to have that contract with me," Tommy interrupted, reaching into his pocket for it. He held up the four page document.

"My contract is with Victor.......*Victor* Slade. See....his signature next to mine?"

It was now James's turn to remain silent.

"Now Victor's dead. I went to his memorial service. He's dead and gone.....officially.....legally. And I have a signed contract with no one. I can do as I please."

Tommy knew he was in control. James took a large swig of brandy this time. Tommy hadn't yet finished, though.

"Now I could, and probably should, tear this up into little pieces. What do you reckon, James?"

Tommy was extremely satisfied with his behaviour. He hadn't sworn, he hadn't raved and ranted, or walked out, or thumped the man, and at that point he knew he'd matured into a businessman, of sorts at least. He looked at James and waited for his reply.

"Oh....and I'll have that brandy now, just a small one mind," he added, sitting down in the captains chair. James smiled and poured his drink.

"Clever Tommy, very smart.....and astute. I'll give you that."

"You're a wily old fox....but a good teacher all

the same," Tommy said.

"I'm my worst enemy then," James replied, "And I accept the back handed compliment."

"What about the contract," Tommy pressed his point home.

"You have a point, I'll give you that," James again replied. Tommy now had the upper hand and was revelling in it.

"You're good James.....still can't get over not calling you Victor, though. No, you're damn good in this business. I need time though, to weigh up the odds."

"So you're not ruling out us continuing to work together then?"

"No, not at all. But if we do It'll be on my terms and with a new contract, I can tell you that."

James looked a lot happier than he did a few moments before and finished his brandy.

"Successful meeting, I'd say," he said getting to his feet. Tommy agreed.

"I'll give you a ring," he said confidently to James as he was escorted to his Lotus. Tommy left feeling ten feet tall and the Devil hadn't been mentioned once.

Chapter 36

The first Saturday of the new football season had arrived and Barchester Utd. were playing at home. An air of anticipation had been building all week, fuelled by the press and media, and the team sheet for that first match included Steve Baker, and the buzz from the supporters leading up to the fixture was almost tangible. They hadn't seen their hero play for so long most were convinced he'd never play again.

Barchester Utd. hadn't won the league as Angelo Mantovani had glibly predicted prior to his attempt at match fixing. The Challenge Cup was another trophy they were expected to win but they didn't even get to the final. All in all it turned out to be a disappointing season for the thousands of fans and once again, with the onset if a new season about to begin, their hopes were high and their expectation for success just as lofty.

For Steve to battle such adversity and pull on the centre forward's team shirt once again was testament to his hard working, professional attitude to believe in himself, and the love, encouragement and support Emma gave him in those dark days during and after he'd left hospital. But here he was, lining up with the team on the opening game of the season in front of a raucous forty thousand home crowd.

Angelo Mantovani wasn't there. His director's box was empty. Disillusionment with the club as a money making enterprise for himself and the Zanetti corporation had set in some time before. He didn't even like the game and his continuing absence and general apathy towards the club hadn't gone unnoticed by his fellow directors and plans were afoot to oust him from the board.

Steve played well and lasted an hour on the pitch before Jock McFadden watched his fitness wane and he was replaced. He hadn't scored but Barchester had a commanding lead and were well on their way to winning their opening fixture. He received a huge ovation as he left the pitch, and a deserved pat on the back from his manager as he found welcome respite amongst his colleagues on the substitutes bench, where he sat out the remainder of the game.

*   *   *   *

Tommy had also given a great deal of thought to his future since his meeting with James Slade, and the big dilemma he had, apart from his decision to accept James as his manager, was whether to tell Carol about the bizarre episode. Even though he'd confided in her over Victor's involvement with the Devil, only he and James knew Victor was the man's alter ego and he came to the conclusion it was one revelation he would keep to himself. There were many aspects of his life Carol wasn't privy to, and by not telling her about this one, he sincerely believed he was doing the right thing.

After a lot of soul searching and deliberating he met James, but at the Blue Boar this time, to discuss the tricky and somewhat delicate matter of his future. He felt more at home meeting him in the environment he was more used to seeing him in, and not in his plush Dene Park home and he took the initiative from the outset.

He made the decision that whatever had happened in the past, he *was* successful and a big part of that was down to James, in whatever guise. As far as James's involvement with Satan and his Devil worshipping was concerned, he felt he had that under control, and so long as it didn't infringe on either his personal or professional life, or on his family, he could live with that.

He told James he was prepared to work with him in the future under two conditions. The first being a new contract would be drawn up by his lawyer, Quentin Hill, and the second being his commission would be reduced to the industry standard fifteen percent for being both manager and agent, and not the twenty percent in his original contract. James really had no option, and he knew it. He'd always got on reasonably well with Tommy as both James and Victor, and respected him for his values and even in a way, his belligerence, and that had been borne out by his actions at the Mill House Cafe which saved Tommy's life. He also knew *Bobby Nelson* was a gold mine and would keep him in the lifestyle he'd grown accustomed to.

James agreed and they celebrated their continued partnership with a bottle of Dom Perignon and it was left to Tommy to sort the details. James did ask Tommy, not as a condition, but as a personal favour, to keep his little secret regarding Victor and not tell a living soul. Tommy had already decided on that course of action and readily agreed. He left James planning a big Christmas television extravaganza in the form of an evening and an audience with *Bobby Nelson*. Tommy chuckled to himself as he left the pub, and inwardly gave himself a pat on the back for the way he handled the whole affair.

*   *   *   *

D.S. Sutherland's extended frustration watching Angelo Mantovani lead a life of opulent indulgence whilst continuingly flouting the law was about to change. It had recently been brought to his attention that the Lucky Seven Casino, owned by the Zanetti Corporation, had been in serious breach of both its gambling and alcohol licenses, and although not strictly a C.I.D. matter, Sutherland was given the task of investigating, with a view to charging

Angelo Mantovani, whose name was on the licenses, with serious acts of misdemeanour if the allegations made against the casino were substantiated.

He was in his office ensconced in that rather mundane and tedious assignment when the uniformed duty sergeant popped his head round the door.

"There's a couple at the front desk asking for you," he said.

"Do you know who they are?" D.S. Sutherland asked.

"A man and a woman.....seen him before. Shall I tell them you're busy?"

"No, I'll be right there," Sutherland answered, happy to have a break from the job he thought should never have been passed to him from Barchester council's licensing authority. To his surprise the couple were Harry and June Nelson.

"Well, I'm honoured," he said, greeting them.

"We've got something to tell you," June said in a hushed voice.

"In here." Sutherland beckoned them into an interview room and gestured for them to sit at the desk. June was watching Harry's hands. The reason became immediately obvious. Fed up with not being able to converse with anyone, Harry had learnt sign language, together with June, and she was now his voice.

"We'll stand," June said. D.S. Sutherland was

impressed.

"Never thought I'd see the day, Harry," he replied to June. Harry wasn't pleased and quickly signed for his wife to reply.

"Harry says he's dumb.....not deaf. You talk to him, not me."

Tim Sutherland chuckled. He knew when he'd been put in his place.

"Yes, okay Harry. Right, what have you got for me?" he asked, not expecting anything of significance. It was nearly five years since the casino bombing and although the case was still open, it had gone cold a long time ago.

Harry and June had rehearsed this particular scene more than once and Harry didn't need to sign on this occasion. He nodded to her though.

"A lot has changed for us over the last few years, sergeant, you know that. We can't change what's happened, but we can do something now," she said. Sutherland listened with interest.

"Harry, and me....have thought long and hard over this, and I can tell you it hasn't been easy."

"In your own time, Mrs. Nelson," Sutherland urged her to continue.

"Harry's decided he'll stand up in court and tell the truth about the bombing."

D.S. Sutherland looked at Harry, "Is this true, Harry......you'll testify in court?" he couldn't quite believe what he was hearing. Harry nodded.

"There's conditions mind," June said.

"I'm listening."

"Conditions are, Harry won't face *any* charges for his involvement, because he was completely innocent, you know that sergeant."

Tim Sutherland thought Christmas had come early and was trying his hardest not to show either his amazement or his elation.

"You said conditions.....plural."

"That's right. We want police protection, for our Tommy and Emma and their families as much as us. That's what we want." Harry signed to June and she continued. "Twenty four hour protection, Harry says. Nothing less.....or he won't do it."

D.S. Sutherland paced around the room. Harry and June were standing awkwardly by the desk.

"Let me get this right. You will stand up in court and implicate Angelo Mantovani in the murder of two staff at the Platinum Casino on the night of the bombing. Is that what you're saying?"

Harry nodded.

"What's made you change your mind?"

"Lots of things," June replied. "It *was* them that cut out his tongue. Well, the one that did it was that Freddie, but Angelo told him to, *and* he was there. Now Freddie's dead and we've got our lives back together, Harry....and me....we both want to see the callous bastard pay.....if you'd excuse my language," she added.

"I'll be honest with you," Sutherland replied, "I'm amazed, I really am, and this puts a whole new complexion on the case."

"So?" June asked.

"I need a day or two. Give me your telephone number.....I'll ring you. Best if I don't come round to the house, in the circumstances."

Harry signed again.

"Harry says we need that protection, is that clear?....or he definitely won't do it."

"I'll see what I can do. Now, follow me, we'll go out the back. You never know whose watching the front entrance. And I can't thank you enough, both of you.....for the courage you've shown coming here today."

Nothing more was said and when D.S. Sutherland got back to his office he cleared his desk of the licensing infringement documents. He had a murder case to concentrate on instead.

He knew he had to secure Harry's signed statement before the Crown Prosecution would even consider charging Angelo Mantovani with murder. He had corroborative photographic evidence from the surveillance camera outside the casino on the night in question, and he could certainly build a strong case for the prosecution. In the meantime it didn't stop him informing his superiors of the important breakthrough, and the head of Barchester C.I.D. the Detective Chief Inspector was soon notified and involved.

D.S. Sutherland was also aware of Angelo's ingenious methods of evading arrest and was leaving nothing to chance. In a bid to outsmart his adversary's huge intelligence network Harry and June were taken in an unmarked police car to the less significant Southfields Police Station where Harry duly gave his written statement to D.S. Sutherland with the verbal proviso that if protection wasn't forthcoming, he'd rescind his statement and say nothing if he was subsequently subpoenaed to appear in court.

D.S. Sutherland was delighted to have the written statement at long last and the wheels of justice were set in motion. Harry and June soon got confirmation of their demands for round the clock protection and the Crown Prosecution office processed the warrant for the arrest of Angelo Mantovani. D.S. Sutherland came up with the name, operation Horatio, After Harry's surname and the arrest was planned for early the following morning at the Zanetti Corporation's headquarters on the top floor of the 'Excalibur' building in the city, where Sutherland hoped an unsuspecting Angelo would be spending just another day at the office.

As was usual since Freddie's death, Angelo's commute to work was by Blue Cloud Charter helicopter which landed routinely every morning on the roof of the 'Excalibur' building. He was the first in the office early that morning and the constantly ringing telephones heralded the sign that something wasn't right. Those calls were from members of his underworld intelligence service warning him his freedom was in peril and the police would soon be knocking on his office door with a warrant for his arrest.

D.S. Sutherland and his men had already surrounded the iconic building. They'd seen the helicopter arrive and take off again, and disappear across the city skyline. Everything was in place. He had the warrant safely in his pocket and operation Horatio was ready to go.

Angelo's business empire hadn't grown to worldwide status through him sitting around idly watching the company grow however, and even though he now knew the police presence was imminent, he wasn't surrendering without a fight and his escape plan was put into action. He picked up the telephone and dialled.

"Blue Cloud, this is Angelo Mantovani. I want a chopper now....roof of 'Excalibur'.....right now," and he slammed the phone down.

D.S. Sutherland gave the orders to raid the building and took control of all four elevators, believing any escape route would be thwarted. He and his men were soon on their way to the top floor. Angelo locked and bolted Zanetti's offices from the inside, grabbed a wad of notes from the safe and made his way up to the roof via a secret internal staircase he'd had installed when the company took the lease on the suite of offices.

It was breezy up on the roof and he could hear police sirens rising from the streets below. But there was no sign of a helicopter. He realised he had only minutes left before the police would be upon him. Suddenly he heard the familiar sound of a helicopter approaching. He listened again. To his amazement he could hear two distinctly different sounds. Two helicopters were heading his way, both from different directions. D.S. Sutherland and his men were now battering down the door to his offices. He could hear the racket even where he was, on the roof.

The first helicopter, the larger of the two, arrived on the scene and circled noisily overhead. Angelo could plainly see it was a police vehicle. His heart sank. In a couple of minutes he knew he'd have company from the officers below and he'd be arrested. The second aircraft, a smaller, more nimble machine, seemed to come out of nowhere and swooped dramatically down at an incredibly acute angle and amongst a cacophony of noise and swirling dust, touched down.

Angelo ran to it. It had no doors and the cockpit glass was darkly tinted. The police helicopter was right above it.

"Jump in buddy," the pilot shouted, his accent distinctly American. Angelo didn't wait for a second invitation and leapt aboard the two seater helicopter.

"Buckle up," the pilot yelled and pulled on the joystick. The machine lifted off, narrowly missing the police helicopter hovering above it. The larger and less manoeuvrable police aircraft was powerless to intervene. It's loud hailer was ordering their surrender but amidst the noise it was hardly audible.

"Let's get out of here," Angelo shrieked. He watched as D.S. Sutherland and the others appeared on the roof. His heart was pounding. He was just seconds from being apprehended and now he was up and away. The police helicopter gave chase but it was far too big, slow and cumbersome and soon gave up.

Inwardly, Angelo was euphoric and revelled in his James Bond style escape to freedom, but the aircraft was strange to him and he'd never seen the pilot before either, so outwardly he remained cautious.

"Blue Cloud Charter?" Angelo asked trying desperately to conceal his adrenalin rush.

"Yep. Where to?"

"Haven't seen you before, or the chopper."

"Special, this one. Others were all busy.....where to?"

"Do you know who I am?"

"Yeah, I do."

"Who are you, then?" Angelo demanded. Barchester city centre was disappearing behind them.

"I'm the Lone Ranger, Mr. Mantovani......the Lone Ranger. Where to?" and he laughed. Angelo wondered what he was on about but he had more important matters on his mind than riddles.

"France.....south of France....near Nice."

"I need to know more than that," the pilot replied.

"Not now you don't. I'll tell you more when we get there."

"I need to radio in."

"What, and have every copper in the country knowing where I'm going. You stay clear of that radio," Angelo said, reaching in his pocket for a revolver which he made a point of showing to the pilot before putting it back.

"You're the boss," came the reply. Nothing more was said as the helicopter swept across the countryside towards the English Channel and onwards to France.

D.S. Sutherland and his fellow officers were gutted. Their own bureaucracy had given Angelo's moles within the system, and that included infiltrators within the police force, ample time to warn him of operation Horatio, and it had failed miserably. D.S. Sutherland also had no idea whose helicopter it was that snatched their man from within their grasp, and he now had his supervisors to face and explain the whole debacle to.

There was one possible saving grace however. He was able to track the aircraft to the English Channel and was aware it was probably heading for France, and even beyond. He set about searching the whole of Europe for possible links with Angelo and the Zanetti Corporation and with this in mind he enrolled the services of Interpol.

He knew it was a long shot though and didn't hold out much hope for its success. Time wasn't on his side either and he realised within hours Angelo could slip away forever. Luck was on his side though and Interpol came up with two French addresses linked to the man. The first was an office in the centre of Paris leased by the Zanetti Corporation, and the second was a chateau in the south of France under the specific ownership of Angelo Mantovani. Interpol told D.S. Sutherland they would send armed men to both addresses, whilst searching for the helicopter over their air space. They also promised to keep the detective sergeant informed every step of the way.

This new course of action gave D.S. Sutherland renewed hope they might still get their fugitive and he made his way to police headquarters to await news from Interpol. Angelo gave the pilot strict instructions to fly at the highest altitude he could, so as not to be spotted by the authorities, which he did, but it was uncomfortably cold so high up, especially as the craft was open to the elements. It was a relief for both of them when the French southern coast came into view with the Mediterranean beyond.

Angelo gestured for them to go down, which the pilot was only too happy to do.

"The town of Saint-Maxine, on the coast, that's where we're heading....just along from Nice."

"West or east....of Nice?" the pilot asked searching for a chart of the area whilst retaining control of the aircraft as it descended rapidly. Angelo was disorientated by the sudden drop and had to think for a few seconds.

"West," he replied finally. The helicopter swooped down towards the resort and levelled out.

"Go past the town, and stick to the coast. You'll see a chateau with a helipad. We land there, understood?" Angelo said pulling out his revolver and scanning the area below. The pilot said nothing. It was now pleasantly warm and sunny and under different circumstances would have been the perfect joyride over the Cote d'azur.

"There......over there," Angelo said, his voice full of enthusiasm.

"Yeah, I see it," came the reply as the helicopter slowed. Chateau De-La Maritime lay ahead, a sprawling country estate set in idyllic wooded surroundings overlooking the sea.

"I need to radio in, we're low on fuel."

Angelo nodded in agreement. His safe haven was seconds away and his mood was buoyant.

"Lone Ranger to Hazeldene, over."

The aircraft came in low over the trees with the helipad now in sight.

"I read you Ranger, over."

Angelo peered towards the chateau.

"Delivering goods. Will refuel at Nice, over."

The helicopter flew slowly over the roof of the

chateau and hovered over the helipad, preparing to land.

"Everything good with you, Ranger, over?"

Angelo's attention was drawn to something on the roof. A French police sniper dressed in black was lying between the roof's ancient castellation.

"Up!" Angelo screamed, turning to the pilot with his revolver firmly in his grasp.

"Take it up.....now!"

He glanced towards the roof. A second marksman caught his attention near a corner turret.

"Is everything good with you, Ranger. Do you read me, over."

The sun glinted off the marksman's rifle. The pilot pulled on the joystick, flicked it right and hit the throttle. The response was instant and astounding and took Angelo completely by surprise.

"Come in, Ranger. Respond. Do you read me, over?"

The Hughes two seater banked and accelerated upwards so fiercely Angelo was thrown from the passenger seat. He made a grab for the cockpit safety rail.

"Told you to buckle up, buddy......didn't I?"

Those were the last words Angelo heard as he plummeted to the ground. He'd arrived at his destination, slap bang in the middle of the helipad. But he was dead.

"Come in, Ranger, is everything okay, over?"

"Everything's good Mr. Slade, over and out."

The helicopter wheeled up and away and the Lone Ranger headed for Nice Airport.

Two simple mistakes had cost Angelo Mantovani his life. The first was his vanity in registering the ownership of the chateau in his name rather than using an anonymous pseudonym. Had he done so the authorities would never have linked him to Chateau De-La Maritime in the first place. The second was disregarding the pilot's instruction to securely fasten his seat harness when he initially scrambled aboard the helicopter on the roof of the 'Excalibur' building back in Barchester.

At twenty seven, with all his wealth and trappings of success, over confidence and youthful inexperience had been his downfall, and for both him and his twin brother, Freddie, death was the ultimate price.

Chapter 37

D.S. Sutherland had snatched victory from the jaws of defeat and with Interpol's help had kept his ambitions within Barchester C.I.D. firmly on track for the future. Although operation Horatio hadn't been a resounding success in as much that Angelo wouldn't be brought to justice for his crimes, inwardly, nearly everyone concerned, including the police, Crown Prosecution and the relevant authorities involved, were happy with the outcome.

It was hoped the restructured board of the Zanetti Corporation would seriously look at the company's future without the Mantovanis at the helm and steer it towards implementing more acceptable trading standards, and away from its gangster led ideology of its past.

James Slade was also satisfied with the outcome of events and finally had his retribution for the cowardly and devastating attack on his casino. He'd always been one step ahead of Angelo, and his acquisition of the air services company, Blue Cloud Charter, shortly after Freddie's death, when Angelo moved out of his penthouse and started commuting to work by helicopter, proved to be a master stroke and one which eventually led to Angelo's death.

Harry and June Nelson, when they heard the

news, were relieved more than anything else. Harry in particular, having witnessed the wrath and mercilessness of the brothers when Freddie cut his tongue out, was genuinely terrified, fearing the reprisals he could have expected from the remorseless Angelo if the cunning gangster found out he was about to testify against him. They had a visit from D.S. Sutherland and it was agreed police protection was no longer needed and the detective sergeant thanked them once again for their bravery and enjoyed another of June's welcome brews before he wished them well and went on his way.

Tommy was another who shed no tears for Angelo. He knew him for what he was, growing up together in Felgate Road, and the well versed cliché, *'live by the sword....die by the sword'*, Tommy felt summed up Angelo's short, intense, and in some ways, fanatical life perfectly. His recent experiences with James Slade had also galvanised his more mature outlook and slant on life, and he and Carol were both happy and content. They were immersed in their careers and any thoughts of having a family weren't even on the horizon. Carol had her sights set firmly on becoming a crew member on the supersonic aeroplane, Concorde, and Tommy was still very passionate about ensuring *Bobby Nelson's* continuing success throughout the world.

Dennis Carter paid them a visit knowing his life was no longer in danger, and he and Tommy had a great time reminiscing over the highs and lows of their respective pasts. It was only a visit however, as Dennis had grown to love Mexico and the wonderful lifestyle he enjoyed in Acapulco and vowed the next time their paths crossed he would have met and married the girl of his dreams.

Steve Baker's single-mindedness and courage had seen him return to Barchester United's first team and his international career flourished. Emma thought her life was complete as a footballer's wife with a loving husband and a child to cherish, in the lavish surroundings of 'Beechwood', and cosseted in the beautiful environs of the Dene Park estate and she could wish for no more.

James Slade, living next door, was a pain to her on occasions though. He would come round at every opportunity to see young Aaron and spend time with him, calling himself uncle James in the boy's company whenever he did so. Emma thought it harmless enough though, putting his interest in her son down to her belief he was a confirmed bachelor and had no children of his own. Other than that, her life was complete.

Chapter 38

Dene Park's preparatory school's summer concert was the highlight of the year for many proud parents living on the prestigious estate and Emma and Steve Baker were no exception. The private school had spawned its fair share of young starlets over the years, and this year, pupil Aaron Baker, who was now five, was to entertain the mum's and dad's with a short recital on the piano.

It was an auspicious occasion and the afternoon show's itinerary was diverse and usually held a surprise or two. The school hall was packed and the atmosphere warm and convivial. The concert began with a satirical, condensed version of Shakespeare's Romeo and Juliet by the older pupils followed by an eight year old girl soprano who sang Simon and Garfunkel's *'Bridge Over Troubled Water'* accompanied by Mr. Stroud, the music teacher, on the enormous Bosendorfer grand piano. Her rendition was simple and evocative and received generous applause.

The scene was set for young Aaron, who was up next, and Mr. Stroud organised his sheet music at the piano, in readiness for his performance. Tommy and Carol sat in the front row with Emma and Steve. Tommy was eagerly awaiting Aaron's short recital of Mozart's Piano Concerto no. 21. Even he knew the elegantly lyrical theme and Emma said he'd been practicing the piece at home for weeks.

Lawyer Quentin Hill was there, as was James Slade, who'd chosen to sit right at the back of the hall. He too, was looking forward to the boy's performance and the young lad walked nervously towards the piano with his mascot, the strange cuddly toy James had given him when he was only a baby, firmly in his grasp. He climbed onto the piano stool, made himself comfortable and placed his furry, goatee friend on the top of the grand piano.

The school hall descended into hushed silence. Emma was on the edge of her seat, tense and anxious. Tommy also sat forward in anticipation. Being a performer himself he was only too aware how scary the moment could be, especially for a five year old.

Aaron began playing. The opening bars were powerful and dramatic, but they didn't belong to Mozart's Piano Concerto no. 21. His music teacher, standing ready to turn the pages of the score, looked bemused and glanced embarrassingly towards the audience. Emma was dumbfounded and Tommy's eyes were like saucers as Aaron continued at the piano. He looked to be in a trance-like state as his arms extended out across the keys and his long, slender fingers brought the Bosendorfer grand piano to life.

Tommy suddenly realised he'd heard the piece of music before. He was horrified. It was the Warsaw Concerto. He looked at Emma, she was in shock. Young Aaron was in full flow and although his playing wasn't perfect, it was a virtuoso performance for one so young and the audience were bowled over and completely captivated by it.

Tommy looked to the back of the hall and caught sight of James Slade. Their eyes met and James nodded to him and smiled. At that moment Tommy knew little Aaron had the mark. James Slade had always known. It was the unmistakeable mark of genius, the invisible, indelible mark of Satan.

The end

About the Author

Gerry Ware was born and grew up in London and has always been fascinated by its people and history.

Since the late eighties he has been a prolific composer and songwriter and his first album of instrumental music was released in 1992. Since then he has written songs for solo singers and choirs, radio jingles, backing music for children's stories and a four movement symphony.

Gerry's talents as an author came to the fore while researching and writing the book for the new musical **'1888'** for which he also composed the music and wrote the lyrics. It was premiered in London in 2011 and received good reviews.

His hobbies include playing the guitar and coin collecting.

Gerry's first novel ***Ruthless Deception*** was published in 2012. His second novel ***Dodgy Dealings*** was published in 2013. His third novel ***Sunset Bay Murders*** was published in 2014 and his fourth novel, the futuristic ***Aster 17*** was published in 2015. They are all available from Amazon in paperback form and as a Kindle download.

The Ultimate Price is Gerry's new gripping, powerful drama.

For more about Gerry Ware and his novels and music please visit his website **www.gerryware.com**

You can also get in touch by emailing him at **gerry@gerryware.com**

Made in the USA
Charleston, SC
09 May 2016